THE
FOURTH
PRINCESS

ALSO BY JANIE CHANG

The Phoenix Crown (with Kate Quinn)
The Porcelain Moon
The Library of Legends
Dragon Springs Road
Three Souls

THE FOURTH PRINCESS

A Gothic Novel of Old Shanghai

JANIE CHANG

WILLIAM MORROW

An Imprint of HarperCollinsPublishers

In memory of Mischa. Forever in my heart.

THE
FOURTH
PRINCESS

FOR SALE OR LEASE: LENNOX MANOR

A five-acre country estate just outside Shanghai, minutes from the junction of Brenan and Jessfield Roads. Fully furnished, all rooms are well-appointed with a tasteful mix of superior European and Asian furnishings. Three-year minimum lease with option to purchase.

Three floors of gracious living. On the ground floor, the impressive entrance foyer features a marble floor, double curved staircase, and a Venetian crystal chandelier. The formal drawing and dining rooms overlook splendid French-style gardens. Other areas on the ground floor include a parlor, billiards room, smoking room, and private library.

The servants' quarters are adjacent to the kitchen, which has been updated with the latest conveniences. On the second floor are three suites of rooms, each with attached bathrooms and dressing rooms, six smaller bedrooms, and two additional bathrooms, plus nursery with nanny room. The top floor boasts a magnificent ballroom with parquet flooring and orchestra platform. Electric lights and fans are installed throughout, fireplaces and stoves for heating.

The grounds include a formal French garden, rose garden, Oriental garden, orchard, tennis court, croquet lawns, and a man-made lake. This is the ideal home for owners who entertain frequently and in style.

CHAPTER 1

Shanghai
March 1, 1911

LISAN WAS NOT doing anything forbidden, not yet. She had managed to get away from the house unseen, granted anonymity by the large black umbrella, the crunch of gravel under her feet muted by thunder and rainfall, water droplets on window-panes making it unlikely that Master Liu would bother looking out. She would face his displeasure only if she was successful, and at the moment, her chances of success seemed less substantial than ripples on a pond.

Luck was on her side. Old Mah the gatekeeper wasn't at his station and she slipped out onto the street. At the intersection, she expected to wait because rickshaws were generally in short supply on wet days, but one pulled up just as she approached and let off a passenger. She hurried over to the corner and the puller held aside the tarp as she climbed onto the seat and huddled under the shelter of its canopy. She had to haggle; it would be a long ride out to the External Roads Area. A horse carriage would've been faster, and a motorcar even better, but she couldn't afford either. The rickshaw puller agreed to wait and bring her back, adding to his fee.

They soon left the busy streets of Shanghai's French Concession, the rickshaw puller jogging at a surprisingly fast pace. The canvas tarp attached to the rickshaw's canopy offered protection against the downpour, but the constant strum of raindrops on its threadbare surface echoed Lisan's agitation and made her anxious. She pulled aside the tarp just a few inches to look at the surroundings.

"Where are we now?" she called.

Rain coursed off the rickshaw puller's cape of woven bamboo and palm leaves. He turned to reassure his passenger with a shout. "We're on Bubbling Well Road, nearly at Jing'an Temple! Then we cut over to Yuyuen Road and up to Brenan Road!"

Lisan flinched as cold rain lashed her face and hair, hastily closed the tarp. She had to look decent when she arrived at Lennox Manor.

Bubbling Well Road had once been just a dirt track used by visitors to Jing'an Temple and its cemetery. The city had improved the road and it was now a wide street planted with shady sycamores. As Shanghai expanded, the building lots along the road were snapped up by wealthy Chinese and foreigners. Some properties were the size of small city parks and held mansions with formal gardens in front and lawns extending far behind. Rose gardens, kitchen gardens, tennis courts, and even horse stables were common features. The McBain residence was one of the grandest, a three-story mansion on ten acres. Farther along was a house familiar to Master Liu, the family estate where he had lived before moving to a modest villa in the French Concession. Lisan had only seen it from the outside, a vaguely Tudor-style complex of mansions that housed the extended Liu household, multiple generations of family and their retainers, some four hundred people.

But she wasn't going to an address on Bubbling Well Road, smoothly paved with stone and illuminated with streetlamps at night. She was due at Lennox Manor on Brenan Road, which was a rutted menace. Like many roads in Shanghai, it was covered with a mixture of dirt and clay intended to smooth out an uneven base of rocks and rubble, but with all the rain this spring, the clay had been washing away in muddy trickles. The rickshaw jounced with every pothole, the puller swearing loudly each time his foot hit a rock.

Lisan risked another peek through the gap in the tarp. Houses along the road grew sparser as the rickshaw made its way farther west. They rolled past Jessfield Park, then the railway station. Brenan Road was becoming a fashionable residential area, but its westernmost environs were still considered too remote—more than an hour by rickshaw; half that time by motorcar. With spindly young trees and empty lots, this stretch of Brenan Road felt like an abandoned territory rather than an extension of urban Shanghai.

Lennox Manor was the last house on the road. The rickshaw stopped and Lisan lifted the tarp to venture another look. The rickshaw waited in front of a pair of gates, all elaborate wrought iron curlicues and pointed finials set into high brick walls. A hedge of evergreen yews a few yards inside the gates created a dense screen that obscured views of the house and garden from casual passersby. Perhaps the landscaper had been Chinese and chose to use greenery in place of a spirit wall to shield the house from evil spirits. Beside the iron gates a wicket door set into a brick arch creaked open and the gatekeeper scurried out, opening a large umbrella as he darted toward her.

"I have an appointment with Mrs. Stanton," Lisan called out to him. If she'd been in a chauffeur-driven automobile, if she'd been a white foreigner, the gatekeeper would've rushed to open the gates without question.

The rain had lightened to a misty drizzle and Lisan kept the canvas tarp pulled open as the rickshaw rolled along an oval driveway of crushed gravel. Inside the oval was what had to be a rose garden. It was a sad sight, grass between flower beds sodden from the rain, shrubs brown and withered from neglect. At first all she could see of the house through the mist was a heavy, hulking shape at the end of the oval. Set so far back from the road, Lennox Manor looked desolate, a solitary outpost against windswept skies. As the rickshaw drew closer, the silhouette resolved into a looming edifice of timber and brick, a bulky, squat building that gave the impression of being perched uneasily on its foundations.

Details emerged as she neared the house: dormer windows, a forest of chimneys, lamplight shining through mullioned windows. Slim pillars and latticework adorned balconies but they seemed tacked on, an afterthought to remedy the mansion's heavy lines. The house was the strangest blend of Chinese and Western elements. Lisan stared in fascination at the swooping eaves of the roof, the faces of reptilian demons that glared down from each corner. At the top of the roof, Chinese spirit guardians shaped from green and yellow glazed pottery paraded around a mansard roof.

Normally such spirit guardians marched atop the ridge of a steep, gabled roof. What was the point of putting spirit guardians up there to fend off evil spirits when the roof's flat top made it easy for evil spirits to land? But of course foreigners wouldn't know any better. It wasn't that Lisan was superstitious, it was more that the jumble of styles was so jarring, odd and disturbing, and not just for aesthetic reasons, though she couldn't have explained exactly why. It made Lisan wonder if the inside of the house was as strange as its exterior.

As the rickshaw drew closer, Lisan felt anxiety and anticipation like a hand gripping her heart, an odd and disconcerting sensation. No doubt she was feeling nerves at the prospect of the interview. A movement drew her eyes to a window on the second floor. A woman in red was standing at the window, her features blurred behind the rain-spattered glass. A blink later, she was gone.

The manservant who answered the door gave the rickshaw puller permission to wait for Lisan under the shelter of the porte cochere, a relief since it was unlikely she would find another rickshaw this far away from the center of town.

The servant stood at the door, patiently waiting. She hurried up the few steps and he held open the door, wordless. Inside, another manservant took her coat and hung it inside a cloakroom just off the entrance. Tall and silent in a long blue tunic vest, his black trousers and cloth shoes immaculate, he beckoned her to follow. They crossed a foyer dominated by a magnificent double staircase that curved down from the second-floor mezzanine to terminate at a broad semicircular landing with a half dozen steps descending to the marble floor. The landing and steps were directly in line with the front door. Lisan could just imagine what Master Liu would say, shaking his head over the lack of attention to feng shui. Luck would run down those stairs and straight out the door like a waterfall.

A thick Persian carpet covered the foyer's finely veined white marble floor and a tiered crystal chandelier was suspended from the ceiling, spanning three stories. Heavy tapestries above mahogany wainscoting covered the walls, and a row of clerestory windows emphasized the height of the entrance. Each corner of the ceiling was decorated with a bizarre figure squatting on a bracket, each one different, carved from the same mahogany as the paneled wainscoting. They resembled gargoyles in photographs of European cathedrals, all sneers and protruding eyeballs. But even without those grotesque faces, the house made her shiver. The rich carpet and tapestries couldn't fend off the damp chill of a rainy afternoon, and the proportions of the space felt wrong. Even the placement of furniture in the entrance foyer seemed unharmonious, everything pushed against the walls.

If she got the job, she would have to live here. If Master Liu allowed it.

The manservant didn't take her up the curved staircase. Instead, she followed him past the grand marble steps to a doorway just behind, which opened onto a corridor with a stairwell at one end. The steep wooden staircase connected corridors on each level, a hidden byway for servants to move between floors and stay out of sight except when needed. They climbed the stairs, Lisan quickening her steps to keep up with the manservant's long, effortless stride. They emerged on the second floor, and the servant led her back toward the main staircase and mezzanine. He stopped at the first room beside the main staircase.

He knocked on the door and the voice that replied was low and musical, slightly husky. Lisan entered a room that was a complete contrast to what she had seen of the house so far. A pair of tall windows looked out to the garden, and instead of dark paneling, the walls were covered in pale yellow wallpaper printed with tiny red roses. A blond woman in soft green rose from an armchair, her smile natural and unforced as she greeted Lisan. She appeared to be in her twenties, not much older than Lisan, but with foreigners it was hard to tell. Her face reminded Lisan of a kitten's, a small pointed chin and wide-set eyes. There was also an older woman in the room; she remained seated on a small sofa, her disapproval so evident even the ruffles on her bright blue gown seemed to bristle with condemnation. The woman in red she had glimpsed was not in this room.

"Caroline, you're wasting your time." The older woman spoke as though Lisan weren't there. "A Chinese secretary? Miss Wallace met all the requirements. Absolutely respectable, familiar with who's who in our social circle. I would not have referred her otherwise."

"Oh, Mrs. Easton," Caroline Stanton said, "it doesn't hurt to interview someone different." Her smile as she turned to Lisan carried a trace of amusement, but it wasn't directed at Lisan. "Now, Miss Liu. You're nineteen, yes? In your letter, you say you graduated from a school called St. Clare's Hall. Tell me about it."

"St. Clare's is the top school for Chinese girls in Shanghai," Lisan said. "It provides a Western education while also making sure we are fluently bilingual."

"Did you really attend St. Clare's?" Mrs. Easton said. "It's a school for daughters of wealthy Chinese, so why do you need a job?"

Lisan ignored the accusatory tone. "I'm an orphan, ma'am. My guardian paid my tuition at St. Clare's as long as I earned good grades. I don't expect him to continue supporting me, nor do I want that." That was as much as she was willing to reveal; they didn't need to know more.

"An orphan," Mrs. Stanton said. Lisan caught an undertone of sympathy, genuine feeling. It was as unexpected as it was warming. "How old were you when you lost your parents?"

"I don't know, ma'am," Lisan said. "I have no memories at all of my life before my guardian took me into his household." No memories, only nightmares.

Mrs. Easton snorted. "Who knows what slum she came from?" as though Lisan weren't fluent in English and didn't understand every word perfectly.

Mrs. Stanton smiled at Lisan. "Can you type?"

Lisan answered Caroline Stanton's questions as succinctly as she could, all the while observing the American woman's face, her voice, the way she moved her hands and body. Unlike Mrs. Easton, whose nest of curls threatened to slide off her forehead, Caroline

Stanton's blond locks were pinned in a simple roll, held in a twist at the back with a tortoiseshell comb. The pale green dress emphasized her fresh complexion, and her only visible jewelry, apart from a wedding band, was a pair of cameo earrings, coral pink and finely carved. With such hair and skin, Lisan had expected Mrs. Stanton's eyes to be blue, but they were strange, even for a foreigner, an indeterminate shade that was neither brown nor green, shifting color as Mrs. Stanton turned her face from window to lamplight.

At the end of twenty minutes, Mrs. Stanton stood up and pulled the bell. "I think you'll do, Miss Liu. Can you start on Monday? Come at noon. There will be a room ready for you by then."

"Thank you, Mrs. Stanton," Lisan said. "Yes, I can be here on Monday. Thank you." She dug her fingers into the palm of her hand to contain her excitement. In just a few days, a new life.

In answer to the bell, the same manservant glided in to show her out. Just before the door to the parlor closed, Lisan heard Mrs. Easton's censorious words. "Really, Caroline. This will hardly enhance your position. What could a girl like that understand?"

Walking away from the door, Lisan couldn't make out Caroline Stanton's reply, only the tone of her voice, and to Lisan it sounded rather amused. But it was clear Mrs. Easton would do her best to make young Mrs. Stanton change her mind.

Not that any of it would matter if Master Liu didn't let her take the job.

CHAPTER 2

THE SKIES WERE clear when Lisan stepped out the door. The rickshaw puller had tied the canvas tarp to one side of the canopy. As soon as Lisan climbed on, he set on his way.

"There's not much business this far out of town," he called over his shoulder, as he began jogging up the driveway. "I could've earned two more fares after all this time if this were in the city."

"I'll make it up to you," she said, not offended by his complaint. Rickshaw pullers led short, brutal lives. She didn't have much money but compared to the rickshaw puller, Lisan was rich. She had an allowance, a comfortable home, and the protection of a guardian, Master Liu, a member of the wealthy Liu clan.

Except that she wasn't actually a member of the Liu family, Lisan thought, settling herself farther back against the padded seat. The Lius were one of Shanghai's most prominent families; they owned land and houses throughout the city, vast tracts of farmland elsewhere in Chekiang and adjacent provinces, mines in the interior of China. There was a shipping company and large shareholdings in banks and railway corporations. Then there were the businesses some family members dabbled in, things that caught their fancy. Master Liu imported luxury automobiles from America and one of his nephews owned *Xinwen Bao* newspaper.

Her guardian was third of five sons, a bachelor who adamantly refused to marry. He only cared about books, paintings, and his *penjing*: miniature trees in shallow pots, which he sometimes referred to by their Japanese nomenclature, *bonsai*. It was a *penjing* collection acknowledged to be the finest in Chekiang. Yet this scholarly bachelor had taken her, an orphaned child, off the streets of Shanghai and dropped her into a life of comfort. It confirmed to his family that he was even more eccentric than they'd first believed.

In his own absent-minded way, he was kind to Lisan, but through all these years had never bothered clarifying her status in the household to her or to anyone else. He hadn't adopted her formally and her status in the household was ambiguous; although she lived in Master Liu's house and had a room of her own, she was not quite family and not exactly a servant. Taking their cue from Master Liu, the servants treated her respectfully. But family was everything, and she didn't belong to one.

As for school, Master Liu had enrolled her at St. Clare's Hall for a Western-style education. Perhaps it was because he'd spent time abroad at university. Or perhaps it was simply because the school was the default choice for daughters of the Liu clan and other prominent families.

A year ago, with her graduation drawing near, she had asked Master Liu rather hesitantly whether she could continue her education by attending college. Unlike the famous Soong sisters, Lisan couldn't even dream of going to school in America, but there was a women's college in Foochow, the first in all of China.

"I'm grateful, Master Liu," she said, "for all that you've given me. I'm an adult now and shouldn't need to rely on your generosity, but there's one more favor I need: I've applied to Hua Nan Women's College and they've accepted me. I'd like to become a teacher . . ."

He held up a hand, stopping her. "College is a long-term commitment and there are other considerations. Let me think it over."

She refrained from pressing her case any further. Master Liu was not a large man, and had wire-rimmed glasses and rounded features that gave an impression of mildness. Yet his direct gaze carried an authority that made him seem taller and made her drop her eyes to the floor whenever it fixed on her in disapproval. As a child, she had found his intense scrutiny disconcerting at the best of times, even when he wasn't upset with her. At that moment it seemed best for her to keep her eyes lowered. She would try again later—after all, her college acceptance was valid for two more years.

As a child, she never questioned her undefined status within the household, as children do, believing their situation to be common, if not normal. When she grew older, her existence felt precarious, at best; borrowed. She noticed how her classmates, privileged daughters of wealthy parents, understood exactly what they owed and were owed. In the rigid hierarchy of family, their positions were clearly set by their order of birth as well as their fathers' rank in their lineage.

"You're like a poor relative," her friend and classmate Ju Ming had concluded when they were thirteen years old, "a charity case. Only even lesser since you're not actually a blood relation. You need to be very obedient and careful so your guardian doesn't throw you out on the street."

Master Liu had never even hinted at any such fate, but for years after and even now, Ju Ming's simplistic assessment of her situation shadowed Lisan's days, heightening her natural caution. He never mentioned college after her first attempt so she didn't bring it up again. However, when St. Clare Hall's headmistress offered Lisan a typing and filing job after her graduation, Master Liu had agreed, saying it was good experience for her to work now that she had finished school. She assumed he meant it was time now for her to support herself. Why else had he given her an education?

And what other options were there for her, a girl of unknown ancestry?

Her only other choice, if she couldn't support herself, was marriage. Thankfully Master Liu had never raised the topic, didn't even seem to recognize she was long past the age when families arranged marriages for their daughters. Lisan hoped he'd remain oblivious for a few more years while she found a way to earn a living. She fervently hoped she was beneath the notice of his sisters and aunts, all of whom would relish making a match for her. Not so much because they cared about her but because it would be a chance to scrutinize candidates from a lower class, a challenge they could complain about over mahjong and lotus seed cake.

But then something happened. Something Lisan was still trying to unravel.

She had been working for Mrs. Gordon at the school since last June, just eight months, when Master Liu called her to his *penjing* room. He had been very quiet of late and she had the distinct impression he was watching her, as though she were a stranger and not the child he'd raised. He hardly spoke at mealtimes these days and when he did, it was mostly about his automobile import business, a hobby more than anything from what she could gather. He employed a full-time agent, a Mr. Zheng, who visited car companies around the world to select vehicles for Master Liu. He spoke quite often these days about Mr. Zheng, someone she'd never met.

Mr. Zheng is in a place called Indiana right now, looking at the American Motorcar Company.

Mr. Zheng has gone to Canada to see whether he can find useful contacts.

The *penjing* room was at the southwest corner of the house. Three large windows made it the sunniest space in the villa. A custom-built L-shaped table, its surface the same height as the windowsills, displayed Master Liu's collection, the most valuable ones planted in antique pottery containers. The only other item of furniture was a long bench of elmwood with carved legs, where Master Liu sat to meditate upon his collection.

"You'll resign from your job at St. Clare's," he said with no preamble when she entered the room. His fingers twisted a fine wire around a slim branch of pine. He didn't look up.

"But . . . for what reason?" she stammered. The work had been simple and undemanding, the pay trivial, but it made her feel less beholden to Master Liu.

"In your resignation letter, just tell Mrs. Gordon you must leave for family reasons," he said. "That should suffice."

No, no, she wanted to protest. I meant, what is the real reason you want me to leave?

But Master Liu's demeanor was even more unyielding than when she'd broached the subject of college in Foochow. Even though he hadn't given her an explanation, she had no choice but to comply. She owed Master Liu everything. Besides, she didn't care to risk angering him right then. In the days leading up to this conversation, he had not been himself, his benign, absent-minded smile replaced by a frown whenever he saw her, as though contemplating a miniature pine that needed judicious pruning.

He picked up a pair of tiny pliers. "You'll stay home from now on. There's work I can find for you here if you want to keep busy."

Lost in her thoughts, she only realized she was nearly home when the rickshaw driver called out. "We've arrived, young miss! We're here!"

The gates of Master Liu's villa opened when the gatekeeper saw her, and the rickshaw rolled straight through. According to Master Liu's family, this house was further proof of his eccentricity. His brothers and cousins lived in an urban estate comprising a half dozen houses. From the street, they appeared as individual mansions, each within its own walls. At the back, however, the gardens were unfenced so that family members and servants could wander freely between houses. The estate was home to three generations of Lius, their servants, and the servants' families. But more than ten years ago, shortly after he picked Lisan off the streets, Master Liu bought this modest villa in the French Concession and moved out of the estate, away from his family. He didn't even bring any of their longtime servants with him, but hired new ones, including an amah for Lisan.

This turned out to have been a kindness, Lisan reflected as she got out of the rickshaw, for at the Liu estate she would've grown up subjected to speculation and constant judgment, always under the scrutiny of the family's appraising eyes.

Appraising eyes.

It came to her all of a sudden. She knew when it was that Master Liu's behavior changed, when he began looking at her as though concerned by her presence.

It was during the New Year, a season of festivities that lasted for weeks. Master Liu rarely entertained and, when he did, tended to host small dinner parties for a few scholarly friends or fellow *penjing* enthusiasts. But during the holidays there was no avoiding his duties, and in the second week of February it was his turn to give a party, just one family celebration of many during the New Year. Master Liu's brothers, their wives and children, the cousins and close family friends, all crowded into the modest villa, the children chasing each other up and down the stairs, followed by harried-looking amahs. Servants borrowed from other Liu households passed around trays of appetizers while the cook sent up platter after platter of food for the buffet table.

Lisan helped, as she always did. She took trays of empty dishes and glasses back to the kitchen, being careful of her new tunic, royal blue silk embroidered with pink peonies. She paused to let a guest put a wineglass on the tray. By now, members of the Liu family barely took notice of her. The novelty of a street orphan being raised by one of their own had long since faded.

"I know buffet dinners are all the rage," one of the cousins said, "but I wish Third Uncle would hold proper banquets. Then we could sit down to eat."

"This house doesn't have a large enough dining room," said another, scoffing. "He bought this house on purpose so he wouldn't have to host big dinner parties for the whole family."

Lisan wove her way toward the kitchen, passing the open door of the *penjing* room, where Master Liu had chosen to hide from his guests. His younger brother, whom Lisan addressed as Fourth Uncle, was with him. There was also a guest, an elderly man wearing a black Manchu-style surcoat. A large square insignia badge embroidered with golden pheasants identified him as an official of the Imperial court.

"This juniper is now forty years old," Master Liu said, slowly rotating the potted plant on a turntable, "and I keep it in a partially shaded spot so that the branches will reach for sunlight, developing an asymmetric shape."

"Master Liu? Gentlemen?" she said, standing at the threshold. "May I take any used cups or plates?"

Fourth Uncle ignored her. The elderly guest stared at her, forehead creased in a frown that looked more like amazement than disapproval. Master Liu shook his head and turned back to the juniper.

On her way back from the kitchen with an empty tray, she passed the door again. Conversation from the *penjing* room drifted out as she walked past.

"The resemblance is remarkable," said a voice she didn't know. The elderly guest in Manchu robes.

"A remarkable coincidence," Fourth Uncle's voice said firmly. "Now here's something truly remarkable, the best of the modern specimens in this collection, in my opinion. A wisteria. It's already setting buds."

Master Liu glanced at the open door and when he saw her, a peculiar expression came into his eyes, a look of appraisal, as though recognizing something he should've seen before. He quickly turned away, almost as though embarrassed to have been caught staring, and continued the discussion with his guest, now bent over the potted wisteria.

The memory came back as clearly as though it had been yesterday. That was the day Master Liu's behavior toward her had changed, and she sensed it was connected to the real reason Master Liu made her resign from St. Clare's Hall, but she still didn't understand why.

CHAPTER 3

A CHINESE WOMAN AS your social secretary?"

Mason Burnett was a large man whose beard couldn't quite conceal heavy jowls. Although his clothing was expensively tailored, the dinner jacket skillfully fitted to his broad torso, he still managed to look unkempt. Perhaps it was his balding pate fringed with wisps of gray, or his thick, bristling brows, at the moment drawn together in skepticism. His voice was his best feature, deep and rich. When she'd first met him, Mason's voice had made Caroline think of fine, fragrant pipe tobacco. Now she flinched mentally at the sound of it.

She took a deep, calming breath and smiled, a carefully poised smile that conveyed nothing more than pleasant interest. Her gown of apricot silk glowed against the drawing room's mahogany panels, and candlelight reflected from the yellow topazes at her throat.

"You need to trust Caroline's instincts, Uncle Mason," Thomas Stanton said. "My wife has her reasons and she knows what she wants." He filled Mason's glass with more sherry. Their guests would arrive soon, their first dinner party since coming to Shanghai just over a week ago. She'd made sure everything was ready and could only hope that Mason knew when to stop drinking.

Caroline was certain she'd made a good decision. She had to

admit she had enjoyed seeing Mrs. Easton's face stiffen with displeasure, but that wasn't why she had hired the young Chinese woman over the other candidate.

"Mrs. Easton seemed to think a Chinese secretary wouldn't understand anything about our social circle," she said, "but that's hardly going to be a problem given that Mrs. Easton and her friends will be instructing me every step of the way. Who's who and which invitations we must accept and which ones we can safely ignore."

"Her English . . ." Mason began.

"Her English is excellent, Uncle Mason," Caroline said. "Her typing is very good, and her penmanship is exceptional, a perfect copperplate. But unlike the woman Mrs. Easton wanted me to hire, Miss Liu also speaks and reads Chinese, which means she can translate for me when I deal with the staff. I need to be sure they know exactly how I want things done, and I won't have them making mistakes just because I can't make myself understood."

"I told you," Thomas said with a proud smile, "my wife has her reasons and they're always good ones. I learned that very quickly."

Thomas was a good fifteen years older than Caroline but he'd maintained the lean physique that spoke of his college days as a rowing champion. A thin face, plain and with a long nose, but pleasant to look at. The few gray hairs he had were nearly invisible under a thick mop of light brown curls, and his dark eyes gleamed, alert and intelligent.

Caroline had other reasons for hiring a Chinese secretary, reasons she preferred keeping to herself. Caroline liked it that Lisan wasn't part of white society. Gossip was a currency generously exchanged in those social circles, extracted from friends, dressmakers, and jewelers like money lifted by a pickpocket. But women like Mrs. Easton would never deign to chat with a Chinese servant—for that was how she would regard someone like Lisan, no matter how well educated. Therefore, Mrs. Easton would never glean any information about Caroline from Lisan.

Lights from headlamps entered the gates and curved around the yew hedge. "Our first guests have arrived," Caroline said. "Shall we go out to the foyer and welcome them?"

She rose from the chair and, as she moved across the room, felt a tendril of cold air settle around her shoulders. The house was beset by drafts. Rain and general humidity had swelled the timbers of the wooden structure, warping planks and window frames out of alignment. Floorboards creaked and window latches rattled, but nothing could be done until the rains stopped. One of the things she quickly realized was that Mason hadn't done a thing in years to keep the mansion in good repair. And now he expected them—because, as he said, the house would be theirs when he died—to bring it back to its former glory. Caroline swallowed her annoyance and prepared to receive their guests.

The dinner was for a small gathering of bankers and potential investors and their wives. Thomas was learning the ropes from these longtime residents, foreigners who considered Shanghai home. "Shanghailanders," they called themselves. They'd acquired decades' worth of business knowledge and Thomas needed that knowledge as well as the connections they had cultivated. He needed to understand the slow grind of Chinese bureaucracy and how much judicious bribery was needed to push through the project to build a railway line from Shanghai to Chengtu. And this rope learning, he had remarked dryly, seemed to require a lot of fine dining, cigars, and cognac.

Caroline and Thomas were hosting this dinner; the house, however, belonged to Mason, so the most politic thing was for all three to receive the guests. It rankled her because this created the impression that Mason and Thomas were equal partners in the railway venture.

Mason picked up the sherry bottle. "Another quick one, then, before facing the hordes."

"Yes, the municipality says we will finally have reliable electricity this year," Mason said, "but I do like it when the power fails. Candlelight is more flattering to my aging looks." He leaned closer to the woman beside him, Mrs. Tennison, whose husband was a shipping magnate. She seemed amused rather than revolted, as Caroline would've been.

"When people first began building along Brenan Road," Mrs. Tennison said, "Lennox Manor was one of the first—and also the farthest out. Do you not find it rather remote, out of the way?"

"Not at all," he said. "I bought this house *because* of its remote location, and I'll be sorry when the lots nearby fill up with more homes. It will spoil the feeling of living in a country home."

One could always count on real estate to monopolize a dinner conversation for at least thirty minutes, Caroline reflected as she signaled her head servant. Chin snapped his fingers and two houseboys took away the soup bowls. Their cook had made a delicious leek soup. Next to come was a fish course of poached salmon with Hollandaise, then a sautéed chicken-and-mushroom dish, then roast lamb with potatoes, carrots, cauliflower, and steamed asparagus. At the end, a compote of pears with cream, and a selection of petits fours. The vegetables and fruit were expensive at this time of year, shipped in from Australia and New Zealand, but Thomas had told her not to worry.

She turned her head to the man at her left, half listened as he described in detail the activities of the Shanghai Paper Hunt Club and why Mongolian ponies were best for the chase. Caroline fixed her gaze on his face but tilted her head to better hear what the couple across from him were saying in low voices. Those were always the better conversations.

"A stroke of luck for Mason, a rich nephew who married an heiress," the woman said. "Do they realize he's almost insolvent?"

"They'll find out soon enough," said the gentleman beside her. "Thomas Stanton is the real thing though. Silver mines, if I recall. Very astute businessman, not like young Charles Burnett."

"And not the sort to fall for the wrong kind of woman. Poor Charles."

A woman's voice, loud and confident, interrupted all other conversation. "Tell me, Mr. Stanton," Mrs. Tennison said, "how did the two of you meet? We've only heard rumors. A rail disaster?"

"No rumor," Thomas said, a wide smile breaking over his face. "Caroline was traveling with her aunt and uncle. We were all on the same train bound for Seattle. But it had been snowing heavily and snow was banked so high on the railway tracks we were stranded for days near a small town in Washington State."

"It was hardly a town," Caroline said, looking across the table at her husband. "It was more like a depot for railway employees, with a small hotel and stables."

"And a tavern," Thomas said, "don't forget the tavern. We were trapped there nearly a week and that tavern kept me and others from losing our minds to boredom. I checked into the hotel just to get off the train. Good thing I did."

"You tell the story, darling," she said. Caroline knew that in Thomas's mind, the avalanche had taken on mythic dimensions because it had brought them together. He had shaped and honed the narrative to make it clear that their romance had been fated. She preferred to sit quietly and listen, recall her own memories of the event that had changed her life.

He beamed at her and turned to his audience. "It was this time last year, almost to the exact date. Our train was on its way to Seattle, but days of heavy snowfall had turned into a fierce blizzard and created such difficult conditions that supervisors of the

Great Northern Railway decided that all trains in the area should stop at their nearest station. But in fact our train really had no choice by then. We were trapped not far from a small town called Wellington, in the middle of the Cascade mountains. It was just a railway town, a depot and a small hotel, a tavern, and a telegraph machine."

The tracks were blocked by snow, and some passengers got out to make the walk to the town, including Thomas, who hoped to use the telegraph to let business contacts know that he was delayed by the blizzard. But the telegraph wires were down, so Thomas decided to check into Bailets Hotel.

"It was just luck," he said, "a lucky impulse that made me take a room in the hotel, for a change of scenery and to be near the telegraph office. I wanted to send messages as soon as the wires were back up again."

"Where was Caroline?" Mrs. Tennison asked. "Did she also check into the hotel?"

Caroline interjected. "I would've liked to walk to the town— not to stay at the hotel, just to take a look and get off the train. But I was traveling with my aunt and uncle and they thought it was too far and too tiring, and we had everything we needed in our carriage."

"The Dominics' private car was very comfortable," Thomas said. "It was quite something, a railway carriage built by the Pullman Company, fitted out as luxuriously as any suite in a fine hotel, and they'd brought their own chef and a maid. Mrs. Dominic invited a few guests for dinner the first evening we were stranded, but I didn't meet Caroline then." He glanced over at her and winked. "She was unwell and in her compartment."

On the third night, it began to rain. To some it was a relief, a sign of warmer temperatures. They hoped the snow would melt enough that they could set off on their way. What it really meant, however, was that rain was soaking into the snow on the mountains above and making it heavier. And in the early hours of the fourth day, a wet slab of snow half a mile wide began sliding down the slope, gaining momentum and scraping up everything in its path until it slammed into the trains.

"Luckily I was at the hotel," Thomas said, "and luckily for Caroline, she wasn't in her sleeping compartment. She had gotten up for a glass of water."

Caroline had been in the carriage's dining room when the avalanche struck. The force of the slide slammed the carriage against a tree and the car broke open at its center. She was thrown out into the snow and lay unconscious until rescuers from Wellington arrived. Thomas and other hotel guests had joined the search for survivors.

"I found her lying on top of a piece paneling from the carriage," Thomas said, "and it saved her life because she wasn't buried under snow. That and her fur coat."

She shivered at the memory. The fur she had pulled on instead of a bathrobe to go out for a glass of water. The fur that had kept her from freezing before rescuers arrived. She was chilled through but alive, and could only cling to Thomas, teeth chattering. The Great Northern Railway's bunkhouse in Wellington was turned into a temporary hospital, and it was days before snowplows finally got through. A special hospital train arrived shortly after to take the injured to the nearest hospital, in Spokane.

"For the first while, Caroline didn't even know her own name," Thomas said. "She couldn't remember anything of her past because she'd hit her head. But we said to her, 'We know you're Caroline Vessey because of your fur coat.' You see, the coat's lining had her name embroidered on it."

At this point in the story, Caroline knew Thomas liked her to jump in. "He visited me every day at the hospital," she said, "until one day I realized who he was. 'I believe you're the man who saved my life, sir. What is your name?' I asked."

"And I replied, 'Thomas Stanton, at your service,' and I meant it," said Thomas. "I was ready to be at her service for the rest of my life, if she would have me."

"How romantic! What a wonderful story!" Mrs. Tennison said, clapping her hands. "And now here you are, starting a new life in Shanghai."

"Yes, a new life," Caroline said. "If only my parents had lived long enough to meet Thomas. If only my aunt and uncle were still alive and could come to visit. They often spoke of traveling to the Far East."

"Oh, my dear"—Mrs. Tennison blinked—"I only meant that out of such tragedy, well, it's a blessing the two of you found each other . . ." Her voice trailed off, embarrassed.

Caroline nodded. "Of course. As you say, how fortunate to have a happy outcome out of such sorrow."

Another woman jumped in, to smooth over this small faux pas. "Cherish your new life here, Mrs. Stanton," she said. "We must return to Chicago soon and I'm lamenting already. I must say I'll miss our houseboys. We will never be so well looked after again. We've been quite spoiled in Shanghai. You must make the most of your time here."

"Oh, I will," Caroline replied, completely sincere. "Sometimes it feels like a dream to be living here."

She had been excited about Shanghai ever since Thomas first broached the idea to her. They had taken a leisurely tour of Europe for their honeymoon, then spent several weeks traveling through California, where Thomas owned a number of properties, mostly silver mines. She refused to visit New York or Boston. She associated those cities with her past, a life of sad events and memories she would rather not relive. Thomas and the lawyers had been very understanding, and they had finished the last of the legal paperwork from San Francisco.

Then he'd told her about Mason Burnett and his offer: the opportunity to be part owner, a major shareholder in a railway, the mansion he would give Thomas, and a chance to experience Shanghai, the Paris of the East, where Westerners lived like royalty.

She never hesitated. Caroline was glad they were going to live in Shanghai, a city where no one knew her, where they wouldn't whisper about Caroline Vessey. *Poor creature, barely survived the Wellington railway disaster, you know, the one where ninety-six people died.* In Shanghai she would simply be Caroline Stanton, wife of millionaire Thomas Stanton.

CHAPTER 4

LISAN TOOK A deep breath. It was better to tell her guardian about the job opportunity now and get it over with. The longer she waited the more it would look as though she was trying to be evasive. But first, she would pay her respects at the small family temple.

Tucked against the side of the house, the temple was very plain, a polished stone floor and a sloped roof held up by four wooden columns. It was connected to the main house by a covered walkway. The name tablets honored Master Liu's ancestors, and Lisan burned incense to them as she had done since she was a child, an easy way to thank Master Liu for taking her into his home. The deity she actually prayed to was the Goddess of Mercy, whose statue stood on an altar adjacent to the ancestral name tablets. The wooden statue was lacquered a rich brown, its carved robes flowed as though lifted by a breeze. Her lips curved up in a gentle, enigmatic smile that Lisan always found encouraging. At some point, someone had draped a string of wooden beads around the Goddess, each bead the size of a walnut and carved with Buddhist symbols.

She took a handful of incense sticks from the box under the altar and lit them. Kneeling, she quietly beseeched the Goddess that Master Liu would allow her to take this job. She murmured her prayers until the sticks of incense burned down, then stood and straightened her tunic, steeling herself for the conversation to come.

When she entered the small dining room, she saw to her dismay that Fourth Uncle was with her guardian. She hadn't heard him arrive, but then, she had been praying in the temple. Out of all Master Liu's brothers, this one intimidated her the most.

In any other family, one brother visiting another would be an unremarkable, normal event. However, Master Liu and his younger brother preferred to stay out of each other's way because they barely got along. Fourth Uncle couldn't hide his exasperation with Master Liu's complete lack of interest in the family's businesses; the two avoided each other whenever possible. Yet they were of the same blood and would always protect each other.

Fourth Uncle turned to scowl at her, his thin face grumpier than usual. Lisan realized long ago that he appeared the elder of the two only because he looked so stern all the time, and because he wore traditional clothing: brocade vests layered over long scholar gowns, a skullcap, and cloth shoes, the sort of grandfatherly clothing someone much older would wear. He carried a cane, an affectation since there was nothing amiss with his legs. Seen closer though, Fourth Uncle's face was unlined, his posture straight and unbent. She had never seen him in a suit, whereas Master Liu often dressed in Western-style clothing, a habit acquired during his university days in France.

"Ah, Lisan," Master Liu said, "my brother and I need to discuss some things in private. Cook is making up a tray for you to take to your room."

She nodded. "Yes, Master Liu. But there's something I wish to tell you." She avoided looking at Fourth Uncle. "May I come see you once Fourth Uncle has left?"

"Tell me now," he said, peering over his glasses at her. "We'll be up quite late."

Heart sinking, she took a deep breath. If Master Liu had even the tiniest inclination to let her take the job, Fourth Uncle's presence would dampen it.

"I found a new job today, sir. As secretary to a foreign woman, Mrs. Thomas Stanton. They live out at the end of Brenan Road. I would start on Monday." She took a deep breath. "And I would have to live there."

A frown marred her guardian's face. "What nonsense! I had you leave the job at St. Clare's and now you turn around and get another one?"

She should've known better. "I thought it was just St. Clare's you didn't think was right." It was the feeblest of tactics.

"Lisan, you've had more advantages than many girls of good family are allowed," Master Liu said. "A modern, Western-style education. Freedom to visit friends. Then you had an actual job at St. Clare's. It's enough."

"Sir, you said that work experience would be good for me," she mumbled, looking down at her feet.

"Well, you've had that experience and it's enough," he said, "so tomorrow you must telephone this woman, this Mrs. Stanton, to let her know you can't take the job after all."

"At the end of Brenan Road?" Fourth Uncle said. "Is that Lennox Manor?"

"Yes, Fourth Uncle," she said, "do you know the house?"

"I own it. It's leased to an American, Mason Burnett." Fourth Uncle turned to Master Liu, effectively dismissing Lisan. "Let's talk about this over dinner, Brother. You can give her a final decision in the morning."

Master Liu paused, looked sideways at his brother, then waved his hand to indicate that Lisan should close the door on her way out.

Her first impulse after leaving the room was to kneel in the corridor with her ear to the door, but there was no hope of eaves-dropping without being noticed by one of the servants. In fact, one of the house servants was approaching now, carrying a tray of covered dishes. She stood against the wall to let him by, then ran upstairs to her room, pulled on a coat, and slipped outside.

It was a winter evening and silhouettes of the garden's bare-branched trees stood out dimly in the gloom. She was the only one outside since none of the servants would willingly brave the cold. The only person who might notice her was Old Mah the gatekeeper, huddled inside his brick alcove. At this hour he would be downing his evening bowl of hot congee and stew, staying close to the clay pot of hot coals that kept his little space warm. But just to be safe, she hurried along while keeping to the shadows of trees and hedges, away from Old Mah's line of sight.

The dining room's window was at eye level, but she wasn't going to risk looking in. Lisan sidled beside the window, staying away from the light cast through its glass panes. She could hear conversation and hoped they were talking about her, because she didn't want to be outside any longer than necessary, not with a light rain starting to fall again.

"I still think ignorance is the best safety measure," Master Liu was saying. "There's no need for her to know. Not yet."

Her? Did they mean her, Lisan? And if so, he wanted to keep her in ignorance. Of what?

Then Fourth Uncle's voice from farther inside the room. She strained to hear but failed to make out his words.

"No, I haven't heard from Mr. Zheng in a while," Master Liu said. "I'm getting a bit worried. We can't make that decision until he sends word. It's up to him."

They couldn't be talking about her now. Zheng had nothing to do with her. Again, Fourth Uncle's voice. His reply unclear.

"Yes, that makes sense. Out of sight somewhere close but unexpected," Master Liu replied, as though in agreement. "An unusual setting where no one would think to look."

"But it's also important to have someone there to keep an eye on things." This time Fourth Uncle's voice was louder and closer. "I'll take care of it. Burnett knows he hasn't kept up his side of the bargain. He'll agree."

"What was the bargain?"

A latch squeaked, and she moved away from the window along the wall as quietly as she could and flattened herself on the other side of a wooden trellis. The window opened and Fourth Uncle's hand reached out to tap the bowl of his pipe against the stone ledge.

"After I bought the house from Burnett, he leased it back from me for next to nothing. The bargain was that in return, he would take on the cost of bringing it back to its original condition, both the mansion and the gardens. He hasn't done a thing so far."

The window latch clicked shut. Lisan caught a glimpse of a blue sleeve as a house servant pulled dark velvet drapes across the window.

She sighed and went back inside the house through the back door. Upstairs in her room, there was a covered tray on her desk, and she sat down to eat, still puzzling over what she'd heard.

She couldn't connect the scraps of sentences into a coherent discussion. She couldn't even be certain they had been talking about her, because they'd also mentioned Mr. Zheng, the man who worked as a buyer for Master Liu's automobile import business. It was unlikely he was part of any discussion about her. She shivered, her feet still cold from going outside in her thin house shoes. She put on her nightgown and climbed under the blankets even though she was too restless to sleep.

As for what Master Liu had said about the freedom he allowed her, she had always thought it because he didn't pay much attention to her. She was free to visit her friends, go to parties, walk around Shanghai unchaperoned. He didn't even seem to care if this meant she would meet young men, her friends' brothers and cousins. Well, she was an orphan, so she had no brothers to escort her to functions. And she didn't have an amah following her anymore, not since she turned sixteen.

"You're lucky, Lisan," Ju Ming often said. "Your guardian is an absent-minded scholar and doesn't care what you do since you're not really his daughter. My mother worries all the time about what others will think. I have to go everywhere with a maidservant or one of my stupid brothers." Ju Ming's virtue had to be unassailable.

Turning over in bed to look out the bedroom window, Lisan reflected that without her small job at St. Clare's, she felt irrelevant, adrift and without purpose. Master Liu had never indicated whether he had any plans for her. *We can't make that decision until he sends word.* He'd been referring to his agent Mr. Zheng, but it crossed her mind that it could apply just as well to her, because sometimes she had an odd feeling that Master Liu was waiting for something to happen, for someone else to say the word before deciding her future.

She shook her head at this irrational notion. The more likely reason was that he simply hadn't thought about her prospects. She wasn't important enough. She wasn't his daughter.

Her classmates all knew what to expect once they'd graduated. Once their time at school was finished, Lisan's friends became very busy young adults. In the first year after graduation, she received invitations to six weddings. Most of the marriages were arranged—some with the young woman's consent, that was true, and always to a husband within their own social class. Some of her classmates, the serious ones hoping to put off marriage, were going to college abroad or in other provinces. Others had entered Shanghai society, daringly modern as they attended dances and dinners, frequented theaters and nightclubs. Escorted by fathers and brothers, some even bet on the horses at the Race Club.

They were from rich families, able to afford such entertainments, their social calendars scheduled so tightly they gave an illusion of purpose. Ultimately, all her classmates would marry, and then they would belong to their husbands' families. They would be under scrutiny, carefully watched for signs of pregnancy, urged to bear sons. So perhaps this nonstop swirl of entertainment was its own purpose, a time to enjoy being free of responsibilities.

Lisan couldn't afford such a life, nor did she want one. After giving up her job at St. Clare's, she passed her days drifting restlessly. She could only read books for so long, could only window-shop so often. Thus when she'd seen the small advertisement in the *North China Daily News*, she applied on impulse, writing a letter in her best penmanship to Mrs. Caroline Stanton. Unexpectedly, she'd received a reply. Then, even more unexpectedly, she'd been hired.

As Mrs. Stanton's secretary, she would indeed earn wages and have a place to live. But this merely transferred all her dependence from Master Liu to a foreign woman. A woman who might not stay in Shanghai very long, a woman who might decide she didn't like Lisan after all—and then she would be unemployed. She knew full well what adversities young women suffered if they lacked family protection. The servants and her old amah often reminded her how lucky she was to have such a kind guardian, how grateful she should be for his generosity.

Ultimately, Master Liu was all that stood between her and the dirty streets of Shanghai, she thought in resignation as her eyelids finally began to droop. So if her guardian forbade her to work for Mrs. Stanton, she had to obey.

In the morning, Lisan found Master Liu in the *penjing* room studying a tiny maple he had recently planted. He'd put the potted tree on a marble turntable so he could look at it from all sides. As a child, she had spent many hours fidgeting beside Master Liu, handing him lengths of wire and pruning tools, and he had explained what he was doing so she knew the correct names. Tree *penjing* were single trees, also called *bonsai* in Japanese. Mountain-and-water *penjing* were miniature landscapes in a container, with rocks added to represent mountains or islands. Master Liu's collection contained both kinds, but he preferred single trees.

"Are you working on a new *penjing*?" she asked. A question about his collection usually put her guardian in a good mood.

"One does not work on a *bonsai*," he said, using the Japanese term. He bent low to peer at the underside of the maple. "You let it work on you. A true master learns from the tree and envisions how to express himself in the decades to come through the medium of the tree."

The oldest specimen in Master Liu's collection was a hundred-and-ten-year-old trident maple. Master Liu had paid a fortune for the specimen, purchased from a family fallen into poverty. Three generations of scholars had cared for the little tree, and the man who sold it to Master Liu had wept on his way out.

He straightened up and wiped his hands on a towel. "Lisan, you may take the job at Lennox Manor."

"Oh, sir! Thank you!" she gasped. This was not at all what she'd expected.

"On one condition," he continued. "On your day off, you'll come back home and spend your day here. No visiting with friends or going to the theater or socializing in cafés. That is all."

"Yes, of course," she said. "Thank you, Master Liu. Thank you for allowing this." She didn't ask why he'd agreed or how Fourth Uncle had reversed his initial reluctance. She didn't want to say anything more in case it made him reconsider.

She could hardly believe it. She had a job again, one where she would live away from home for the first time. It would be an adventure, or at the very least, a first step toward independence.

"One more thing," he said, turning back to the miniature maple tree. "It seems that Fourth Uncle's tenant has finally hired a gardener. He's hired Yao, on Fourth Uncle's recommendation."

Yao.

She could barely hold back an audible intake of breath. Yao would be there. She would see him again.

MASTER LIU HAD his driver take Lisan to Lennox Manor in his newest American motorcar, a Cadillac. Traditional though he was in many ways, Master Liu had a weakness for the latest in automobiles. Lisan suspected he'd started an import business to indulge his love for cars and hired Mr. Zheng to visit European and American motorcar factories, inspecting and purchasing the latest luxury vehicles. The garage at the villa currently held three shining automobiles.

This time, at the vehicle's approach, the gatekeeper at Lennox Manor hurried to open the gates. Lisan suppressed a surge of panic. What was she doing here? She had never spent a single night away from her home, and here she was moving to a strange house filled with strangers. It no longer felt like an adventure or a step toward independence; it felt like a mistake.

The door opened and the thin, stern manservant she'd met on the day of her interview frowned at her. "The servants' entrance is at the back," he said, "but you may as well come in now. Quickly. I'll take you to your room. I'm Chin, Number One Boy."

She had to treat him carefully. The Number One Boy was the head servant, someone whose goodwill she needed to win even after she had established her status in the hierarchy. Had she been a white secretary, her authority would've been just below that of the Stantons, far above that of the Number One Boy. As a Chinese employee and a woman, her standing had yet to be defined even though she was categorically not a servant.

"I'll leave my luggage there and then pay my respects to Mrs. Stanton," she said, struggling to keep up with his long strides. He paused and took one of her valises.

"There's no one home right now except servants," he said, striding ahead of her. "Master Thomas and Missy Caroline left an hour ago for a dinner engagement and Master Mason is staying at his club in Shanghai. So when you've unpacked, come down to the kitchen and meet the rest of the household staff over lunch."

"Will all the staff be there?" she couldn't help asking, a frisson of excitement traveling up her spine as she thought of Yao.

Chin shrugged. "Probably. They never miss a meal."

The floorboards creaked under his cloth-soled shoes as he walked along the hall; he spoke rapidly, pointing at the doors of the various rooms.

"Except for the ballroom, which is on the third floor, all the public rooms are here on the ground floor," Chin said. "On this side of the main hall are rooms that look out onto the back terrace and tennis courts: large parlor and dining room, library, small breakfast room. This door here is the servants' entrance from the back terrace. On the other side of this hall are rooms with windows facing the front of the house: the drawing room, billiards room, smoking room, a small parlor for the ladies."

Walking to the end of the main hall, he took her through a door that opened to a narrower corridor with a steep wooden staircase. "The servants' hallway and stairs. Through this door is the kitchen, where we eat, the pantry, butler's pantry, storage. Down the stairwell is the basement and the servants' quarters for the houseboys. Now, take these stairs up to the next floor."

Lisan hoped it wouldn't take her too long to learn the layout of this huge mansion. She hurried behind Chin; the steep and narrow staircase led to a small landing and two doors.

"This is your bedroom," he said, opening one door. "It's supposed to sleep two or three maidservants. It's close to the mistress's room, which is through that door to the main hall. Missy Caroline put a desk in your room so you can use it as bedroom and office. Your bathroom is through the other door. Come down to the kitchen for lunch as soon as you've put away your things."

She barely heard him descend the stairs, so silently did he move on his cloth-soled shoes. Lisan looked around the room, which was small and made smaller by heavy, dark furniture. At least there was a window with a view of lawns and a small lake with willows. She quickly put away her garments and piled her books on top of the desk. She would take a closer look at her new living quarters later. She didn't want to be late to her first lunch with the rest of the household servants.

But something drew her back to the window, where her gaze fell upon the lake. The willows leaned toward the water, the tips of their branches brushing so close to the surface they almost touched. Then the light shifted and for a moment she saw a ripple of red behind the willows. She blinked and it was gone.

LISAN WENT DOWN the staircase and found the kitchen by following the sound of lively conversation and the smell of food. Two long tables were in the middle of the space, and the air was fragrant with the scent of steamed rice and a savory stew. The noisy talk she'd heard from the corridor stopped as soon as she stepped inside. The servants were seated around the shorter of the two tables. Head servant Chin wasn't there, and neither was Yao. An older man with a kerchief tied over his bald head bustled up to her and began making introductions.

Old Zhao, the senior cook, lost no time informing Lisan that he had cooked for the cream of Shanghai society, having trained in the kitchens of the Astor House Hotel, where the chef had been brought over especially from France.

"That's my son and assistant—just call him Young Zhao." His son was lanky and pimpled, busy at the stove adding some final seasonings to a pot of spicy pork stew. He nodded in Lisan's direction as his father continued with introductions to the four house servants.

"Liao is Number Two Boy," he said as a middle-aged man bobbed his head and grinned at her. "His brother, Little Liao, is Number Three Boy. Then there's Da Wu, Number Four Boy. And his baby brother, Xiao Wu, Number Five. I call them by number, who can remember these idiots' names?"

The house servants laughed good-naturedly, not at all offended. From Little Liao on down, they were all young men in their twenties. Xiao Wu, the youngest, looked no more than twelve. "Old Zhao, you can call us anything as long as you feed us," said Da Wu. "Xiao Wu, a chair for Miss Liu."

The boy stood up with a shy smile and moved a chair into place for her. "What about you, Miss Liu?" his brother, Da Wu, asked. "Where did you work before this?"

"At a foreign school, St. Clare's Hall," she said, and they all nodded at the mention of the famous school. "But what can you tell me about our employers?"

"The owner of this house is Mason Burnett," said Liao. "The new arrivals are his nephew Thomas Stanton and wife, Missy Caroline, your boss. The nephew is already very rich, a millionaire who made his fortune in mining, and now he's here to get into railways. That's the gossip I've heard, anyway."

"But we really don't know much," Da Wu chimed in, "because except for Chin, we're all new. We were hired only a couple of weeks before the Stantons came."

"So Master Mason lived here alone, without any other staff?" Lisan asked, confused. "For how long?" The name Mason Burnett started niggling at her. There was something about that name. A troubling something that crept along the edges of her mind.

"Chin has been here the longest," Little Liao offered. "He's been with Master Mason the whole time. You should ask him. We've tried but he just ignores us and makes it clear he doesn't want to chat. He's a good house manager but not very friendly."

"This has not been a happy house," said Zhao the cook, "and there's a strange feel about the place. But it's livelier since the young couple arrived. A dinner party the other night. Excellent menu. Soon there will be loud music and dancing, as is the way of foreigners."

"Not a happy house?" she prompted.

"You know this house is cursed, don't you?" said Da Wu, leaning forward eagerly. "My auntie warned me against working here, but how does one turn down steady employment?"

"Cursed how?" Lisan smiled. She prided herself on her St. Clare's education, one that disparaged superstition. "Tell me what you know."

The servants talked over each other in their impatience to repeat the gossip and rumors they'd heard about the house. It had acquired a reputation years ago from its first owner, the man who built Lennox Manor. He was a Scottish opium trader who hired an architect to design a stately mansion enhanced with Chinese flourishes. But Shanghai's high life trapped him in its decadent whirl and gambling debts eventually forced him to sell Lennox Manor ten years later. He died shortly after, penniless and friendless.

Mason Burnett then bought the house for a pittance and lived there for a time. When his son, Charles, came of age, he gave him Lennox Manor along with a large sum of money to start his own business. He wanted Charles to prove himself and to marry well. But Charles went bankrupt, his businesses failed, and his debts dragged him down. Then his wife left and he took his own life. People said he had been madly in love with her and couldn't take the loss. After this tragedy, only three years ago, Mason Burnett moved into Lennox Manor and had lived here alone since.

"This house is badly designed, that's why it's unlucky," said Liao. "Look at the main staircase, directly facing the front entrance, allowing luck and wealth to pour downstairs and out the door." There were murmurs of agreement, heads shaking at such disregard for basic feng shui.

"Imagine, a foreigner committed suicide right here in this house!" Little Liao said, his bright eyes agog at the thought. "Miss Liu, do you think his ghost follows Chinese rules or foreign ones?"

There followed a spirited argument about whether the souls of foreign people who died in China returned to their native land or remained here until the body was sent home. If Charles Burnett's ghost was bound to the laws of the Chinese afterlife, then everyone living at Lennox Manor was in peril, since death by suicide created the most dangerous kind of ghost. Only by getting another soul to replace it in the afterlife could such a ghost move on to reincarnation; thus it was compelled to drive another victim to self-destruction through madness or despair. It begat a never-ending cycle of death.

"If Mason Burnett is so rich," Lisan said, changing the subject, "why did he let his son go bankrupt? Why didn't he help? With money, advice, connections?"

"Father and son were estranged," Old Zhao said. "Master Mason didn't approve of the woman his son married. She was a nightclub singer, not a real lady. They say she only married him for money, and when that was gone . . ." He shrugged.

"The son hanged himself," said Young Zhao, bringing a vat of pork stew to the table. "Tied the rope to a post on the third-floor mezzanine and jumped. They say he dangled there all night until the last remaining servant found him."

Lisan shuddered at the thought. To walk in and find a corpse hanging in the foyer. The uneasy sensation when she'd heard the name Burnett now made sense. "I remember now," she said, "the story was in the newspapers, did you say three years ago?"

"We shouldn't talk about him," Xiao Wu said. His small face was serious and concerned. "It's been very quiet but we don't want to wake up bad spirits by talking about them. You should paste a pair of *fu* scrolls to either side of your bedroom door to ward off ghosts, Miss Liu. Just in case the ghost follows Chinese rules. You should put a vase of willow branches in your room too."

"I don't think Missy Caroline would approve of Chinese good luck scrolls glued to her wallpaper," Lisan said to the boy, "but I'll consider the willow branches."

"There's a willow tree by the lake. I'll cut some branches for you in the morning," Xiao Wu said. Then he pulled a wooden bangle from his wrist and handed it to her solemnly. "Peach wood, carved with amulets to fend off evil spirits. I have another one for myself. My auntie gave me all sorts of good luck charms and amulets when she learned I would be working here."

She smiled at the boy and slipped the bangle onto her wrist. "I promise to wear this at all times. Thank you, Xiao Wu."

"Now, where is Chin," Old Zhou said, "and that new gardener, Yao? Number Three, stop being such a glutton, leave some rice for them. Ah, here they come." The tall head servant entered, a young man following behind.

Lisan's heart skipped a beat, as it always did when she saw him.

Yao had a square and pleasant face. Like the others, he wore servant's garb, a blue tunic with a high collar over loose black trousers. Unexpectedly and unlike the others, his hair was cut short in the Western style instead of long and pulled back in a queue. But his good looks were not what flustered her, because she knew him, though not very well.

Each time she saw him, Lisan was flooded with a sensation of familiarity, of instant trust and security. Yet at the same time, his presence filled her with dread, a premonition or a memory, something intangibly disturbing. She had so many questions for Yao, but the conflicting emotions assailed her so forcefully that she didn't know where to begin. He was also an orphan, another stray picked up by Master Liu, who then sent Yao to be trained as a gardener in Soochow, a city famous for its exquisite classical gardens. She wasn't quite sure exactly when she'd first met Yao; she had the impression that he had joined the Liu household before her. Yao visited Shanghai every so often, and although he and Lisan exchanged friendly greetings, he mostly spent his time with Master Liu, talking about landscaping and *penjing*.

The gardener nodded at the diners and filled his bowl with rice and stew. His eyes lingered on her as Zhao made the introductions, but he didn't volunteer that he already knew her so Lisan took her cue from him. For the servants at Lennox Manor, the knowledge that Lisan and Yao knew each other might spur inquisitive questions, and at least for now, she didn't want to fend off their curiosity. She sensed that Yao felt the same; he'd always been friendly but kept his distance, and not just from her.

She concentrated on her lunch, barely listening to the lively voices around her, trying to decipher the odd feeling that came over her whenever she saw the gardener. She chanced a quick look at the end of the table where Yao sat eating. He was listening to Young Zhao, the assistant cook. He took his eyes away from Young Zhao for a moment and smiled at her.

CHAPTER 5

WHEN THOMAS HAD first told her about it, Caroline was excited at the prospect of living in China. "Your uncle Mason is very generous, offering to let us live with him," she said, "and he's promised to leave his house to you. Do you know why he quarreled with your mother?"

"My mother never said much," Thomas said, "only that he'd wanted her to marry someone else. She wrote to him when I was born, but he never replied. The only reason I contacted Uncle Mason last year was to let him know she'd died. He wrote back saying he regretted falling out with her. Then he told me that his son, Charles—who I didn't even know existed—died a few years ago. I'm Uncle Mason's only surviving family now and he says he wants to make up for lost time."

"I suppose he's hoping you can replace Charles," Caroline said. "He wants an heir and business partner. He won't be disappointed, my darling. Without even knowing Charles, I'm sure you're every bit as clever and astute. How did he die?"

"I'm not sure," Thomas said. "Uncle Mason didn't want to talk about it. Who can blame him? I do know that the house once belonged to Charles. That is, Uncle Mason bought it for him, and after Charles died, Mason moved in. It's called Lennox Manor. Uncle Mason said he'd be happy for us to take over the house. He wants you to run it as you please, entertain as you like. He'll just live in a suite of rooms there."

She recalled her first excited views of Shanghai, of sunrise gilding the ripples of water on the horizon, the distant and tantalizing view of its waterfront coming into focus as their ship neared the port. She and Thomas had rushed to stand on deck with the other passengers, some eagerly taking in the sight of the city, others sighing with relief at the familiar skyline.

They descended the wharf to a scene of chaos: disembarking passengers and the people welcoming them, swarms of porters and coolies, rickshaws and carts, uniformed sailors threading their way through the crowd, red-turbaned Sikh police keeping beggars and vendors away from the arrivals area.

And then there was Mason Burnett. Thomas's uncle, the man who would make her husband heir to the Burnett fortune, including the mansion. She noticed him even before he put up his hand to wave, a large solitary figure who stood out from the clusters of families and friends waiting on the wharf. Not because he was alone, but because of the look on his face, anxious rather than joyfully expectant; he broke into a wide smile as they descended the ramp.

"Welcome, welcome to Shanghai, the Paris of the East!" He kissed Caroline's hand and shook hands vigorously with Thomas. "The heavens will open soon, let's get into the carriage. Is that your luggage?" He snapped his fingers and a Chinese man in a dark green uniform hurried up to direct the porters. Soon two coolies were loading their steamer trunks and other belongings onto carts that would follow them to Lennox Manor.

They climbed into a large horse carriage and Mason gave Caroline a woolen lap robe to drape over her legs. "I know you're wearing a warm coat," he said, "but the damp here makes the cold air sink into your bones."

"I've brought over a motorcar, Uncle Mason," Thomas said, leaning back, "so I need to come back to the wharf tomorrow and make sure it's been unloaded."

"A motorcar, well, well," Mason said, "yes, of course. I'll have the carriage come around to the house tomorrow morning and we can go together." He turned to Caroline. "And you, my dear, I suppose you'd like to spend tomorrow resting and looking at your new home. I'd be happy to take you around Shanghai once the rain stops."

The two men dived straight into a discussion about railways and investors while Caroline stared out the window, avid and curious. China was exciting, noisy and full of life. She had never seen such traffic, never even imagined such a mix of conveyances. Motorcars and horse-drawn carriages of all sizes shared the road with rickshaws and donkey carts. There didn't appear to be any traffic lanes; people simply made their way along the street in whichever direction suited them. Warning shouts and cries of exasperation mingled with horns and bells as vehicles of all kinds nudged each other along the rain-covered streets.

It was another world. She had never seen people of so many nationalities within a single city block. Laborers pushed wheelbarrows piled high with sacks of goods, vegetables stacked for delivery, furniture, and, often as not, half a dozen passengers whose legs dangled over the wheelbarrow's platform. Other workers carried heavy loads in baskets swinging from the ends of bamboo poles hefted across their shoulders, the men nearly bent over from the weight but still threading their way deftly through the crowds.

Yet amidst all this confusion there was enough that was reassuringly familiar to Caroline, especially in the buildings along the Bund. She had seen postcards and guidebooks about this part of the waterfront, a street where banks and embassies dominated the shore, with buildings that could've been transported from a European city. Farther into the city, inside the French Concession, Chinese buildings and shops alternated with Western-style structures. Bakeries and nightclubs existed side by side; delicious smells tickled her nose, some familiar, others strange and tempting.

They left behind the noise and traffic to roll along what looked to Caroline like a country road. Wrought iron gates opened as the carriage approached and through the misty drizzle, Caroline caught her first sight of Lennox Manor. She squeezed Thomas's arm in excitement. Her new home. A porte cochere sheltered the few steps up to the mansion's front door, and when the carriage stopped, Mason got out and spoke to the lean Chinese manservant who had come out to greet them.

"Welcome, welcome," Mason said, "welcome to your new home." The Chinese servant bowed and held the door open. "This is Chin, our Number One Boy. Anything you want, ask him first."

A line of house servants, all men, stood by the staircase, dressed in blue cotton tunics with high necks worn over loose black trousers. Their eyes were alert and inquisitive as they bowed to the new arrivals. They ranged from an older man, whose spotless apron proclaimed him the cook, all the way down to a boy, a child of perhaps twelve who stared openly at Caroline until Chin rapped him on the top of the head.

"It's been a long time since a lady took charge of this place," Mason said. "It's good to have you here, my dear." His accompanying smile expressed welcome but Caroline glimpsed a shrewd gleam in his eyes that made her uneasy.

Her unease was justified within a few days. Caroline quickly came to the realization, one she had not yet shared with Thomas, that Mason Burnett wasn't so much leaving the house to them as ridding himself of a white elephant. During her first day of exploration, she recognized immediately how expensive it would be to bring Lennox Manor back to good repair; the more she saw of the building, the more worrisome the situation, especially since Thomas had also agreed to take over all household expenses.

Caroline soon realized that if she were to do a good job of running the house, she would have to train the staff, and for that she needed help to do it quickly. For some reason, the servants were all new except for the head servant. Chin spoke a little English, the rest of the staff none at all, and the list of things she needed to do grew longer each day.

But now she had Lisan, which made life much easier.

STANDING AT THE window of her parlor, she shook her head at the memory of her first days in Lennox Manor, when the sight of the sodden lawns and the rivulets running along the gravel driveway had dismayed her. The garden had been left to grow wild for too long. She suspected Mason had brought in workers before she and Thomas arrived to mow down the tall grass. Lisan said they now had a gardener, an actual trained gardener, not just some manual laborer, and he was tidying up the hothouse.

Caroline was pleased with her young secretary, whom she found quiet but forthright. After just a few days, Caroline could tell they would get along very well. There was nothing forced about Lisan's pleasant demeanor or her deferential manner. She hoped the young woman would grow more talkative once she settled into the role and the household. During her time living with the Dominics, Caroline knew that some of the best information came from servants' gossip.

Lisan unraveled some of the mysteries of domestic help in China for her. She had trailed behind Caroline, translating and offering suggestions, explaining to her why the servants did things a certain way and explaining to the servants how Caroline wanted some tasks done differently. She could already tell that the house servants were quick and intelligent. With Lisan's help, it wouldn't take long for them to learn how she liked things done. Between Miss Fielding's Finishing School for Young Ladies and living at the Dominics', she'd acquired a very thorough education in the practicalities of running a large house, but it was helpful to have Lisan vouch for a different perspective. After all, Shanghai was not New York.

For one thing, Caroline felt they had too many servants.

"If you're worried about the cost, Mrs. Stanton, there's no need," Lisan said. "I understand that compared to America or Europe, in China a large household staff is extremely affordable. You don't have too many servants, I promise you, not for a house of this size."

"But there's head servant Chin, four houseboys, and two cooks," Caroline said, "and Uncle Mason has a carriage and driver."

"And the new gardener," Lisan reminded her. "The main thing, ma'am, is to think of Chin, your head servant and Number One Boy, as the equivalent of a butler. His command of English is basic but for most housekeeping chores he is completely able to convey your instructions to the other house servants. If you have any problems with the house servants, he will replace those who don't meet your standards. House servants, cooks, kitchen help, and so on. Remember the other day, when you mentioned hosting a party? He offered to borrow some extra servants. He has good connections."

"All right. But another thing—except for our youngest houseboy, the servants are all grown men," Caroline said. "But we call them 'Boy' and by number. Number Two Boy. Number Three Boy. Don't they mind?"

"It's very kind of you to ask if they mind," Lisan said, looking startled. "I'm not sure they believe there's a choice. Westerners have a difficult time learning Chinese names and find it easier to call servants by number. It's been going on since . . . oh, ever since foreigners first hired Chinese servants." Her voice and expression were deliberately very polite.

And indeed, when Caroline looked into it, the house servants were quite affordable. The cost of keeping them was minuscule compared with the cost of restoring the house to good condition. If Mason wanted Thomas to pay for that, she would at least compile a list and get some idea of the expense. It would also be a good way to start a conversation with Thomas about Mason. They had to be careful. His uncle was not a benevolent father figure even though Thomas wanted to think of him that way.

THOMAS AND MASON would be in the city all day, so it was a good time to make a thorough tour of the house and all its rooms. Caroline had Lisan accompany her with a notepad. Their first task was to inventory the food and supplies stores in the kitchen and pantry. Rice and beans, flour, sugar, salt, oil, vinegar, potatoes, and apples. Hams and tinned kippers for Mason's breakfast. Lamp oil, candles, soaps, various polishes, tea towels, and brushes.

Zhao the cook and his son shopped at the market every day for fresh food, and vendors delivered supplies such as lamp oil. There was no existing list to work from as far as she could tell.

"Lists are so important." Caroline sighed. "At school we were taught to make sure the pantry never ran out of essential food and supplies. For example, there's eight metal jerry cans of lamp oil and I've no idea how long it lasts."

"You'll know in time, Mrs. Stanton," Lisan said, "just ask Chin to keep an eye on things. What matters is that you've made a list."

"Let's take a tour of the house," she said. "I've a feeling it's been neglected for too long." She paused, looked more closely at Lisan. There was a bruised look around her eyes, and her shoulders slumped slightly, as though she was tiring. But her secretary's smile was bright and her responses immediate. "Let's work our way from one end of each floor to the other," Caroline continued, deciding not to show concern. Not yet. "Top to bottom."

The house's foundations were stonework, the house itself timber. It had been built for luxury, no doubt of that. The ballroom was on the third floor, along with powder rooms for guests and a salon where female guests could rest and freshen up. On the second floor, the entire west wing was reserved for the Stantons. Their suites faced each other across the hall, each suite consisting of bedchamber, bathroom, and dressing room; Caroline's dressing room was much larger, lined with shelves and wardrobes. She had claimed another room, the one closest to the main staircase, to use as her private parlor and office.

Her parents' house had been in poor condition too, so Caroline knew what to look for. At first glance the house seemed solid, especially the rooms for entertaining. But upon closer inspection, she saw that rain had seeped in through warped window frames, too many floorboards creaked, and the plumbing was erratic. Caroline ran her hand along the wallpaper in her dressing room and felt something give underneath. Kneeling down in a corner, she picked away at an edge and realized that wallpaper had been recently and hastily applied to conceal crumbling plasterwork.

Mason's quarters were in the smaller east wing. Caroline knew she shouldn't enter his quarters unless invited and expected the same from him when it came to the west wing. But she felt no compunction about taking a look around to assess the state of the house.

In the rooms that Mason used, fireplaces and stoves kept the air warm and relatively dry. But in rooms where sheets covered furniture, evidence that they were not used, the air was dank, condensation dripping down windowpanes and mirrors. They found strips of wallpaper that showed signs of mildew. One window frame was starting to rot. Clearly Mason had made superficial improvements to dress up the Stantons' rooms and the public rooms. But his own quarters revealed the true state of Lennox Manor.

It was making her head ache. "Let's go outside now," she said to Lisan, "I really need some fresh air." She had examined the property from various upstairs windows and now it was time to descend into the gardens.

It was clear to Caroline what a huge amount of work it would take to care for these five acres if they were to be returned to beautiful condition. She shuddered to think of the effort needed to revive the derelict shrubs and flower beds. The parklike setting held south-facing lawns and a small orchard. A beautiful grove of birch trees had been planted by the western perimeter of the park, and a formal French garden grew below the terrace. Behind the formal gardens a flat expanse of ground contained the croquet lawn and tennis court, then sloped up on the south side to meet an earthen berm topped with a row of poplar trees, marking one edge of the property.

Then there was the shimmering oval beyond the croquet lawn, a man-made lake rimmed with banked turf and a stand of willows. Today, its waters rippled with gusts of wind and willow branches swayed on its shores like mourners singing hymns.

On some other fine day, she would walk around the property with Thomas and have him take an inventory of what needed repairing on the exterior. Surely he'd have Mason pay a share of the costs once he saw how much was involved. That is, if Mason had any money at all.

AFTER THE INSPECTION, she felt she needed a cup of tea or maybe a glass of sherry. She sat in her small parlor with Lisan. The Number Two Boy, whom Lisan addressed as Liao, brought them a tray of tea and biscuits.

"It's going to cost a fortune to bring this pile of lumber back to its original glory," she said with a sigh.

"But that is the arrangement, isn't it?" Lisan said, kneeling by the table to pour Caroline's tea.

"Yes, it's our responsibility to fix up Lennox Manor," she said, thinking of Mason and his infuriating assumption that the Stantons would take on all the household expenses, the staff as well as repairs. Equally infuriating was that Thomas had agreed.

"Perhaps you could negotiate with Mr. Liu?" Lisan said.

"What do you mean?" Caroline said. "Who is Mr. Liu?"

The girl looked up, flustered. "The owner of this house," she said. "I was told Mr. Burnett leased Lennox Manor from Mr. Liu. But perhaps I'm wrong. My apologies."

"Who told you, Lisan?" Caroline said. She noticed the concern on the young Chinese woman's features. "Don't worry, it's not your fault if you're mistaken. And if you're right, I'm better off knowing. Tell me."

Her secretary looked down in embarrassment, then, after much coaxing, mumbled that she had overheard talk that a Mr. Liu owned Lennox Manor, that in fact he had bought it from Mason Burnett, then leased it back to him for next to nothing. Part of the lease agreement was that Mason would pay for its upkeep and restore it to its original condition.

LISAN'S REVELATIONS INFURIATED Caroline, but she was careful not to let it show. She didn't want the young Chinese woman to think she blamed her for anything. Instead, she set Lisan to work addressing invitations for the party, giving her the list of names that Mason had drawn up, with a few more Thomas had added.

Then she eased herself into the armchair by the tall arched window of her parlor to still her mind. She wouldn't allow herself to stew over Mason's duplicity. She had a party to plan.

The menu, written in Lisan's flawless copperplate, lay on the side table and she picked it up to review for the umpteenth time. The party would be her first real foray into Shanghai society as a hostess.

Lisan had helped things along immensely by recommending the city's best French pâtisserie to supply the desserts. The cook was exceptional, but she had doubts that he was able to produce the elegant pastries and desserts the occasion demanded. He had indeed looked more relieved than affronted when Caroline informed him she would be ordering desserts and pastries from Pâtisserie Bontemps.

Unfortunately, neither the beautifully written menu nor the memory of sampling delicious pastries the day before was enough to dampen Caroline's anger. Even in China, the cost of upkeep for such a property was ruinous, a cost Thomas was taking on because Lennox Manor would be theirs one day. Except that it wasn't Mason's property, according to what she'd learned from Lisan. And even so, she wasn't going to tell Thomas or confront Mason, not until she had the evidence to confirm this information; but she believed Lisan more than she did Mason.

Outside, the wind was picking up. Dull rays of sunset stained the pale yellow wallpaper a dim beige. Even though the fireplace was burning and the lamps turned on, her little parlor felt dreary. At least she had exchanged that heavy secretaire desk for a smaller one, a dainty kidney-shaped desk with a veneer of golden walnut burl. With Lisan handling most of the correspondence, she didn't need a large desk. She'd put the bulk of her stationery and writing supplies in the secretaire desk, which was now in Lisan's room.

She had placed a miniature pine tree on the walnut desk. It was something she'd found in the hothouse. There were two other such small trees and she would ask Lisan about them sometime. Such beautiful little curiosities. Caroline got up from the armchair, moved away from the window. She really needed to get ready for yet another dinner engagement.

The Stantons were now part of Shanghai's international society, newest members of the elite, and everyone wanted a look at them. Invitations had poured in, dinners and charity auctions, the Race Club, musical performances. Thomas was attending almost every social event right now to meet potential business partners, potential sources of funding.

Caroline began picking out the jewelry to wear that night. Later, she would ring for Lisan to help her into her corset and dress. She could manage everything else; at boarding school, she'd learned to do without a lady's maid, and now that she could afford as many servants as she wanted, she decided she didn't want one. It would be just another person nosing around. Caroline had also decided she wouldn't drink any wine or champagne for the next several days. Alcohol disturbed her sleep and whenever she woke up, she found it hard to settle down again. There was something about this house, about its location so far from the city—the nights were utterly and silently dark, no neighboring lights or streetlamps, no music from nightclubs or cries of farewell as friends parted company. The silence magnified every small noise inside the house: the rattle of a shutter against its latch, the creak of floorboards, the low whistle of wind blowing through one of the chimneys, a sound like a woman crying.

As soon as she could, she thought, brushing out her hair, she would find out who really owned Lennox Manor. There had to be a land titles office somewhere in Shanghai.

CHAPTER 6

I'D LIKE TO discuss something with you, Caroline," Thomas said
at breakfast the next morning. Mason always took breakfast in
his room, citing the need to give young couples as much privacy as
possible. Caroline suspected it was because Mason needed time to
recover from his habitual hangovers. Thomas probably knew this,
but kept up the pretense. He felt sorry for Mason, she knew, but
she also suspected something more—that Thomas felt protective
of Mason, an older relative, his only remaining family.

"Yes, darling," she said, scanning the morning post. Shanghai's
postal system was surprisingly good, with deliveries three times a
day. There were a half dozen invitations on the silver tray. "Is there
a problem?"

"I've reconsidered how to go about raising funds for this railway venture," he said, "now that we're here and I've seen for myself it's an incredible opportunity. The Chinese government wants
to expand railway networks using foreign companies and foreign
money to do it. We want a larger controlling share, and for that
we'd need to put in more capital."

"Are you thinking of selling your silver mines, Thomas?" she
asked, putting down the paper. She opened her eyes wide, a guileless young woman. She had a horrible feeling she knew what was
coming.

"No, not at all," he said, "those are doing well."

"Oh. So does it mean Uncle Mason is putting in more capital?" she said, still in her most innocent voice.

"Uncle Mason," and here Thomas cleared his throat, "he's, well, he isn't prepared to invest any more. In fact, he's backed off a bit on the amount he'd promised to invest."

"Wasn't it his assurances that made this a good move?" she said. She clenched one hand in her lap and rested the other on the newspaper. But she had to stay calm, appear trusting. "Has he changed his mind? Thomas, exactly how much is Mason investing?"

"Very little," he said, reluctantly, "less than I first believed. Now, Caroline, your inheritance is yours to use as you wish, always. But I would be very grateful if I could borrow some. I'll return it, of course, once the railway is making money."

Thomas explained he was looking at a scheme where the company would loan money to the Chinese government, and the government would then use those funds to finance the railway's building and development. Then Burnett and Stanton Ltd. would run the railway and retain most of the profits until the government paid back the loan in full.

"But given the state of the Imperial finances," Thomas said, "the Chinese won't be able to pay back the loan, not in our lifetime anyway. It's going to be a cash cow, earning more than any other venture out there, any stocks or savings. But for this to work, I'd want our family to control a majority shareholding."

He continued cutting up his ham and eggs. *Our family.* He meant Mason. But wasn't she, his wife, also family? Did he want her money because he had such confidence that he was willing to go ahead even if Mason put in less than promised? Or was it because he needed to make up the difference for what should've been Mason's share? Either way, now he needed more money and he wasn't going to raise it from selling his own silver mines. A wife's inheritance was like found money, easier than a bank loan, not to mention interest free.

In New York, whenever the Dominics threw a party, she had loitered at the peripheries. Guests oblivious to her presence, she had become an expert at invisibility and she had listened. Listened and then pondered, lying awake in her bed musing upon the secrets that New York's society ladies revealed to each other in quiet corners, behind screens and potted plants.

The Ingraham sisters, for instance. Their conversation had been a truly useful lesson, a cautionary tale. One sister confessed to the other that she had loaned money out of her inheritance to her husband, who needed funds to get over a rough patch.

"But there was no end to the rough patch, Ida," she said. The two huddled together on an upholstered bench partially screened by a large potted bamboo, their voices low. "And then he borrowed more, throwing good money after bad, but I didn't want to hurt his feelings by saying so. Now my legacy from our parents is gone and he can't ever pay it back. I've nothing of my own anymore."

Nothing of my own.

Those four words haunted Caroline. The Dominics moved in circles where young women entered a marriage with money of their own or the anticipation of an inheritance. Caroline had witnessed how the kindest of husbands could turn when it came to money. Money and pride. When that happened, they inevitably presumed their wives' money was there for the taking. When his debts mounted, a husband could ask, even demand, that his wife hand over her wealth. He might use words such as "borrow" or "just until it gets better," but "asking" for a loan was only a formality. What choice did women have but to comply? To maintain their marriage and family, to avoid the shame of bankruptcy. To keep up appearances.

Caroline had vowed she'd never let that happen to her. No

one would control her money, however little or however much she had. The Dominics' will had appointed one of their lawyers as Caroline's legal guardian, charged with managing her inheritances until she turned twenty-five or married. She'd married Thomas Stanton, a millionaire in his own right who didn't need her money.

Except now he did.

CHAPTER 7

THE NIGHTMARE WAS utterly familiar and that's what made it worse each time for Lisan. She knew what would happen but she was helpless to change things. The dream swept her along, relentless, inexorable.

First, a large hand grasps hers and pulls her up a long staircase. Her legs pump desperately to clamber up each step, calves aching with the effort to keep up. She reaches the top of the stairwell and there's a view of rooftops. Black smoke billows in the distance, loud noises boom from the streets outside, and screams shred the air. She stands looking down and it's a familiar sight: a beautiful courtyard garden with an arched bridge that spans a large pond. What's not familiar is the activity in the courtyard, women running through the garden in all directions, a confusion of movement. And then there's nothing to see as gentle hands tie a cloth over her eyes and a voice, quavering but insistent, says, *Now jump.*

But Lisan doesn't jump. She never jumps, because that's when she always wakes up.

She sat up gasping for breath, panicked for a moment when she didn't recognize the room, then after a few more breaths remembered. She was in Lennox Manor. Swinging her legs out of bed, she stumbled to the window and struggled to push it open just an inch, cursing the humidity that had swollen the wood. Cool, damp air entered, calming the jumbled riot of emotions pounding at her heart. Through rain-spattered glass the sky was momentarily clear of clouds, swept away by windy gusts that seized leaves off branches and sent them flailing through the air.

Lisan couldn't remember a spring as cold as this. The newspapers said it might even snow. She pressed her face against the glass, clouding it with her breath. She wiped it clear, wished she could wipe away the terror of her nightmare as easily. It had been years since that particular one had materialized so vividly, affected her so forcefully. It was the strain of the past weeks, she told herself. First Master Liu forcing her to leave her job with Mrs. Gordon—which she hoped had not caused a rift between her and the headmistress. Then coming here to Lennox Manor, the effort of adjusting to a new life, a new employer. To this house. A house whose every creaking floorboard and rattling casement seemed to cry out to her.

And there was Yao. So strong was the impression of familiarity that whenever she saw him, she fell into confusion, unable to voice her questions. She had sifted through her memories and found nothing that could warrant such feelings; she'd never spent more than a few minutes in Yao's presence whenever he came to see Master Liu. They'd only ever exchanged polite greetings, the most superficial of conversations.

And yet she could feel his eyes on her whenever she turned to leave a room. And he had always treated her respectfully, almost deferentially, even when she was a little girl and he a mere teenager. Perhaps because although Master Liu had not adopted either of them, she lived as a member of his household while Yao had been sent off to apprentice as a gardener.

She considered the possibility that somehow, he had known her before Master Liu took her in. She had no memories of that other life. She had tried at different times to gather her thoughts and move backward, deeper into the past, but her mind always shrank away from that darkness like billowing black curtains of dread that prevented her from seeing—seeing what? Remembering what?

She had told Master Liu about her nightmares once. She wondered if they had anything to do with her past. He listened to her inarticulate, childish outpouring. She was still a child then, and when she finally stopped, he patted the seat beside him, and she sat down on the long elmwood bench.

"You were all alone when I found you," he said very gently, "and I think that your life must've been very harsh or perhaps you saw something terrible. Perhaps you forgot everything because it was just too sad, made you too unhappy, but sometimes memories pop up in those bad dreams. In which case, it's best you don't try to remember, *neh*?"

Master Liu didn't know about her past but perhaps Yao did. She had to talk to him, ask if he recognized her. What if he had known her real family? But surely he would've said something if that was the case. She wouldn't get her hopes up, but if she didn't ask, she would always wonder. She had to work up the courage to ask him.

Why do you seem so familiar, Yao? Why do I trust you without knowing anything about you?

She had hardly slept this past week. When awake, she forced herself to smile and pay close attention, hide her exhaustion from Caroline Stanton. Lisan never realized how much she missed the familiar sounds of the only home she could remember, how she'd fallen asleep to the household's nighttime routines at Master Liu's villa. To the quiet shuffle of cloth slippers as the house servants checked each room, banking fires and turning out lights; the soft thuds as doors pulled shut; the faint sweet trills of Master Liu's bamboo flute from the other side of the house as he practiced a new piece of music.

But out here at the far end of Bubbling Well Road, Lennox Manor sat in splendid, if rather bedraggled solitude. Since following Caroline through the entire house, Lisan understood why she heard so many strange noises in the night. Warped floorboards, gaps in door and window frames, clogged chimneys and loose latches. Every shift in temperature made timbers expand or contract to grind against each other, every puff of breeze outside moaned its way through cracks, and unsecured shutters thumped like footsteps.

Yet even knowing all this, those nighttime noises still put her on edge.

She coughed. Her throat felt parched and painful, the way it did before coming down with a cold. She needed a drink of water. The jug in her room was empty and Lisan wasn't going to risk a drink from the bathroom tap. She'd find her way to the kitchen, where there was sure to be a carafe of clean, boiled water.

She didn't want to disturb anyone by turning on the electric lights, so Lisan lit the oil lamp beside her bed and pulled on a quilted robe. She padded out to the landing and down the narrow staircase, trying not to cough. Opening the door to the kitchen and work areas, she paused. Someone was crying. The sound was faint, and she could've sworn it was the sound of a woman sobbing. Woman or child? Could Xiao Wu, the youngest house servant, be unhappy or ill? But it seemed to be coming from the other side of the house, beyond the servants' quarters.

Her feet moved from polished hardwood planks to cold marble as she followed the sound, crossing from the main hall to the foyer, the lamp flickering in her hand. She stood there, uncertain of what to do next. The sound of crying had stopped. The drawing room doors were wide open, and for the first time in what seemed like weeks, the moon was visible, its cold, silvery light glimmering in a long streak of brightness on the floor below each window. She went to a window, beguiled by the sight of skies swept clean of all but a few wisps of cloud. Out on the lake, the moon's reflection rippled on the water's surface as though trapped and struggling. Moonlight fell on a hazy shape weaving between the willow trees, a shape that resembled a woman. A woman in a long, flowing red dress. Startled, Lisan backed away from the window. When she looked again, the figure had vanished.

Trembling, she lifted the lamp and made her way back across the foyer, back to her room.

"Rosa?" A man's voice, slightly slurred. Puzzled. "Rosalie?"

From the second-floor landing, a large figure looked down on her. He swayed a little, steadied himself on the handrail. A large, balding man in a long dressing gown.

"It's Lisan Liu, sir," she said. "Mrs. Stanton's secretary. Are you all right, Mr. Burnett?"

"Not Rosalie." He shook his head, then stumbled as he turned away. He paused and looked down at her again. "No, you couldn't possibly be Rosa," he said, and left the landing, his footsteps ponderous, heavy. He turned to the east wing, mumbling words she couldn't make out.

Could he have been the one she heard weeping? No, it had been a woman's voice, she was sure of that. Returning to her room, she climbed back under the blankets, shivering. Who was Rosalie? Was she the one who was crying? She closed her eyes and exhaustion from all the sleepless nights finally claimed her.

LISAN WOKE AT daybreak, the light still hesitant and muted, the skies sullen. Scraps of memories. A woman had been crying. Had Mason Burnett really been speaking to her? The events of the night seemed so unreal now. But there was soot on the glass shade of the oil lamp beside her bed, proof she had used it. She pushed herself up and looked around.

It was still hard to think of this room as her own. She had rearranged the furniture a bit, and now a low chest of drawers beside the bed doubled as a night table. She had moved a wooden chair to a spot beside the door where she could sit to remove her shoes. At some point someone—she suspected Xiao Wu—had put a single stem of orchid blooms in a slim pewter vase by her bed, a small act of kindness that made her smile. Lennox Manor felt more familiar now, but the disquiet that curled around her whenever she was inside the mansion refused to dispel and she didn't know if it ever would.

There was something she did know: it was time to talk to Yao. The act of asking him the question, she realized, mattered as much as his answer, whatever it might be.

In the normal course of a day, she had no reason to speak with the gardener; the only time they were in the same room was when the servants ate together, and she had no intention of starting a personal conversation with others avidly listening in. But this morning, she had an opportunity, a perfect excuse to seek him out.

Lisan pulled her clothes off the chair where they had been warming in front of the fireplace and dressed quickly. She had ample time to herself each morning. Caroline always had breakfast with her husband, and after Thomas left she would go upstairs to change out of her housecoat and into a day dress. Caroline didn't have a lady's maid and said she didn't need one.

"I don't need a maid, Lisan," Caroline had said, laughing, when Lisan asked. "I was at boarding school for years and learned to do for myself. Just come to my room at nine o'clock each morning to button me up."

Entering Caroline's small parlor, she picked up the tree *penjing* from the walnut desk and carried it down to the hothouse. It was a magnificent structure, a long hall of glass and iron with glass-paneled walls rising above a base of waist-high stone. Cast-iron medallions decorated corners where slim metal pillars intersected to support a peaked glass roof. Hot water pipes set into the ground heated the space, and the hothouse was warm and humid, stiflingly so. Condensation dripped from metal beams and fogged up glass panes. Long tables held porcelain pots of orchids and ginger lilies. Ferns grew everywhere, springing from containers and hanging baskets. A riot of pink and white jasmines clambered up one trellis and coral-red bougainvillea covered another.

"Hello?" she called. "Yao? Mrs. Stanton has a request."

Yao emerged from behind the bougainvillea trellis, holding a tray of seedling pots. "Miss Liu? Does she want more ginger lilies in the breakfast room?"

She shook her head and held out the miniature tree. "I told her these could be quite old," she said, "so she wants to know what type of tree this is, and how old it is, if you're able to tell."

"I've studied horticulture and landscaping," he said, "and *penjing* was part of the training. Let me see."

He set down the tray and examined the tree. He put it at the end of a table and crouched down to view it, lifted it up and examined the bottom of the pot. "It's a Japanese white pine," he said, "roughly fifty years old." He tilted the container toward her very carefully, lifting it so she could read what was etched into its unglazed bottom. "The person who first potted this marked the date."

"I won't give away your secret," she said, laughing.

Did she imagine it or was there warmth in his smile? She wanted to keep talking, continue the conversation and learn more about his past. There was an old copy of *Shenbao* newspaper on the table, spread open under some empty pots. She pointed at the headline, hoping it was a topic that interested him.

"There's a lot of anger at the government for their plans to nationalize provincial railways and use them as collateral to borrow money from foreign banks," she noted.

"In Sichuan there's talk of riots," Yao said. "Sichuan province raised money for their railway project by selling shares to ordinary people. Thousands of merchants and gentry are furious they'll lose their investment. Not to mention that the railway will then be handed over to foreigners."

She studied the article. "The writer condemns the Sichuan railway company for being so badly run that they've laid less than ten miles of track in four years. At the same time, he condemns the government for taking over local railways to pay back debts. It seems hopeless."

"Yes," he said, "this cannot continue, Lisan. China cannot continue like this or we will pawn away our future. The question is what model best serves the common citizen, not emperors and aristocrats."

The Imperial government was beset by infighting, and newspapers such as *Shenbao* no longer held back criticism. Residents of Shanghai had the advantage of subscribing to foreign-owned papers that covered the news independently. Of these, *Shenbao* was the most reliable, according to Master Liu. Next to the family-owned *Xinwen Bao*, of course.

"I'm not an expert in politics," she said, "but I feel it must be a democracy of some sort, a complete break from empire. We Chinese have had absolute rulers for thousands of years and are so accustomed to an emperor that if we merely change to a constitutional monarchy, I worry we will drift back to an absolute monarchy."

"Are these revolutionary views because of your foreign school?" he said. She could tell he was teasing. "Do all your classmates think as you do?"

Lisan laughed. "No, not at all. Some don't ever think about politics and others belong to families with close ties to the Imperial government. What do you think, Yao?"

"I'm only a gardener," he said, "and what I mostly think about is what to do about this hothouse. It's a wilderness. Chin doesn't know how to prune or thin out plants. He did water and keep the heating system going for the past three years, but I'm still trying to get the humidity right."

"How long has Chin been at Lennox Manor?" Lisan asked, hoping to nudge the conversation in a different direction. "He keeps very much to himself. Have you ever talked to him?"

"He does keep to himself and never socializes with the house servants," Yao said. "He thinks the cook gossips too much. He's willing to chat with me though, and I did ask why he stayed here for so long looking after Mr. Burnett on his own. He said he couldn't work anywhere else, he won't leave Lennox Manor. And that ended the discussion."

"There's nothing in Chin's manner to make me think he's particularly devoted to Mason Burnett." Lisan's brows creased. Chin was an extremely capable head servant. She doubted he'd have trouble finding work in any foreign household.

"Do you know whether he was here when . . . when Mr. Burnett's son died?" she asked.

"I don't know if he was here when young Mr. Burnett lived at Lennox Manor or only since Master Mason moved into the house," Yao said. "All I know is that Chin believes all other cities inferior to Shanghai." He smiled, a slow, amused lift of his lips that made her want to move closer. His smile reassured her, gave her the courage to ask what she'd been wanting to know since she first saw him.

"What about you, Yao?" Lisan said. "Are you originally from Shanghai?"

"No, not at all," he said. "I'm from the north. Peking. I came to Shanghai when I was, well, perhaps fourteen."

She paused before asking. "Your family?"

He shook his head. "They gave me up, sold me as a bond servant to . . . to a wealthy family. During the Boxer Rebellion, they fled the city, leaving their servants behind."

Lisan knew the history of what had happened in 1900. Every school child knew. The Chinese Army, aided by fanatical rebels known as the Boxers, attacked Peking's foreign residents, who took shelter inside the grounds of the Foreign Legation. There, Western military units as well as civilians defended themselves for nearly two months under siege until troops from an alliance of eight nations arrived to defeat the Boxers and the Chinese Army. The victorious foreign powers then forced China to make reparations of more than three hundred million dollars, effectively putting the country into a permanent state of debt.

Foreigners weren't the only ones affected; many of Peking's local residents also fled the fighting.

"I joined a group of refugees heading for Shanghai," he said, "and that's how I ended up here on the streets, where Master Liu found me."

After a few months, Master Liu noticed how much Yao enjoyed helping the gardener and sent the boy to live with a friend in Soochow, a rich and cultured scholar whose garden was famous throughout China. There he apprenticed with the head gardener.

"So you're not from Shanghai," she said, disappointed. "It's just that I've always wondered whether we've met before we came to live with Master Liu. Have we?" There, she'd said it. Asked the question that had been unsettling her since he first walked into the kitchen.

He smiled, a smile that gave nothing away. "I don't believe so, but I have a very ordinary face," he said, "very common features."

No, not common, she wanted to say. I could find your face in a sea of faces.

She picked up the plant and said, "Thank you. I'll tell Mrs. Stanton this is a fifty-year-old Japanese white pine."

"Bring that white pine back in about two weeks," he said, opening the door of the hothouse for her. "I'll pinch back some of those buds."

COME FIND ME, a soft voice whispers urgently.

That was all she could remember, except for scattered scraps of images: the lake and the willow trees, a red dress. It took all Lisan's willpower to pay attention to the task in front of her. She closed her eyes momentarily, pushing away the nightmare that had woken her up just before dawn, tangled in her sheets and moaning. The voice lingered at the edges of her mind, whispering those three words whenever she let her thoughts slip or her focus drift away from Caroline's seated figure.

"Most of the guests are people Uncle Mason said we should invite," Caroline said, scanning the sheets of paper on her desk. RSVPs had started coming in for the party since the invitations went out two days ago, and she was checking them against the guest list, something Lisan had offered to do but Caroline wanted to do it herself. "We'll just have to trust that Mason has invited all the right people. They're probably all 'old China hands,' as he calls them. And their wives," Caroline added with a sigh.

"Almost all have accepted," Lisan said, "and I suspect the rest of the RSVPs will arrive tomorrow morning."

"I nearly forgot." Caroline picked up a business card from the corner of her desk. "Uncle Mason gave me this. It's the architect who's renovating his office. Add Mr. Grey to the guest list and make sure the invitation is delivered to his hotel today. The hotel name is on the back."

"Yes, Mrs. Stanton. I'll write him an invitation right away," Lisan said.

The American woman was easy to work for and unexpectedly kind. Lisan had soon realized that Caroline was probably no more than four or five years her senior. Yet there were times when Lisan caught a glimpse of Caroline's face deep in thought, her eyes more green than brown, an expression that spoke of knowledge beyond her years.

"Lisan, something I've been meaning to mention," Caroline said. "When we were inspecting the house the other day, I noticed the servants have pasted paper with writing and pictures beside doors to the kitchen and servants' quarters. I want them taken down."

"Ma'am, unless it really offends you, please don't do that," Lisan said, "it would upset the house servants. They're meant to ward off evil spirits."

"Goodness, why?" Caroline laughed. "Is the house haunted? Oh come now, Lisan. You blush so easily. I can tell you know something."

"The servants get nervous, Mrs. Stanton," she said, unsure of how much to divulge, "because there was a suicide in this house, and they worry about the ghost. They're superstitious and believe the ghost of a suicide to be the most dangerous type of evil spirit."

"Really? How interesting." Caroline tilted her head to one side. "And do you know who it was that committed suicide?" She looked intently at Lisan, who fidgeted with the pen before finally looking up.

"It was Mr. Burnett's son, Charles," Lisan said, deciding there was no way to reveal just one part of the story. "He was heavily in debt, lost his friends, and then his wife left him."

There was a long silence. "Uncle Mason never talks about how

Charles died," Caroline said, "or that he had a wife. We assumed he died of some illness. How did Charles die?"

"Apparently, he hung himself." She looked away from Caroline.

"And where is Charles's wife, do you know? Is Mason still in touch with her?"

"I don't believe Mr. Burnett cared to stay in touch," she said. "He didn't approve of his daughter-in-law. She was a singer."

"Well," Caroline said, "that certainly explains why people keep asking how I enjoy living here. I thought it was because Lennox Manor is so out of the way, but they were fishing to see what I knew about Charles Burnett. Thank you for telling me, Lisan. Now I won't get ambushed by some supposedly well-intentioned person. What was her name, the wife?"

"I don't know, Mrs. Stanton," Lisan said, but she remembered Mason Burnett's confused voice. *Rosa? Rosalie?*

"No matter, I'm sure some helpful gossip will tell me all the lurid details," Caroline said. "Well, that's all for now, Lisan. Oh, and can you please telephone the dressmaker? Since we will be in the city tomorrow anyway, I may as well drop in for a fitting."

"Certainly," Lisan said. "And I will update the guest list with Mr. Grey's name before you go out tonight." The Stantons were attending a musical that night, a fundraiser put on by one of Shanghai's many amateur music societies.

"Oh, that stupid charity performance," Caroline said with a groan. "I despise Gilbert and Sullivan. I would pay the same price as those tickets—no, more than the ticket price—to not attend. Our headmistress always chose a Gilbert and Sullivan for the spring musical. She put me in a lead role my final year."

"You must have a very nice voice, Mrs. Stanton," Lisan said.

"It was *The Pirates of Penzance* and I sang the role of Mabel," Caroline said, "in an awful puffy yellow dress and bonnet. Well, at least I'll be in the audience tonight and not onstage."

CHAPTER 8

THAT EVENING IN the kitchen, the servants' talk was all about the party, only two days away. Chin had borrowed three extra house servants to help serve and wash up. Florists would be bringing out-of-season flowers to fill large urns and vases. The cloakroom had to be staffed at all times.

Chin drilled the servants on the order of events and how they were to behave toward the guests.

"Xiao Wu, Little Liao, you'll clean the powder rooms every thirty minutes," he said, fixing them with a stern eye. "All of them. And Da Wu, you'll be stationed on the second-floor landing to direct guests upstairs to the ballroom."

Zhao the cook spoke up. "There will be platters of cakes and I want to scatter edible blooms on the platters. Anything suitable, Yao?"

"I can find you something." Yao nodded. "Violets or dianthus and marigolds. Enough for a bowl of petals."

As she dipped another dumpling in spicy-sweet soy sauce, Lisan watched Yao from under her lashes. She had just realized something else about him. His words and the way he spoke were those of an educated person, not a mere gardener. She knew that in the city of Soochow, famed for its glorious classical gardens, landscapers and gardeners were held in high regard; they often worked closely with the owners of such gardens, men of refinement and scholarship. Could he have acquired his manners and speech from being around such people?

The two Wu brothers were whispering to each other and Chin startled them with a rap on each of their heads. "Da Wu, Xiao Wu," he said. "Are you listening?"

"Yes, Head Servant," Da Wu said, "only we are a bit worried about all the noise from the party."

"Yes, the music and talk," Xiao Wu said, "so much louder than anything we've had before. What if it wakes the ghost? Music he remembers and conversation in his own language."

Chin gave them a withering look. "Even if a ghost comes screeching through the ballroom, you'll still make sure all the champagne glasses are filled."

Lisan took her leave of the servants, taking a mug of hot sweetened soy milk to the bedroom with her. There was a bit of work she wanted to finish. She kept a duplicate copy of Caroline Stanton's plans for the party, and now that most of the RSVPs were in, she might as well update her copy of the guest list.

The fireplace was more than adequate for heating the room, yet she couldn't shake off the chill that clung to her, draped like a damp shroud. She cupped her hands around the mug of hot soy milk and moved to the window. Wind rippled the willow trees by the lake and rattled her window latch. She would deal with the loose latch in the morning. Lightning spiked, and in the sudden light she saw a slash of red between the trees. She frowned. How could anyone be out there in all this rain? Thunder rumbled and then the slight figure was gone. It had been nothing more than a trick of the light, a movement caused by a torrent of windblown rain.

If only the rain would stop. A watery veil streamed down the roof, curtaining off the house from the rest of the world. Although at the moment it didn't matter since she wasn't interested in going out. The names on the RSVP list blurred. She rubbed her eyes, desperately tired. She would lie down, just for a few minutes, then get back to updating the list.

SHE IS CLIMBING the staircase again. Even though she knows it's a dream, even though she knows what will happen, she can't take control of the dream, can't break free. The hand that grasps hers is soft-skinned, a little damp with sweat, and she wants so badly to look up and see who she is following but she has to keep her eyes lowered and concentrate on negotiating the steps. If she looks up, she might trip and they'd both tumble down. When she finally reaches the top of the stairs, the sun blinds her with its brightness and she can't see the face of the person who pulled her up the steps. Sharp cracks of sound and screams as she is hurried along smooth wooden floors and then the blindfold is tied over her eyes, the weight of something drops onto her shoulders and a gentle voice, a voice she trusts, says, *Now jump.*

This time when she woke up, it was because she'd been jolted awake by sounds of crying, anguished sobs that tore into Lisan's heart even though she knew she was dreaming. Or at least she thought she was dreaming.

Then a woman's voice whispered in her ear, the words soft but the tone urgent. *Come find me.*

And this time, she truly woke up.

After a few minutes of restless dozing, she realized it would be impossible for her to fall asleep again. Heaving a sigh, Lisan got up, wrapped a shawl around her shoulders, and turned on the desk lamp. She may as well get back to work.

The large secretaire desk was an expensive piece of furniture, far too good for someone in her position. She'd spent considerable time arranging the desk to make her work more efficient: drawers in the lower half held writing paper, envelopes, and file folders.

The upper part of the desk was a bookcase flanked by pigeonholes. A leather desk pad covered the work surface and just above it were shelves holding Caroline's expensive monogrammed stationery. A dictionary and thesaurus rested on the top bookshelf, as well as a Shanghai business directory. The two most important items, always out on the desk, were an address book and a notebook, her copies of Caroline's address and appointment books.

There were brass inlays set into the wide band of carved molding that adorned the top of the bookcase. At the center, a brass medallion stood out in relief. Lisan admired the beautiful rose design etched on the brass, touching it gently. Lamplight glanced across the circle of rose petals and she noticed the center of the flower was slightly tarnished.

A faint idea nudged her consciousness and she pressed her index finger against the center of the medallion.

A soft click and a section of the ornamental molding sprang out a couple of inches, revealing a shallow drawer. It slid out smoothly when she gave it a light pull. Lisan scrambled up onto the chair and looked inside cautiously. She lifted out a cheap notebook with a plain gray cardboard cover, similar to the one she used to keep track of Caroline Stanton's appointments.

She flipped it open to the first page. And drew in her breath.

Rosalie Burnett. Above it, crossed out, *Rosalie Roussel.*

Charles Burnett's runaway wife. Her name had been Rosalie. *Rosa? Rosalie?* The name Mason Burnett had mumbled when drunk that night. Rosalie Roussel. And this was her diary.

10 Fevrier 1907

Avec la nouvelle année, un nouvel agenda. Je ferai de mon mieux pour y écrire chaque jour et pratiquer mon français . . .

French had not been Lisan's best subject; she had only taken two years of it at St. Clare's. She heaved a great sigh of frustration. She needed a dictionary to translate Rosalie's words. Why had Rosalie left her diary behind? Didn't she care who found it, or had she simply forgotten it in the rush to leave?

ROSALIE'S DIARY

10 February 1907

With the new year, a new diary. I will do my best to write
in it every day and practice my French. When the Bandman
Opera Company came, I went to audition because to sing
opera is my dream. One aria, I begged, just let me
perform one aria. But I couldn't even get in to see their
music director. I've auditioned for all the bands at all the big
hotels and nightclubs, but they don't want a girl like me.
They want American singers for popular dance music.

So today, at last, I have a job singing at the Golden Rooster,
which is not a five-star nightclub, or even a three-star. But my
money's running out and I must pay the rent on this room or
share with other girls and I would hate that. Always worrying
about them stealing my things, borrowing without asking,
gossip and meanness. I know it too well.

Father worries but what can he do? My voice could be
my fortune but my face will never allow that fortune to
materialize. But enough melancholy, it's a new year and I will
be onstage in a few hours.

CHAPTER 9

CAROLINE'S DRESSMAKER WAS one Lisan had recommended. "I have some very fashionable friends who use this tailor's shop," her secretary had said. "All they do is give him magazine pictures and his seamstresses copy the outfits perfectly."

On his first visit, the tailor had come to Lennox Manor bringing bolts of silk, embroidered fabric panels, and his head seamstress. The entire experience had proven wonderfully convenient. The shop was in the Chinese district of Shanghai, not in the International Settlement.

"I much prefer your Chinese tailor to the English one Mrs. Easton said to use," Caroline said. "There's no risk that any of my secrets will get back to ladies such as Mrs. Easton. Lisan, I order you to keep this tailor a secret from those busybodies."

They both laughed, Lisan at first just giggling, hand in front of her mouth, then a loud guffaw. Caroline, who had never seen her rather solemn young secretary like this, laughed even more.

And now she was going into Shanghai with Lisan for a final fitting. Normally the tailor would've come out to Lennox Manor again, but Caroline was curious about the Chinese City, or the Old City, as Lisan called it, the oldest part of Shanghai. Embedded within the foreign concessions, the Old City remained under Chinese authority, unlike the areas surrounding it, where a

Western police force and law courts operated according to their own conventions.

Besides, they were already going to Shanghai for other errands, so why not take a look? She had the use of Thomas's motorcar every day because each morning, after he and Mason went to the office, Thomas sent the driver back with the car for Caroline.

"Thomas and I can hail a taxi or rickshaws to come home if necessary," Mason said. "It's more important that you get around in comfort, Caroline." His smile was a bit oily, nervous. It turned out that the horse and carriage he'd been using were hired from a stable and not his own. By now Caroline knew he was barely keeping up appearances.

Thankfully, the enclosed carriage of the Pierce Arrow kept out rain and wind and they had a pleasant ride all the way into Shanghai, Lisan pointing out the city's landmarks, which Caroline was starting to recognize. As they neared the Old City, Lisan explained there had been walls encircling the Old City during the Ming dynasty, built during the sixteenth century to fend off pirates. But raiders had not been a problem for three hundred years.

"Now the old wall is an obstacle," Lisan said, "even though there are ten gates to let traffic through. Every year there are arguments for and against demolishing the walls."

The dressmaker's shop was on a street just inside the wall. Its windows were papered over with fashion magazine covers, and the interior was cramped and disorderly, filled with rolls of fabric and notions, with a curtained-off area for customer fittings. Lisan translated as the head seamstress tucked and pinned, checking with each adjustment whether it was to Caroline's satisfaction. When the seamstress finished, Caroline rotated slowly to admire her reflection in the tall three-way mirror. The gown of pale celadon-green silk trimmed with jet beading was French—or at least the design was French. The dress was deceptively simple, an empire-waisted sheath adorned with gauzy billowing sleeves. A short train of the same pale green silk fell from the shoulders in soft pleats. The design was by Callot Soeurs of Paris. The dress was a perfect copy that had taken just a week to complete.

Lisan helped her out of the dress, which the head seamstress took away. "The gown can be finished in fifteen minutes, Mrs. Stanton," Lisan said, "if it's not too inconvenient to wait?"

Caroline nodded. "Yes, I can wait. I wanted to look at his collection of fabrics anyway. They're as good as anything I've seen in New York. My goodness, what is this lovely blue cloth with black under weave?"

"That's silk from Siam, Mrs. Stanton," Lisan said. "It's hand-woven and appears to be cotton cloth until you notice the sheen and that two-tone effect."

The door of the tailor shop opened to a tinkling of bells and a voice squealed, "Liu Lisan!" There followed a cascade of greetings in Chinese that Lisan returned with smiles and exclamations. Caroline stared admiringly at the stylish young woman who had flounced into the shop, followed by a middle-aged servant who immediately sat down to flip through the pages of a fashion magazine.

The young woman was exquisitely dressed. She wore the latest in winter coats, and the leather boots peeping out from under the hem exactly matched her navy blue hat and the colors of her cashmere scarf. The conversation was rather one-sided, with Lisan mostly nodding at what her friend was saying, responding occasionally with an appreciative gasp. When Lisan finally got a word in, she said something that made the young woman twirl around to face Caroline.

Lisan switched to English. "Ju Ming, I'd like you to meet Mrs.

Thomas Stanton, my employer. Mrs. Stanton, my friend Ju Ming Lee."

"Mrs. Stanton. I'm so delighted to meet you." The young woman spoke perfect English with just a touch of an accent, similar to Lisan's. "I see so little of Lisan these days. But now I understand. She has a new job!"

The owner of the shop rushed out from the back, pouring out a torrent of words that made it clear Miss Lee was a valued customer. Following quickly behind him, the head seamstress brought out a garment bag, handed it to Lisan, and bowed to Caroline.

"I have so much more to tell you about Princess Masako Kyo," Lisan's friend said. "Oh dear, my father was so scandalized. But I see you're finishing up here, so I won't keep you. So nice to meet you, Mrs. Stanton. May I have permission to visit Lisan one day, when it's convenient?"

The driver sprang to attention as soon as Caroline and Lisan came out of the shop, held the door open for them. Caroline looked at Lisan curiously as they climbed into the automobile. "Your friend is delightful. How do you know her?"

"Ju Ming and I were classmates at St. Clare's Hall," she replied, settling into the passenger seat beside Caroline.

"Is she a close friend?" Caroline said.

Lisan hesitated. "She's one of my better friends. She's very kind and invites me to her parties, but I can never truly be part of their circle, Mrs. Stanton. No family, no lineage, no wealth."

"Women don't have an easy time making our way in this world." Caroline's voice was soft. "We must take hold of any opportunity that comes our way, make the most of every lucky break. I understand more than you know."

Lisan nodded, but Caroline could tell what she was thinking. Her secretary doubted that a woman like Caroline could truly understand. To her, Caroline had been born to wealth, had inherited wealth, and married wealth. Lisan seemed dejected by this turn of conversation, so Caroline changed the subject.

"Lisan," she said, "your friend mentioned a princess? Can you tell me more?"

"Just some gossip." Lisan brightened. "Ju Ming's father gave a banquet last night for Count Kato Komei, who is here from Japan on his way to the royal court in Peking. Princess Masako Kyo, who is notoriously scandalous, came unannounced, declaring she was part of the count's diplomatic staff, even though she isn't."

Lisan explained that Masako Kyo was infamous in Japan and China. Born in Peking, she claimed her parents were members of the Manchu royal family. On his deathbed her father had asked a close friend, a Japanese artist, to adopt her. Raised in Tokyo, she was a great admirer of all things Japanese, but she'd also been taught to cherish her Manchurian origins. Princess Kyo, as she styled herself, dressed in Japanese, Chinese, or Manchu robes as the mood took her, claiming affinity with all three cultures. Sometimes she wore Western clothing, and when she did, often donned menswear. She reveled in scandal, and because of this, gossip columnists sought her out.

Her beauty and eccentricity were renowned, as was her loudly proclaimed goal of making the Qing monarchy into a constitutional monarchy like Great Britain. Yet if she hoped to gather allies for a political cause, she was her own worst enemy. Her morals were considered a disgrace: she'd had numerous lovers of all ages from all walks of life and nationalities. Her credibility was no better: she offered to spy for any country willing to pay her, somehow oblivious to a spy's first requirement of discretion.

"My guardian says she's just a social climber," Lisan said, "from a very minor branch of aristocracy, so minor she doesn't have any right to a title. She exaggerates her connections to the royal family. And now she's in Shanghai."

"Well, on your day off," Caroline said, "you must see your classmate and hear more about this fascinating creature. Because I want to know more too."

Lisan looked away, but not before Caroline caught the resignation in her eyes. "On my day off, I must go to my guardian's home," she said.

AFTER THE DRESSMAKER'S, they went to the Pâtisserie Bontemps to confirm last-minute details, then to the florist and the perfumers. After this, Caroline declared she needed a cup of tea and a pastry to keep herself going, so Lisan found a café.

"I can't imagine getting ready for this party without you, Lisan," Caroline said, teasing her. Yet she meant it. "How do other foreign women get by in China without someone like you?"

"They have someone like Chin," Lisan said rather distractedly, her gaze directed out the café window. Then she turned and smiled at Caroline, once again attentive. "They have a Number One Boy like him who speaks enough English, trains the others, conveys your wishes. Helps you plan parties."

"I've heard from other ladies that after some time, the servants who've learned some English get poached," Caroline said.

"Yes, it happens," Lisan said, "because when they go work for another foreign family, it could be higher up the ladder, perhaps as head servant. But for the most part, servants prefer a secure position and are very loyal. Some Chinese families have servants whose own families have been part of the household for generations."

"Lisan, I must ask. Are you sleeping well?" she said, pouring herself another cup of tea. "You seem rather tired and preoccupied. Is your bed comfortable?"

"I apologize if you feel I haven't been giving the work my full attention, Mrs. Stanton," said the young woman. "It's just a bit strange sleeping in a different room. In a few more days I'll be used to it." Her smile and words dismissed Caroline's concerns, but there was a nervous undertone to the young woman's voice.

"No, no, my dear," Caroline said, "your work hasn't suffered at all, it's just that you seem rather fatigued. As for sleeping badly, it's how I felt during my first few weeks at boarding school. Until then I'd only ever slept in my own little room at home." She dabbed the napkin against her lips. "Listen, Lisan, now that the errands are done, I'd like to explore Shanghai a bit on my own, with the car. Please take a rickshaw or carriage home and go through the arrangements again with Chin."

CAROLINE HAD LOOKED up the address for the Shanghai Land Titles Office and copied it down, so her driver had little problem finding it. At the desk, she asked if she could take a look at the survey map and deed to Lennox Manor. She gave the elderly British clerk her most radiant and pleading smile, and he was more than happy to pull out the information she wanted.

"Here we are," he said, returning from a room at the back. He beckoned to her from a door near the entrance, where he laid out some maps on a long table. "Ah, as you can see on this map, here is Lennox Manor, the property reference number is marked right here. And here is the folder with the deeds. Excuse me, there's someone at the desk. I will leave you to it."

Caroline pulled out the deeds. Lisan was right. The current owner was a Mr. Liu Fanzhu. Before that, Charles Burnett. Before that, Mason Burnett. Before that, a Malcolm Armstrong had bought the land from Liu Fanzhu, the same man who now owned the property.

At one time Mason actually did own Lennox Manor, but now he was merely leasing it and the property wasn't his to bequeath. Did Mason think he would buy it back someday without Thomas ever finding out? Once she told Thomas, surely he would take a step back from his dealings with Mason. She had proof now that Mason was taking advantage of her and Thomas.

It was a good thing she'd sent Lisan home. She wouldn't have been able to chat or act normally. She needed the time to take control of her emotions. She would keep her outrage in check and speak calmly to Thomas later. She would convince him to get out of whatever business contract he had with Mason and get back to mining, a business he understood. She had to do it. The motorcar sped along Bubbling Well Road, passing rickshaws and street vendors. The skies were clear, the air warmer than it had ever been since she'd been in Shanghai. Branches on trees were no longer bare but covered in a haze of pale green. To her this had always been a joyful first sign of spring.

Upon her arrival back at Lennox Manor, two houseboys darted out the door and hurried to take the boxes and bags of shopping from the car. Lisan was at the top of the steps waiting to greet her.

"Two things, Mrs. Stanton," Lisan said. "Your car has arrived and also a driver. Mr. Stanton hired him for you. The car is in the garage and the driver is sharing a room with Mr. Stanton's own driver. Also, more of your belongings have arrived. Two big wooden crates from New York. I had them taken upstairs to the attic above the west wing. Here's the letter that came with the crates."

She handed Caroline a sealed envelope, and Caroline ripped it open. It was from her lawyers in New York, who had been the Dominics' lawyers.

In accordance with your instructions, we have sold the contents of the Dominic apartment and appointed a property manager to lease the property to a suitable tenant. Regarding the two crates we have shipped to you, although you asked us to dispose of "everything inside the apartment that isn't nailed down," we did find some personal and family items you may want to keep. Perhaps once the pain of your loss has lessened, you may even be glad of these reminders of your aunt and uncle, of your parents and your life before its tragedies.

"Oh dear," Caroline said, with a sigh of displeasure. She was sure that if Thomas had expressed such wishes, the lawyers would've obeyed to the letter. But she was only a young woman, befuddled by tragedy. "I told the lawyers to sell everything, I don't want any of it. But, evidently, they had other ideas. I may as well go up and take a look, see what they considered worth sending all this way."

They followed the head servant up the service staircase to the attic. Chin switched on the lights and they stepped over the threshold. Two bare bulbs hung from the sloped ceiling. Empty steamer trunks marked with *Stanton* and sets of luggage sat neatly stacked against one wall. The newly arrived crates were lined up against the adjacent wall. Miscellaneous bits of furniture, some broken, were pushed against another wall along with framed pictures, presumably unwanted. Unwanted by whom? Charles Burnett? His runaway wife? Or perhaps Mason. She would look through them later, just out of curiosity.

The tops of the wooden packing crates were still nailed down and Chin used a claw hammer to pry them open. He bowed on his way out, leaving the hammer on the floor. Lisan lifted the top off the first crate so Caroline could look in. It was filled with smaller boxes, straw and paper stuffed around them.

"The crates are labeled," Lisan said, pointing to a piece of cardboard at the top of the open crate. "*Silverware. Porcelain. Crystal.* Shall I ask Chin to bring those down to the butler's pantry and put them with the rest of your table settings?"

"No. Because I won't ever use them," Caroline said. "I don't want these place settings on my dining table. They can stay here in storage. All this belonged to the Dominics and I don't want to be reminded of that life. And besides, they're so ugly. Look."

She pulled out a box of polished wood and set it down on top of the other crate, opened the hinged lid. It was a canteen of silverware, the inside of the box lined in blue velvet, the cutlery expensive and heavy, ornate swirling patterns on the handles traced in gold. She opened another box, which contained a carving set, a long fork and matching straight knife, both with antler handles.

Caroline opened another box and handed Lisan a cut crystal champagne coupe, every inch covered in a diamond design. "Truly hideous," she said to Lisan, who handed it back silently, nodding assent.

"I asked the Dominics' lawyer to sell everything at auction," Caroline sighed, "the apartment in Manhattan and all its furnishings, everything. But the lawyers advised keeping the apartment for now and Thomas agreed. And now they've sent me what they decided is of sentimental value."

"Perhaps they thought you would change your mind," Lisan said, "once you were grieving less. They were being kind."

"Well, since these things are here," Caroline said, "let's see what they considered of sentimental value."

Lisan moved aside the lid of the second crate, which was labeled *Caroline Vessey bedroom*. Caroline rummaged through the boxes inside. She unwrapped small knickknacks that she recalled had been on a fireplace mantel: a collection of ceramic cats, some seashells, and a Dresden shepherdess. She shook her head and Lisan wrapped them up again, put them back in the crate.

Caroline took out a pair of cushions embroidered with petit point roses. "I made these," she murmured, sinking to the floor beside the crate. "Mrs. Dominic was adamant that young ladies should be skilled at decorative needlework. I'll take these, they'd suit the chairs in my parlor. Oh, and this Waterford crystal water jug and matching tumbler. They used to sit on the bedside table. I always liked them."

She found a desk set, the base a two-inch thickness of green onyx holding a fat gold fountain pen and an oversize paper knife. "Italian, a gift from Mr. Dominic. It's too heavy and completely wrong for my desk," Caroline remarked. "I may give it to Uncle Mason. Or ask Thomas to take it into his office. Put it over there."

The small pile of items on the floor was growing. She stood to lean into the crate and took out another cardboard box. A school photo album. Bad memories. She would burn those.

Something brushed past her feet and she gave a startled cry. Her legs gave way and the box dropped back into the crate. A small, dark creature ran along the wall and vanished through a gap between the floor and wall. Caroline could hardly breathe as she shrank back against the rough wood of the crate. She pressed a hand against her heaving stomach.

"I'll have Chin put down some rat poison," Lisan said, kneeling down beside her, "but I'm afraid you can't avoid rodents or cockroaches in Shanghai. The best we can do is keep them from being obviously visible."

"Yes, yes, tell Chin to put down poison. We can't have vermin running over our guests' shoes." She struggled to calm herself, took a deep breath. She moved away from the wall where the rat had gone to hide. "I'm done for now with these crates. Lisan, let's look through the bits of furniture over here. Maybe I can find a little footstool to put by the fireplace. And there are some pictures, let's see them."

Lisan nodded and began sorting through the pile of miscellaneous furniture.

"Nothing useful here in the way of furniture, Mrs. Stanton,"

Lisan said, "but you might find this picture interesting." She pulled out a framed painting, a fan-shaped watercolor of chrysanthemum flowers painted on silk. "Look closely," she said, bringing the picture into the light so that Caroline could inspect it. "This isn't a watercolor—the flowers and leaves are all embroidery. It's probably from Soochow, a town famous for fine needlework as well as its gardens."

"Astounding," Caroline said. "The workmanship is exquisite. The petals look so real. My goodness, there are actual veins on the leaves. My petit point roses are ridiculously crude compared to this. The wall above my parlor fireplace is empty. This will look very fine. What else do we have?"

"Some more paintings," Lisan said.

A landscape of windmills. A still life of autumn fruits and a dead grouse. Caroline made a face and they both laughed. The last picture in the stack was an oil portrait, a woman in a red dress. The portrait was in a square frame, about two feet wide. The woman was Chinese. At least, Caroline thought she was Chinese. She was young and entrancingly beautiful, eyes dark and serene, cheeks rounded. Her lips were slightly parted, as though about to speak, lending a schoolgirl innocence to her features.

"How interesting," Caroline said, leaning in for a closer look. She pointed at the brass plate fixed to the lower edge of the frame. "*Rosalie Roussel as Tosca.* Tosca, as in the opera. This Rosalie must be an opera singer. Isn't she beautiful?"

There was no answer. Lisan was staring at the painting as though mesmerized.

ROSALIE'S DIARY

20 February 1907

There is one good thing about the Golden Rooster. I had heard that the owner, Mr. Huang, doesn't touch the girls and it turns out to be true because he likes boys. I've asked Huang to let me sing some arias during intermissions, when the band is taking a break, and he said he would think about it.

It's not La Scala but at least I'm singing. It's not what I hoped for, but I've realized what a naive dream that was. There is not an opera house that would ever take me, even in the chorus. In China, no amateur musical society would ever have me. And now I'm a nightclub singer, and in people's eyes, only one step up from a prostitute. I would have to move to another city and find another career to be rid of this taint.

CHAPTER 10

LISAN SANK BACK on her knees. She couldn't move, could only stare at the woman's face. Then she realized that Caroline Stanton was looking at her, and she collected herself. She touched a finger to the brass plate.

"If this portrait is true to life," she said, "then I think that Rosalie Roussel is only part Chinese. It would explain the last name, Roussel. Charles Burnett married a singer. This must be her, Rosalie. It also explains why Mr. Burnett didn't approve. Not only is Rosalie a singer, she is also of mixed race."

It surprised Lisan that Mason hadn't thrown out or destroyed the painting, given how he must have felt about this unwanted daughter-in-law. The young woman's complexion was pale as ivory, a striking contrast against her dark hair. Her features were sweet, the small nose well-defined, although the jawline hinted at stubbornness. Her European-style dress, deep red and high-waisted, was a costume. An oval pendant with a red gem in its center hung on a gold chain, nestled just in the hollow of her throat.

This was the face of Rosalie, the owner of the diary she'd found. She needed to get a French dictionary and start translating.

"It's very skillfully done," Caroline said, examining the painting. "The eyes are especially expressive."

Lisan thought the dark eyes seemed anxious, adding tension to the woman's features. Her sweet demeanor hinted at a tragic fate. It was the face of a woman confronting terrible decisions. But was that Rosalie's own expression or had she summoned the role of Tosca for this portrait?

"Will you hang this somewhere downstairs?" she said.

"Heavens, no," Caroline said, turning away to look at the remaining pictures. "I hate portraits, especially when it's people I don't know looking down at me from the wall. Anyway, I suspect Uncle Mason had it stored away here because he didn't want any reminders of his son's wife. It would be in poor taste to hang it up."

"May I take it to hang in my room?" The request had burst out of her before she'd even had time to think. "Mr. Burnett would never come into the room, so he'll never see it."

"Why, Lisan," Caroline said, teasing, "do you really want the portrait of a scandalous woman in your room?"

"I don't think she looks scandalous," Lisan said. "I think she looks lonely. It must've been hard to be the cause of estrangement between father and son, between her husband and his friends."

"Well, I'm not planning to hang it anywhere so go ahead and take it," Caroline said. "Let's head down. I want a word with the cook before tomorrow's luncheon with Mrs. Easton and Mrs. Franks."

LISAN STARED UP at the ceiling, then looked over to the portrait, which she had hung on the wall beside the desk. It was dimly lit by the desk lamp. What had come over her, that she should hang the portrait of a complete stranger on her wall? What had compelled her to be so bold and ask Caroline Stanton for permission to take it? All she could say was that something about Rosalie's portrait had called out to her and she had responded. No, she had obeyed.

She was desperate for a good night's sleep. She was so tired. She had been drinking strong tea all day to stay sharp but she was so exhausted tea hardly made an impact now. She feared appearing slow-witted in front of Caroline Stanton when she needed to be alert. Constant fatigue plagued her, prevented her from thinking clearly. At the same time, sleep meant dreams.

The portrait of Rosalie drew her gaze again. Even though the painting was not very large, it seemed to dominate the room. The dramatic red of Rosalie's dress was at odds with her gentle features. Looking at the young woman's face, at the proud tilt of her chin, Lisan couldn't believe Rosalie had been a gold digger. The dark eyes challenged her, told her not to believe everything people said.

Rosalie seemed to be observing the room. Hands folded in her lap, her expression seemed rather melancholy to Lisan, her eyes pleading, as though she wanted to confide in Lisan. What secrets did Rosalie want to share? Her gauzy red shawl left one shoulder bare, the other carelessly covered. Who had put away her portrait and stored it in the attic? Could it have been someone else besides Mason Burnett? Had Charles taken it off a wall after she left him?

Lisan got up and turned off the desk lamp. Why had she ever imagined a house far away from the city would be quiet? At night, the sounds of human activity were stilled, but the quiet only amplified the house's own noises, gusts of wind forcing their way inside, timbers creaking from too much damp. She'd get used to the nighttime noises, she thought, as she fell asleep.

SHE PRESSES HER face to the windowpane and cold dread raises the hairs on her arms. A figure walks toward the lake. A woman in a red dress. *Rosa? Rosalie?* And there is something different about the lake. Lisan peers through the droplets of rain at the rowboat tied to a small dock. But she has seen the lake in daylight and there is no boat, no dock.

She looks again and the woman is now seated in the boat, which begins gliding slowly across the lake. Now that the figure is still and no longer moving, Lisan can see the long dark hair, unbound and whipped by the wind, the rain-soaked crimson dress clinging to her slim body. The boat stops on the opposite shore and the woman gets out, her feet barely touching the ground. She drifts up to the edge of the lake, stops by the stand of willows.

Then, looking straight at Lisan, she beckons. *Come find me*, a sweet voice beseeches. Lisan is overcome by a sensation of despair so intense she wants to weep. A moment later, the crimson of the gown fades to gray and she melts into the rain.

Now Lisan is standing by the door of the drawing room. Notes from a piano drift through the air. Is Caroline in the drawing room playing the grand piano? Lisan pushes open the door and there is a young man, a foreigner, standing at the piano, looking through sheets of music with a slight frown. He looks up at her and when he sees her, a joyous smile transforms his features. There's something familiar about him, something she can't define.

The music stops and she wakes up.

Getting out of bed, she tried shaking off the strange dream. She longed for daylight to filter through the windows and give her permission to leave her room and the confusion of her dreams. It was clear she wasn't going to fall asleep again so she pulled aside the fire screen and put two more logs onto the embers, then turned on the desk lamp and took out Rosalie's diary from the hidden drawer.

Between the messy handwriting and her rudimentary knowledge of French, the task of translating Rosalie's entries was beyond her. What she needed was a French-English dictionary from the library. She pulled on her robe, lit the oil lamp, and made her way down the staircase to the ground floor. Past the entrance foyer, past the closed doors of the drawing room and dining room, until she reached the library. The door was slightly ajar. Inside, tall mahogany bookshelves lined the walls.

She lifted the oil lamp and gazed at the shelves. She had come in only once before with Caroline, who'd been hunting for something on the history of Shanghai. She'd seen a set of encyclopedias on a bottom shelf somewhere; perhaps that's where the dictionaries were too.

"Who's there?" a voice rasped from the corner. She gasped, almost dropping the oil lamp.

A light turned on and a brass floor lamp cast stunted shadows on the carpet. Mason Burnett rose from an armchair, still dressed in his evening clothes from the night before. There was a decanter and glass on the side table next to the armchair.

"It's Lisan Liu, Mr. Burnett," she stammered. "I'm sorry to disturb you." She turned to flee out the door but he called out.

"Wait. Come back." Reluctantly, she stopped.

"What are you looking for, Miss Liu?" he said.

"A dictionary. A French-English dictionary," she said.

"A French dictionary," he repeated. "Do you understand French as well as English?"

"I only studied it at school for two years," she said, "not enough to be useful."

He turned to a shelf beside the window and pulled out a book. "Take this one. In case you need them, all the dictionaries are on this shelf. German. Spanish. Latin. Greek."

"Thank you, sir." She turned to leave again and this time he stopped her with a hand on her shoulder.

"This is the second time we've met before daylight," he said. "Aren't you too young to be suffering from insomnia?"

"I . . . I think it's just being in a new place," she said. "It will pass."

"I've lived here for years," he said, downing his drink, "still can't sleep. Well, off you go."

SETTLING IN THE padded leather seat of her desk chair, Lisan found she was still shaking from the encounter with Mason Burnett. He was so large, his presence so forceful. He'd been trying to be helpful, but it just made her want to back away. Taking a deep breath, she opened the diary and took out a pad of paper.

An hour later, Lisan rubbed her eyes, dropped her head in her hands, and sighed. She had managed to translate only a few pages; it was slow work. Thankfully Rosalie's entries were brief. It was two o'clock in the morning. Perhaps she could get a few hours of sleep.

Anyway, why should she care about Rosalie? she thought, climbing under the blankets. And why should she be seeing visions of a woman when Rosa had run away and Charles had died? If anyone was doing the haunting, it would surely be poor Charles, in which case she should be seeing the apparition of a man, not a woman. This was proof that the disturbing visions and strange sounds were all due to her imagination, fueled by fatigue.

Unless. Unless she was seeing Rosalie's phantom because Charles's ghost had conjured its appearance, because he still longed for his faithless wife.

She snorted, dismissing such foolishness, and turned on her side to burrow into the blankets. She wished she could find Yao, get some time with him on his own. She longed for his reassuring smile and good humor. But with the party coming up, like all members of the staff, he was busy every minute. There were signs of his work inside the house. Flowering plants had replaced sad-looking specimens and all the overgrown ferns were now beautifully trimmed.

Caroline wanted the gardens to look tidier for the party, so Yao had been out in the rain for the past two days, an oilskin cloak fixed to a wide bamboo hat so that he could use both hands to gather dead branches and leaves. Xiao Wu had been eager to help and the two of them had been out in the rain chatting away like old friends. All the servants liked Yao, seemed to respect him. Lisan envied the houseboy for being able to spend so much time with the gardener.

She finally drifted into sleep as thunder rumbled to accompany crackling forks of lightning. Out on the ornamental lake, wind rippled the slate-gray water and tore the few remaining leaves off poplar trees. And inside Lennox Manor, it spoke through cracks and crevices, reverberated down chimneys, called out for release.

ROSALIE'S DIARY

25 February 1907

Huang regrets hiring me, he says. He let me sing some opera pieces when the band took a break. Some uncouth clients howled their displeasure and exited the club, losing the club money from more hours of drinking. He handed me a stack of Golden Rooster business cards and told me to bring in some new business or else I'm fired.

When Father came to see me, I told him. He could've said "I told you so" and many more cruel things but he didn't. I gave him some Golden Rooster business cards and asked him to distribute them at every opportunity. I don't hope for much. What comes next? Domestic service for some foreign family, I suppose. My languages put to use at last. Perhaps I can look after children and teach them songs, how to play the piano a little.

CHAPTER 11

CAROLINE FOUND IT hard to be in the same room with a man who could deceive his own nephew and business partner. Thomas deserved so much better; he was a good man, so decent that he'd shown no anger when she told him over breakfast that Mason didn't own Lennox Manor.

"It's all right, dearest," he said, "I'm sure Uncle Mason knows it was only a matter of time before we learned the truth."

"But Thomas, you can't continue to—" she protested, but he put a finger to her lips.

"It will be all right," he repeated. Holding back a sigh, she stood up and squeezed half a lemon into a cup of hot water and handed it to him. Good for the liver, Thomas believed. He downed it in two quick gulps. "Do you like your motorcar? The driver?"

He was changing the subject on her. "Yes, the Adler coupé is very nice," she said, "and although my driver doesn't speak much English, Lisan says he understands more than he speaks."

"That sounds like Mason coming down the stairs," he said. "We're off, then. Who is coming to luncheon today? Mrs. Easton, I think you said."

"Mrs. Easton and Mrs. Franks," Caroline said, making a face and following him out to the foyer. "They want me to join the board of a women's club they're founding. They practically pounced on me a few days ago when I ran into them at the jewelers'. Thank goodness Lisan rescued me by pretending we were late to another appointment."

"Good morning, my dear," Mason said. "Thomas, ready to go? By the way, Caroline, how is your secretary? English good enough?"

"Excellent English," Caroline said, smiling as pleasantly as she could. "In fact, she's far too qualified to be just a social secretary. She's helping me train the staff, so if there's anything you'd like them to do differently or better, Uncle Mason, please let me know."

"No need, no need, I'm happy with whatever you think best," Mason said. "It's been a while since a lady took charge of the house. I leave its running in your care. Any changes you make will all be to the better, I'm sure."

Thomas kissed her. "Good luck with your ladies' lunch. I wouldn't care to spend that much time with Mrs. Easton."

UPSTAIRS IN THE small parlor, Lisan was waiting for her to start their day.

"First, help me dress," Caroline said. "Those women are coming for lunch so I have to make an effort."

Lisan buttoned Caroline into a day dress of pale yellow silk, its skirt draped in translucent chiffon hemmed with embroidered roses. Caroline thrust both arms straight out to make it easier for Lisan to adjust the falls of lace at the sleeves. For earrings, she chose something simple, pear-shaped drops of yellow topaz dangling from small, diamond-studded medallions.

Then they went to the small parlor, where Caroline rang for Chin. Together the three reviewed arrangements for tomorrow's party, as though Caroline hadn't already been through the details several times already.

"You have nothing to worry about, Mrs. Stanton," Lisan said, after the head servant left them. "Chin is extremely reliable and the house servants are very excited. They'll do their utmost for the honor of Lennox Manor."

"Of course you're right," she agreed. "Actually I'm rather more concerned about getting through this lunch. Two of them and only one of me." She gave Lisan a rueful smile. "Let's try and enjoy the next few minutes before our guests come. The latest issue of *Vogue* magazine should keep my mind off things for a while."

"I don't know if you have a few minutes," Lisan said, standing up. "Someone's coming."

Caroline joined Lisan at the window in time to see the gates of Lennox Manor open to admit a gleaming automobile. Mrs. Easton and Mrs. Franks were starting an American Ladies Club and assumed that Caroline would want to be one of its founding members.

"If all they wanted was money, it would be fine," Caroline said, "but they want me to *participate*. And now I'll spend most of luncheon fending off their attempts to include me. Mrs. Easton reminds me so much of Mrs. Dominic."

"Mrs. Dominic. You mean your guardian?" Lisan said.

"Yes, determined to have her way," Caroline said, "with the goal of climbing to the top of New York society. Nothing and no one else mattered. I'm speaking ill of the dead, which one shouldn't do, but I was dreadfully unhappy in New York because of her. Well, I should go down to greet my guests."

"I'm sure the lovely lunch will distract them," Lisan said.

Caroline knew the meal would be excellent. There was grapefruit, followed by a clear consommé. Chicken timbales with mushroom sauce, slices of beef fillet with a Spanish sauce, croquette potatoes, a salad with French dressing. Olives, pickles, cheese balls, and brown bread on the side. A dessert tray of fruit parfait and individual angel food cakes. Bonbons and meringues to go with coffee.

Everything for this lunch was ready, except for her.

"I'm rather hoping the meal will put them in a stupor that forces them to go home and take a nap," Caroline said, sighing. "You'll have a better time than I will, eating lunch in the kitchen. But please wait in the parlor once you've finished your lunch. I may need you."

LUNCH FELT INTERMINABLE. Mrs. Easton now considered herself Caroline's closest friend and mentor; her questions were relentless, direct, and unapologetic, as though she were entitled to know everything about Caroline's life. Caroline chose her words carefully to give away as little as possible about Thomas's plans for the railway venture, her own life, and what Mason Burnett was like.

Finally, Mrs. Easton poured herself a second cup of coffee, signaling her readiness to leave the table. Caroline motioned the Number Four Boy to follow them into the drawing room with the tray of bonbons.

"A spacious house, Caroline," Mrs. Easton said, settling herself into an armchair. "I hope we can hold some committee meetings here in the future."

"But don't even think about it until after your party," Mrs. Franks quickly added. "Don't worry about anything until after that. You must have so many preparations."

"No one will ever call it your 'coming out' party, my dear," Mrs. Easton said, taking another bonbon from the tray, "but you do realize how important it is to make a good first impression as a hostess. Given your husband's status, your party will be much discussed in society afterward. I hope I'm not being too direct, but you're so new to Shanghai."

Mrs. Easton's opinions, bluntly delivered over the past hour, made it clear that Mrs. Easton considered herself the leading lady of Shanghai's American community.

"I'll keep that in mind, thank you," Caroline said. She turned to Mrs. Franks. "Will you take more coffee?"

"I wish you'd consulted me about this party, dear Caroline," Mrs. Easton continued, not changing the subject, "but I understand, you're far too polite and didn't want to presume upon my friendship. But from now on, you must let me advise you. Food, drink, decorations, who to invite, what to wear, and so on."

"Well, for tomorrow everything is arranged, Mrs. Easton," Caroline said. "Thomas has some very definite ideas, even down to my dress." Her smile remained bright as she dropped a spoonful of sugar into her coffee.

"Do feel free to call on us for advice about managing your staff," Mrs. Franks said. "Those Chinese can be so deliberately obtuse."

"Mm-hmm," Caroline said, dabbing her lips with a napkin. "Actually, my servants have been nothing but excellent."

"Good to hear, good to hear." Mrs. Easton didn't seem at all convinced. She leaned forward with a predatory gleam in her eyes. "You know, don't you, that this house has a reputation? You may have trouble keeping staff once they know."

"Yes, I heard about Charles." Caroline smiled sweetly. Thank goodness Lisan had warned her. "I'm aware that people think this house is haunted. But I don't know all the details. After all, it's a sad topic for Uncle Mason, so I never bring it up."

"I've met them—well, we all did one time or another," Mrs. Franks said. "Young Charles Burnett and Rosalie Roussel. That was before they married, of course. When she was just his . . . companion."

"She was a musician of some sort, wasn't she?" Caroline said, putting on her best schoolgirl face. "I seem to recall something like that."

"A singer," Mrs. Easton said, sniffing, "or she thought of herself as one. She was part French or Italian from her mother's side and took her mother's maiden name for the stage. She trained in opera. Or at least she had taken voice lessons. She was a beauty, I'll admit. It wasn't her voice but her looks that caught Charles Burnett's attention."

"He doted on her," Mrs. Franks said, "even paid one of the touring opera companies to put her onstage when they performed in Shanghai. By all accounts, she did well enough, for an amateur."

"I was at that concert." Mrs. Easton sniffed again. "Her voice was rather nasal and thin, that Oriental quality of singing, you know."

"Well, Mason was appalled when the dalliance turned serious," Mrs. Franks said, "then Charles married the girl without telling his father or his friends. Mason cut him off and set him adrift without financial support, hoping he'd come to his senses and divorce Rosalie.

"She was marginally acceptable as his mistress." Mrs. Franks said the word *mistress* in hushed tones. "But marrying a mixed-race girl—well, you can imagine. And Charles had a gambling habit, his ultimate undoing."

Desperate for money, he made risky business decisions until finally he had to put Lennox Manor on the market. The house was already mortgaged to the point where he could no longer hold on to it. Friends stopped visiting, discouraged by his bad temper as much as his constant pleas for loans.

And then Rosalie vanished. The prevailing theory was that she'd been a gold digger and wanted nothing more to do with Charles once he was bankrupt. Popular opinion was that heartbreak had pushed Charles over the edge into suicide. Mason then paid off Charles's debts and moved into Lennox Manor, turning into a recluse who emerged only for business meetings.

"What a terrible, sad story," Caroline said, spoon tinkling as she stirred milk into her coffee cup. "And did Rosalie ever come back?"

"No, she hasn't been in Shanghai since," Mrs. Franks said. "After all, she couldn't come back to the city where she'd been the cause of her own husband's death. What future does she have here with that sort of scandal following her around?"

"Enough of that," Mrs. Easton said. "Everyone is delighted that you and Thomas are here now. It's brought Mason back to us; he's a man of renewed purpose. A new partner and new business ideas. Perhaps you've lifted the curse from this house."

"I don't believe in ghosts or curses." Caroline smiled and finished her coffee. "Another sweet, Mrs. Easton? And I must say, I saw your automobile as you came in. It's beautiful. Brand-new?"

Mrs. Easton beamed. "Very new, and the interiors are fitted out beautifully. My husband knows an importer, actually a rich Chinese man, who brings in just a few luxury motorcars each year for his own collection and as a favor to others. A Mr. Liu."

"I have heard that name," Caroline said. "Isn't there a Liu family that owns a great deal of real estate in Shanghai?"

"My dear," said Mrs. Franks, "land in Shanghai and all over the province. They are old, old money with tentacles reaching into every business. Half of Bubbling Well Road used to belong to them before they sold the land for huge sums."

"Goodness," Caroline said, "but enough gossip. Let's discuss this committee. But first, I'll send for my secretary."

Caroline winked at Lisan when she entered the drawing room. "My secretary, Lisan Liu," she announced cheerfully. "Lisan, this is Mrs. Easton and Mrs. Franks. Now, ladies, I asked Lisan to join us and take notes. Meeting minutes, if you will, since this is an important discussion and I don't want to forget anything. Do sit down, Lisan."

Mrs. Easton stared with disapproval at Lisan, who merely settled on a chair by the window with her pencil and notepad.

"You won't even know she's there," Caroline added. "Now, where were we? The most essential facilities we will need?" For the next forty minutes, Caroline nodded and smiled, offered suggestions, and Lisan scribbled diligently on her notepad.

AFTER THE GATES closed on Mrs. Easton's automobile, Caroline turned to Lisan and sighed in relief. "That woman. I hope there aren't many more like her in Shanghai. A city can only take one of her kind."

"Would you like me to write out the notes from your meeting?" Lisan said. "I can type them up and make copies for Mrs. Easton and Mrs. Franks if you want something more official as a record."

"You can crumple them up or use them to light the stove." Caroline grimaced. "I wanted you there so I wouldn't feel so . . . so outnumbered. Yes, I suppose you're right. Please type them up and send copies to the ladies. Minutes of the meeting and all that. There's no hurry. Now I need to lie down, that was such a grueling experience."

"Shall I help you undress, Mrs. Stanton," Lisan said, "so you can rest?"

"Goodness no," Caroline said, "I wasn't serious. Go type up the notes. But yes, do help me undress. I need to get out of the house, go for a drive to the city. I'd like to change into something plainer."

LISAN HELPED HER out of the pale yellow silk dress. "Oh, don't move, Mrs. Stanton," the young woman cautioned, "a button just caught on my bracelet. One moment. There."

"Let me see that bracelet, Lisan," Caroline said. It was a simple wooden bangle, decorated with a few Chinese characters. "Most unusual, carved wood."

Her secretary blushed. "It was a gift from Xiao Wu, the youngest house servant. He was quite insistent that I wear it all the time."

"As a sign of your devotion to him?" Caroline teased.

"No, because he worries about Charles Burnett's ghost." Lisan held up the cheap bangle. "It's made of peach wood, which wards off ghosts, and carved with amulets of protection. Charles killed himself, which in Chinese folklore makes his ghost very dangerous. They are trapped in the Underworld, and unless they find someone to take their place, they can't move on to reincarnation. So they must compel another person to commit suicide, usually by driving them mad."

"That sounds like a never-ending chain of death," Caroline said.

"It is never-ending and endlessly tragic," Lisan said. "The servants have an ongoing debate whether Charles Burnett's ghost, because he's foreign, would behave the same way as a Chinese ghost."

"What's their conclusion?" Caroline said, amused and also curious.

"Undecided. Some feel he is bound by whatever the rules are in his homeland. Others think that since he died in China, his spirit must follow our rules."

It was most interesting, Caroline thought, after Lisan went to call for her car and driver. The Chinese have no problem with multiple belief systems. Or, in this case, multiple schools of superstition. She wondered when Mason would tell them about his son's death. Surely he must realize that by now they would've heard most of the story for themselves from all the gossipmongers. Perhaps he was content to leave it that way, for them to learn about it through rumor and secondhand chat instead of recounting the painful tale himself.

She almost felt sorry for Mason. But then she remembered that he was defrauding his own nephew.

CAROLINE DECIDED TO broach the subject again the next morning, after Thomas had spent the night in her room. He watched her from the bed, smiling contentedly as she brushed her hair.

"Don't be nervous about this evening," he said. "You've put such attention into planning this party, everything will be perfect."

"It's not the party that worries me, Thomas," she said, sitting on the edge of the bed. She took his hand. "It's Mason. He's living a lie and dragging you into it."

"Caroline," he said, "I know you're unhappy that Uncle Mason isn't going to put in the funds he first promised, but a railway to northern China is undoubtedly a fine business venture. I've spoken to the Chinese officials . . ."

She shook her head. "No, Thomas. That's not what bothers me. I mean, that's not the only thing that bothers me. If Mason's backed out of his promise to fund investment in this railway venture, if he's promised you a house he doesn't own, what other lies has he been feeding us?" She took both his hands in hers. "Thomas, get out of this. Nothing's been signed yet, nothing's under contract. We can't afford any more surprises."

He sighed. "You're the surprise, Caroline. You understand more about money than any young woman should ever need to know."

"My father . . ." she said. "Well, I learned. He was rather more trusting than he should've been when it came to money."

"I'll speak to Uncle Mason tomorrow," he said, kissing her on the forehead. "Give me some time to think things over. Let's enjoy the party tonight. I must get to work now, just a half day. Don't worry. I'll be back in plenty of time."

The door closed behind him and Caroline put her face in her

hands. Thomas wouldn't do anything. He might get the truth out of Mason, but he would let it go. Because Mason was family. Even though he had estranged himself from Thomas's own mother for years, even though he had lied to Thomas about the house, lied about sharing in the cost of a railway, Mason was family, and important to him.

And what was she to him?

ROSALIE'S DIARY

1 March 1907

A young American came to the club. He asked me to his table after I finished my set. He had one of those business cards with him and showed me. "Someone gave me this," he said, "and I thought I might as well give this place a try. And I'm very glad I did."

He gave me one of his cards. Charles Burnett. He is handsome, kind, and cheerful. But most of all, he is rich. Huang is beside himself—never has a client of such quality entered his club before, so my immediate future is assured. Perhaps beyond immediate since Mr. Burnett has promised to bring all his friends to the Golden Rooster.

Most unexpectedly, after I told Charles that I'd had operatic training, he requested that I sing him an aria, and applauded loudly after. Huang was not pleased but what could he do?

CHAPTER 12

THERE WASN'T A single flower arrangement out of place or crystal wall sconce that didn't sparkle. Caroline had ordered masses of floral decorations, so gorgeously painted porcelain planters of jasmine, ginger lilies, orchids, and gardenias rested on tall stands at eye level, making their beauty and fragrance easier to admire. Tropical plants and flowers filled the rooms, commandeered from the hothouse as well as florists in Shanghai. Niches held huge vases filled with out-of-season flowers and spring bulbs, some forced into opening early. A round table at the center of the foyer held a magnificent arrangement of purple orchids. Yao had fixed each stem to thin bamboo supports so that the purple blooms stood upright. Caroline had been thrilled.

Lisan knew the flowers were to draw people's eyes away from the walls, where damp patches were starting to show on wallpaper, where wooden panels had warped from the humidity. She understood Caroline's concerns over the state of the house.

But enough of that, she thought. Just get through today. Everything is perfect. The foyer looks beautiful.

On the second-floor mezzanine, Caroline had instructed the servants to set two large porcelain planters at either side of the landing. Each planter held a blooming lemon tree, a miracle Yao had wrought. The flowers' fresh, clean fragrance lightened the air, and like sentries, the lemon trees impeded access to the hallways that led to the east and west wings, a subtle hint to guests that they should continue up to the ballroom on the next floor. Using ornamental trees as barriers had been Lisan's suggestion, but just to be on the safe side, Chin had stationed Da Wu on the landing. There, he would bow to guests and wave them upstairs just in case anyone missed the hint that the Stantons' private rooms were off-limits.

"Perhaps I'm too careful," Caroline had remarked, "but in New York, sometimes guests went into rooms and pilfered things. Imagine. Some of the richest people in the city and they'd 'accidentally' wander into private chambers and bedrooms."

All the servants were aware that this event had to establish Mr. and Mrs. Thomas Stanton as worthy members of Shanghai society. Lisan knew the servants felt the household's honor was at stake. Caroline had hosted a few small gatherings, but this evening, there would be seventy guests, the elite of Shanghai society.

Once she was satisfied with the state of the house, Caroline returned to her chambers, where Lisan helped her finish getting dressed. Caroline had styled her hair simply as usual, but with hair ornaments of gold set with precious stones instead of her usual tortoiseshell combs. All she needed was some help from Lisan to fix a few more jeweled hairpins to the twist at the back.

"It's far more than a little welcome party, of course," Caroline murmured, opening a box of bracelets. "I didn't need Mrs. Easton's lecture to know what this means. It's a chance for Shanghai society to judge whether or not I'm worthy of being one of their leading hostesses. If not for Thomas, I wouldn't care at all."

Caroline touched the collar of pearls and jade, the jade beads at her throat the same pale green as her new dress. She smiled at Lisan's reflection in the tall glass. "Now, Lisan, are you ready for our guests?"

"Are you sure about this, Mrs. Stanton?" Lisan said. Caroline had decided Lisan would help Little Liao take the guests' coats and put them in the cloakroom.

"You want to get a good look at the guests, don't you?" Caroline said. "And afterward we can compare notes."

There was a knock on the dressing room door and Thomas entered; he smiled with pleasure as Caroline stood up and twirled to show off her gown. "Our first guests will be here soon—we should head down," he said, kissing the inside of her wrist. "Your perfume is delicious. Something new?"

"Created for me especially," she said. "Ginger lily. Lisan knows a perfumer who specializes in custom fragrances."

"Delicious," he repeated, "and we'd better go downstairs to greet our guests, side by side, wearing our most welcoming faces."

"A united front against the barbarian hordes," Caroline said, taking his arm, "or like the guards at Buckingham Palace."

After Caroline went downstairs, Lisan lingered a bit longer in the dressing room and used the full-length mirror to check her own appearance. She had put on a plain woolen skirt and blouse, a change from her usual Chinese clothing, and had wrapped her long plait around her head like a crown, a hairstyle that suited her Western clothing better than a single braid down her back. She made sure her white shirtwaist was tucked neatly into the navy blue skirt and touched the modest pearl studs at her ears, a graduation gift from Master Liu. She looked tidy and, more importantly, inconspicuous.

In the foyer, Lisan joined Little Liao in the cloakroom. She murmured words of welcome as guests arrived, helping them take off coats and hanging them up. Most of the arrivals paused for a moment to straighten hair and jackets at the tall mirror by the cloakroom door before continuing on to greet their hosts.

"Were you ever here when Charlie Burnett was still alive, Freddie?" a young woman asked her husband, as she brushed a speck of something off his shoulder. Little Liao took away the man's coat. Lisan loitered for a moment to hear the man's reply.

"A couple of times," Freddie said. "He gave wild parties. Too wild for my taste. Then he got serious about Rosalie and worked hard to clean up his act. He wanted to be respectable so that respectable society would accept her."

"If his father hadn't abandoned him, it might've come right in the end," she said. "Money takes care of most problems." They moved off and another group of guests arrived.

Lisan hoped the Stantons were pleased. Everything was going smoothly. Seated just inside the open doorway of the drawing room, a trio of musicians played a lively medley of popular tunes. "To the End of the World with You." "I Wonder Who's Kissing Her Now." The three were very good, Thomas's contribution to the party, a touring American group he had heard at a restaurant. Her gaze moved across to the Stantons.

Caroline, Thomas, and Mason stood at the foot of the staircase. Caroline stood beside Thomas, a pretty picture of confidence in her green silk gown. Lisan thought she looked beautiful, her dress elegant and well suited to both her complexion and her slim figure.

Lisan realized that Caroline was smiling at her. When she saw that she'd caught Lisan's eye, Caroline gestured at the musicians. Lisan nodded. It was time to move the trio upstairs.

Stepping away from the cloakroom, Lisan crossed the foyer and stood between the staircase and the drawing room door. When the musicians finished playing the set, she would show them upstairs to the ballroom. In the meantime, she had a good view of the arrivals, and if she moved away slightly from the musicians and tilted her head just right, she could hear the Stantons greet their guests as well as keep an eye on the front door and cloakroom, in case Little Liao needed her again.

Hushed whispers filled the foyer. She saw the woman enter.

Everyone did. There were avid stares on every face, a name on everyone's lips. It couldn't have been anyone else but Princess Masako Kyo.

It was clear that Masako Kyo liked making an entrance and it didn't matter if her audience consisted of two or two hundred. Sweeping into the marble-tiled foyer, she threw back the hood of her cerise cloak as though oblivious to the gaze of the Stantons' guests. The last thing this crowd of white foreigners expected was this petite, exquisite Asian woman. Kyo's face was dusted with white powder, eyebrows darkened to the shape of a willow leaf, lips a perfect crimson bud. When she slipped off the cloak, she revealed not a beribboned and ruffled gown but resplendent Japanese robes with wide, long sleeves, royal blue watered silk embroidered with purple and silver irises. Her hair was slicked back, pulled into a high rolled bun at the top of her head secured with a pair of jade pins.

CHAPTER 13

THE STREAM OF guests had slowed down. Caroline went through the guest list in her head and judged that only four or five remained. She watched Mason chat with an older couple, his laughter jovial and welcoming. The more she pondered the situation, the more convinced she had become that Mason had something else to hide. Something besides ownership of Lennox Manor, something besides lying about his finances. She would find out once this party was out of the way. Something *had* to change, even if she had to force the situation.

Thomas touched her arm and she wrenched her attention back to receiving guests. She set her lips in a smile of delighted welcome and prepared to greet the next arrivals. But first, she caught Lisan's eye and indicated with a tilt of her chin that she wanted the musicians to move up to the ballroom. It was good to have someone like Lisan, intelligent and intuitive. She was more than a good secretary; she had become a good companion.

There was sudden silence in the foyer, a collective intake of breath, then whispers.

An Asian woman in a stunning red cloak had entered. She shed the cloak and began making her way across the foyer with gliding footsteps, her blue kimono shimmering with purple and silver irises. As she approached, Caroline saw that even though the woman's face was heavily powdered, she was exquisite, with delicate features that were somewhat boyish and heavy brows that lent her features an androgynous beauty.

Her escort, who had hovered unnoticed during the woman's spectacular entrance, doffed his coat and hurried to join her.

Caroline's breath clawed at her throat and she struggled to hold her welcoming smile. She knew the man. She didn't know his name, or where she knew him from, but they'd met before and it had not been a pleasant encounter.

"Andrew, thank you for coming," Mason said, taking the lead. "You already know Thomas, of course. This is his wife, Caroline. Caroline, Andrew Grey is the architect I told you about, my dear." Caroline murmured words of welcome.

Andrew Grey's long face was almost handsome. Almost, because his features were too sharp and his dark reddish hair made his pale, freckled skin look pasty. His eyes were what made him memorable, an unusual shade of light brown, fringed with dark lashes.

"Thank you for the invitation," Grey said. "May I introduce Princess Masako Kyo?"

"Your Highness," Caroline said, making a graceful curtsy. Thomas bowed deeply. Mason merely inclined his head with a polite, slightly amused smile.

"There's no need for ceremony," the princess replied. Her English was slightly accented, her voice pleasant. "I'm actually Manchu and I don't believe in titles. Please, just call me Kyo."

"If I may ask," Thomas said, "your dress is magnificent, and it's Japanese, am I correct? But you say you're Manchu?"

"I'm Manchu, raised in Japan," she said, "which makes me uniquely qualified to be part of Count Kato Komei's diplomatic mission to the Forbidden City."

Caroline pretended she was listening to the conversation between Mason, Thomas, and Kyo, pretended she didn't notice how keenly Grey was looking at her. But she couldn't avoid him when he spoke to her directly.

"Mrs. Stanton," he said softly. She had to face him. "Mason mentioned your maiden name was Vessey and that you're related to the Dominics of New York. I believe we've met before, at one of the Dominics' parties. Very briefly."

His words managed to sound like a threat.

"I don't recall," she said, brightening her smile even more. "Do forgive me, but I've never been good with names or faces. And there were so many parties in New York, so many people to meet."

The thing was, she did remember him. He was heavier, his auburn hair a little thinner, but his freckled complexion and strange light brown eyes were the same. If only she could place him. If only she knew what he remembered.

"Come, Andrew," Kyo said, "there's other guests arriving and we mustn't monopolize our hosts."

Grey turned to her with an adoring gaze; clearly he was besotted by this fascinating creature, barely taking his eyes from Kyo as he escorted her toward the staircase. Then Kyo stopped, as though yanked back by a harness. She walked with gliding steps toward the musicians. Toward Lisan.

Caroline tore her eyes away; two more guests had come to the door.

"Well, this will make for a memorable party, whatever else happens," Mason whispered to them. "Andrew shows up with a princess of ill repute. She claims to be a member of Count Kato Komei's diplomatic mission. Word is she's nothing of the sort. Nor is she a real princess."

"I've heard of this woman," Thomas murmured. "Is it true she was mistress to one of the northern warlords?"

"Whether or not it's true, what on earth is Andrew doing with her?" Mason said. "She'll have him for breakfast." He sounded amused, not annoyed.

"I didn't know you'd met Grey before," Thomas said, turning to Caroline. All the guests had arrived and he took her arm to mount the staircase to the ballroom.

"Honestly, I don't remember him at all," she said. "He says we met in New York, but the Dominics gave so many parties and I never enjoyed them. I always left as soon as it was decent to do so."

Caroline wanted to plead a headache, go hide in her room. But she couldn't do that. Furthermore, it was better to face Andrew Grey. Whatever was on his mind, whatever threat he represented, the sooner she found out, the sooner she could deal with it. She had to learn what Grey remembered, what he might do or say. Taking a deep breath, she straightened her shoulders, forced yet another smile to her lips, and, with her hand tucked in the crook of Thomas's elbow, entered the ballroom.

CHAPTER 14

L ISAN COULDN'T STOP staring at the princess, whose beauty and spectacular clothing made all the other women seem lackluster and mundane. Her escort could barely take his eyes off her. She watched the woman and her escort greet the Stantons and Mason. When the man saw Caroline Stanton a puzzled expression crossed his face. He spoke with Caroline while Thomas chatted with Masako Kyo. The polite conversations ended as another group of guests arrived, but Lisan had the distinct impression that Caroline had been disturbed by the brief encounter.

In Western etiquette, it was rude to stare. Lisan turned her full attention to the musicians seated by the drawing room door. They were now putting their instruments into cases. Once she'd taken them up the service staircase to the ballroom, her duties would be over for the night.

She spun around at the touch of a hand on her shoulder and found herself face-to-face with the princess. Masako Kyo stared at her with wide and curious eyes. It was intimidating.

"Who are you?" Kyo said, addressing Lisan in Mandarin Chinese. "Surely you're not a house servant?"

"I'm Liu Lisan, Mrs. Stanton's secretary." Lisan dipped in a slight curtsy.

Without asking, the princess put two fingers under Lisan's chin and tilted her face up, then sideways, as though she were a horse.

Lisan was so startled she didn't protest being touched. But her distress must've been evident.

"I've offended you," Kyo said, stepping back, "and I apologize. It's just that you look so familiar I couldn't help myself. Your family?"

"I'm an orphan," Lisan said. *You look so familiar.* But she was sure she had never met the woman before. How could anyone forget such a creature? She dropped her eyes, not wanting to meet the woman's forceful gaze. Kyo was slightly older than she'd first thought, with fine lines at the corners of her eyes and a softening around the jawline. She looked tired. Yet she was so beautiful that these were but minor deficiencies.

"Tell me, have you always lived in Shanghai?" Kyo said, still scrutinizing Lisan with disturbing intensity.

"Living in Shanghai is all I remember," she answered, wishing she had ducked into the hallway under the staircase instead of lingering in the foyer. The princess's attention was unnerving.

"Do you know," Kyo said, "you look exactly like someone I knew many years ago in Peking. Someone very special."

"I've never been to Peking." Lisan shook her head. "I have some other duties to attend to for Mrs. Stanton. If I may?"

"Well, don't disappear, Miss Liu. I want to speak with you later. In private," the princess said, an unmistakable air of command in her voice. Lisan felt intense scrutiny and something else from Kyo. Excitement.

The false princess returned to her escort, whom she'd left standing bemused by the staircase.

"You know, Andrew," Kyo said, taking his arm, "I never forget a face. It's why I would make a good spy. But as I was saying, an American thoroughbred makes a poor hunter for the paper chase. The climate here does not suit American horses, darling boy. You need one of those tough little Mongolian ponies. I can borrow one for you from a friend at the Japanese consulate."

Andrew. The man must be Andrew Grey, the architect Mrs. Stanton added to the guest list at the last minute. But he seemed preoccupied, unlike a few minutes ago when his entire attention had concentrated on the princess.

"There's no need, Kyo," he said. "I'll ask Ballard for one of his ponies." Grey glanced back at the Stantons, who were greeting the latest arrivals. Was it Lisan's imagination, or had Caroline's smile of greeting become fixed and artificial?

The musicians had finished packing up their instruments, and as Lisan led them through the service stairwell up to the third-floor ballroom, her thoughts lingered on the princess. Why would someone like that bother puzzling over why Lisan looked familiar? Masako Kyo must meet hundreds of people every year. She guided the musicians to a small platform, where they set up quickly and swung into "Moonstruck."

Then Lisan hurried down to the hothouse for one final task. It was something Young Zhao the assistant cook could've done, but it was a chance to see Yao so she'd offered to do the errand.

Yao had done a great deal of work since he arrived. The hothouse was no longer a tangled mess. He had grouped potted plants neatly on the brick floor, creating islands of greenery like a series of flower beds. Bamboo trellises held up climbing vines, and palm trees in huge tubs added height and interest to the look of an indoor garden. Pots of orchids hung along bamboo poles fixed to brackets, and a table at one end held more orchids. Several gardenia shrubs bloomed on a brick platform at the center of the hothouse, along with large pots of the ginger lilies that Caroline admired so much.

She found Yao in the utility area at the very back of the hothouse. Enclosed by trellised vines of jasmine and bougainvillea, the space was hidden and almost invisible to the casual visitor unless one made an effort to look behind the vines. Then they'd see a worktable, gardening tools in boxes on the ground, and a collection of rakes hanging from its walls. Yao was at the table snipping marigolds and filling an enamel bowl with their petals, the bowl she would take back to the kitchen for Young Zhao. The cook's assistant would scatter these fragments of edible color across platters of dainty desserts. The gardener looked up inquiringly, one hand holding a pair of scissors.

"There's no hurry," she said. "Young Zhao won't be plating the desserts for a while yet."

"Nearly done," and he returned to the marigolds.

"It's quite the party tonight," she said, drifting to the entrance of the utility area to sniff the jasmine, "with an interesting addition. One of the guests brought a lady friend—the notorious princess Masako Kyo. And something very odd. She sought me out." Lisan leaned to breathe in the strong, almost overpowering scent of pink jasmine. "She said I looked very familiar and reminded her of someone she used to know in Peking. Someone very special. She asked about my family."

There was a muttered curse. She peeked back at the worktable, where Yao was wrapping a handkerchief around his finger. He'd nicked himself with the scissors.

"And what did you tell her?" he said. He pointed at the bowl of petals, indicating that he had finished.

"I told her the boring truth," Lisan said, pulling a flower-laden vine closer to her nose, "that I'm an orphan. Yao, there was something most disturbing about her attentions. I felt like a . . . a target."

"Well, maybe she'll lose interest if you don't catch her attention again," he said, putting the scissors inside a drawer. "Do you have much more to do?"

"No, I'm finished now and I'll stay away for the rest of the evening," Lisan said. She let go of the vine. "Yao, can I cut some jasmine for my room?"

But the gardener had gone. There was just a fleeting cold draft, then a click of the door to the garden, and through the glass she saw his figure walking around to the back of the mansion. Doubtless he had other tasks and chatting with her wasn't one of them. She took the bowl of petals down to the kitchen. That was her final task. She could do whatever she wanted now.

CHAPTER 15

A SWIRL OF MUSIC, a warm gust of air, a relentlessly bright room, electric lights that reflected and refracted from hundreds of cut crystal pendants. The minutes crawled past as Caroline drifted between clusters of guests, sometimes with Thomas by her side, sometimes on her own. She felt under siege by the babble of conversation, the constant clink of crystal and silverware, by the smell of food on the buffet tables. Only a few hours ago, the jasmine blooms arranged along the center of the long buffet table had seemed so charming, their long twining stems woven between the line of candelabras. Now their heady scent stank in her nostrils, pungent and revolting.

The press of bodies was overheating the room and she signaled Chin to open a few windows. She barely paid attention to the effusive compliments, even from Mrs. Easton.

"You have such wonderful taste and you're a generous hostess," the older woman said, with only a slight tone of reproach. "From flowers to food, it's just perfect. And what a delightful string ensemble. Americans? Mr. Stanton's idea, I believe you said? Splendid."

"Yes," she said, "yes, he has so many wonderful ideas. Shanghai quite inspires him."

Mrs. Easton promenaded her around the ballroom, taking charge of each conversation as though Lennox Manor were hers and Caroline a pet being put on display. Caroline watched for Grey, cast her eyes furtively around the huge room, all the while allowing Mrs. Easton to carry on; no one seemed to notice how little she spoke.

Mrs. Easton deposited her with two women. "Mrs. Peters and Mrs. Cole. They came to Shanghai only a few months ago." Then the formidable matron bustled off to assail another cluster of guests.

"Tell me, Mrs. Stanton," said Mrs. Peters, "how do you like living in this house? It's an absolute chateau!" From her accent, Mrs. Peters came from somewhere in the Midwest. She laughed, a tinkling bell-like peal.

"It has its quirks but I find it delightful," Caroline said. Mrs. Peters laughed again.

"Do you not find it rather far from the city?" Mrs. Cole said.

"With a motorcar, the city doesn't seem that far," she replied, "and I rather enjoy living on a country estate."

Another laugh from Mrs. Peters. She laughed often, Caroline noticed. Doubtless she'd been told at some point that she had a pretty laugh and now brought it out at every opportunity.

"Do you know the dramatic history of this house, Mrs. Stanton?" Mrs. Cole said. "The young couple who lived here committed suicide—oh, three or five years ago? A young man, heir to a fortune, and his bride, an opera singer."

"No, no," Mrs. Peters said, jumping in to correct her friend, "it was only the husband who died. After the opera singer ran off and broke his heart."

"But I heard she wasn't really an opera singer, not a properly trained one," Mrs. Cole said. Her gown of saffron silk was beautifully made and she had been eyeing Caroline's dress the whole time. "She was part French, part Chinese. Something like that. What was her name? Nora, something with an *R* in it."

"Her name was Rosalie Roussel," Caroline said, "and the young man who killed himself was Charles Burnett, our uncle Mason's son."

This effectively silenced the bell-like laughter, and the small group broke up, the other two making excuses about wanting more champagne. Caroline sighed in relief as they moved away from her. She'd forgotten how much she disliked large gatherings.

CHAPTER 16

NOW THAT HER duties were done, Lisan wanted to see how the party was doing in the ballroom. She walked along the service corridor to the stairwell that led all the way up to the third floor, where a similar corridor ran alongside the ballroom. This narrow hallway allowed servants to enter the ballroom through an unobtrusive door disguised as paneling. A peephole allowed servants to make sure guests were not standing by the door before opening it.

She put her eye to the peephole and squinted at the brightly lit room. Wearing immaculately-pressed white tunics and soft, cloth-soled shoes, the house servants moved quietly among the guests, holding out silver platters of bite-size sandwiches and savory pastries, some filled with smoked salmon, others with curried beef. At the far end of the ballroom Chin directed them like a conductor, pointing a white-gloved hand at a guest whose champagne glass was empty, causing Liao to rush up with a chilled bottle to refill the glass.

A burst of laughter diverted Lisan's attention to a corner of the ballroom where Princess Kyo held court, surrounded by a half dozen male guests. Grey was nowhere to be seen, at least not close to Kyo. Then her view was cut off by Chin moving quietly and purposefully across the room. He was coming toward the service door. She backed away quickly, dashing along the corridor and down the service stairwell.

She thought of going down to the kitchen to get herself a plate of leftovers, but suddenly felt very tired and very cold. It had been a long day and she still needed to update Caroline's dinner party logbook, which was on the walnut desk in the small parlor. She would build up the fire in her room to get warm, then do a bit of work. Then she would translate a bit more of Rosalie's diary.

The wall sconces along the hallway to the private rooms were unlit, another of Caroline's precautions against errant guests. One hand touching the wall for guidance, Lisan moved carefully from the servants' stairwell to Caroline's parlor. She found the dinner logbook on the walnut desk. On the way along the hall to her room, voices on the landing made her stop. One of the voices belonged to Caroline. The other to a man. Whatever was being discussed, Lisan was sure it was meant only for the two of them. Even though it was unlikely they'd see her in the depths of the dim hallway, she slipped down the first few steps of the servants' stairwell, where she could look out toward the mezzanine.

Above the circular staircase, the chandelier blazed with light. Da Wu was still stationed between the lemon trees. Caroline stood on the mezzanine by the landing. Her delicate green dress contrasted with the almost military rigidity of her posture, her back so straight it brought to mind a violin string stretched taut, ready either to vibrate or to snap from the tension.

The man was Andrew Grey. He leaned back on the curved balustrade, cigarette in hand.

"Oh, I doubt you'll mention anything to Thomas," Lisan heard him say. "I promise to keep this between us until I decide what to do about what I know." He began walking up the staircase, back to the ballroom, then paused and looked down at Caroline. "I know your secret."

Lisan heard very distinctly both the words and their gloating tone. Caroline's back stiffened even more, if that was possible. She spun around in a swirl of green silk and, to Lisan's relief, went directly into her bedchamber without a glance down the darkened passageway. Holding tightly to the handrail of the service stairs, Lisan returned to her own room. She realized she was trembling, so strongly did she feel the threat behind Grey's words to Caroline, even though she had no idea what it could mean.

CHAPTER 17

I T TOOK ALL Caroline had to stand upright as Grey strolled back up to the ballroom. When he was out of sight, she walked across the landing with as much dignity as she could muster. Past the houseboy, who gave no indication of having understood the exchange. Past the lemon trees and down the hallway to her rooms. Once inside the privacy of her bedchamber she rushed to the bathroom. There she collapsed on the floor tiles, then crawled to retch into the white porcelain toilet bowl again and again, gasping and wiping back tears until all she could do was crouch on the floor, trembling.

She rinsed out her mouth and brushed her teeth. She had to get back to the party. But first, she needed to get hold of herself. If there was even a chance Grey had been bluffing then she still held the cards. Her mind ran through the past fifteen minutes. Mere minutes, that's all it had taken to send her life spinning.

There had been a lull in the ballroom as servants carried away trays of half-eaten savories and cleared away used silverware and napkins to set out fresh ones in preparation for filling the long buffet table with platters of fruit and pastries. During this break, Caroline had slipped down the staircase. She had to get away from all those gossipy women, had to gather her thoughts about Andrew Grey. She'd planned to lie down for a few minutes in her room, then return to the party.

Caroline looked down from the third floor and saw the house-boy still standing guard on the landing by the lemon trees. He looked up, beaming, and she smiled. Her first genuine smile in what seemed like hours. But when she descended the curved staircase and saw who else was on the landing, she stopped dead. Andrew Grey was leaning on the handrail, a cigarette held languidly between his fingers. He grinned up at her as she descended the last two steps.

Somehow, she'd known they would confront each other before the evening was over. This moment had been inevitable. He regarded her with apparent amusement. Caroline paused in front of him, put a hand on the railing.

"Mr. Grey, I do hope you're not here by yourself because you don't like the music," she said, playing the hostess. "I can ask the trio to play something you enjoy."

"The music is quite acceptable," he said. "I'm here by myself because I wanted to think about something. Something that's been bothering me ever since we met. But now I remember. And it means I know your secret."

"Mr. Grey, you're teasing me." She lifted her chin a little higher. "I have no secrets. You said we've met before at the Dominics'."

"This life must mean a lot to you," he said. "So I'm going to let you think things over for a day or two. After that, I'm going to ask you for something and you're going to give it to me."

She twisted the gloves in her hands, felt the heat rise to her cheeks. "Sir, I'll tell my husband of your impudence . . ."

"Oh, I doubt you'll mention anything to Thomas," Grey said. "I promise to keep this between us until I decide what to do about what I know." He dropped his cigarette butt into the lemon planter and brushed past her deliberately as he took the stairs back up to the ballroom. Then he turned and smirked down at her.

"I know your secret," he repeated.

And perhaps he did, Caroline thought as she sat in front of her vanity. She pinched some color back into her cheeks and dabbed a little more ginger lily perfume on her wrists. Perhaps he did know, but he couldn't intimidate her. Thinking back on their conversation, she was satisfied that she had not spoken a single word or given away with a single gesture anything to confirm Andrew Grey's assertion that she had a secret.

ROSALIE'S DIARY

6 March 1907

Charles Burnett wants me to call him Charlie. He has been
to the club every night since that first time, refuses to leave
when all his friends move on to other clubs. He says so
many sweet things. He promises to buy me an apartment,
he wants me to be his mistress. He laughed when I told him
that I'd rather have voice lessons with a good teacher than an
apartment. Then he apologized for laughing and told me to
find the best voice teacher in Shanghai. He would pay for the
lessons.

I accused him of mocking me but he said he was perfectly
serious and would do anything to win my love. So far I've
refused to have dinner with him and I've only danced with
him at the club, nowhere else, as one of my duties. I'm not
one of those girls.

His friends get louder and louder the more they drink. They
talk as though I don't speak English. They teased him about
a girl he was supposed to marry, Miss Vera Drummond. What
would Vera think of Charles if she knew he spent all his spare
evenings chasing a nightclub singer?

CHAPTER 18

THE RAIN HAD stopped—in fact, it hadn't rained for two days since the party—but even so, Lisan's room felt damp. There was a dankness to the curtains and bedclothes, and each morning she still draped her clothes on a chair in front of the fire to warm them a bit before getting dressed. She worried about catching a cold and had been feeding wood into the fireplace, but the chill simply wouldn't go away.

Little Liao, who brought her a stack of wood each morning, expressed confusion. "Miss Liu, I have stood in this room and I can't feel any drafts—I mean, nothing worse than in any other room."

She sighed. "Well, maybe you need to be here when the wind blows in from a particular direction to feel it. Don't worry, just bring lots of wood."

What Little Liao and the servants did worry about was Charles Burnett's ghost. They worried the noise and gaiety of the party had roused the dead man's specter.

"I saw his ghost by the lake after dark," Xiao Wu insisted, "a man walking beside the willow trees."

"That was Master Mason," Chin said. "He often goes for walks in the evenings."

"But I've only seen the ghost since the party," Xiao Wu said, "for the past two nights, never before. It must be the spirit of the dead man—it's awakened. Foreign musicians playing familiar tunes, foreign voices speaking his language, perhaps even gossiping about him."

"Calm down, Xiao Wu," Yao said. "It was Master Mason you saw. It hasn't rained for the past two days since the party, so now he can stroll around the garden in the evening. He's spoken to me. It's not a ghost."

The older servants hooted with laughter, but to Lisan, their amusement hid relief. And to tell the truth, she felt relief as well that what Xiao Wu saw had been Mason Burnett and not a phantom.

It was getting to the point where she dreaded the night, but the last thing she wanted was to let anyone know about her dreams or that she was hearing things, like the sounds of a woman sobbing. Especially since half the time she wasn't sure whether she was awake or still dreaming. Was it better to be superstitious or going mad? If she believed in ghosts, she would say that Charles's ghost had chosen to haunt her by sharing his obsession with Rosalie. He had died in despair, alone with his anguished thoughts, abandoned by the woman he loved; so now he assailed her sleep by reliving his final days in her dreams and disturbing the twilight moments of early morning with the sounds of a woman's wailing. Charles, staying invisible while conjuring up his memories of Rosalie.

Yet even after hearing all the gossip about Charles and Rosalie, whenever Lisan looked at the portrait, she couldn't find it in her to put all the blame on Rosalie for Charles's tragic end. Charles had been a poor businessman, he had gambled and drunk too much, and he had taken opium to forget his troubles. No wonder Rosalie had run away. There were too many examples of opium addiction driving families into total poverty.

Back in her room, Lisan looked up at the portrait.

"We have something in common, you and I," she said. The

sweet, melancholy features gazed down at her. "You don't belong to either Chinese or Western society and I don't know where I belong. I'm not part of the Liu family and I'm not a servant. Nor can I ever truly belong to Ju Ming's crowd, even though they were my classmates."

Rosalie's expression seemed to commiserate with Lisan; her dark eyes suggested sympathy.

Lisan climbed into bed. Had she brought this on herself with the portrait and the diary? No, she recalled how she'd felt the first time she entered the gates of Lennox Manor, the rickshaw puller's feet splashing through puddles, her first glimpse of a woman in red at the window. The odd sensation of being drawn to the house. Even before she found those left-behind fragments of Rosalie, before she knew of Lennox Manor's history, she'd felt a gentle coercion.

Come find me.

A coercion that had developed rapidly into compulsion, along with an obligation that cramped itself around her heart and fogged her thinking. She did not know what the obligation entailed. Those three words. *Come find me.* A woman's voice. Did Charles want her to go look for Rosalie? And there was something else. Lately, the thought of leaving Lennox Manor, of setting foot outside its wrought iron gates, caused her to flinch, as though she didn't deserve to be free, not yet.

THANK-YOU NOTES HAD started arriving the day after the party. Caroline told Lisan to bring them to the breakfast room in the morning instead of to her parlor; she wanted to share them with Thomas before he left for work. Almost all of the thank-you notes also included invitations to dinner, to join clubs and attend charity functions, offers to sponsor their membership to the Shanghai Race Club.

The breakfast room smelled comfortingly of buttered toast and coffee, and one of the flowering lemon trees stood in a corner, perfuming the air with its delightful fresh scent. But Lisan sensed something else in the air, a tension that contrasted with the warmth of the room.

"Thank you, Lisan," Caroline said. "Will you come back in about ten minutes? I want to sort through these before you take them up to the parlor." Her words were pleasant and polite, but her voice was strained, her expression rigid.

Lisan saw Da Wu in the hallway, coming up from the kitchen with a jug of hot water. "Da Wu," she said in a low voice, "did you hear anything in there? Are those two having an argument?"

Da Wu had been working hard to learn more English. He listened carefully and whenever he was in the kitchen, often repeated sentences he had heard to ask Lisan what the words meant. He was illiterate but had a good ear and a good memory, and Lisan had been impressed with his progress.

"Oh yes," he said, "no shouting or throwing things, but Missy Caroline is very, very upset."

"Do you know why?" she said.

He frowned in concentration. "Something to do with Master Mason, because I heard her say his name. And then Master Thomas said something, he used the word 'family' and Missy Caroline grew very quiet." Da Wu continued on to the breakfast room, knocking softly on the door before entering.

When she returned to the breakfast room for the letter tray, Thomas was just getting up from the table. He folded his newspaper and dropped it on the sideboard.

"I'm off to work, my darling. Uncle Mason is probably coming down right now." He seemed impervious to his wife's mood, to the fact that Caroline's features were carefully composed and gave away nothing of how she felt.

"You haven't had your hot lemon water yet." Caroline took the carafe from the sideboard and poured hot water into a cup, squeezed in half a lemon. Thomas grimaced at the sour taste. "If you drank less while entertaining investors, you wouldn't need this for your liver," she said, and he chuckled, kissed the top of her head in farewell.

Caroline pointed to the letter tray, and Lisan took it up to the parlor and set it down on Caroline's walnut desk. She glanced through the two piles: one of thank-you notes, the other of invitations that would need replies. That would be their work for the morning, as it had been for the past two mornings since the party.

It occurred to her that there had been a blue envelope printed with a hotel's name: *Les Trois Lanternes*. Now the pale blue envelope was not in either pile. The hotel's cheap stationery had caught her attention when she'd glanced through the mail earlier before delivering it to the breakfast room. It stood out from the other envelopes, which were of heavy, expensive stock, most of them monogrammed.

She checked her address book, which contained the contact details of every guest who'd received an invitation, and she was right, Les Trois Lanternes was Andrew Grey's address. Caroline had removed his letter from the pile. Was it so that Thomas wouldn't see it?

What was behind Grey's arrogant insolence, the way he'd behaved and spoken to Caroline? His sneering tone of voice, as though she were a maidservant or shopgirl, not the wife of a respected man. *I know your secret.* What sort of secret did Caroline harbor that she seemed so vulnerable to Grey?

In Caroline's dressing room, she found her employer very quiet, brushing her hair and gazing at her reflection in the vanity mirror. "Thomas is so forgetful about his lemon water," Caroline said, leaning closer to the mirror to smooth her eyebrows. "He dines out so often I worry that he is drinking too much these days."

"Master Thomas is lucky you take such good care of him," Lisan said, standing by the window. "There's someone at the gate, it's just opened. Goodness, it's a sedan chair! How very odd. Hardly anyone rides in sedan chairs anymore, they're actually extremely uncomfortable. Only officials and aristocrats use them, and mostly for ceremonial occasions."

Caroline joined her at the window. The sedan chair advanced at a slow and stately pace toward the house and vanished under the shelter of the porte cochere.

"We shall know soon enough who it is," Caroline said. "How very curious."

A few minutes later, Chin knocked on the parlor door. "The visitor wishes to see Miss Liu," he said, "and only Miss Liu." He held out a calling card.

Princess Masako Kyo

"How astonishing," Caroline said, when Lisan showed her. "Why do you think she wants to see you?"

"I've no idea," Lisan said. She remembered the woman's avid, almost predatory attention. She looked at Caroline pleadingly. "Won't you come with me, Mrs. Stanton?"

But Caroline shook her head in playful reluctance. "You heard, Her Highness wants to see you alone."

MASAKO KYO STOOD with her back to the door of the drawing room. At the sound of Lisan's footsteps she turned around, and Lisan saw that her clothing today was nothing like the gorgeous robes she had worn at the party. She wore men's clothing: a tailored suit of fine brown wool tweed, a brown paisley cravat tied around a stiff collar, a waistcoat of brown silk brocade, and trousers tucked into polished knee-high boots. A tight bun pulled her hair back from her pale face; she looked like a beautiful boy playing dress-up in his older brother's clothes.

When she saw Lisan, Kyo dropped dramatically into a deep curtsy. "Forgive me barging in without an appointment," she said. "I know it isn't done in polite society. But I was so excited when I figured it out, I just had to come see you, to see your face again, just to be sure. And now I'm sure."

"Sure of what?" Lisan was so startled by the curtsy she didn't resist when Kyo guided her to the settee.

"It was only after I left the party that it came to me. The Forbidden City." She peered at Lisan, and received only a puzzled look. "When I was a child, my parents were invited to court and stayed for a month. The year was 1898. I was only twelve, restless and fidgeting. One of the Empress Dowager's ladies-in-waiting was very kind. She took charge of me so that my mother could attend functions without worrying that I would get into trouble."

She cocked her head and looked at Lisan, who waited, puzzled, for Kyo to make her point.

"The lady-in-waiting was Princess Tsai. You look exactly like her. You're the youngest daughter of Prince and Princess Tsai. You're the missing fourth princess. Oh, Your Highness!" Kyo knelt on the floor and, this time, didn't get up from her obeisance. "I'm just a lowly aristocrat and I admit, I lie about my title. But your father is a true prince of the Third Rank." She looked up at Lisan, excitement coloring her cheeks bright red, her eyes glittering with an intense, fanatical light.

"I've no idea what you mean," Lisan said, pushing herself as far back as the settee allowed. "I've never heard of a Prince and Princess Tsai. Or a missing princess. I'm an orphan."

Still kneeling, Kyo reached inside her handbag and took out a photograph. She proffered it with both hands, head bowed. The photograph was of a group of court women, the Empress Dowager seated in the middle. Kyo pointed to a young girl standing at the edge of the group. "I never go anywhere without a copy of this photograph. That's me, twelve years old, in full Manchu court dress. And that, just behind me, is Princess Tsai. Your mother."

Lisan gazed at the face of the woman Kyo claimed was her mother. Hair elaborately styled, face lightly powdered, two small dabs of color on her lips that gave her mouth a pursed-up look. The woman did somewhat resemble Lisan, the broad forehead and small nose, rounded cheeks on a wide face. She shook her head and handed the photo back. "It could be anyone under that makeup."

"You're only seeing her in this picture," Kyo said, finally rising to sit across from Lisan, "but I was in her company every day for a month in person. I knew what she looked like without that headdress, without the lip stain. You look just like her. Let me tell you a story and then I'll tell you what I learned over the past two days."

Without waiting for Lisan to reply, she continued. "In 1900, Boxer forces and the Imperial Chinese Army attacked the Foreign Legation in Peking."

"I know the history," Lisan said.

"Then you know—we all know—what happened when the foreign armies occupied Peking," Kyo said. "Violence and looting. Properties plundered and torched. It wasn't just foreign soldiers committing these crimes: diplomats, journalists, even missionaries joined in snatching what they considered the spoils of war."

"I still don't understand what any of this has to do with me," Lisan said.

"You're a part of an unsolved mystery," Kyo said. "Prince Tsai, a well-respected diplomat, was in Paris on a diplomatic mission. But with French citizens in Peking under attack, it was impossible for the prince to carry out his mission. Furthermore, he feared for his family's safety, so he left Europe and returned to China. He brought with him only a small staff. And here is where the mystery begins, because all anyone knows after this is what the newspapers reported."

When the prince reached China, he boarded a train to Peking, shedding what remained of his staff in order to travel faster on his own. Then somewhere along the way, Prince Tsai vanished. The last people to see the prince alive were the customs officials who met him at the border and his six clerks.

Newspapers speculated the most likely reason behind the prince's disappearance was that he'd met with misadventure. There had been all sorts of confusion on the roads and railways surrounding Peking. Chinese soldiers and Boxers trying to escape, foreign troops executing people they merely suspected of being Boxers, ordinary civilians fleeing the destruction of their homes. There had been uncontrolled looting everywhere around the capital and assaults on homeowners trying to defend their families and belongings.

Had the prince made it back to Peking, to his small palace near the Forbidden City, he would've found his courtiers and servants dressed in mourning. Three princesses—his wife Princess Tsai and their two older daughters—lay in three coffins. They'd hung themselves, fearing what foreign soldiers would do to them.

But the youngest daughter, the fourth princess, was missing. When questioned, the household servants believed the girl had been abducted or killed. She had been missing since the day her mother and sisters committed suicide.

This gave rise to more speculation: that Prince Tsai did reach his home and had taken his last surviving child away from Peking, never to return, for the city held nothing for him now except sorrow. There were rumors afterward, sightings of father and daughter, but nothing concrete. Gradually other calamities displaced interest in the story of one missing prince and his child.

"You're the missing princess," Kyo said. "Your face, even your voice, tells me so."

"So you believe this?" Lisan said. "Just on the basis of a passing resemblance to a woman you knew more than ten years ago?"

"Not merely a passing resemblance," Kyo insisted, "a near-exact resemblance. But you're right, looks can be mere coincidence. So I've spent the last two days making inquiries."

What she had learned was that Master Liu had bought himself a villa in Shanghai's French Concession a few weeks after Prince Tsai disappeared, effectively cutting himself off from his own family and the estate where the Liu clan lived. A short time after, he brought a little girl into his household. A little girl who remembered nothing of her past.

"But ask yourself, Highness, why would Master Liu Fengmu of the rich and powerful Liu clan adopt a street urchin?" Kyo said. "Did you know that your guardian spent some years in Paris, as a student? And did you know that Prince Tsai was there at the same time? They became close friends. Did he never mention this?"

"No, and . . . and I'm not adopted," Lisan said, starting to feel unsure. "I'm more . . . like a servant in his household. And I still don't know how any of this . . ."

"Liu Fengmu may not have adopted you officially," Kyo continued, "but he's treated you very well. For one thing, he sent you to an expensive school. Why do that for a child picked up off the streets?"

"He's eccentric, everyone knows that." But a slow knot of anxiety was tightening at her throat. There was something in what Kyo had been telling her that both tugged at her memories and at the same time made her want to run away.

"I believe that Prince Tsai did survive, and he did take his daughter away," Kyo said, "and you've been hiding at Master Liu's, living as private citizens. But the prince needs to step out and lead, Your Highness. This is why I've come to see you. Between the Nationalists, the warlords, and infighting among the nobility, our nation is on the edge of revolution."

"This is nonsense," Lisan said. "For one thing, there isn't anyone in Master Liu's household who could even remotely be the prince. Secondly, suppose Prince Tsai is in hiding. It means he doesn't want any part in politics anymore."

"Please understand, Highness," Kyo said earnestly, "your father was a man of such sterling reputation even his political enemies respected him. He was a man of great integrity and intelligence. He also admired Japan. If he endorsed a monarchy guided by Japan, the nobility would follow, it would be a bloodless revolution that could save China. But if we don't move quickly, the empire will fall and we'll lose the chance to establish a modern Chinese empire."

"If this Prince Tsai were alive, and if I were his daughter, he would be the one taking care of me, and not Master Liu." Lisan got up from the settee. "As I've said, there's no one at Master Liu's who could possibly be the prince. Also, I'm not this fourth princess, and I'm of absolutely no use to you."

"All this must be very bewildering for you," Kyo said, her smile radiant, "and you need time to get used to the idea. I'll leave you now to think things over, but know that I'll be speaking with important people in Peking next week and you'll be part of the conversation. It would be ideal if your father is alive, but if not, I'll find a way for you to be helpful to our cause. There's always marriage to a noble house."

She left the photograph on the coffee table and practically sashayed out of the drawing room.

The sedan chair lurched as the chair porters found their balance, then moved off, taking away Masako Kyo and her absurd declarations. Lisan closed her eyes and put her hand on the windowsill to steady herself, then sank into an armchair to take another look at the photograph.

"She's gone, has she? My dear, what was it all about?" Caroline said, coming into the drawing room. "You're quite pale. What did that woman say to upset you?"

Lisan tucked the photograph into her sleeve and looked up at her employer. "She claimed to know my mother. She thinks my father is still alive. She told me things about my supposed family."

"I see," Caroline said, sitting on the chair on the other side of the window. "And what do you think?"

"It's all preposterous. If I don't know anything about my early years, how could she? And certainly nothing about my family," Lisan said. "My guardian said he found me on the streets in Shanghai. I don't understand why Masako Kyo would say things that can't possibly be true."

Caroline leaned forward. Her voice was gentle. "But does a part of you hope it might be true? That you might have a father who's still alive?"

Lisan didn't answer immediately and turned to look out the window again. "A little bit," she admitted. More than a little bit, in fact. But what worried her most was that she wasn't sure who to believe anymore. Master Liu, who had been her benefactor all these years, or this woman with her ridiculous stories? The fact that she even doubted Master Liu was beyond disloyal.

Yet there was the photograph of the court ladies. And Kyo's claims that Master Liu had bought his house shortly after Prince Tsai vanished, then brought her into his household. It couldn't be anything more than a coincidence of timing. Perhaps it was true that Master Liu and the prince had known each other in Paris, yet how could Masako Kyo say for certain that the two men had been close friends? Close enough for Master Liu to shelter a prominent member of the royal court for all these years?

"I'm not sure what it means if what she told me is true," Lisan finally said. "I'd like to believe I still have a family somewhere, a father. Yet at the same time . . . oh, Mrs. Stanton, I don't know what to think right now."

"This must be very distressing for you," Caroline said. "I don't understand what sort of mischief that woman hopes might come of this." Then a pause. "But if I may say something, Lisan, because I also lost my family. Sometimes, without family obligations or expectations, you can do more with your life. Your decisions affect only you. You have more choices."

"Perhaps that's true for American women, Mrs. Stanton," Lisan said, "but in China, family is everything, for better or worse. Without a family, I'm nobody."

"Never say that about yourself, Lisan," Caroline exclaimed, "you're an intelligent, educated young woman."

"China is different from the West, where the self-made man is much admired," Lisan said. "If I could be simplistic about it, in our society one advances only with the help of family and family connections. In return, it's one's duty to enrich the entire family. Education, career, and marriage. So much is enabled by one's family and the family's position in society, especially for women."

"I stand by my words," Caroline said. "As an orphan you need only consider yourself, not carry your family's burdens with you. You have more choices."

Spoken like a woman of wealth, Lisan thought, stifling a groan. Words from a woman who came from a country where women were allowed to earn a living, like the missionaries and schoolteachers she'd met, or the female doctors and nurses at the Margaret Williamson Hospital. They didn't depend on the goodwill of a male relative or on charity. She didn't expect Caroline Stanton to understand. Yet she didn't hold it against the American woman. She meant well. She was better than most foreign women Lisan had met.

Lisan touched her sleeve, felt the photograph tucked there. Her mother's image. No, how ridiculous. Outside, Yao was walking down the driveway, an umbrella on his arm. His light gray raincoat stood out against the dark green cypress hedge. Wherever he was going, Lisan wished she could go too, get out of this house. She needed to talk with someone, not Caroline. Not even Yao.

"I wonder, Mrs. Stanton," Lisan said, "may I be allowed to take my day off now, a few hours early?" She had to speak with the one person who could tell her the truth: Master Liu.

"Of course," Caroline said. "Lisan, you've worked so hard since you've been here. The party is over and there's nothing going on that I can't handle myself for a couple of days. Go home for the whole weekend and don't come back until Monday. I insist. Get some sleep, you look so tired."

ROSALIE'S DIARY

12 March 1907

Even though Charlie has been coming to the club every night and bringing his extravagant friends with him, Huang still hasn't given me a raise. He says why give me a raise when Charlie will tire of me and then he'll stop coming? He did give me a small bonus this week, very reluctantly. The Golden Rooster and other clubs like it are the best I can hope for. Huang doesn't know I'm now taking voice lessons from Madame Taddeo. She has been very kind and encouraging, so at least I know I've got talent even if nothing comes of it. But with more professional training, and with Madame Taddeo's support, perhaps I can get somewhere.

Charlie is being very kind. I'm starting to believe he really is sincere. He is so guileless, so desperate to be liked. He buys drinks for all his friends and I can tell they take advantage of him. "You brought us to this rotten club, Charlie," they say, "so drinks are on you." The poor boy. For that's what he is, still just a boy.

I must not fall in love with him. There is no future in being the mistress of such a man.

CHAPTER 19

I T WAS ONLY after Lisan left the house that Caroline admitted to herself what a relief it was to be completely alone. Much as she liked Lisan, her sincerity and forthright manner, Caroline needed to be alone and think through what might come next.

At breakfast that morning she had pressed Thomas about Mason and they'd argued.

"It's a good thing you told me about the house, sweetheart," Thomas said, "forewarned is forearmed. But I believe Uncle Mason's intentions are good. He must have a plan to buy back the house from this Liu person. I've decided not to bring it up, not unless it becomes necessary. I don't want to embarrass him. We are his family and all he has in this world now."

"It isn't just about the house, Thomas," she pleaded. "What else might be going on with Mason? What if there are more issues with the railway business than he says?"

"Caroline," he said, with just a touch of impatience, "the railway venture is sound. I've looked into all its aspects myself. And if you're worried then I can tell you that once I've put money from your inheritance into the business, I'll have more than enough of a controlling stake to make all the decisions. Mason will be just a very minor shareholder."

He wouldn't take any money from her, not just yet, Thomas said. First, he would make a trip to the north with an engineer and a surveyor, travel along the path of the proposed rail line and map the terrain. It was the sort of due diligence she'd come to expect from Thomas when it came to his business ventures; yet he still seemed to have a blind spot when it came to Mason Burnett.

But Mason wasn't her biggest problem, not at the moment.

She looked around the small parlor, her favorite room. She always kept the drapes pulled back to allow in as much daylight as possible and had made the space more welcoming with plants brought in from the hothouse: a small plumeria tree, orchids and ginger lilies arranged on a wrought iron table, all potted in blue-and-white porcelain of varying sizes. Her favorite was a miniature Japanese white pine, which Lisan told her was fifty years old, a marvel of botany.

She liked the furnishings in this room, less formal, more delicate in scale, the upholstery all in light-colored fabrics. It must've been Rosalie's room. Rosalie Roussel, the mysterious woman Mason never mentioned, his son's wife. She wondered what this room had witnessed in the weeks and days before Rosalie left, whether Rosalie had found solace in this cozy space. Had she sat in this chair, deciding what to do about her future? Would she tie her fate to the man she'd married or strike out on her own? Had there been one incident that made her decide to run away from Charles or had there been a series of escalating events?

Even though Rosalie had abandoned her husband, Caroline's sympathies lay with the young wife.

Outside, a high wind pushed a bank of clouds together, dimming the day. Despite the cup of hot tea in her hands, Caroline shivered. Rather than ring for the youngest houseboy, she added more wood to the fireplace herself. She stood beside the mantel and held her hands out to the heat. Dampness seemed to have settled into her bones. All of Shanghai was cold and damp right now, though many of her guests had assured her this was preferable to the summers, when clammy air worked in tandem with stifling heat, bringing days of unbearable humidity, insects, the miasma of unsavory smells from the river, and outbreaks of disease. Illnesses borne by parasites and infections that could kill.

Worst of all were the vermin. The house servants had put rat poison in the attic, and for good measure, she'd also had them set traps and lay down more poison under large pieces of furniture in each of the rooms, as inconspicuously as possible. She shuddered at the memory of the rat in the attic.

"Speaking of rats," she murmured to herself, and turned her attention to the envelope in her skirt pocket. Andrew Grey and the immediate threat he represented far surpassed any menace from Mason Burnett.

The note was written on pale blue hotel stationery, Les Trois Lanternes on the Rue Voisin, an address in the French Concession. Grey's words were polite and innocuous, thanking the Stantons for the party and concluding with the statement that he looked forward to their next meeting, which he hoped would be soon, just name the date and place. Bland words for what amounted to a summons, for that's what it was. He was telling her to choose a time and place.

"What should I do?" Caroline murmured, looking out the window. Opening a drawer of the walnut desk, she took out some stationery, folded a sheet of paper into an envelope and put a stamp on the envelope. She tucked it in her handbag and after a moment's thought, dropped her diary into her bag as well. She selected her plainest coat and a hat with a wide, low brim, and pinned a veil onto the hat.

Now that she had her own car, she could go to Shanghai anytime. Her driver was a broad, muscular man named Gu. Even when dressed in a forest green chauffeur's uniform he looked like a bodyguard; she suspected Thomas had hired him for both purposes.

Her first destination was Dauphin Jewelers in the French Concession, where she dropped off a bracelet with a broken clasp. The owner brought a tray of bracelets to show her, but she waved him off with a smile.

"I'm not in the mood to try on jewelry right now," she said. "Another time, Monsieur."

She put up her umbrella against the light drizzle and glanced back at the car. Gu was reading a newspaper and smoking a cigarette. He would wait, uncomplaining and indifferent, until she returned. Caroline strolled around the block slowly, looking in shop windows and reading menus posted outside restaurants. She widened her explorations along the side streets, away from the fashionable Avenue Paul Brunat, umbrella pulled down low against the rain and against curious eyes.

Caroline found what she needed a few streets off Avenue Paul Brunat, a small and rather sad-looking café with a faded awning, improbably called the Café Royale. It was empty. Adjusting her veil to cover more of her face, she ordered a hot chocolate and some cake. When her order arrived, she found the beverage unexpectedly good, although the slice of vanilla cake tasted dry, at least two days old. She wrote the address of the tea shop in her diary and penned a reply to Grey on the stationery she'd brought from home. Just a date, time, and place. Three days from now at two o'clock in the afternoon, the Café Royale on Rue Lemaire.

She dropped it in the mailbox on the corner, then returned to the car.

On the driveway of Lennox Manor, Caroline saw that Thomas's motorcar was parked under the porte cochere, something unexpected because Thomas and Mason were supposed to be at a meeting with potential board members for the railway. When her car pulled up behind it, she caught a glimpse of Thomas being helped up the steps into the house, a house servant propping him up on one side, another one carrying his briefcase.

"Why, Thomas," she exclaimed, hurrying into the foyer after him, "what's wrong? Are you ill?"

He waved off her concerns. "An upset stomach, nothing more. I've felt queasy all day and by the afternoon decided to come home."

"But have you called for a doctor? I'll do that," she said.

"Leave it, leave it," he said, wincing. "Just something I ate." Sweat beaded his face and he lurched against the staircase railing, pushing aside the houseboy at his elbow. She gave a small cry as he vomited over the stairs, foul-smelling liquid splattering the marble. Immediately, Head Servant Chin called out orders, and as Caroline followed Thomas into his bedroom, a houseboy came running with a mop and wooden bucket.

"I'm calling a doctor," she said. Mason's doctor was listed in the address book by the telephone but first she helped the houseboy take off Thomas's soiled clothing and put him to bed in his nightshirt. For good measure, Caroline had them line up two chamber pots beside the bed and ordered Chin to make sure they were replaced every hour.

"There's no need to call a doctor," Thomas said, wiping his mouth with a washcloth. "I've had food poisoning before and it passes." But his skin was the color of raw dough, and he convulsed with pain as he said this.

"You've no choice," she said firmly. "I'm going to call. Where is Mason, by the way?"

"I asked him to chair the meeting with potential board members. It's important." Thomas retched into the chamber pot; she pressed a cool towel against his forehead as he sank back into the pillows.

This was a meeting he had not invited Mason to attend. He'd told Caroline this over breakfast to show he was taking her concerns seriously. But now Mason would be representing Burnett and Stanton Ltd. and who knew what he would say, what he would promise. But that wasn't her first worry now.

Caroline found the number for Mason's doctor, a Dr. Ellis, who reassured her over the phone that this was probably something Thomas would get over on his own and that he would be at Lennox Manor as soon as he could.

She met Dr. Ellis at the door. He was a rotund and red-faced man who stared at Caroline with unconcealed curiosity. He'd arrived in a rickshaw. "You can send away the rickshaw, Doctor," she said. "My driver will take you back.

"Have you been here before, Dr. Ellis?" she asked, leading him up the staircase.

"Only once," he said, "when Mason was a little under the weather. Is he here, by the way?" He spoke Mason's name as though they were old friends. "Not to worry, Mrs. Stanton. Newcomers to China frequently fall prey to all sorts of stomach upsets that don't bother the Chinese or longtime foreign residents. After a while the body adjusts to food and local germs."

At Thomas's bedside, Dr. Ellis was jovial and reassuring. "You must drink only boiled water, Mr. Stanton, and drink it hot. Did you by any chance forget one time?"

"I always drink only boiled water," Thomas replied, "here and at the office. Beer or wine when I'm in restaurants."

"A good idea in places where hygiene is suspect," the doctor said, "but this sort of thing is rarely serious. Do remember that raw vegetables and fruit could've been washed in tap water. Also, ice is suspect. A few doses of emetine should fix you up soon. And

I'll send over a bottle of my own formulation as soon as I get back to my surgery. In the meantime, I'll give you something for the pain and nausea and something to help you sleep. I'll telephone tomorrow to see how you're doing."

"I feel better just being home," Thomas said. He mustered a weak smile.

"Doctor, is it all right to give him hot water with lemon?" Caroline said, as she showed him out. "Thomas takes that every morning for his digestion."

"It can do no harm," said Dr. Ellis, putting on his hat. "I've taken some samples from his chamber pot to test for parasites. The hospital laboratory will provide the results within a day or two. Ah, it's stopped raining. And here is Mason."

The two men greeted each other. "And how is Thomas doing?" Mason said.

"He should be fine by tomorrow—or the day after, worst case," Dr. Ellis said. "Just his first brush with local stomach bugs." They both laughed. "And now I must get back. I've a dinner engagement."

Mason mounted the stairs. "I'll give Thomas a quick summary of the meeting."

"Can it wait, Uncle Mason?" Caroline said, hurrying to catch up with him. "He is so very ill right now."

But Thomas was eager to learn how the meeting had gone. He winced as he pushed himself up to sit against the pillows. "Tell me all about it, Uncle Mason. And then I have some blueprints to show you, they're in that brown portfolio. Caroline, could you bring it over here, please?"

"Oh, Uncle Mason, couldn't this wait until Thomas feels better?" she said.

"No, no, it's all right," Thomas said, "it will take my mind off how awful I feel. And I'm actually better right now, those drugs from Dr. Ellis are helping." He reached eagerly for the papers Mason pulled out of a briefcase.

"Then I'll go see about getting you some clear broth," she said, but Thomas wasn't listening anymore. Both men were completely absorbed in conversation and looking at the documents, Mason on a chair beside the bed, nodding and explaining.

Out in the corridor, the youngest houseboy was just coming up the service stairs, carrying a coal scuttle. He bobbed his head to her and knocked on the bedroom door, two taps that signaled a servant wishing to enter; he pushed it open upon hearing Mason's impatient "Come in." And then, with the door left ajar, Caroline distinctly heard Mason say her name.

She moved back quietly and stood by the partially open door where she could hear but not see the two men.

"We do need more funds," Thomas was saying, "but I won't dip into Caroline's money until it's absolutely necessary."

Mason's voice. "Thomas, you have it all. A beautiful heiress, twice as wealthy as we'd hoped. But we need to make use of that inheritance. That was the plan. What's changed?"

"I love her, that's what has changed," Thomas said. "She's nowhere as meek and mousy as you said she would be."

"Dear boy." Mason's rumbling tones. "You married her *because* of the money, so that we could afford this venture. You got on that train, met the Dominics and Caroline, then came very close to losing your life in that avalanche. Make it count."

She stuffed her fist against her mouth to stifle a cry. She wouldn't think about it, would not think about what this meant, or what to do about it. She would think about it later.

THOMAS WAS ASLEEP, in a stupor from Dr. Ellis's drugs. Caroline and Mason took supper by themselves in the breakfast room, a simple meal for two. Their conversation was superficial, Caroline listing all the engagements in her diary and Mason commenting on the people who would be there.

"You're very subdued, my dear," he said. "You mustn't worry about Thomas. Most of us get a tummy upset or two during our first months here and then we acclimate."

"That's also what Dr. Ellis told us," she said, "and I hope that's all it is."

"Thomas needs to recover quickly—things are moving at top speed." Mason finished a glass of wine, poured himself another. "And he will recover, so cheer up. Put a smile on that sweet face."

Caroline couldn't hold back anymore. "Uncle Mason, I feel you've deceived us," she said. "We agreed to pay for fixing up this house, and it's in a terrible state, far worse than you led us to believe."

"Ah, well, I admit the state of things surprised me too when I took a closer look," he said, "however, it's all repairs that you'd have to do anyway once the house is yours, and far better to take care of things now than later."

"We agreed because you promised Thomas this house would be his," she said, "but I've learned that you don't own Lennox Manor. It belongs to a Mr. Liu. And I've told Thomas."

A long silence.

"I see you're as thorough as your husband when he decides to look into something," Mason said. He was silent for a moment. "I live here, in the house where my son died. For his sake, I can never leave this place. And it will belong to me in a few years' time. I'll buy it back."

"With what, Uncle Mason?" she said.

"With my share of profits from the railway," he said. His speech was starting to slur. "Thomas is clever, the most astute businessman I've ever met. Even my small share will prove extremely valuable."

"Did you lure him here, Mason?" She dropped the "uncle." "Did you promise him great things in Shanghai?"

"Not at all. I laid out the opportunity and he gave it careful consideration." Mason's face was shadowed, turned away from the firelight. "I gave him advice and he took it."

Caroline stiffened. "What was the advice?"

"When I told him about the railway opportunity, I said we would need more funds." Mason chuckled. "And he married you, an heiress twice over. What a treasure you are, Caroline."

He took a decanter from the sideboard and opened it. The fragrance of fine whiskey drifted across the space between them. She couldn't seem to take in enough air to fill her lungs.

"Is there anything you've done that was for Thomas and not yourself?" she said, standing up. He had preyed upon her husband, holding out family ties like silken ropes when he sensed Thomas's longing for a family, his need to take care of an older family member after losing his mother.

"You wouldn't understand," he said, "you were born into wealth, never a day's worry. But I must say, someone taught you about money. Your father perhaps? Or Mr. Dominic. In any case, Thomas is a lucky man."

"I'm going to sit with Thomas," she said, pushing her chair away from the table. "Good night, Mason. Please don't disturb him again tonight. He needs rest." He raised his glass to her, firelight sparkling red and gold on the cut crystal.

At Thomas's bedside, Caroline turned on the lamp. He slept deeply, his color much improved now that he was no longer in pain. Did Thomas truly love her? Did she hold any sway over him at all?

She moved about the room, as familiar to her as her own. There had been nights when Thomas wanted her here, in this bed, under the velvet canopy and with all the drapes pulled open. She thought of the words he'd murmured after making love to her. How he described the life they'd have together, the children who would bring them even more joy.

The drapes were open and it was a rare clear night, moonlight casting shadows on the ground and glinting off puddles, water droplets hanging on twigs like tiny crystals. Out by the lake, someone was walking under the willow trees. The burly figure couldn't be anyone else but Mason. It was beyond her why he would want to stroll where the ground was soaking and muddy, the man-made lake so swollen by rain its waters sloshed up to the willows' roots. Yet there he was, and as she watched him circle the slate-gray oval of the lake, it seemed to her that Mason's every step spelled dejection.

Behind her, Thomas groaned. She moved swiftly to bring the chamber pot beside him, then wiped his mouth with a damp towel. She rang for a houseboy to bring hot water and a lemon, then helped Thomas sit up to swallow a bit of food, washed down by hot lemon water.

Thomas. And Andrew Grey. She knew what she had to do.

ROSALIE'S DIARY

15 April 1907

I no longer work at the Golden Rooster. Charles rented an apartment for me near Madame Taddeo, so it's very easy to walk to her place for voice lessons. She says I'm making wonderful progress. I'm so happy. There is an opera company coming next month, and Madame Taddeo knows the conductor, Rudolph Buck. As a favor, she will ask him to hear me sing.

If Buck likes my singing, he might be willing to put me on the program—not in an actual opera, but these traveling companies also present recital concerts in addition to full operas, and that's when they sometimes add local artists to the program.

To be perfectly honest, she did mention that a little cash helps things along. When I told Charles, he told me not to worry. If Rudolph Buck wanted payment to put me on the program, then he would pay.

I'm so nervous. I'm only an amateur. But at the same time, I want this so very much. Do I even dare dream that Buck will hire me? I would be quite content to be a member of the chorus, travel the world, get out of Shanghai.

I told Father about the voice lessons. He warned me that the more Charles gave me, the more he would expect in return.

CHAPTER 20

LISAN SHIVERED AS she passed through the gates of Lennox Manor, but her need to know the truth about her past was so overwhelming it overcame the compulsion to turn back. She walked to Jessfield Station and from there took a rickshaw to Master Liu's home. To her home. The pull of the house, the urge to go back, lessened the farther away the rickshaw took her from Brenan Road and Lennox Manor.

She had never felt such relief as when the rickshaw turned into Rue Molière, the street she knew so well. Her fists unclenched at the familiar sights: the newspaper stand on the corner, rickshaw drivers clustered at the intersection, and the vendor making deep-fried tofu puffs regardless of the season. She walked up the brick-paved driveway to the house, taking in every shrub and tree, each one an old companion. She asked Master Liu's house servant to let him know she was home and would go see him as soon as she had put away her things.

In her room, she washed her face and for the umpteenth time rehearsed the words she would say to ask Master Liu for assurances that Masako Kyo's claims had no merit. Then she could continue her days as before.

The door to the *penjing* room was slightly ajar. She entered, but the words she'd been preparing to say evaporated when she saw the person standing beside Master Liu.

It was Yao.

"What are you doing here?" she blurted, unable to take her eyes off the young man. But it was Master Liu who answered.

"Yao is here because of Masako Kyo," Master Liu said, his voice mild. "Close the door, Lisan. Then sit down."

She managed to lower herself into a chair beside the door, too confused to ask anything. All she could do was stare at Yao, whose sympathetic gaze only served to aggravate her confusion.

"Yao came to me because Masako Kyo confronted you at a party," Master Liu said, "and then she visited you this afternoon. She went to Lennox Manor because of you. What did she say?"

His voice prompted the habitual obedience of years. "She claimed to know my parents," Lisan said. "According to her, they were Prince and Princess Tsai. I've never even heard of them."

Master Liu nodded for her to continue and she repeated everything she could remember of that disturbing conversation. When she finished, there was only silence. His expression gave nothing away. She had salvaged her composure while recounting Kyo's claims, and now she dredged up the words she had rehearsed.

"She's wrong, isn't she?" Lisan said. "It's all just coincidence, isn't it? That you found me on the streets just a few weeks after the Forbidden City fell? That you and Prince Tsai were classmates in France? I mean, if my father were Prince Tsai, if I were really the missing fourth princess, you would've told me."

She looked from Master Liu to Yao and back again. One of them was a millionaire many times over, the other merely a gardener. Yet looking at them today, she realized for the first time that even though Yao only came to Shanghai on occasion, the two knew each other quite well. Not only that, both of them knew about her past. It took everything she had not to scream, not to demand answers.

Master Liu sat back in his chair, looked at Yao, and sighed. "We didn't tell you because it was better for you not to remember. It was better and safer for all of us."

Hardly believing his words, she gripped the arms of the chair. "Tell me the truth," she said, "I deserve to know it. All of it." She had never spoken with such ferocity to her guardian.

Master Liu cleared his throat. "Lisan, I didn't find you in the streets of Shanghai. Your father brought you here to me. And yes, your father is Prince Tsai."

She pressed herself against the back of the chair as he spoke, but she heard his words as though from far away, almost drowned out by the pounding of her heart.

Everything Masako Kyo had told her was true, and Master Liu was able to fill in the details.

Before going to France, Prince Tsai could tell that the Boxer Rebellion was going to escalate. He instructed his wife to abandon Peking and take the family to their summer estate in the hills outside Peking at the first sign of trouble. The route there was familiar to the entire household.

When news came of the attack on Peking, Prince Tsai returned home immediately. But partway through his journey, he realized how dangerous the situation had become and changed course from Peking to his summer home northwest of the city. Dressed in ordinary clothes and carrying only a small bag of belongings, the prince had to travel by foot before reaching the estate. But the summer house stood quiet. His wife and children weren't there. Nor was anyone else from the Peking household. Or so he thought until a servant boy emerged from hiding. He told the prince what had befallen the rest of his family.

The youngest princess had been running a fever, so his wife was reluctant to leave home. Princess Tsai had dithered and hoped for the best, trusted reports coming from the Palace claiming that all was well, that the fighting would cease very soon, that the Chinese

Army was winning and foreign soldiers would never enter Peking. When it was no longer possible to deny the evidence of her own eyes and ears, it was already too late to gather the household for an orderly evacuation. There was no hope of getting their carts, carriages, or motorcars through streets choked with panicked citizens.

Princess Tsai had the gardeners take out a section of railing along the veranda on the third floor of her quarters. Accustomed to following orders absolutely, the gardeners never questioned why. While they carried out this task, the princess ordered her servants to run away and hide.

Down in the courtyard, a young gardener's assistant set down the section of railing he'd carried from the third-floor veranda and chanced to look up. He realized what Princess Tsai was planning. She had blindfolded her daughters and was pulling nooses over their heads. He ran up the staircase as Princess Tsai lined up the three girls, hand in hand, along the edge of the veranda. He grabbed the girl closest to him, tearing her from her sister's grasp just as their mother jumped, taking the two older girls with her.

The boy carried the youngest princess down to the courtyard. Inside the walls of the small palace, sounds from outside reverberated, the sharp retorts of rifles punctuated shouts of pain, and the booms of cannon fire seemed to ricochet between buildings. Everywhere, desperate cries for help. What servants still remained were too intent on escaping to pay attention to the boy and his burden. Some were running out with valuables from the palace. The youngest princess began screaming, and he realized too late that she had pulled off her blindfold. She had seen her mother and sisters swinging by their necks. Then she fainted.

Carrying the unconscious child on his back, he hurried through the embattled city, ducking into side streets and avoiding crowds, walking until paved city streets turned into dirt roads and the houses he passed were roofed with thatch instead of tiles, until the sounds of gunfire no longer battered his ears. He walked for hours, stopping only to drink some water, eat one of the steamed buns taken from the palace kitchens. By now it was bandits he feared more than soldiers and he didn't stop to rest. He walked and walked until finally the prince's summer home appeared on the mountain path, its whitewashed walls glazed by moonlight.

He did his best to take care of the youngest princess, hoping the prince would return before their food ran out. The child was un-communicative, stunned into muteness by all she had witnessed. She sat stone-still and silent. She refused to eat. When the prince arrived, she didn't recognize her father and clung to the young gardener. It was days before she let Prince Tsai hold her.

"Prince Tsai wanted to disappear, for people to believe him dead," Master Liu said, "and to do that, he couldn't return to Pe-king, not even to see his wife and daughters buried. He wanted no more to do with the Imperial government. He blamed their igno-rance for policies that had weakened China, for their arrogance that gave rise to the rebellion that ended with the storming of the Foreign Legation."

The most plausible way Prince Tsai could disappear was for people to assume he'd come to harm on the road. He took advan-tage of the turmoil and left on a train filled with refugees bound for Shanghai, taking his daughter and the young gardener with him. After they arrived in Shanghai, he contacted his friend Liu. Master Liu readily agreed to shelter the prince and keep his iden-tity a secret until they had come up with a plan.

Lisan looked at Yao. He was the boy who had rescued her. She didn't remember everything, not yet, but now she understood her nightmares. And she understood why she trusted Yao instinctively.

"Where is Prince Tsai?" she said. She couldn't say *my father*; those words were suddenly more alien than when she believed herself an orphan. "Is he still alive?"

"He's alive and does not live in China," Master Liu said. "He's in America right now. We correspond only as necessary. He's taken the identity of an employee, as my agent for the automobile import business."

"Mr. Zheng," she said, "your agent Mr. Zheng." A man who traveled to automobile manufacturers in America and Europe.

"It's a role that allows him to travel and make contact with Chinese living abroad," Master Liu said. "Many are impatient for political change. He's raising money from overseas Chinese communities to support Sun Yat-sen and the Nationalists. He supports the overthrow of the Imperial government."

"But if he returned to China now and his identity came to light," Yao said, speaking for the first time, "he would be in danger. Your father was a remarkable diplomat. When he was at court, members from different factions tried to recruit him for the credibility he would bring to their side."

Yao, she realized, was in awe of Prince Tsai. Her father. *Father.* She rolled the word in her mind, considered how it made her feel. "No, no more about him," she said, putting her head in her hands. "All I want to know right now is why you haven't told me any of this before."

"It seemed like a blessing that you lost your memory," Master Liu said. "Your father was relieved you couldn't recall the horrors of your last day in Peking. Of seeing your mother and sisters dead. He felt it was an omen, a sign to forget that life and leave it behind."

"Furthermore," Yao said, "you were so young we weren't sure you would understand the need for secrecy."

For weeks, newspapers printed supposed sightings of the prince and his daughter: a man and a little girl on a steamship bound for South America, a father and daughter seen at a silk shop in Singapore, or riding on horseback across the Mongolian grasslands. Lisan could inhabit her new identity far more easily and safely if she didn't remember the past, if she didn't refer to her father as a prince.

"And the problem and the danger," Master Liu said, "which this woman, this fraudulent princess, does not seem to understand, is that each faction would prefer your father dead than have him support a rival. And since the prince is on the side of the Nationalists, then all the Royalists—all of them, regardless of stripe—would want him dead."

"But how can he still be of consequence," Lisan said, "when he's been gone more than ten years?"

"Masako Kyo was correct when she said our nation is on the edge of revolution," Master Liu said. "China stands on the edge and any small nudge could tip it in any direction. Any one person, any one incident. Prince Tsai is one such person. Or at least that's what desperate men think whether or not it's true. It's what they want to believe because killing dissent is easier to them than admitting their mistakes, their own crimes. Easier than the effort needed to remake China."

"Masako Kyo has put you in danger," Yao said. "She may be keeping quiet for now, but she won't be able to resist telling others she's found the missing fourth princess once she gets to Peking. She said as much herself."

"Why would I be in any danger?" Lisan said. "I'm not important."

"You're his daughter," Master Liu said gently. "They could kidnap you, use you to force him out of hiding. His most dangerous enemy is a powerful man called Prince Duan."

A hard-line conservative who considered Prince Tsai and other progressive members of the court traitors, Duan had often clashed with Prince Tsai. In 1900 when the Boxers and the Chinese Army attacked the Foreign Legation, they did so with the blessing of the Empress Dowager, advised by Prince Duan. Duan gave Chinese troops instructions to attack the homes of foreigners and also those of his political enemies—Prince Tsai's included.

"Duan is a hero to hard-line royalists," Yao said. "All he has to do is give the word, and assassins will target you and your father, for no reason other than Duan's hatred. If Duan takes you hostage, you will not be treated kindly."

"But it would only be Masako Kyo's word against yours," she said, "and her reputation is scandalous. Tell everyone I'm just an orphan you rescued from the streets. I'm nothing."

"The trouble is, you have your mother's features," Master Liu said. "The guest who saw you at my New Year's party remarked on it. He's a court official who has met your parents. And now Masako Kyo has noticed." He shook his head. "I should've noticed it myself, but I see you every day, and somehow . . ."

"Why did you make me leave my job at St. Clare's?" she said. "Was it because of this?" And she swept a hand over her face.

Her guardian nodded. "At first, I just wanted you to stay home as much as possible so that no one else would see you. But you got the job with the Stantons, and Fourth Uncle pointed out you'd be safer living with foreigners."

"The Stantons were unlikely to invite anyone except other foreigners to their home," Yao said, "and they wouldn't look at you twice, let alone connect you to Prince Tsai. But then Masako Kyo . . ."

"I can't talk about this anymore. I'm going to my room," Lisan said, standing up. "I've not slept well in weeks."

As she made her way along the corridor, almost running, she heard Master Liu's voice. "Let her get some rest, Yao. This is unexpected and disturbing to her."

SHE LAY ON the bed in the room where she'd slept for more than ten years. Lisan wished the sturdy door could shut out the confusion, put a barricade between her and what she had just learned. She sank under the covers and turned on her side, curled up until her knees nearly touched her chest. The bedroom was cozy, just enough space for a bed and chest of drawers, a tiny armoire, a schoolgirl-size desk and chair. This bedroom was her first memory. She remembered waking up one morning and seeing daylight through gauze-curtained windows. The scent of sandalwood soap on her skin. A middle-aged woman looking down with an inquiring smile. Her amah. One time, there had been a man who watched while the amah fed her congee and pieces of fruit. She never saw that face again, and sometimes she wondered whether she'd dreamed it. Now she realized it must've been her father. Other than that, she had only flashes of memory from dreams.

And now she was back, trying to gather her thoughts, regain the feeling of safety she'd felt here as a child. But with all that she'd learned since leaving Lennox Manor she could barely think. What she had learned and what it meant. She didn't know how she ought to feel instead of simply numb.

She sat up and looked at her feet. Another revelation. All these years, her big feet had been evidence that her origins were lowly, her dead parents so poor they expected a daughter to labor and walk long distances. Foot binding was still practiced by the Han Chinese, but more and more, families shunned the custom. At St. Clare's her classmates were a mix of girls with bound feet, bound feet that had been "let loose," and normal feet. Now she knew why she had normal feet. She was Manchu. Manchus never bound their daughters' feet.

As a child, whenever she felt lonely, she'd make up stories about her parents, about why she had been abandoned. Perhaps her family had once been wealthy but lost their fortune. This was a common enough tale, and when it happened sometimes families sold off their daughters. More often though, she wanted desperately to believe she was Master Liu's daughter, an illegitimate child. After all, he had given her a good life and sent her to school for an education no servant would ever need. In an absent-minded way, he was even affectionate to her.

Her emotions churned. What she needed was a visit to the Goddess of Mercy at the family temple. There she would light some incense, whisper her requests, and sit for a while on the floor to contemplate the goddess's carved features, the string of wooden beads draped around the wooden shoulders. As a child she'd been sorely tempted to play with those beads, but even then, she knew Master Liu would've frowned on her touching anything in this sacred place. She would visit the Goddess of Mercy in the morning.

Lulled by the familiarity of her own bed, the comforting weight of woolen blankets, she gave in to exhaustion and let her thoughts drift until sleep took over. And yet, even here at home, she could feel a strange tugging at the edge of her consciousness, something that urged her to go back to Lennox Manor. *Come find me.*

SHE IS IN the garden at Lennox Manor, but it isn't winter. The skies are a cerulean blue. Early blooming roses flourish on shrubs in the formal garden, the fresh, elusive green only found in springtime tints leaves and grass, and the plum trees behind the house are in flower, some already dropping pink and white petals on the grass. Lisan recognizes the season—late spring is her favorite time of year, days of soft sunshine and turquoise skies. But she had never seen the gardens of Lennox Manor at this time of year.

A flash of color and it's Rosalie, kneeling on the grass by the water's edge; the crimson train of her dress spreads out behind her like a pool of blood. She stands up when she sees Lisan. She isn't very tall. Barefoot, she is more petite than Lisan.

Rosalie smiles, looks up at the sky, and Lisan hears laughter, a man's happy voice. A young man across the lake is pointing to a family of ducks clambering up from the water and onto the grass. He's the same man Lisan saw by the piano in a previous dream, and she realizes he's a younger version of Mason Burnett, not as broad or as tall but with the same unruly brows and deep-set eyes. His dark head is bare, his chin covered with a short beard.

The young man and the lake fade out of her dream but a voice lingers in the air, murmuring words Lisan can't make out. A red dress flutters, then vanishes into a stand of silver birches growing in front of a row of poplars.

Come find me, the voice says. Rosalie's voice, she now realizes. Red fades to gray, this time vanishing completely.

LISAN ROLLED OVER in bed and opened her eyes. How would she even know what Charles Burnett looked like? There were no portraits of him in the house, no photographs, nothing at all. When she and Caroline had stolen into Mason's rooms, she had peered at the artwork on his walls, mostly landscapes and hunting scenes. On a side table she'd found a sepia-toned photograph of a young woman with smiling eyes and hair piled in a pompadour, her dress dark with a fall of lace at her throat. Another beside it of the same woman, a little older, a more elaborate hairstyle, a collar of pearls. Both were in silver frames. She thought this was probably Mason's wife, who had died more than twenty years ago.

Shadows fell on the wall and fluttered as trees outside shook with every gust of wind. Even here, where she had always felt safe, Lennox Manor still reached out to haunt her. It was because of the diary and the portrait; they had taken up residence in her thoughts even though she had no interest in finding Rosalie. She had to stop reading the diary, stop letting Rosalie's story intrude on her reality.

She had her own future to consider, but how was that possible when she didn't know who she was anymore? She had a father but no memory of him. Her father had a family and a clan, but it was a lineage lost to her if she followed his wishes and kept their identities hidden. She had a royal title, which gave her entry to the Imperial court, but like so many young Chinese, she scorned the antiquated regime that had ruled and ruined China. She had to know more about her past before she could feel comfortable about the future others were shaping for her.

MASTER LIU'S VILLA was in the middle of Shanghai, its garden a tenth the size of Lennox Manor's parklike setting. The garden shed was at the very back, almost completely covered in ivy; the vines were clipped away from a large window so that sunlight could shine through. She had seen Yao go in earlier. She carried a tray with bowls of hot soy milk and scallion pancakes.

"How did you carry me?" she said, entering without greetings or small talk. "You walked for hours—didn't your arms hurt?"

Yao put down the miniature azalea, hot pink blooms on tiny branches that gave off a scent like incense. "I put you in a baby sling left behind in the servants' quarters."

He'd wrapped her in a maid's tunic to hide her silk clothes, took off the embroidered red satin shoes, and hoisted her onto his back. He tied the straps of the sling to his chest, and started walking.

"How old were you?" she said.

"Fourteen and very strong," he said, grinning. "Fortunately, you were small for an eight-year-old, and unconscious most of the way."

"How did you get into the summer house?" she said. "Weren't there guards?"

"Yes, four guards, just enough to watch the gates," Yao said. "One of them recognized me because I used to help with the garden work there. They knew nothing about what was happening in the city. The three younger guards had family in Peking and rushed back to protect them."

Yao never told the guards her identity. What he had seen on his flight out of Peking cautioned him not to reveal anything of value—including a small princess. All people saw was a boy in straw sandals and ragged trousers running away with a younger sibling slung on his back, no different from countless other refugees, with nothing of value to rob. Yao and Lisan lived in the servants' quarters with the elderly guard for two days until the prince arrived, a humble-looking man in shabby trousers and cloth-soled shoes.

"Your father realized he was safer as a commoner," Yao said, "and this made him unrecognizable to the guard, who had always cast his eyes down and bowed low whenever he crossed paths with a member of your family. I took my cue from Prince Tsai and never addressed him as 'Prince' until we were alone. Your father told the guard he was a clerk from the prince's household and I vouched for him."

Yao had the sad duty of telling Prince Tsai about the fate of his wife and other daughters. Then he led the prince to the mute little girl, his last remaining child. Before the prince had known what happened to his family, when he still believed he would find them at the summer house, he had already decided he wanted nothing more to do with the Imperial court. A day after reuniting with his daughter, he took them to Shanghai, first on foot, mixing in with another group of refugees. Then they traveled by horse and cart, then by train; when they finally reached Shanghai, they stayed in a cheap hotel until the prince was able to contact Master Liu.

Master Liu bought the villa and hired servants, new ones without any connections to the Liu clan. This allowed privacy and concealment for Prince Tsai. After a few weeks, when Lisan came out of her silence and became aware of her surroundings, the prince decided to slip into a new identity and go overseas, entrusting his daughter to Master Liu's care. He would live apart from her for a while because people were on the lookout for a father and daughter.

"You're wondering why your father didn't keep you with him," Yao said. She didn't reply. "You were still sick and in shock, Lisan. You needed a stable home and medical attention."

Then as the years went by, Lisan seemed content living with Master Liu. In her mind, she had never known another home. As for Master Liu, he was content as well. He'd led a solitary, bachelor life and the villa was a good distance from the rest of his family; the separation suited him perfectly. The prince remained overseas, traveling to raise money and support for the Nationalists, always introducing himself as Mr. Zheng, purchasing agent of the Liu Motorcar Import Company.

Yao sipped the warm soy milk, all the while keeping his eyes on Lisan as though worried she might break down.

Prince Tsai. As his child, she owed the prince her duty. But what about her affection? And should she expect affection from him? She was only a daughter, only a girl. She thought about Lee Ju Ming and how the few times she'd seen Ju Ming with her father, her classmate had been subdued and respectful, her father distant. But Mr. Lee's face lit up when Ju Ming's brothers were around. He took an interest in his sons' activities. They were young men, the ones who would carry on the Lee lineage and take over the family business. Ju Ming and her sister were only daughters, girls who would marry out, their loyalty pledged to their husbands' families.

Was this how her father felt about her and her sisters? Had he held them at arm's length? A mother would've loved her child, boy or girl. But her mother had killed herself and taken Lisan's two older sisters with her. She couldn't even fathom this right now.

Lisan knew she was supposed to feel grateful her father had left her in Master Liu's care, and after a while perhaps she would be.

Perhaps all would be different after seeing her father again. But at the moment, her life felt like a rough path bounded by tall hedges through which she could catch only glimpses of some other life, some other road.

"Yao, were you really in Soochow these past years?" she said. "Or have you been here in Shanghai all along?"

"I really did go to school in Soochow," he said, "and I really did train there in gardening, landscape design, plants, and *penjing*. I had the pleasure of working at one of the great classical gardens there. Then Master Liu called me to Shanghai and put me into the job at Lennox Manor. Fourth Uncle's doing."

"How very convenient that Mason Burnett is indebted to Fourth Uncle," she said. "I suppose it was to keep an eye on me?"

"It was to protect you," he said, without any sign that he'd heard her indignant tone. "That is my sworn duty, Princess."

Princess. The first time he'd called her that. The title grated on her nerves and even worse, placed her far too high above him. "Don't call me that," she said. "I want nothing to do with this regime. I'm only an ordinary citizen, like you."

He bowed his head.

"Masako Kyo says my father admires Japan," she said, "that he might persuade the monarchy to follow Japan's guidance."

"Many Chinese admire Japan since they won the Russo-Japanese War," Yao said. "It allowed us to realize that an Asian nation could be the equal of a Western power. But he would never want Japanese interests to rule China from behind the throne."

"What now?" she said. "What should we do about Masako Kyo? When will I get to see my father?"

Yao dusted off his hands, wiped them on an old towel. "Master Liu will confer with his brother about Masako Kyo. As for your father"—he hesitated—"Master Liu hasn't heard from him in weeks. Your father's missing, Lisan."

ROSALIE'S DIARY

20 April 1907

The apartment, the voice lessons, and now a chance to sing onstage.

Charles hasn't pressed me at all to be his mistress. He would like it, of course, but avoids pushing. I think he really means it when he says he loves me. And despite promising myself I would not fall in love with him, I am. He is generous and thoughtful and believes in my talent.

Madame Taddeo has arranged for me to sing in front of Rudolph Buck. It's too much to hope for. I must prepare. She is giving me extra lessons. I will sing an aria from *Tosca*—which Madame says is Buck's favorite opera.

22 April 1907

I'm so happy—my audition was successful!! I'm going to be a guest artist with the Town Band, conducted by Rudolph Buck! One performance only but it means a lot of preparation! Charles is paying for my costume, jewelry, extra voice lessons. And of course, he paid to put me onstage. It's not a bribe, he assures me—these touring companies need to turn a profit any way they can and it's common practice. I'm so happy. Afterward, Charles is going to commission my portrait, dressed as Tosca. Vissi d'arte. Vissi d'arte!

CHAPTER 21

D R. ELLIS BROUGHT over a bottle of medicine to the house, purgatives that left Thomas exhausted and even paler than before. The mixture, Ellis explained with a touch of pride, was his own formulation, a mineral-based tonic that accelerated the expulsion of digestive acids from the patient's system.

"It's just as I thought and the laboratory results proved your husband suffers from intestinal parasites," he said. "It's affecting Mr. Stanton more severely than usual, but everyone's different."

"Parasites," Caroline said, "you're absolutely sure?"

"Yes, my dear," he said, "the lab results are very definite so it's nothing to worry your pretty head about. Your husband will recover on his own, and for now, just make sure he stays in bed, eats only bland food, and drinks lots of liquids to prevent dehydration. I'll leave more laudanum so he can sleep."

"Doctor, he's in so much pain," she said. "I didn't think it would be so painful and I can't bear it. Is there anything stronger you can give him? The laudanum isn't enough. I used to give my mother morphine injections during her final illness."

"An injection of morphine?" he said. "It's addictive, but for just a few days, it should be fine. It will allow him to sleep comfortably."

"Thomas, my dear," Caroline said, leaning over him, "are you willing to take an injection?"

He groaned and doubled up. "Anything."

The morphine was like a small miracle. Thomas's body unclenched and he fell into a deep sleep. Dr. Ellis left some vials and a syringe behind for Caroline. "Purgatives and some proper rest will help him get rid of the parasites."

Thomas had been taking the medication for two days with no signs of improvement, but the doctor remained undaunted and very certain. That made it easier for Caroline to turn down Mrs. Easton's offer when she telephoned the older woman to explain why she couldn't go to the American Ladies Club board meeting. Mrs. Easton had inquired which doctor was treating Thomas.

"Dr. *Ellis*? You didn't say Ellis, did you?" The woman sounded horrified. "Why, Caroline, he's an old soak. Only good for prescribing laudanum and medicinal tonics that are mostly alcohol. I'll send you my own doctor."

"According to the laboratory results, Thomas has a case of intestinal parasites," Caroline said, "and my understanding is that it's the sort of thing people get over by themselves, with or without a doctor. It's hit him harder than most people but I'm sure he'll be all right. Please don't worry."

When conscious, Thomas suffered terribly, groaning so loudly sometimes the sound of his pain echoed through the corridor. She gave him Ellis's tonic twice a day, washed down with lemon water. Then morphine to ease the pain and make him sleep.

Mason spent less time at home, often staying in the city for dinner. "I'm terribly busy these days," he said, "since I'm also doing Thomas's work."

Caroline guessed it was because Thomas's illness distressed him. Well, she no longer cared about Mason. It was actually very convenient to have him out of the house so that she could deal with other problems. She had been lying awake over her upcoming appointment with Grey, the days both dragging on and winging by too quickly. Grey could take all this away from her.

Which was so unfair because the thing was, she hadn't actually planned to take over Caroline Vessey's life.

HER PARENTS HAD been in catastrophic debt. She learned this once they died, both at the same time and from the same undiagnosed illness after a holiday. A holiday to Italy they couldn't afford, as she learned while they were away and she saw for herself the payment demands and bills that poured in. Her parents died leaving her next to nothing. She wrote to classmates from her time at boarding school, girls she'd counted as friends.

Caroline Vessey, also recently orphaned, had been the only one to reply. In a gesture of empathy, Caroline offered to bring her to New York and into the Dominic household as a companion. This offer almost didn't succeed, thanks to Mrs. Dominic, who gave in only because Caroline refused to leave the apartment unless she agreed.

Caroline Vessey considered her a friend, their bond forged as roommates during boarding school. Mrs. Dominic, however, considered her merely another girl of good family come down in the world; the woman was not inclined to charity, not unless there were social benefits involved. But for once, the timid and self-effacing young woman stood up to her aunt and insisted on giving her former classmate a job. She stated firmly that she would pay the wages from her own trust fund.

"My aunt says you can be a maid," Caroline said. She was almost in tears when they met at Grand Central Station in New York. "But I won't treat you as a maid, you know that." From Caroline's demeanor, anyone would've thought she was the supplicant and not the other way around.

In the Dominics' apartment, she lived in a closet-size room beside Caroline's huge bedchamber. She came to know the city well, often running errands because Caroline had developed a terror of leaving the huge apartment. She soothed Caroline through her frequent fits of anxiety, calmed her before Mrs. Dominic's parties, where Caroline was expected to shine and attract eligible suitors. She helped Caroline get ready, rolling the fine straight hair into something approximating the latest style, selecting dresses and jewelry to flatter her pallid complexion, all the while making light of the guests who would be there, hoping laughter would dispel Caroline's anxious expression long enough to get her through the evening. Mrs. Dominic soon understood how much her pale, peculiar niece depended on this impoverished school friend, especially since Caroline often descended into hysterics at the thought of meeting new people.

How tired she became of all this, of being grateful for her small room, the hand-me-down clothes. For the first two years in New York, she had moved through a fog of confusion and distress, humiliated by her changed circumstances. But now, after four years, the numbness had subsided and it was getting harder not to snap at Caroline and her whining insecurities. *You have everything,* she wanted to scream at the petulant mouth, the blinking eyes. *Enjoy your life instead of hiding in your room!*

She was achingly aware of her dependence on the Dominics' goodwill. Aware also of Mr. Dominic's growing interest in her. During the cross-country train journey, he managed to be in the carriage's corridor whenever she walked through, placing himself in her way so that she had to squeeze past him. She held herself in as much as possible to avoid pressing against his paunch, but even so, his hands always brushed her hips even when there was ample room for them to pass each other without touching.

Perhaps things would change when they reached Seattle. Mr.

Dominic had bought a construction company there. Seattle was expanding and housing could barely keep pace. He planned to build a mansion in Seattle, a grand villa, so that Mrs. Dominic wouldn't miss their Fifth Avenue apartment whenever they were out West.

She would take a look around when they arrived in Seattle. Somehow she would find a way to be free of the Dominics. After all, she wasn't without skills. Music, dancing, etiquette, which fork to use. How to manage a household of servants. She could teach the daughters of social-climbing mothers all the social graces her expensive boarding school had provided. She was prepared to do the work. She had learned some hard lessons after her parents died, sorting through the tangle of their debts on her own.

In the meantime, however, she couldn't complain and she still had to be careful. So on their journey, when Caroline came to her compartment that night, she made lively conversation while they snuggled to keep warm. She made Caroline laugh, recalling how they'd hidden Katherine van Dusen's white stockings before a dance recital. They argued over which of their teachers had been the worst, until finally Caroline yawned.

"Could you get me some water?" Caroline asked, already half asleep. "You know how I like to have water by my bed at night."

"Of course," she said, swinging her legs out of bed. She reached for her bathrobe, found Caroline's fur coat instead, and put her arms through it, felt the fine, luxurious mink warm her almost instantly. On the way back from the dining room, she stumbled and fell, sprawling to her hands and knees, dropping the glass of water. The rail carriage shuddered. There was a creaking sound, then a rumble, not of engines or thunder, but something deeper and slower and unfamiliar. She heard screams. Then the world rolled over on its side, over and over, and then there was only oblivion.

And then Thomas found her.

Snowplows finally arrived, bringing more rescue workers and doctors. Along with other survivors, she was carried to a railway carriage that had been set up as a hospital ward. The train took them to Spokane, where she stayed in the hospital for a week. The hospital was blessed with an active group of volunteers who turned up in force, women who supplemented the beleaguered staff, helping to feed and bathe survivors, keeping them company, praying with them or for them. One of these volunteers now settled herself on a cane chair by the bed.

"I'm Helen Cannon, president of the hospital's volunteer organization," the woman said. She was well-dressed, a fur stole pinned around her shoulders. "How's your head today?"

"I still don't remember much," she said, "but I think my head hurts less than yesterday."

"You were asleep earlier when Mr. Stanton came by," Mrs. Cannon said. "He has never missed a day. He said to tell you he would come by again in a few hours."

Blushing, she looked away from Mrs. Cannon.

"Rescue crews are still digging and finding more of the dead every hour," the woman informed her. "You're one of the lucky ones, Miss Vessey. Lucky also that we were quickly able to identify you from the clothes you were wearing. With help from Mr. Stanton, of course."

The fur coat with *Caroline Vessey* stitched inside the lining, the hand-me-down nightgown with *CV* embroidered on the cuff. Yes, lucky that she'd happened to grab the fur coat before leaving her compartment. Its warmth had saved her. Lucky that she had left to get a glass of water, that she hadn't been in her compartment when the avalanche hit. Lucky that apart from a concussion, some bruising, and a sprained wrist, she had no other injuries. Not even frostbite.

"You're due for discharge tomorrow, but you still need rest and quiet," Mrs. Cannon said. "My husband and I would like you to stay with us until you're feeling better. Until you remember more. He's notified your guardians' lawyer. Mr. Danby is on his way here."

Not only were the Cannons one of the town's most prominent couples, but Mr. Cannon was also its leading lawyer. She stayed with Edward and Helen Cannon for several days before the Dominics' lawyer arrived. She didn't go into the parlor to meet Danby until Mrs. Cannon sent for her.

In the room adjoining the parlor, piles of papers were spread out on the dining table, where Mr. Cannon was reading his way through a stack of documents. Another man sat beside him, a pair of glasses in his right hand. The lawyer from New York.

The man who would take one look and announce she was not Caroline Vessey. But they couldn't blame her for losing her memory. They could only blame themselves for making assumptions.

"Ah, here is Miss Vessey," Mrs. Cannon said. "Now, Caroline, I've told Mr. Danby that your health is still delicate, physically and mentally. He knows you don't remember everything so he's not to question you as though it's a cross-examination." She shot a stern look at Danby, who put the glasses down and hastened to greet her.

"Miss Vessey, my sincere condolences," he said, taking her hand. "Your guardians were clients for decades, friends as much as clients, if I may presume to say. I shall miss them very much."

Danby was tall and lean. His gray mustache was neatly trimmed, his clothing expensively tailored, and his hair neatly slicked back. Even though it was the middle of winter, there was a fresh rosebud in his lapel. It gave him the air of an elderly dandy, but when he peered at her through watery brown eyes, she thought he looked kind.

"How do you do, Mr. Danby," she said. "I'm afraid that if we've met I don't quite recall; my head still hurts and I remember things only in bits and pieces sometimes . . ."

This was a lie. Her memories had come back while in the hospital but it had been useful to feign confusion. For one thing, the Cannons thought she was a wealthy heiress and had insisted she stay with them until she had recovered completely.

"Nothing to worry about," he said gallantly, "I'm eminently forgettable. And we met only once, very briefly, at your guardians' home on Fifth Avenue shortly after you went to live with them. It was your uncle's birthday. You joined the party for a few minutes and then left. That was four years ago when you were still . . ." His voice trailed off and he looked awkward.

". . . still in mourning," she said, finishing the sentence for him. She remembered Danby now. She remembered that he had squinted with myopic eyes at the tray of hors d'oeuvres she had been carrying.

"I do remember something about that party, Mr. Danby," she said slowly. "You didn't like caviar, so you took the smoked trout canapé."

"That's right," he said with a pleased smile. "I abhor caviar. I'm astonished you remember. That's a good sign that your memory is coming back, isn't it?" He beamed and blinked.

"Only in bits and pieces," she said.

"Shall we set out the tea, Caroline," Mrs. Cannon said, "while the men keep talking business?"

She helped Mrs. Cannon lay out the teacups and sat down on the settee to slice cake, all the while keeping her ear tilted toward the dining room, where the lawyers were talking.

"Poor little rich girl," Mr. Cannon said, "first she loses her parents and then her guardians. And in such a horrific way. She's a sweet thing, clever too. You can tell even though her memory's a bit vague."

"When I met her that one time in New York, she was really still a child, not long out of boarding school." Mr. Danby sighed. "A pinched little face, in shock after losing her parents. All in black, thin as a wraith. Stared down at the floor the whole time, long fringe of hair hanging over her eyes. She's certainly improved now that she's grown up and put on some weight."

"Can you confirm this is Caroline Vessey?" Mr. Cannon said. "We've never doubted it, but you're the one who knows her."

"She just remembered a detail only Caroline Vessey would know, from the one time we met," Mr. Danby said, "something I had forgotten myself until she brought it up."

That was when she realized how easy it would be to simply become Caroline Vessey. And now she was Mrs. Thomas Stanton. Caroline Stanton. Grey would not take this life away from her.

ONCE AGAIN, CAROLINE had the driver drop her off near Dauphin Jewelers with instructions to return in an hour. She picked up her bracelet, now repaired, and strolled away from the jeweler, away from the main street toward the Café Royale.

For this meeting with Grey, she had dressed in the most nondescript clothing she owned, muted colors, a charcoal-gray coat with the collar turned up, a plain black hat with a drooping brim and veil. The Café Royale, tucked into a small side street, was a far cry from the kind of establishment that attracted the better class of clientele. Its dingy fly-specked windows were streaky with grease—most definitely not the sort of place where she would run into anyone she knew.

Caroline took a quick look above the café curtains and drew a deep breath. He was there, at a corner table by the window, a spot where he could peer through the cheap curtains to watch the street. That was all right; she had expected him to arrive earlier than the appointed time. The bell on the door tinkled when she pushed it open.

He stood up when she approached the table, and even though she didn't want to exchange pleasantries about the weather or the newly renovated dining room at the Astor House Hotel, Grey thought he was holding all the cards and she had to play the game as he wished. He obviously wanted to make this encounter look like a rendezvous between friends. Only after their coffee arrived did he lean forward and change to a low, confiding voice.

"So, my dear." He put his hand over hers as she reached for her steaming cup. She pulled back, splashing dark liquid on the tablecloth. He grinned at this and withdrew his hand. "How did you do it? How did you get away with it?"

"I don't know what you mean, Mr. Grey," she said.

"Stop pretending, Caroline, or whatever your name is," he said. "I've contacted a detective in New York and he's doing some digging around for me. I'll soon have evidence that you were the Dominics' maid. So again, how did you do it?"

What slim hope she'd dared entertain crumbled. Hope that perhaps he was mistaken, that what he thought he knew wasn't her real secret, that she could somehow still evade his grasp.

"It was remarkably simple, given the circumstances," she said, holding back nausea. "Everyone assumed I was Caroline Vessey and I let them. They all tiptoed around and didn't question me too much, not wanting to upset my fragile state of mind after the avalanche. I refused to get on a train back to New York. Everyone was very understanding of this and a very kind lawyer brought all the paperwork to me."

Grey sat back, waited for her to say more, but she merely put the cup to her lips and regarded him as she drank.

"So the opportunity fell in your lap and you decided to take it," he said. "I applaud your initiative. And then marrying Thomas Stanton for his money. Or did he marry you for yours?"

"Thomas doesn't need money," she said, carefully judging how much to say. "He was a millionaire before we married."

"Is that what you think?" Grey shook his head. "He owns mines, but some of them are no longer producing. He's worth less than he was a year ago. That's why he's in China, rolling the dice on railways. Using your money, which he can have you sign over to him." He licked his lips and smiled again, watched for her reaction to his words.

Caroline managed to put her cup and saucer down, hands steady, no rattle of porcelain, nothing to give away the fear clotting around her heart. "All I need to know is why we are meeting today."

"Ah yes," he said, "so here's the thing. My fortunes have slipped since those heady days in New York. If the awe-inspiring Mrs. Dominic were still alive, she wouldn't invite me to one of her dinner parties. Though to be perfectly frank, I barely scrambled my way onto her guest list even back then." Grey snorted, then sat up straight. "I need your husband to invest in my land development company. Fifteen thousand dollars. I've asked him but he refused."

"I don't tell Thomas what to do," she said, "and anyway, why would he listen to me? I know nothing about business."

"Perhaps you don't know anything about business," Grey said, "but I think he'd do anything for you. He's absolutely smitten. If a man of Stanton's stature invests in my business, others will jump on board too."

If only it were true that Thomas would do anything for her. If only he'd listened to her, stayed away from Mason and his grasping, greedy schemes. She dabbed the napkin to her lips. "If Thomas doesn't think your business is a good investment, it doesn't matter how smitten he might be," she said, "he won't do it."

"Actually, I really don't care where the money comes from. If you can't persuade Thomas, then just get it for me yourself." Grey leaned back in his chair, stirred his coffee. "Of course, it's better if Thomas could lend both his money and his name to my business, but I'll take just the money. You must have plenty."

She picked up the cup again and kept her eyes steadily on Grey's. When Thomas had proposed, she didn't know that Caroline was sole heir to the Dominics' fortune. She only knew what Caroline had told her, that the Vessey inheritance was held in trust until she turned twenty-five or married. She'd married Thomas and now he could call upon both fortunes.

"But how on earth would I get that kind of money without Thomas noticing—" she began to protest, and stopped when he waggled a finger at her.

"Now, now. Not my problem. And I want it in two weeks, Caroline. Or whatever your real name is." He leaned closer across the top of the small round table. "That gives you enough time to gather the money, doesn't it? You've proven how clever you are; you'll come up with some scheme, send cables to your banks and lawyers and such. If not, I'll tell him about you. And then I'll threaten to expose you to the world. That would snarl things up, wouldn't it? He won't want scandal, so he'll pay. But at what cost to your happy marriage?"

"It won't come to that," she said.

"No, it won't," he agreed, "since you'll get me the money. And by the way, I want to see you before then. I want a small deposit soon. Two weeks is rather a long time to wait." His lewd grin made it clear what he meant by a small deposit.

"I'll get the money," she said, keeping her voice even. "And you don't need a deposit."

"Oh, but the deposit is essential. It sweetens the payment. I'll send for you, Caroline." He rolled the name on his tongue as though licking cream from a pastry. He stood up and pulled out his wallet from the back pocket of his trousers, dropped some coins on the table. "Don't worry, I know how to be discreet. Even though you don't deserve it."

She left the café fifteen minutes later, her mind ice-cold. She had prepared herself for the worst and that's what it had been. Grey's intentions would ruin her, take this life away from her. And she didn't trust him at all. The blackmail would never stop. She climbed into the car exhausted, her nerves ready to shatter, thankful the long ride back would give her time to compose herself.

He wanted money. And he wanted her. Not because he truly desired her, but because he enjoyed her fear and revulsion, enjoyed knowing he could force her into submission. That he could force the wife of a more successful man. She would get the money, somehow she would find a way. But the problem was, would he stop there? Would he ask for more from her? More money, more . . . She shuddered.

A blast of music interrupted her thoughts as the door to a nightclub opened. In Shanghai, some nightclubs stayed open long hours, giving clients all the time in the world to spend money. An unruly group of young men tumbled out and clustered on the sidewalk. One of them had pulled a hostess out of the club, a Chinese girl who was clearly uncomfortable though trying to smile and joke. She couldn't afford to offend clients. Laughing, the young man let her go back inside.

The scene loosened a fragment of memory. Now she remembered when and how she first met Andrew Grey. It was at Mrs. Dominic's annual opera party, always held the weekend just before the start of the new opera season. Mrs. Dominic had achieved the coup of securing both Arturo Toscanini, the new conductor of the Metropolitan Opera, and its general manager, Giulio Gatti-Casazza, as guests of honor.

All the household staff, from scullery maids to butler, had been pressed into service. Instead of the usual fifty guests, more than a hundred people had been invited to witness this social triumph. She had been hurrying down the hallway to the ladies' salon with a bowl of scented potpourri when a man stopped her, his hand held out to block her passage. She thought he was a guest who'd gotten lost and needed directions back to the drawing room. Instead, he circled his arm around her waist and pulled her against him, making her gasp.

"You're a pretty one," he said, slurring his words, "prettier than any of those overdressed debutantes."

"Sir, I have my duties," she replied, trying to twist away. He refused to relax his grip and his smile grew wider, his strange light brown eyes glittering. His breath reeked of whiskey. He was enjoying her resistance. She marshaled all her control and smiled back.

"This is an uneven struggle, sir," she said, forcing a flirtatious smile. "If I drop this bowl, it will cost me my job."

At that, he laughed and let her go. "Prettier and spunkier than any of them," he said, "especially that mousy, morose little Caroline Vessey. Go on, get back to your duties. I won't be responsible for putting you on the streets."

He patted her on the bum and she continued along the corridor, felt the tingle of his light brown eyes on her back, felt rage at her own helplessness. That was how she'd first met Andrew Grey. And at Lennox Manor, when he'd threatened her in her own home, she was again a helpless servant.

ROSALIE'S DIARY

15 May 1907

What joy. To be onstage, to sing as though it was my only purpose in life. I know I sang well. Randolph Buck himself complimented me afterward and I know it wasn't just because of Charles's payment. Charles bought tickets for the best seats in the house and escorted Madame Taddeo to the concert. She was so pleased and Charles was bursting with pride.

But the biggest news. After the concert, he proposed. I said yes. After all, we love each other. I will be his wife, not his mistress.

Never mind my father, he said, he'll get over it. And look at the McBains—a mixed-race family who are accepted in society.

I didn't remind him that the McBains are so ridiculously wealthy no one can afford to snub them. But we must keep it quiet from his father for a little while. His father will relent, Charles promises.

Tomorrow, I will tell Father. He should be happy—he's been worried that Charles just wanted to make me his mistress.

16 May 1907

The review in the *North China Herald* was good. Reluctantly so.

The last aria of the evening was performed by Miss Rosalie

Roussel, who sang 'Vissi d'Arte' from Tosca. A student of Shanghai voice teacher Giulia Taddeo, Miss Roussel has a fine soprano and did a creditable job, displaying both the technique and the intensity required of the role.

This is as good as it can get for someone like me. Madame Taddeo was very frank before the concert. She warned me not to expect wonderful reviews no matter how well I sang. What mattered was that I should deliver a performance she and I both knew was my best. And I did.

I told Father that Charles proposed and that I said yes. He was extremely upset, furious even. In the end, he said, "Daughter, all I want is your happiness. Life with Charles Burnett will not be easy."

CHAPTER 22

THE COOK HAD made beef noodle soup, the hot broth topped with slices of tender meat and slivered scallions, a dish of cucumber pickles on the side. The cook mentioned to her that Master Liu had ordered this meal especially because he remembered it was Lisan's favorite noodle dish. It had never occurred to her that he even knew this or that he cared enough to remember.

What did her father know about her?

Lisan said nothing during lunch and listened to Yao and Master Liu talk about *penjing* and the Soochow garden where Yao used to work. They said nothing about Prince Tsai until the dishes had been cleared away, a spoonful of Dragon Well tea set to steep in Master Liu's favorite teapot, and the door to the small dining room firmly shut.

"Does he ever ask about me?" she said, hands clenched tightly in her lap.

"In every letter," Master Liu said. "We don't mention you in business correspondence. Yao is the intermediary for personal letters. So your father knows about you. He knows that history was always your favorite subject. How you cried so hard when your cat died that you were sick for days. He asks every so often if you still miss your cat. He knows you love beef noodle soup and the smell of freshly cut grass."

Lisan wanted to reach over and grasp his hand. Master Liu was the one passing on this information to her father. He was the one who knew her well. Absent-minded though he appeared to be, distant though his affection seemed, he had been her protector all these years. Caretaker, guardian. And father. He had taken the place of her father. Prince Tsai was the parent of her blood but she didn't remember anything of him. He'd gone away for her protection, so they'd never be seen together and recognized as father and daughter, a sacrifice she didn't doubt was hard on him, knowing that Master Liu was watching his daughter grow up and he was not.

"Yao tells me my father is missing," she said. "Is he in danger?"

Master Liu looked even wearier. "As Mr. Zheng, he has been raising money from overseas Chinese. His last telegram said he was going to Mexico. There are towns in Mexico where Chinese have prospered."

But it wasn't easy or safe for Chinese to travel in America, even though the prince carried all the right papers and licenses identifying him as a merchant, the agent of a Chinese import company, with ample cash and bank accounts at well-respected banks. He'd cut off his queue when he left China and dressed in suits like any Western businessman. He telegrammed once a week. But Master Liu had not heard from Prince Tsai in three weeks, so Fourth Uncle had hired the Pinkerton Detective Agency to search for her father in Mexico.

Master Liu showed Lisan the telegram from "Zheng" that stated his intention of visiting the towns of Ensenada and Torreón.

Lisan looked up from the paper. "If Masako Kyo hadn't confronted me, when were you going to tell me about my father? When was I going to meet him?"

"Your father decided it would be this year, whether or not you regained your memories," he said. Her father felt it was time. His plan was for the two of them, father and daughter, to settle in Canada and make it their home. Unlike America, Canada still accepted Chinese immigrants, and "Mr. Zheng" had decided to move to a well-established Chinatown in a city called Victoria, on the west coast.

For years, Master Liu had kept a set of forged identity papers in readiness for the day Lisan joined her father.

"I was expecting a telegram from him any day now, once he came back from Mexico, and when that happened I would tell you everything. But nothing's arrived and . . ." Master Liu's voice trailed off and he shook his head. Obviously, he feared the worst.

"So what now?" she said. "Do I carry on as though nothing has changed? Do I come back here to hide for the rest of my life? Or do I leave China and wait for my father to be found?"

Father. Still such a strange word on her tongue, taking up an even stranger place in her heart. It seemed impossibly cruel that he had disappeared just as she learned of his existence.

"Master Liu and your Fourth Uncle have been making arrangements all this time," Yao said, "getting in touch with contacts in Canada."

"Fourth Uncle's been monopolizing the telegraph machine at *Xinwen Bao*," Master Liu said. "A newspaper in the family can be so useful. We must proceed assuming your father is all right. In a week's time you'll get on board a freighter to Victoria, Canada—a ship of the Jade Star Line, which our family owns. Your father—or one of our contacts—will meet you in Victoria. Since Masako Kyo knows who you are, we need to get you out of China."

"What if something has . . . happened to my father?" she said. "What then? What would I do all by myself in Canada?"

"You won't be alone," Yao said. "I'm going too. I'm coming to Canada with you, to join you and your father. I have papers that say I have an uncle who runs a broom manufacturing company over there. It's a company owned by the Lius."

He was coming with her. She hadn't realized until that moment just how unmoored the thought of leaving China made her feel, or how fiercely she'd been pushing away the fear that she might never see Yao again. But Yao would be there too, someone familiar. Someone who made her feel safe.

She sighed. But it was Prince Tsai, not her, who held Yao's loyalty and affection. She was merely his duty.

"And even if something has happened to your father," Master Liu said, "I will always take care of you. You'll never be in need of money or help. You are my dearest friend's only child and have been my daughter these past years." His voice broke for a moment and he looked away quickly, taking off his glasses to polish them. "You simply cannot stay in China much longer, my dear. I can't risk your safety."

"You think you're insignificant, Lisan," Yao spoke up, "and though we live here in Shanghai, which seems to revolve around money, entertainment, and gambling as if nothing has changed, everyone knows our country is about to experience enormous, possibly violent, change. There are people who stand to lose everything, and are therefore willing to do anything to gain some advantage. They would not consider you insignificant."

She nodded, remembering Master Liu's words. *China stands on the edge and any small nudge could tip it in any direction. Any one person, any one incident.*

"I want to go back to Lennox Manor," she said. The statement startled her; it was as though someone else had spoken the words. As soon as Master Liu made it clear that she had to leave Shanghai, she had felt the pull again, the compulsion to return to the mansion on Brenan Road. A feeling of obligation, of unfinished business. Back to working for Mrs. Stanton until they put her on board a ship heading for a foreign country and a father she didn't know.

"Yes, I think the best thing is for you to continue there as though nothing has happened," Master Liu said. "We should know the prince's situation soon, and when we do, we'll know what to do."

"What about Masako Kyo?" Yao said. "She's in Peking now. Should we worry about what she'll do when Lisan goes missing?"

"She has a reputation for being annoyingly persistent," Master Liu said, with a sigh, "but my Fourth Brother claims he can deal with her. It's best we don't ask how he will do that."

Lisan ran to her room. She packed up her belongings and put on her coat. When she opened the bedroom door, Yao was there in the hallway.

"Leaving right now?" he said, taking in her coat, the valise.

"I've been away from my job for two days," she said. "Mrs. Stanton has been very kind, giving me extra time off, and I should get back."

"I should get back too," he said. "Are you taking a rickshaw? It's cold and it's pouring with rain. Let's ask Master Liu if he'll let us borrow his car and driver. I don't want to catch a cold before we go."

WHEN THEY NEARED Lennox Manor, Yao got out of the motorcar. "Let's arrive separately," he said. "I'll walk the rest of the way. And Lisan, try and carry on as though everything is normal. There's nothing either of us can do until Master Liu and his brother find your father."

He opened the umbrella and began trudging down the road. As the automobile drove past him, Yao gave her an encouraging smile.

As though everything is normal. What was normal now? Lisan got out at the front gate, tapped at the gatekeeper's door to let her in. "What was that automobile?" he said, craning his neck as Master Liu's motorcar drove away. "Are you rich?"

"No, not at all," she said, and walked past him, through the gates.

Almost as soon as she set foot on the driveway, she felt it. The sensation of being drawn to the house, of a task left undone, and it was stronger than ever; there was now an undertone of urgency to the feeling. It had become more insistent.

Come find me.

What made Charles, if he was the one behind the dreams, think she was in any way equipped to search for a woman who had wanted to leave him and leave Shanghai behind? And why was she even thinking about ghosts as though she could reason with them?

She entered the house through the servants' entrance, where Xiao Wu rushed up as though he'd been watching for her. Every inch of his small person quivered in agitation. "Master Thomas is very, very sick," he said. "The doctor has come. Missy Caroline is with him almost all the time."

She had him take her bag to her room and hurried upstairs to see Caroline. She reached Thomas's bedroom door at the same time as Little Liao and Da Wu.

"We're taking turns changing sheets and replacing the chamber pots," Little Liao said, "several times a day, and whenever Missy Caroline rings for it. Aiya, the laundry!"

"There's something truly wrong," Da Wu said. "We've all been talking about it. This isn't just a stomach upset, but the foreign doctor keeps saying things will get better. Miss Liu, Master Thomas's hair has started falling out."

"Surely the doctor has seen this," Lisan said.

Da Wu shook his head. "We clean up everything as Missy Caroline orders. Sheets, blankets, pillowcases. We brush away the hair and take it away."

"I'll make sure to tell Mrs. Stanton," she promised, "in case it's important."

"And he had convulsions earlier today. Master Mason is more worried than he appears," said Little Liao, "and in the evening, after supper, he sat with Master Thomas so that Missy Caroline could eat dinner and have a rest."

Lisan found it surprising that Mason would have the patience to attend a sick person. She'd put him down as the sort who avoided unpleasantness, and from the sounds of it, Thomas's condition was extremely unpleasant to witness.

"The house is cursed," Da Wu said, and added hastily, "I don't mean the illness is anything supernatural, only that if any bad luck was to fall, it would be here."

The door to Thomas's bedroom was ajar, and Lisan called out softly, "Mrs. Stanton? I'm back. And the house servants are here to take care of the sheets and chamber pots."

When Caroline opened the door, an overwhelming stink almost made Lisan retch. The Caroline Stanton who stood aside to let the servants in wore her hair tied back in a simple braid, a pinafore over her dress. The pinafore was dark blue, splashed with stains.

"He's unconscious now," Caroline said, as the servants began their work. "Morphine and laudanum. He's in terrible pain otherwise, and quite frankly I can't bear watching it."

"Can I bring you something, Mrs. Stanton?" she said, shocked at Caroline's appearance. "Tea or broth? A meal perhaps?"

"No, no. But as you can guess, Lisan," Caroline said, "I'd like you to cancel all my appointments for the coming week. And if people come to the house, let them know we're not taking visitors. Especially not Mrs. Easton." Her smile was brief and rueful.

"I'll start telephoning to cancel engagements scheduled for

tomorrow and the day after, Mrs. Stanton," she said, "and write notes of apology for the ones that come later; those we can send by post. "

"Perhaps I should make those telephone calls," her employer said, sighing. "There will be so many questions. But not right away. It's still light out. I'm going to take a walk in the garden now that there's a break in the weather. Number One Boy will be up shortly; he helps keep an eye on Thomas. Would you come with me?"

The lawns squelched under their feet. They kept to the gravel paths that wound through the garden, stepping over puddles, avoiding fallen branches and patches of mud. As they walked across the garden, Lisan felt as though no other world existed outside the walls of Lennox Manor, no other reality. Her father and Master Liu, and the plans to leave China, they all slipped to the back of her mind, pushed away by the persistent throb of three words. Soft but insistent. *Come find me.* She really was going mad.

"Let's go up there and take a look," Caroline said, pointing to the western side of the property. "See where the path splits and runs up to that berm? It's on higher ground and won't be as soggy."

The garden sloped up and the path took them all the way to the long line of poplar trees atop the earthen berm that marked the western edge of the property. They looked down on a broad, flat expanse of paved surface with short poles set at opposite sides of faded perimeter lines.

"This was the tennis court." Caroline shook her head, surveying the marshy ground. "But then, everything here needs work. It's too bad. It could've been . . . must've been wonderful. At one time." There was something wistful in her manner.

"In another month, it'll be springtime," Lisan said. "Under sunshine and bright skies, this will look completely different.

The magnolias will be in bud, the fruit trees covered in pink and white."

How did she know that? Only from her dreams. A quick movement at the far end of the garden beyond the poplar trees caught her attention. A fox trotted out, glanced at the two women, and vanished down the berm, reappearing in the empty field next to Lennox Manor. It ran into the tall grass, solitary and secretive. The late-afternoon sun was surprisingly bright and birds were making the most of the weather. A flock of black-collared starlings foraged on the lawn, and as the women approached, they rose up in alarm, settling in the bare branches of a magnolia tree. Lisan lifted her eyes to follow the flight of a greenfinch, yellow wing patches flashing as it soared over the garden, its high-pitched stuttering call echoing behind as it flew out of sight. A feral cat lurked under the box hedge bordering the formal garden, completely still except for an uncontrollable, agitated twitch of its tail. It sprang. There was a flap of wings, then silence, and the cat hurried off to deal with its prize in private.

Caroline pointed down to the lake and Lisan followed her there. They stopped by the willow trees. The lake was almost a perfect oval and rain had made it overflow; the edge of the lake now lapped against the base of the willows. This was where she'd seen Mason Burnett walking at night, obsessively circling the lake. This was where Rosalie had knelt by the shore saying *Come find me*. Lisan shivered.

"The lake is fed by a natural spring, according to Uncle Mason," Caroline said. "It used to be just a small pond, but when the grounds were landscaped, they enlarged and deepened it. I would miss this house if we had to leave. Don't you love the willow trees?"

"They're beautiful," she said, even though something pulsed

in her consciousness, the memory of another lake in another garden, another stand of willow trees, arched stone bridges and carved veranda railings. A sensation of bewilderment and fear. She pushed it to the back of her mind.

"Let's go in now, Lisan," Caroline said. "I'll start making those phone calls and you get a start on the cancellation notes."

She had to carry on as though everything were normal. If only that were possible.

WRITING THE NOTES took Lisan longer than usual. Her mind wandered back continuously to her father, to Yao and Master Liu, to the lost years locked inside her memories, willing them to come out of hiding, but each time she tried, her thoughts slid away around a corner of her mind, a dark alcove, a constant loop of fruitless effort.

Lisan had hoped the tedious, repetitive work of writing apologies would calm her mind, requiring as it did both concentration and control to form perfect loops and letters slanted at precise angles, but the pen kept slipping from her fingers. An ink blot and a misspelling forced her to rewrite two of the notes.

It didn't help that Rosalie's diary, lying in its hidden compartment, enticed her far more than the list of addresses and engagements. She gave up and pulled out the sheets of paper where she had been writing down her translation of Rosalie's diary, then read through the pages she'd translated so far. It was barely past eight o'clock but she was so tired. She glanced up at the portrait. Rosalie's expression was confiding, a woman about to share her secrets with a friend. She didn't mind Lisan reading the diary; in fact, she wanted her to read it.

Lisan shook her head. She was imagining things now, imagining what Rosa might say or want, just because she felt guilty about reading her personal diary. "Rosalie, I hope you're all right," she murmured. "Where did you go when you ran away? Are you safe? I hope you are."

Rosalie's dark eyes shone with urgency, willing Lisan to ask the right question. Lisan sighed and got up. Why was she wasting time thinking about a woman who had run away from her marriage years ago?

She was dazed by the events of the last two days. By her past, which Master Liu had finally revealed to her. By her future, which apparently was all arranged for her. She had so much to think about, yet it was the presence of something in the mansion that overwhelmed her, stronger than before, an urgent summons to do something. As though her own life had receded into some archived past. As though Charles's ghost knew she was leaving soon and urging her to do something.

Her head pounded from the strain of resisting. Resisting what? She had rubbed Tiger Balm ointment on her temples but it didn't help.

Come find me.

Rosalie didn't need her but Caroline did. Lisan walked along the corridor to Thomas's room. Da Wu was just leaving with a chamber pot and whispered, "Master Mason is in there with them," before heading down the corridor toward the servants' staircase. Lisan paused by the partially open door, preparing to knock and call out. But the sound of raised voices rooted her outside, pressed against the wall.

"There's always bureaucracy to get through," Mason said, "and very importantly, we need to have a look at the lay of the land, due diligence and all that. I'm not an engineer, I need money to hire someone to do the survey if we're to continue the project."

"If you've spent all the company funds then you'll just have to wait, Mason"—Caroline's voice, like a whip—"I've no interest in opening my pocketbook to this railway project. It's up to Thomas."

"Thomas would want to continue," he said, "he'd want to keep the momentum going even though he's ill."

"You'll just have to wait until he recovers," Caroline said.

"Caroline, I know Thomas is totally committed," Mason said, "because you should know that in his will, he left a large sum to Burnett and Stanton Ltd. to continue the project should anything happen to him."

"I know about the will," Caroline snapped, "and I don't doubt you'll be using that money for your own debts and not for the business."

Silence.

"Caroline, let's not quarrel." Mason's voice. "You're overwrought because Thomas is ill."

There was silence, then heavy footfalls. Lisan shrank away from the door and felt her way along the dim corridor, slipping down the servants' staircase just as Mason came out. Back in her room, she thought of Mason, his voice so rich and amiable when he was out to charm. This time, that rich voice had been edged with anger and it made Lisan worry for Caroline. Did her employer recognize the threat in his words?

It was the sobbing that woke Lisan. She had meant to close her eyes for a moment, but against her will, sleep had overtaken her. And now it was as though she'd been jerked out of a hazy memory. Where was it coming from? Caroline was the only other woman in the house. Lisan hesitated, then swung her legs out of bed and pulled on her dressing gown to walk along the hallway. The lights in the hallway were off and she put her hand against the wall as she moved along the corridor toward the light switch. The cries seemed softer, fading as she reached the main staircase, then stopped. Had she been imagining them? Oh, she was truly going mad.

A chilling draft pushed its way through gaps in window and

door frames, gusts from the north that bent the pointed tips of cypress trees and shook the weeping willows until their branches swayed like the unkempt locks of a woman in mourning.

She returned to her bedroom and fell asleep, the crying still echoing in her dreams.

Her legs ache from climbing the staircase. Someone's hand grasps hers tightly, and now that she knows more, she wonders if the hand belongs to one of her older sisters or her mother. But she is trapped in this dream and she can't look up. Sounds of gunfire echo just as she comes out of the stairwell.

And then she is climbing a different staircase. She recognizes that it's the main staircase at Lennox Manor and the dream pushes her along the hallway and she opens the door to the small parlor.

The room looks different, and after a moment she realizes why. Rosalie's portrait hangs above the fireplace mantel. Why hadn't she realized before that the portrait was meant to hang above the fireplace? And now, she is seated in a chair across from the fireplace, back rigid and stomach churning with dread. She looks down at her hands in wonder, at the gold ring on her left hand, at the rubies on her wrists, at the dress she's wearing, red silk. Charles likes her in red. A young man is pounding his fists against the marble mantelpiece. He turns around, eyes blazing and unfocused, face unshaven. He grabs a pewter vase from the mantel and smashes it on the marble.

A corner of the mantel falls to the floor. He drops the vase and stumbles to her, puts his head in her lap, begs forgiveness. She watches madness take hold of Charles, feels her heart gripped by sorrow, recognition that her love for him is now submerged beneath a crust of fear.

LISAN WOKE TO the sound of window shutters rattling in the wind. She lay stiffly under the covers waiting for terror to subside.

At long last, a faint glow of daylight crept through the curtains. Morning arrived and sunshine brought sanity. She pulled open the drapes and scolded herself for the absurd worries she'd entertained while lying in the dark. She dressed and ran some cold water in the bathroom basin and splashed her face. Her reflection in the mirror extinguished what little assurance she had managed to coax into being. Haggard features looked back at her as she brushed her teeth, and the dark circles under her eyes looked like bruises. She had lost weight in just the short time she'd been at Lennox Manor. Rinsing a small facecloth in cold water, she returned to her room and lay down with the towel folded over her eyes.

Her nightmares were bleeding into each other. She couldn't let the servants know what was plaguing her, for they'd take it as evidence of evil spirits and they would flee, leaving the Stantons without staff. As for Yao, she desperately wanted to confide in him, but he was so sensible; she couldn't bear it if he thought she was being hysterical.

She would continue on, stand with a straight back and smiling lips, concentrate fiercely on the task at hand, whether it was taking notes or writing out invitations in perfect penmanship or just listening to Caroline talk. And if there were dark circles under her eyes, her expression would be alert, her movements precise. She wouldn't let Caroline know, not when her husband lay ill. She couldn't let anyone think she was going mad.

In a week's time she might not even be here anymore, she could be on a ship steaming across the Pacific. Yet each time the thought of leaving Lennox Manor came to mind, a dreadful urgency pressed down on her. Reading Rosalie's diary had made things worse. She wouldn't do it anymore, she would not. Yet even as she glanced at the clock and saw she had a half hour before going down to breakfast, she reached for the French dictionary, her hand moving as though compelled.

She forced herself away from the desk, then hurried to Caroline's parlor. There was something she just had to know. She looked at the corner of the pink marble mantel over the fireplace. It wasn't broken. Breathing a sigh of relief, she turned to leave, then paused. She turned on the floor lamp beside the fireplace and looked more closely.

There was a crack visible in the pink marble where the corner had been mended.

ROSALIE'S DIARY

17 June 1907

I'm now Mrs. Charles Burnett. We were married on 15 June while his father was out of town, just a very quiet wedding at St. Francis Xavier. Madame Taddeo and her husband were there—she was my matron of honor. A few of Charles's closest friends attended. His British friend Will Reiss was best man.

Now Mr. Burnett is back and he's furious with Charles. I stood outside the library door and listened. He had wanted Charles to marry the daughter of another American, a lawyer. He says that until Charles annuls the marriage, he is no son to him. I'm sad to have caused such a rift between father and son. At the same time, I'm happier than I've ever been. Charles loves me enough to defy his father and ignore his friends. I'm not his mistress, I'm his wife. His wife.

CHAPTER 23

W HEN CHIN BROUGHT in the post, Caroline forced herself to leave the silver letter tray untouched. After breakfast she carried the tray upstairs and shut the parlor door. She rummaged through the pile of mail, looking for the threat she knew would come. And there it was, the pale blue envelope, and even though she'd been expecting it, she couldn't hold back a gasp. Caroline told herself she just had to move through the rest of the day as normally as she could. She tried to keep from constantly touching the pocket of her skirt where she had crumpled the note from Grey, the paper lurking like a scorpion.

Since Caroline was not expecting visitors or going out, she didn't need Lisan to help her dress, not for a simple blouse and skirt.

"I can help with Master Thomas," her secretary offered, "read to him or just sit with him in case he needs anything." The girl looked miserable and distinctly under the weather.

"You don't look very well yourself," Caroline said, "so you should get some rest. Don't worry about helping with Thomas. The servants are doing everything that's needed."

Mason came home for lunch, bringing Dr. Ellis with him. He seemed to have forgotten he had argued with her earlier over money, or at least pretended all was well between them while in the doctor's company.

"Dr. Ellis wanted to check on Thomas, my dear," Mason said, "so I invited him for a bite of lunch."

"I'll have the houseboy put out two place settings in the dining room," she said. "I've been eating in Thomas's room so I won't join you, gentlemen; my apologies."

"Ah, well, without a lady present we'll have an extra whiskey and soda," Mason said. "I need it after meeting with those bankers. Donald? Shall I pour you one?"

"Yes, but I'll go see Thomas first," Dr. Ellis said. "I don't blame you for wanting a drink. Bankers, always trying to gouge you for whatever they can."

"Go ahead and have a drink, Doctor," Caroline said. "Give me ten minutes to have the houseboys clean things up a bit before you see Thomas."

Later, when Dr. Ellis examined Thomas, he found his patient dull and confused. The doctor confessed himself baffled that Thomas hadn't recovered yet, but maintained he was confident in his original diagnosis. After all, the laboratory had come back with undeniable evidence. "Stomach parasites," he said, "definitely that's what it is. Well, keep going with the purgative tonic and give him a bit more time."

"Yes, Doctor," Caroline said, "whatever you advise." He was extremely certain, that much was clear.

She didn't join the men for lunch and went downstairs only after they'd left. She hadn't eaten much lately, and it wouldn't do for her to get lightheaded, not when she needed all her wits and strength. There was soup in the tureen, and she ladled herself a small portion and nibbled on some bread. Thomas was unconscious most of the time now and she made sure he stayed that way. She couldn't have him notice the anxiety that thrummed through her, the tenseness of her voice even when she kept it low, how she had to clutch her hands together for them to remain still in her lap.

In her small parlor, she rang for Lisan.

"I just want to tell you that I'm going out this afternoon, but not for very long," she said, when Lisan came in. "I just want to get out of the house for a bit on my own. I'm happy for you to spend your time reading, or you could go out and see friends."

Lisan nodded. "I'll go over your invitations again and make sure I've canceled all your appointments. Will there be anything else?" Caroline shook her head.

As Lisan's footsteps receded along the hallway, Caroline realized the young woman's unobtrusive manner had become discreet to the point where she practically receded into the walls. Her gentle features bore her usual polite smile, but there was no sweetness in the curve of her lips, no liveliness in her eyes. Whatever Masako Kyo had done or said, it had disturbed Lisan greatly.

Caroline sensed something else bothering Lisan, but right now, she had other worries. She put her teacup and saucer down on the walnut desk. Taking a deep breath, she pulled the blue envelope out of her pinafore pocket and read it one more time.

It was a brief note, just a where and when. The "where" was Les Trois Lanternes, the hotel in the French Concession that Grey called home because he didn't have enough money to rent a real apartment. The "when" was tomorrow, late morning. Obviously, he expected her to simply drop whatever plans she had. Blackmailed for money, that was one thing. But this other—she wouldn't let the situation come to that. The mere thought of it, the prospect of submitting to him, made her clench her fists so tightly her nails left crescents of red when she opened her hands.

If she allowed emotions to intrude, she wouldn't be able to take control of her next meeting with Grey. She knew the time and place, and now she would survey the surroundings and consider how to prepare. She guessed at his state of mind, which she judged to be one of supreme confidence. That was to her advantage.

Caroline opened her diary, which Lisan had updated after canceling appointments for the next week. On the date of her meeting with Grey, she wrote a time and place, his initials, and nothing else. Even though the details were engraved on her mind, she wanted it down in writing. The note was a promise to herself, not a capitulation. Then she crumpled up Grey's letter and tossed it in the fireplace.

The most useful gift Thomas had given Caroline, purchased the week they had arrived, was a guidebook of Shanghai. It described the city's sights, its parks and neighborhoods, its significant buildings, hotels, and restaurants. Most useful of all, there were small maps of different areas in the back pages. She unfolded one of the maps and looked for the street where Grey lived, noted the names of some nearby restaurants and shops. She wanted a look at Grey's hotel, its surroundings. There were few things she could control about the meeting, but at least she could know what to expect about the location of Les Trois Lanternes.

CAROLINE GOT OUT of the car in front of a restaurant and told Gu to pick her up in an hour and a half at Dauphin Jewelers on Avenue Paul Brunat. Inside the restaurant she paused to read the menu, all the while peering out the window to make sure Gu had driven away. Then she smiled at the maître d' and shrugged as if the menu didn't please her. She walked just three blocks and found the street she was looking for, Rue Voisin. The street itself was quiet but looked shabby, due to the run-down appearance of its restaurants and shops. Les Trois Lanternes was a third-rate sort of hotel. She peered at it from under her umbrella as she walked past, at the threadbare blue awning over its entrance, sagging from its own rain-soaked weight. The mildew-streaked brick walls and aging curtains in its windows made her suspect it was more boardinghouse than hotel.

Next door to Les Trois Lanternes was a bar, its door in need of a fresh coat of varnish. An alley separated the two establishments, and a side door of the hotel opened to the alley. From the amount of rubbish there, this narrow passage was used for dumping unwanted items. Two large garbage bins leaned against one wall; piles of empty wooden crates were stacked up against the other. Anyone entering the alley would have to weave between the stacks of crates and garbage bins.

There was a small tearoom across from the hotel and she went inside. She ordered a pot of tea and drank it slowly, looking through the steam-fogged plate glass at the hotel entrance, at the alley, at the bar. A neon sign attached to the second floor of the bar proclaimed a gambling parlor upstairs. She observed the number of passersby at this hour of the day. She hoped it would rain tomorrow, that it would be a day like this, with not many pedestrians, all of them hurrying to get to their destinations, shoulders hunched against the cold, umbrellas pulled down to protect against the driving rain. None of them paying attention to anything except puddles. Tomorrow, she didn't want anyone to notice her, witness her shame.

Caroline put some coins on the table. It was time to make her way to Dauphin Jewelers and wait for the car. It was time to keep watch over Thomas.

SHE HEARD LISAN's soft tap on Thomas's bedroom door and called for her to enter. Chin and another house servant had moved a small table and armchair to the window and she sat there to read books, magazines, and the letters that continued to arrive. It was better than sitting by Thomas when he was asleep.

"Just how many charities are there in Shanghai?" Caroline said, forcing a playful tone as she opened another envelope. "When I met these ladies at their various functions, I had no idea they only wanted me for my donations." Requests for donations she expected, but also requests to join the board of an orphanage for mixed-race girls, to be patroness of a mission school. And of a hospital. "What do you know of this hospital?" she asked Lisan.

"The Margaret Williamson Hospital for Women?" Lisan said, taking the letter from her. "It's the only foreign hospital Chinese women will use."

In some very traditional families, her secretary explained, women remained inside their homes and went out only to pray at a temple or to visit female friends and relatives. The only men they ever saw or spoke to were relatives. Traditional Chinese doctors examined female patients from behind a curtain, making their diagnoses by taking the woman's pulse. It was only when the Margaret Williamson Hospital opened, staffed entirely by female doctors and female nurses, that families allowed their women and girls to leave the house for Western medical treatments.

"Would you like me to write a response, Mrs. Stanton?" Lisan asked.

Caroline shook her head. "Leave it for now. I'm not in the mood to decide about any of these requests. None of them are urgent and none as important as . . . as other things. Oh, there's so much keeping me up at night. All sorts of things seem to disturb my sleep."

"What sort of things, Mrs. Stanton?" Lisan turned away from the window to look at Caroline, her eyes wide and troubled. "Have you also had bad dreams since coming here?"

"Also? Are you having bad dreams, Lisan?" she asked. "I notice you seem tired lately."

Her secretary flushed. "I suffered from nightmares as a child, and since coming to Lennox Manor, I've been having bad dreams again. That's all."

"Well, don't tell the house servants," Caroline said. "They would worry about ghosts, and then who knows, we might lose them all."

Lisan nodded, quite serious. "You're right, they would leave. Now that Mr. Stanton is so ill, their main topics of conversation have been about the supernatural, and whether or not Lennox Manor is haunted. Zhou the cook is very superstitious. I would never mention nightmares in front of them, or the . . ." Her voice trailed off.

"Or the what, Lisan?" Caroline prodded gently. She wanted to make light of things but it appeared her secretary was genuinely worried.

"Or the sounds at night. Sometimes I hear sounds of a woman crying," Lisan said, "but it must be my imagination from being overtired. It's the wind. Because if there's a ghost, it would be the ghost of a man, of Charles Burnett, wouldn't it? I should be hearing a man's voice."

"Go to your room, Lisan," she said gently, "get some sleep. I mean it."

"Is it all right if I take your diary, ma'am? I'll update my copy of your schedule, if you don't mind," Lisan said, "all those cancellations."

"Yes, of course," she said, "it's in my parlor. But after that, take a nap."

Perhaps poor Charles Burnett's ghost really did wander at night, Caroline thought. If only it were a mere ghost she had to fear and not Andrew Grey, a far more potent danger. She didn't need any distractions right now—Grey on his own was enough of a worry. She poured a second cup of tea and took it to the window. Thomas's bedroom looked down on a small Chinese-style garden, a walled courtyard where a stand of green bamboos swayed with each gust of wind and droplets of rain dripped from the bare branches of a plum tree. There was a tranquility about the enclosed view, a simplicity that calmed her, helped her think. Beyond the small courtyard was a view of green lawns, the lake and its willow trees.

After her second cup of tea, she knew what she had to do. There was no way around it.

ROSALIE'S DIARY

26 July 1907

I haven't written in my diary in weeks. After the wedding Charles took me to a mountain retreat in Mount Mogan, which has become a fashionable place for foreigners to build summer homes. It was cool, both the weather and the people we met. In marrying me, Charles has lowered his status in white society. He said he didn't care, that I was all he needed in this life.

Mr. Burnett has cut ties with Charles. At least Lennox Manor was a gift, the deed signed over to Charles, and it can't be taken away, so we have a place to live. Yet I wish we didn't live here. It's my home now but I can't tell Charles I hate living here. It's so far away from Shanghai. At night it creaks and drafts seem to whistle their way in, and the wind practically howls as it funnels down the chimney. I heard the servants gossiping about the previous owner, who went bankrupt. Mason Burnett bought this house for Charles, expecting him to marry Miss Drummond. Lennox Manor is unlucky.

CHAPTER 24

CAROLINE HAD BEEN right, Lisan thought, upon waking. She had needed a nap. For once, she had slept peacefully. Then she realized from the amount of daylight coming through the window that she had slept through supper and it was now the next morning. She got up, aghast at having missed her morning meeting with Caroline. She rushed to wash her face and get dressed. A knock on the door, and she opened it to Chin, holding out an envelope.

"A note from Missy Caroline," he said, standing on the threshold. "She went out and left this for you. I'm supposed to wait for your instructions."

Lisan, I need to go out for a bit this morning. Could you please work with Chin to take turns sitting with Thomas? Please call Dr. Ellis if he changes for the worse. I'll be home in a few hours.

"She would like us to take shifts watching Master Thomas while she's out," she said. "She'll be away for just a few hours. How is he today, Chin?"

"Worse, I would say," Chin said. "And you should know that both Liao and Little Liao left this morning. Liao was most upset after Missy Caroline complained to me that things have been moved around in her parlor. Small ornaments on the mantelpiece, a footstool, her sewing box. She's had to put them back. Liao looks after that room and swears he doesn't move anything. He decided it was the suicide ghost."

"Mrs. Stanton has been under a lot of strain lately," she said. "She may be forgetting that she moved things around herself. Perhaps Liao was just offended at the accusation?"

She never knew that Caroline was experiencing strange incidents. Why hadn't Caroline told her? Probably for the same reason she hated confiding in Caroline—for fear of the other person thinking she was going mad.

"No, Miss Liu. He was genuinely afraid." The head servant paused. "There's something else, Miss Liu. Do you recall when Missy Caroline told me to put rat poison in the attic? And under all the furniture?" He hesitated again. "I keep the poison in a metal canister in the butler's pantry, locked in a cupboard."

"What are you saying, Chin?" she said, catching his unease.

"There's less in there now than last week," he said. At her skeptical frown, he sighed. "I know how much was in that can. I'm very careful."

"Are you saying someone has stolen rat poison?" Lisan said.

"I don't know." He looked uncomfortable. "I'm the only servant with keys to the butler's pantry. Missy Caroline has all the keys, since she's mistress of the house."

"What about Master Mason?" she said, thinking of the conversation between Mason and Caroline, the menace in Mason's voice. "Would he still have all the keys from before?"

Chin looked thoughtful. "Yes, he would do. He never used the pantry keys though; he never went into the butler's pantry or kitchen to check on stores."

"Have you asked the other servants?" she said. "Perhaps somehow they took some of the poison to put down in their own rooms, when the cupboard happened to be unlocked?"

But Chin didn't answer. He had turned slightly and was staring at Rosalie's portrait. All color drained from his face, and he put one hand on the door frame as though trying to steady himself. Shock and distress contorted his features. At her questioning look he stood straighter, regained his composure.

"I've questioned all the house servants, and they all said they didn't take anything," he said, "and Da Wu pointed out that they have a canister of their own for the servants' quarters. Miss Liu, I can sit with Master Thomas for the next two hours."

INSIDE THE HOTHOUSE, the pink jasmine was still in bloom, but the flowers were beginning to age. The vines sent out a pungent, cloying perfume. Lisan had always preferred the white variety of jasmine, a lighter scent.

Yao was at work in the utility area, a space hidden by screens of trellises, and at her approach, he looked up. His smile was the same as always, welcoming and friendly. Just the sight of that smile used to make her feel better, safer. More grounded. Only a few days ago, his calm presence would've been a solace to the turmoil in her mind.

But it wasn't the same anymore. At one point she'd believed there was something special, fateful even, in the way the sight of his smile warmed her. Now that she knew more, it left her wondering what it was exactly that she had felt for him. He was part of machinations that had kept the truth from her all these years, a betrayal that hurt less today than it did when she first found out.

When she thought of Yao, of Master Liu, she wavered between trust and doubt, the opposing emotions washing over her one after the other like a river tide. The relief she'd felt upon knowing Yao would be coming to Canada had now ebbed away, leaving behind the realization that his kindness and attention had been for Prince Tsai's daughter, not for her, Lisan. Yet despite this, she still wanted to be near him.

Yao was examining a *penjing*, a red pine, one of his own that he'd potted since coming to Lennox Manor. She climbed onto a wooden stool and watched him work from across the battered wooden table. Yao belonged here in the gardener's domain, between aisles of greenery, a place where he pruned unruly shoots, or coaxed a twist of vine to cling onto a bamboo support. He was at such ease here.

"Parallel branches," she said, pointing at one of the graceful stems. "Will you remove the upper or lower one?"

"You have a good eye," he said. "Master Liu's training?"

"Just from watching him all my life," she said. "I would remove the upper branch."

Master Liu's gentle voice echoed in her mind as she watched Yao take small *penjing* shears to the plant. *Branches that cross, overlap, that are parallel or symmetrical should be cut short or removed to achieve a good shape. Wiring may be needed to bend them to the desired shape.* At the time she had admired the artistry of *penjing*. Now it made her shudder. A life bent and shaped by force.

"What will you do with your collection when you leave?" she said, indicating the shallow containers of miniature trees. Not "when we leave"; he wasn't leaving China for her, he was doing it for his master, for her father.

"I'll leave them with Master Liu," he said, "but I'll take one with me to Canada."

Canada. She rolled the syllables around in her mind. A country that spoke English. Master Liu had explained this was why he'd sent her to St. Clare's; it had been part of their plan for her to learn foreign language and customs, foreign histories. To understand countries where emperors didn't ruin lives through arrogance and petty whims. To make sure she would never want to be a princess, a member of the royal court that was now blundering to survive.

Between St. Clare's Hall and the cosmopolitan culture of Shanghai, she couldn't help but be aware that a tidal wave of change was imminent. China had to change. The Qing empire was failing, all of China knew it was only a matter of time, the only question being whether or not civil war would come first. Her own father, once a prince, was working toward the fall of the Imperial government.

"Do you remember any more of your childhood now," Yao said, as though sensing her disquiet, "from before Shanghai?"

"No, nothing at all," she said. Only grayness and fog, an impression of chaos, dirty streets. And for some reason, a maple seedling blown by the wind, spinning like a small pinwheel as it descended onto gray paving stones. "Nothing. But I do get nightmares."

"Still?" he said. She nodded.

But now she knew the nightmares were fragments of memory, of her last moments with her mother and sisters. She yearned to see their faces, not stiffly posed in a photograph like the one Masako Kyo had given her, but with their eyes meeting hers, lively and loving, lips on the verge of breaking into laughter. And yet the thought of regaining those memories terrified her so much her mind virtually shut down if she even tried.

During her time at Lennox Manor, those nightmares had become more vivid. Now the dreams were more physical. She could feel the ache in her short legs as she hurried to teeter up the steps. When she looked down at her small feet, the details on her shoes were so clear, bright red silk embroidered with bats. Bats for good luck. She could even feel the discomfort of a fold in her left sock. Booming sounds and screams, a smell of sulphur and smoke. Through cloth soles, her toes could feel the edge of the veranda. And the voice, which she now realized must've been her mother's, saying those terrible words in the kindest, gentlest manner. *Now jump.*

Even now, just remembering it, she flinched. They were beginning to feel more real than her waking life, and worse, now her childhood nightmares were merging into troubled dreams about Rosalie. She felt certain that if she stayed much longer at Lennox Manor, the dreams would persist and overtake her. She might not wake up in time and she would step off the veranda. She might remain trapped under the willow trees, her hair dripping with rain, forever wandering through the garden, crying for rescue. *Come find me.*

But then she looked at Yao, at his capable hands, his strong, stocky torso, his generous smile, and clarity returned, morning light lifting her gloom.

"Master Liu used to say perhaps I couldn't remember my past because it was too terrible," she said, "but now I know and still I can't remember. Yao, did you know my mother? My sisters?"

"I knew who they were. I was just a gardener," Yao said, "and not even that. Just a gardener's helper, never allowed to speak to any of you. But you loved the garden, you know. One day you wanted to plant camellia flowers and took my trowel to do it. I had to tell your maidservant to explain to you that flowers wouldn't grow."

She rummaged for an image of herself, a little girl holding pink camellias and a trowel, found nothing. "I don't remember. I wish I could remember my mother's face."

"You only have to look in a mirror," Yao said, very gently. "When I walked into the kitchen and saw you, it was like seeing her again."

"All this time, Yao, all this time, Master Liu knew my father was alive, and so did Fourth Uncle. So did you. Anyone else?"

Yao shook his head. "Prince Tsai's safety depended on our

silence. What's more, he commanded it of us. I'm his loyal servant, Master Liu is his good friend. And Fourth Uncle, well . . ."

"What about Fourth Uncle?" she said.

"It's best we don't ask what he does or how," Yao said. "He is necessary and his loyalty is to the Liu family, absolutely. He moves through people's lives like a phantom, unseen. Most never realize what he arranges behind the scenes, at the peripheries. No one is ever sure if it's their imagination or a coincidence when things work out."

"At least he's alive and not a real ghost," Lisan said. She hesitated, then, "You know that Liao and his brother Little Liao quit today because they think the house is cursed. Do you know if the servants have seen things or are having nightmares?"

"Liao mostly frightened himself." He put down the shears carefully and wiped his hands on a clean rag. "But no, no nightmares. If they were, we'd be hearing about every single one at mealtimes."

"I don't sleep well in this house, Yao," she said. "I'm starting to believe it's haunted. Mrs. Stanton says she's been missing small items in her parlor and then they turn up again. She asked Chin and he asked Liao. Apparently, that was the final omen for him and he left, taking his brother."

Yao shook his head. "Liao. He talked about suicide ghosts so much he convinced himself he was in danger."

"What do you believe about dreams, Yao?" she said. "Do they mean anything?"

"Ah. There are many schools of thought on that subject," he said. "I think our dreams are an expression of our own thoughts and intelligence. When awake, our thoughts are controlled, directed like a harnessed horse. But in sleep, the horse is free to run away across distance and even time, and when it comes back, it brings new insights. A Ming dynasty scholar believed that what we perceive in dreams can be more perceptive than what we notice when awake."

No one else heard crying in the night. No one else dreamed about Rosalie. It was just her. She truly was going mad.

"There's something else he said that I really liked," Yao said, "which is that when two people dream about each other, they may be thousands of miles apart but in the dream their spirits can be together. Lisan, you look upset. What's wrong?"

"There's so much I want to talk about with you, Yao," she said, "but I can't even sort through everything in my head. I barely know what to say and how to say it."

"You look tired, Lisan," he said, "you'll do better with some sleep. Perhaps you need something to eat?"

No, it's not sleep or food, she wanted to say. Can't you tell I'm going mad? My head won't stop throbbing and when the room is silent I hear voices.

Now jump. Come find me.

"I should join the others for breakfast," she said, feeling overcome by yet another wave of fatigue. "Chin is watching over Mr. Stanton."

Breakfast was laid out on the kitchen table and Zhao was already cooking lunch for the staff. While he stirred and chopped, Zhao grumbled that Caroline had hardly eaten anything lately. He sent up trays of clear broth and newly baked bread rolls, thinking these would be easy to eat.

"Just that," Zhou said mournfully, "not even sandwiches. Sometimes stewed fruit. Perhaps she eats when she goes out?"

"I wish she'd go out more often," Lisan said. "She needs some fresh air and distraction from the sickroom."

The house servants came into the kitchen one by one and ladled out bowls of hot congee cooked in chicken broth for extra flavor. Young Zhao put out pickles and leftover pork stew. Lisan felt her headache recede slightly with the soup's rich, delicious fragrance. They ate in silence. There was none of the good-natured joking and gossip that usually filled the kitchen. The Liao brothers' departure—and their reason for leaving—had put the remaining servants in a somber mood. She noticed furtive looks. Would anyone else leave? she wondered.

"Does anyone know where the Liao brothers will be looking for work?" she asked. A murmur of talk started up, relief at having some gossip to share.

"They're going to try the Kwong household," Da Wu said, "you know, the owners of the Great China Department Store. They've a cousin there."

"That family has a terrible reputation," Young Zhao the assistant cook added. "They have a very bad time keeping servants. The children are very spoiled; the mistress is mean and finds reasons not to pay. And yet they're so rich."

"If they do land at the Kwongs' they won't stay long," Da Wu said. "They'll find another household to work for when Mrs. Kwong fires them. Being fired from the Kwongs is a commendation, not a black mark—all the head servants in Shanghai know that."

"Mrs. Kwong's head servant must be a very patient man," Lisan said, and the servants all burst out laughing.

"There is no head servant there," Da Wu said, "that's a big part of the problem. Mrs. Kwong fired him two years ago and has been trying to run the staff on her own." The mood in the kitchen lifted perceptibly as they traded anecdotes about the famous Kwong family.

Lisan put her empty bowl in the sink and returned to sit beside the youngest houseboy. He looked up at her, his eyes bright and anxious. Lisan held out one arm and pulled up her sleeve. "I always wear your amulet, Xiao Wu," she said, giving him a smile as she sat down at the kitchen table.

"I've just pasted scrolls with protective spells on your bedroom door," he said. "Missy Caroline is too busy to notice, so you can keep them for a while."

"All right," she said, "I'll leave them on. Thank you."

"Miss Liu," he whispered, "don't say anything to Chin, but my brother and I are leaving soon as well. So I won't be able to look after you anymore. You should leave too."

"Take care of yourself, Xiao Wu," she whispered back. "I'll be fine, don't worry." The Liao brothers and now the Wu brothers. That left only Chin, Zhao the cook, and his son. And within the week, she and Yao would be gone as well.

BACK IN HER room, Lisan sank down on the bed. She felt bad for Caroline, who didn't know that all her staff was abandoning her. If Chin stayed on, as he had for Mason, there was a chance of hiring new staff. The portrait of Rosalie gazed down at her but her expression was one of reproach, as though she knew Lisan would be leaving Lennox Manor soon without fulfilling her obligation. *Come find me.* But Lisan had no idea what it meant.

Lisan pulled down the Shanghai telephone directory from the top shelf of the secretaire and went downstairs to the telephone. Did she dare make the call? How could she make up a convincing story?

"Hello?" The woman's voice was warm, melodious.

"Madame Taddeo?" Lisan said. "I am a friend of Rosalie Roussel. I'm hoping you can help me."

"Rosalie's friend?" Madame Taddeo sounded eager. "Have you heard from her?"

Lisan was taken aback. "No, Madame, I haven't. I was hoping you could tell me where she's gone."

There was silence. "So you don't know either. But why has it taken you so long to ask this question?"

"I've been away from Shanghai," Lisan said, offering up the story she'd prepared, "and I lost touch. All I heard was gossip, and knowing Rosalie, I couldn't believe it. I wanted to know she was all right."

"Do not believe any of it." Madame Taddeo made a disparaging noise. "She was a very good person, a talented soprano. She loved her husband, that Charles Burnett. She was not a, what you call it, gold digger. But he had many problems and he was too weak to deal with them."

"Where do you think she might've gone, Madame Taddeo?" Lisan said. "I thought that of all people, she would've told you."

But Madame Taddeo didn't know. "She never contacted me, just vanished from Shanghai," she said, "but please, if you learn anything, if you find Rosalie, please give her my love and tell her I would be most pleased to hear from her."

Lisan hung up the telephone, then went upstairs to take her turn watching Thomas. He tossed and turned, moaned in his sleep. She brushed away some of the hair on his pillow. She'd told Caroline about Thomas's hair loss and Caroline said she would tell the doctor. Lisan sat in the armchair by the window, picked up a magazine. The air was stuffy, the room overheated. Soon her head drooped.

A STRONG GUST shakes the trees and a movement in the garden catches the corner of her eye. Lisan peers into the darkness, knowing it's a dream yet unable to break free. Was there someone walking under the trees? Was it just the wind shaking bare branches? Or her own imagination? The figure moves away from the shadows, a woman in red. Rosalie. *Come find me.* There was a mournful quality to her voice. The woman drifts, as she always does, to the stand of willows by the lake before dissolving into rain.

But Rosalie, Lisan calls out in her dream, *you didn't tell anyone where you'd gone.* The only reply was the rattle of twigs battered by the wind.

Lisan sat up, found herself in an armchair, the magazine fallen from her lap. The air was close and clammy, smothering. She yanked the window open, just an inch, and a welcome rush of cold air chilled her. She pulled the window wide open and leaned out, just for a moment. She breathed in deep gulps, not caring about the raindrops soaking into her hair.

I'm going mad, she thought. Charles is sending me these dreams to drive me mad. I just need to hold on until Yao and I leave Shanghai. And I need to get rid of Rosalie. She means nothing to me.

She wanted to rush to her room and take down Rosalie's portrait, but waited until Chin came back. He lifted one eyebrow in silent query, and she shook her head. No change.

Back in her room, she stood on the chair and removed Rosalie's portrait from the wall. She should never have brought it down from the attic in the first place. Its presence had disturbed her sleeping and waking hours, and it was her own fault for hanging it in her room. She took the portrait up to the attic and leaned it against the wall where she'd first found it, turned it around so that it faced the wall.

Back in her room, after only a moment's hesitation, Lisan took out Rosalie's diary and put it into the fireplace, pushing it in with a poker until it caught fire from the last remaining coals. It flared up and she put some more wood on top of the blaze. There. That was the end of Rosalie Roussel's hold over her.

But she didn't throw away the sheets of notepaper with her translations of the diary.

ROSALIE'S DIARY

12 September 1907

I've learned that Charles is in debt. Men have come to the house demanding money. His father used to pay his gambling bills, and knowing this, the gambling houses extended him a lot of credit. So he ran up huge debts but now he can't pay. He says it's all right, he will borrow against Lennox Manor and work harder at his business. He bought a fleet of riverboats that carry goods up and down the Yangtze River, but what does he know about river transport?

He's started using opium.

I can't bear to write in this diary. There's nothing good to write about anymore.

10 January 1908

Oh Charles, Charles. My poor darling. He borrowed against the house and now the bank wants to foreclose. He was losing money on the riverboats, so he sold the fleet to a competitor, but it still wasn't enough to pay his debts. The servants are gone, unpaid for so long. We have no money for food but he sells my jewelry for opium.

I said we could rent out rooms, take in boarders, but he shouted me down. His home would never become a boardinghouse. He would not allow it. What if his friends found out?

Then I said I could go back to the Golden Rooster and

sing, earn a little money. You're my wife now, he said, and no wife of mine will ever go onstage. But how are we to eat? I said. We need money for food. Charles was even more furious, he was so angry he slapped me. He stormed off and locked himself in his bedchamber. I could smell opium, sickly sweet coming through the gap in the door.

Father brought me food every few days, but we argued and he hasn't come by all week. I don't care what Charles says, someone has to keep us from starving. Tomorrow, I'm going back to sing at the Golden Rooster. For better or for worse, he is my husband and I love him.

CHAPTER 25

SHE HAD LEFT Lennox Manor in good time for her appointment with Grey. Her mind used the term *appointment*; it was dispassionate and businesslike. Her hand rested on a large leather handbag. It was just the right size and, among other things, held all the money she'd been able to gather so far. She'd brought it in case she could placate Grey, perhaps use the money to delay him. There was a chance he was desperate enough to take ready cash and forgo the sexual conquest he had in mind.

Caroline had gone to the bank after her first meeting with Grey—had it only been two days ago? She'd taken a quantity of gold coins and ingots from her safe-deposit box and withdrawn as much as she'd dared from her housekeeping account. The bulk of the fortune from the Vessey and Dominic inheritances was not in Shanghai but still in New York. Funds and investments, assets that needed legal letters of instruction to liquidate, all of which would take too long and raise too many eyebrows.

When the motorcar reached Shanghai, she had Gu drop her off at the perfume store and instructed him to head back to Lennox Manor. She would take a taxi home; she didn't know how long she would be. If the doctor came to see Thomas, she wanted Gu to be at the house and drive the doctor back to the city.

At the perfumery, she bought a small bottle of cologne, a blend of Parma violet and lilac. A dab on her wrists for courage, another dab above her upper lip to fend off malodorous smells. She dropped the bottle into her bag, where it fell to the bottom with the tiniest of clinks. From another store a block away, she bought a cheap oilskin raincoat and pulled it on over her own. She didn't feel ready, but how could anyone feel ready to face what she knew she had to do?

It was time. She crossed the street and began walking toward Les Trois Lanternes, putting up her umbrella against yet another shower, drizzling down from a sky as dull as pewter. Blessed, blessed rain that hid her from unwanted eyes. The thought of being recognized unnerved Caroline, had almost drained her resolve. But there was no other way.

She arrived early on purpose.

It wouldn't do now to be seen near the hotel so she waited across the street, where she could watch from under the canopy of a florist shop. She cast another glance at the bar beside the hotel, at the narrow alley separating the two buildings, its walls still lined with untidy stacks of wooden crates and overflowing garbage bins.

When she felt she'd loitered under the florist's awning long enough, Caroline moved a bit farther down the road to another storefront, still keeping the hotel in sight. The rain never let up; if anything, it was falling harder than ever. A blessing. Tucked under the black umbrella, clad in a nondescript raincoat, she was anonymous, unidentifiable, just another passerby taking shelter from the downpour.

A man staggered out the hotel door and her heart lurched. It wasn't Andrew Grey. No, of course not. How could it be? He was Chinese. His open raincoat revealed evening clothes, as though he hadn't yet changed since the night before.

The man stumbled to the alley, one hand already unbuttoning the front of his trousers. He took a few steps in, not caring or oblivious that anyone who saw him would know he was urinating against the wall. But when he came out, trousers still undone, he wasn't stumbling anymore. Shouting loudly, he rushed back to Les Trois Lanternes, opened the front door, and ran inside. A few moments later, people came running out of the hotel and followed him into the alley. Soon, a crowd gathered on the sidewalk, pouring out from nearby buildings and shops. Caroline walked away. There were too many curious bystanders on the street now and she couldn't risk being recognized.

Pulling the raincoat tight against her body, she lowered the umbrella even more to hide her face. Turning the corner, she hurried back along Boulevard de Montigny toward Avenue Paul Brunat. She paused by a building where a beggar woman shivered under a wide window ledge, a soggy piece of cardboard tented over her head to fend off the rain. Caroline shrugged off the cheap raincoat, tossed it at the woman, and continued on her way.

She entered Dauphin Jewelers, where she feigned interest in the trays of gems and sketches of jewelry from Parisian designers. The owner did his best to persuade her to commission something.

"A significant piece, a custom design, Mrs. Stanton," he said, "as a memento of your time in Shanghai? The workmanship in Shanghai is superb, if you have the right people, which is what we have. I supervise the work myself, of course, and costs are extremely reasonable compared to what you'd pay in New York."

"I'll think on it," she said, "but may I take the drawing for this necklace to consider the design a bit more? Now, could one of your assistants go out there and get me a carriage?"

ALL THE WAY home, Caroline kept seeing images from Rue Voisin unspooling like scenes on a movie screen. The man rushing out of the alley, waving his arms in panic, shouting to attract attention. The crowd swarming out, eager to be first on the scene. The entrance of Les Trois Lanternes, its blue awning soggy and limp in the rain. All she could do now was wait.

Caroline leaned back and closed her eyes. It was easier for her to think while listening to the rhythmic clip-clop of the horse-drawn carriage. She'd been foolish to think she could avoid the past. She should've realized she would always have to stay one step ahead of the Andrew Greys of this world. It had been sheer luck that of all the lawyers at Blackwell and Danby, it had been Mr. Danby who came to Spokane, Danby with his myopic vision. But there were just too many people: the Dominics' society friends, her classmates at Miss Fielding's Finishing School for Young Ladies, all the servants and neighbors.

When she reached her bedchamber, she closed the door and pressed her back against it, light-headed and drained of emotion. If she were at all superstitious, if she believed this house was cursed, she might blame her situation on Lennox Manor. But, of course, the house had nothing to do with it. She'd taken a risk and now she had to deal with the consequences. She had to, because she was not giving up her life as Caroline Stanton. She wished she could run away, as Rosalie had, but that wasn't possible.

She took off the skirt she'd worn. Its damp hem would take a while to dry; she draped it over the back of a chair and moved the chair closer to the fireplace. She tidied her hair and crossed the hall to Thomas's room. Lisan was there, reading quietly in the chair by the window. She rose when Caroline came in.

"It's all right, Lisan, please sit down," she said. "Any change?"

"No, he's completely unconscious now," Lisan said. "Mrs. Stanton, perhaps you should get a different doctor? This is more serious than intestinal parasites, don't you think?" The young woman looked nervous.

"I've been wondering too." Caroline dipped a washcloth in a basin of cold water and wrung it out, placed it on Thomas's forehead. "The thing is, the results from the laboratory are quite clear; Dr. Ellis showed me the actual report. Parasites. I don't know what else it could be. But yes. Perhaps another doctor. Tomorrow."

Lisan nodded. "It's just that the servants noticed that his hair is falling out, Mrs. Stanton. Is that significant? What did Dr. Ellis say?"

"I'll mention it again to Dr. Ellis. Thank goodness for morphine—that laudanum just wasn't enough." She sighed and looked down at Thomas.

She moved to the window and gazed at the small courtyard and bamboo grove below. The green stems swayed gracefully, their long leaves whipped by wind. She gestured to Lisan, who joined her. Together they watched the storm gather strength, surges of rain that beat against the glass, black clouds massed above, the cracks of lightning. In the garden, puddles were turning into ponds.

"Even ducks might complain at this weather," Caroline said, but her smile was insincere. "Lisan, have you ever wanted to leave all your troubles behind? I loved being on honeymoon with Thomas. I thought it was because I loved seeing all those different countries, their art and monuments, but now I think it was the freedom of moving on to the next place, leaving nothing of myself behind, no obligations, no consequences. Like stepping in and out of a puddle. A ripple of water, and afterward, nothing to show your foot had ever been there."

"You had a wonderful time," Lisan said, "and you'll have wonderful times again with Mr. Stanton when he is well."

"But what if he doesn't get well, Lisan?" Caroline said. "Could I ever be happy again? And do you know what occurred to me? Travel. A wandering life. But with a companion. With you, Lisan.

Would you come with me?" She spoke quickly, excitedly, the idea forming in her mind. "We would travel. We'd have such a good life, Lisan, and when we've had enough of one place, we'd move on to a new city, a new country. Venice and London, Istanbul, Athens. Trust me. I'll take care of everything."

"Mrs. Stanton, I pray it doesn't come to that," Lisan said, her face puckered in astonishment. "Mr. Stanton will recover; the doctor doesn't seem alarmed. And please don't take this the wrong way, but I don't want to depend on your goodwill for the rest of my life."

"I do understand that"—Caroline's features softened—"oh, believe me, I understand more than you would think. After Thomas is gone, if you come with me, you'll be paid a good salary as my companion, but I'll also give you a large sum for you to do with as you wish. Then if you decide to leave, you'll still have money of your own to start over."

"Why, Mrs. Stanton," Lisan said, leading her to a chair, "you mustn't say such things. You're feeling anxious and overwrought. Your husband will recover. He will. Otherwise Dr. Ellis would be far more concerned. Think on it again after you've had some sleep."

"Lisan, you're the model of common sense," Caroline said, "that's why I want you by my side. Everything has been so . . . strange. I'm so tired."

"Mrs. Stanton, I thank you for such a kind offer," Lisan said, "travel and a generous wage. But I refuse to take advantage of you when you're going through such difficult times. You're feeling distraught because of Mr. Stanton's illness."

"There's something else, Lisan." Caroline wiped her eyes. "I'm experiencing strange things, things I can't understand. It makes me wonder if I'm going mad."

"What sort of strange things?" Her secretary looked at her, her eyes intent.

"Perhaps I'm just tired, forgetful," Caroline said, "but do you remember my gold fountain pen? I lost it, then found it later, back on my desk by the inkwell. This sort of thing keeps happening."

Her words came out in a rush as she told the tale. Usually in the small parlor, but sometimes in other rooms, she'd notice that things had moved around, a vase here, a footstool there. When she looked later, sometimes no more than thirty minutes later, everything was back in its usual location. Two candlesticks switched places, then switched back. A clock on the mantel gone missing, then appearing later.

"Have you reported this to Head Servant Chin?" Lisan said. "Perhaps one of the house servants is up to mischief." Although her voice was soothing, reasonable, Lisan's expression barely hid her alarm.

"It couldn't have been one of the boys." Caroline shook her head. "The last of these incidents happened last night, after the staff had gone to their quarters. Forget I said anything. I can't afford to worry about ghosts. It's Thomas who matters."

And all she could do about Andrew Grey was to wait.

THE NEXT MORNING, Caroline decided to go into town and take Lisan with her. "I need to go to the bank, Lisan. Then let's go for tea, just quickly, a little treat someplace quiet and not too fancy, the sort of place people like Mrs. Easton wouldn't even know existed."

"That would be good for you, Mrs. Stanton," Lisan said. "You should get out of the house at least once a day."

Lisan stayed in the car while she went to the bank. There, she put the gold and cash back into her safe-deposit box. She didn't like having so much money in the house, let alone in her purse. Then Lisan directed Gu to a café in the French Concession where the customers were mostly Chinese. They saw only a few Westerners. A fashionably dressed couple at the table beside them finished their coffee and stood up, leaving behind a newspaper. Lisan reached over and took it.

"Today's edition of *Xinwen Bao*," she said, "the best Chinese-language newspaper in all Shanghai. I will read it in the car on the way back."

The young Chinese woman always seemed to know when Caroline needed quiet. As the car rolled through Shanghai, Lisan sat reading the newspaper while Caroline gazed out the window. As always, she enjoyed the bustle of Shanghai's streets. Even in rain the traffic never ceased, a parade of carts, horse carriages, and cars. Rickshaws with tarps pulled down to protect their passengers, vendors splashing through puddles with baskets swinging on shoulder poles. The city was endlessly in motion, always fascinating to her. She wondered what it would be like to live in the middle of the city, in one of the new luxury apartments.

A gasp from Lisan jolted her away from idle daydreams.

"Mrs. Stanton, such unbelievable news!" the young woman said. "This is the morning edition of *Xinwen Bao*. Let me translate for you."

Yesterday afternoon, a man was found fatally stabbed in an alley beside Les Trois Lanternes hotel. He had no wallet or papers on him. However, an employee of the hotel identified the man as long-term guest Andrew Grey, an American architect from New York. Police are asking for witnesses to come forward.

Dead. Andrew Grey was dead. Relief washed over her like a cleansing rain.

The scene on the Rue Voisin rolled through her mind again. The man who'd stumbled into the alley to relieve himself. He'd found Grey's body. The crowd that had milled around on the sidewalk. They'd gathered out of morbid curiosity.

"Stabbed." Caroline kept her voice steady. "How horrible."

"Violent death in Shanghai is all too common," Lisan murmured, "gambling and gangs, opium, brothels. Political conflicts. But a white man murdered—the Shanghai Municipal Police won't let go of that easily."

No, Caroline thought. The police would not. "Is there more, Lisan? Do continue."

"Only that apparently, Grey was a frequent customer at the bar beside his hotel," Lisan said, scanning the article. "The bar owns a gambling parlor upstairs. Its owner said Grey had run up large gambling debts. That's all."

Caroline wondered if Grey had needed money for a business investment or if it was to pay off his debts. She wondered also whether Grey's friend Masako Kyo knew what had befallen him. Had he mattered to her at all? When would this news come out in the English language *China Press*? But it didn't matter. She sank back in the seat and waited for the pounding of her heart to subside. She was free now, truly free, of Grey. But she still didn't feel safe.

Back at Lennox Manor, the head servant greeted them with the news that Dr. Ellis had been and gone. This time, the head servant informed them, the doctor had been extremely agitated. He'd left her a note.

Mrs. Stanton, I'll confer with a colleague about your husband's situation. In the meantime, keep him sedated and out of pain. I'll telephone later today.

"Oh, Thomas," she whispered, leaning over his unmoving figure, "will they ever find out what's really wrong with you?"

CHAPTER 26

L ISAN HAD HUNG up her clothes and changed her shoes. She tried to sit at her desk and read, but the compulsion would not go away. It was different though. Instead of pulling at her, it gave Lisan the feeling that she had to leave Lennox Manor. She found herself climbing the stairs up to the attic, and next thing she knew, she was looking at Rosalie's portrait again. She sighed, studied the exquisite features. Rosalie couldn't have been more than twenty or twenty-one when the artist painted her. Whether it was the change of light or the onset of madness, Lisan thought with grim humor, Rosalie's expression seemed to change each time she saw it, imperceptible changes that begged her to understand. Right now, a worried gleam shone in Rosalie's painted irises. The faint lines between her brows seemed to have deepened, signaling a warning, telling Lisan to be careful.

Lisan shook her head and turned the portrait to face the wall again. She would not give in to madness. It was her own fault. Hanging the painting on her wall, reading the diary, those were the reasons why Rosalie kept intruding on her dreams, why she couldn't turn her thoughts to her own future, a reality that loomed ever closer, and one she wasn't completely certain she wanted. A future that deserved more timely consideration.

She stood up to leave, then saw that one of the wooden crates was open, its cover pushed aside ever so slightly. It was the crate containing the Dominics' silverware. Caroline had been adamant she'd never use the ugly silver place settings and Lisan clearly recalled pulling the wooden lid along the top of the crate until it sat snugly closed. Had one of the servants been poking at its contents? Pulling the cover off, she looked inside to see whether anything had been disturbed. It was all as she remembered, polished wooden boxes of silverware neatly stacked.

Except for the long, slim box that held the carving set. It was out of place and lay on top of the other boxes at an angle instead of being tucked alongside. Opening the box, she saw the long fork nestled in its velvet-lined slot. But the knife was gone. Could one of the Liao brothers have stolen the knife before they left? Had any other silverware been taken?

She took out each box to check. The boxes had slots to fit each piece of silverware, which made it easy to see if all the pieces were present. She put them all back in the crate and left the lid as she'd found it, slightly offset. Then she went to look for Chin.

The head servant was in the butler's pantry, the cabinets open and a list on the table beside him. He was hand-polishing wineglasses. When he saw her, he inclined his head slightly. "Miss Liu. Does Missy Caroline need something?"

"No, no," she said. "Just a question for you, Chin. Have you sent any of the servants up into the attic?"

He frowned. "No need. Only Yao the gardener, who went to put down rat poison. Why?"

When she told him about the missing knife, he shook his head in dismay. "No, it wouldn't have been one of the Liao brothers. I'll look into the matter, Miss Liu. Have you told Missy Caroline?"

"Let's not say anything, for now," Lisan said. "She's already so worried about her husband. I trust you to find out what's happened. When you're certain, we can tell Mrs. Stanton, if we need to."

Chin nodded his thanks. An accusation of stealing couldn't be made lightly. Word always got around among the servants, and it upset the careful balance that existed belowstairs. The accused, whether or not he was the wrongdoer, would find his reputation tainted. There would be hostilities and resentment, concerns that the crime had brought suspicion upon all their heads. Their reputations were all they had. It was Chin's job to investigate and uncover, in his own way. Although there was hardly any staff left.

"The foreign doctor came by again," Chin said. "He left a note for Missy. And he said something while he was here."

"What did he say?" She knew that Chin understood more English than he spoke.

"That Master Thomas is dying, that's what I heard the doctor mutter," Chin said, "and he seemed more worried about himself. He kept saying 'what this'll do to my reputation' and 'second opinion' and he helped himself to a whiskey before leaving."

"How do you think the servants will react?" she said, already knowing the answer.

"I think we'd be lucky to keep any of them. Da Wu and Xiao Wu are leaving soon." He sighed, the first time she'd seen him show any emotion or admit to weariness. "I'll stay and do everything I can. And you, Miss Liu?"

"As long as I can," she said. "Miss Caroline needs . . . companionship."

Caroline knew her husband was dying. Lisan could see it in the tired bend of Caroline's slim neck, her slumped shoulders. The American woman's fatigue was palpable and there was a resignation about her that seemed in keeping with the melancholy atmosphere of the house. Lisan could almost believe that a curse had fallen on Thomas. She thought of Rosalie's portrait, those soft lips, the reproachful expression. *Come find me.*

Yet somehow, she didn't think Rosalie's presence, sent by Charles's restless spirit, was part of the curse. But what if, the thought occurred to her, what if Rosalie was dead? Perhaps she had died after leaving Shanghai. What if it was Rosalie's ghost that had been haunting her? Not the wraith of Charles, but Rosalie.

"And how is Mr. Burnett?" she said.

"The same," Chin said. "Goes to work in the city each day as though nothing's happened. Comes back for supper on his own, since Missy Caroline takes a tray in her husband's room now. Then he sits with Master Thomas for a bit so she can have a rest."

"Chin," she said, "I'm not sure if I should bring this up, but why have you stayed with your master for all these years, even when you were the only servant looking after everything? Mason Burnett is not an especially . . . pleasant employer."

"It's not Master Mason," he said, "it's this house. I have to stay here."

"Why, Chin? Why do you say that?" Was the house compelling Chin to stay? Is this what would happen to her? Would she become so bound to this house that she wouldn't be able to leave?

"I'm waiting for my daughter to come back," he said. "When she comes back to Shanghai, I must be here where she can find me. At this house."

Suddenly the room shifted, went off-kilter. "Chin, is your daughter Rosalie? The one who married Charles Burnett?"

CHAPTER 27

DR. ELLIS TELEPHONED that afternoon, humble and apologetic. He had followed through on what he'd promised in the note and consulted another doctor.

"I simply don't understand it," he said. "Thomas should be getting better. He did rally at first, didn't he? Mrs. Stanton, I'm making arrangements for your husband to check into the hospital. I will come with the ambulance in about an hour, sooner if possible."

"Oh dear, the hospital?" Caroline said. "Are you sure?"

Hospitals were for those who couldn't afford house calls and private physicians. Some doctors even performed minor surgeries at patients' homes. Even though Shanghai's newer hospitals provided the most advanced care and owned the latest medical equipment, many foreign residents still preferred home care and their own doctors.

"I know, I know, my dear Mrs. Stanton"—the doctor sounded even more apologetic—"I wouldn't do this if it weren't so serious and puzzling. Only in such an extreme situation would I do this. They have more diagnostic equipment, you see, more ways to test."

"Of course, Doctor. I rely on your professional judgment. I have every faith in you." She hung up the phone and walked up the stairs slowly to Thomas's bedroom. Chin was there with a houseboy. She nodded at Chin to let him know she was ready to sit with

Thomas again. The houseboy carried away a laundry hamper piled with soiled and sweaty bed linens. She shut the bedroom door.

"Mrs. Easton warned me about Dr. Ellis," she said. She gave Thomas another injection and dabbed his face with a cool washcloth. "I can blame everything on Dr. Ellis's lack of attention. He's careless as well as arrogant. Another doctor would've gone for a second opinion sooner, or examined you for another diagnosis. And, of course, some will blame me for trusting Ellis this long."

She sat in the chair down by the window, turned on a table lamp, and picked up a magazine. But she had barely settled down to read when Chin rapped on the door. He entered and held out a calling card.

Princess Masako Kyo. She sighed. The Manchurian princess had caused Lisan so much distress. "Tell her that Miss Liu is not available," she said, "that she is out."

Chin shook his head. "It's you she wants to see, Missy. I wasn't able to keep her out. She is in the drawing room." In the short time they had lived at Lennox Manor, it never failed to amaze her how Chin, even with his limited English, seemed able to anticipate her orders. The drawing room, more formal, nothing of their personal life on display there.

"Tell Miss Liu to stay in her room. Tell her Masako Kyo is here and to avoid going downstairs until I've made that woman go away." She stood up and walked over to Thomas's bed. She leaned over and kissed his forehead, then paused for a moment to stand in front of a mirror and tuck away a stray tendril of hair.

The double doors leading to the drawing room were decorated on one side with carved panels in the Chinese style, landscapes of cliffs and waterfalls, pine forests so finely detailed she could almost see every needle on every tree. Chin had left the doors wide open and Masako Kyo stood posed in the drawing room, perfectly framed by the archway of the door.

She wore a fox fur stole draped over the shoulders of a black three-quarter-length cashmere coat. The fox's eyes were yellow glass and matched the topazes in her earrings. Caroline admired the sham princess's elegant ensemble even as she remained wary of her reason for coming to Lennox Manor.

"Did our servant not take your coat?" Caroline asked, reaching out to help Kyo take off her fox fur.

"I'm keeping my coat on, Mrs. Stanton," Kyo said, "because I'm not staying long. For one thing, you won't want my company after I've said what I've come here to say. For another, I must be at the train station soon after this, so there's no need to bother with the usual courtesies."

"But are you not here to speak with Lisan?" Caroline said. The intensity of Kyo's gaze, her slightly triumphant smile, made her back away. Casually, she moved behind a chair so that it stood between her and Kyo. Caroline put one hand on the chairback. Kyo's brilliant smile sent a growing unease coursing through her body.

Kyo shook her head. "No, not dear Lisan," she said, "dear little Liu Lisan, who doesn't understand how important she is, who is wasting her life as your secretary, Mrs. Stanton. One day you'll understand why I say that. No, Lisan can wait until another day. Today, my business is with you."

"You perplex me, madam," Caroline said. "Business? We've only met once before, and that was at our party. A social event."

"You had business with Andrew Grey," she said, "and now that he's gone, it falls to me to complete the transaction. You seem astonished, Mrs. Stanton. He was more than my lover. We were also business partners."

"My condolences," Caroline said. "I heard he had died. But what business do you mean? His only business was with Mason, as architect for an office renovation." A growing unease now chilled her to the bone, and her heart beat faster, a familiar thrumming of fear.

"If only poor Andrew hadn't owed money to the wrong sort of people," Kyo said. "The police seem certain gambling debts are behind his murder. But he left me some very valuable information about you. You promised Andrew fifteen thousand dollars, Mrs. Stanton, in exchange for him keeping your secret."

"Why would I promise him fifteen thousand dollars?" Caroline said. Her nails dug into the upholstery, but she kept her voice even. How much did Kyo actually know? Was she bluffing?

"I have some information he shared with me," Kyo said, "information that allows me to extort money from you. I won't be coy and call it anything else but blackmail, since I'm dealing with a woman who isn't exactly honest herself."

Caroline tensed. But what could Kyo prove anyway? Unlike Grey, she had never met the Dominics or any of their circle.

"I can't prove anything right now," Kyo said, as if reading her mind, "since it was Andrew who met you back in New York. But he knew he needed evidence to support his claims, especially when facing your husband. And that evidence is on its way from America."

She paused to see the effect of her words on Caroline, who said nothing, just tilted her head inquiringly as if waiting for Kyo to continue. "I will be picking up mail from his hotel as soon as I'm back from Peking, Mrs. Stanton. They know to hold it for me."

All Caroline said was "What sort of evidence?"

"Photographs, documents, who knows?" Kyo shrugged. "And until such evidence arrives, which should be next week, I have nothing. Admittedly nothing. But I'm telling you now so you can finish getting the money together. Which you may already have done. Well, I should leave now and let you think it through. You don't need to show me out."

But Caroline followed her out to the foyer anyway. She had to see for herself that the woman really was out of her house. The sedan chair porters jumped up from the steps to carry the chair closer to the door. Kyo stood at the threshold, then turned to face Caroline.

"Mrs. Stanton, I want you to know the money isn't for myself," she said. "I'm working with Japanese interests that are trying to reshape the Manchu Empire into a monarchy guided by Japan. And since I've discovered someone who could make a real difference to our efforts, it's urgent that I have the money to do something about it."

"So you're conniving against your own emperor," Caroline said.

Kyo smiled. "And you're impersonating Caroline Vessey."

The sedan chair moved ponderously down the driveway. Caroline stood on the steps until the iron gate closed. She shut the front door, leaned against it, and closed her eyes, heaving a quiet sigh.

"What did Masako Kyo want, Mrs. Stanton?" Lisan faced her from the bottom of the marble staircase.

Caroline recalled Kyo's last words. *And you're impersonating Caroline Vessey.* Had Lisan heard the accusation?

"She didn't mention you, Lisan," she said, "so don't worry. I've never met anyone so full of nonsense. She was making up all sorts of unfounded accusations trying to extort money. Something about needing it to rebuild China now that she's found someone who can undermine the current government. What rubbish."

The young woman's face remained troubled. Caroline brushed past her and climbed the stairs back to Thomas's room. Inwardly she cursed Andrew Grey. And Mason, who had hired him.

THOMAS HAD DETERIORATED shockingly. His original nausea, stomach pains, and diarrhea had compounded with severe headache and delirium, more vomiting and weakness. His breathing was increasingly labored, his skin clammy and cold. Without morphine, he cried out from horrible stomach pains, and his eyelids opened and fluttered shut, more in response to her touch on his wrist than anything Caroline said. A rapid, irregular heartbeat. His only relief was morphine.

He would never make it to the hospital, she was sure of that now. It was very likely that it had been too late even a day ago. She propped a cushion behind her back and pulled a blanket over her legs. Thomas was dying and Ellis hadn't recognized how serious it was. No doubt people would blame her—and Mason as well— for not seeking a second opinion sooner, for not taking him to a hospital sooner. But Thomas had deteriorated so quickly. And although she wanted to be awake, to know the exact moment her husband drew his last breath, she felt herself dozing off. Just for a few minutes, she thought. Just a few minutes.

When she woke up, Mason was beside her. When she met his eyes, she knew. Her husband was dead. She leaned over and took his hand. Still warm, but no pulse. His eyes were closed, a relief.

"Dr. Ellis wanted to take Thomas to the hospital," she said. "It's what he should've done before. It's what he should've done sooner. Why did we trust him?"

Mason sat heavily on the bed, put his head in his hands. "Is Ellis coming?"

"He telephoned to say he would be coming with the ambulance," she said, wearily rubbing her eyes. "Please, Mason, perhaps you could go downstairs to wait for Dr. Ellis."

"Yes, of course, of course," and Mason hurried out. She heard his loud footfalls along the corridor, down the staircase. She closed her eyes and leaned against the chair. It was over. This part of her life anyway.

Only when Dr. Ellis hurried into the room did she look up. Outside, daylight was fading. It was late afternoon, nearly evening. An hour later, she was officially widowed, a copy of Thomas's death certificate on the side table, signed by the doctor.

CAROLINE WANTED THE funeral to be held as soon as possible. Dr. Ellis agreed, as she knew he would. He didn't want any delays, any opportunities for questions that might accuse him of incompetence.

"Your husband was very dehydrated," he said, speaking hurriedly, "which made it harder for him to fight infections. It looks as though he caught some form of amoebic dysentery, which the lab tests didn't catch, I must point out."

Mason was furious. "I'll make sure this ruins him," he said, after the doctor left. "Why couldn't he see something was seriously wrong? Something worse than a case of parasites? We should've called in a second opinion sooner."

"You're right about the second opinion," she said, "but we all thought that Thomas was rallying, improving after taking his medications. We trusted Dr. Ellis. And then Thomas went downhill so suddenly. What could anybody have done?"

"He's an incompetent idiot, that Ellis," Mason said, still fuming. "I'll make him sorry he didn't do a more careful diagnosis. I'll ask for an inquest."

"Uncle Mason, please," Caroline said, "it won't bring Thomas back. Who's to say another doctor could've done better? It's over now. I just want a little peace." Also, an inquest wasn't up to Mason. She was Thomas's wife and she didn't care to launch an inquest.

"My dear, I'm sorry for showing such temper," Mason said. "No one could've nursed him with more devotion. You're exhausted." He reached over and patted her on the hand. "We'll speak no more of it, my dear. I didn't mean to rage, but he was my heir and business partner. Now there's no one to carry on my legacy. Only you, Caroline. You're all I've got left."

She sat by Thomas's bedside while Mason made calls to the funeral parlor. Despite the weariness that dragged at her shoulders and neck she sat stiffly upright. If she allowed herself to slump, she would simply collapse. The waiting, the wondering, it was all over. Mason came upstairs, loud footsteps signaling his return. She looked up and caught the expression on Mason's face, just a glance in her direction before Chin came up behind him and said something; then Mason and Chin went back down the stairs.

It had been an appraising look. That was the word that came to mind when she recalled Mason's face.

CHAPTER 28

LISAN AND CHIN settled in the privacy of the butler's pantry, the head servant's domain, where Chin told her everything about Rosalie.

"My wife—that was how we thought of each other, husband and wife—was half-Italian," he said. "I was cleaning rooms in the same hotel where she worked as a laundress. After Rosalie was born, we decided we could do better working for a foreign family."

Having learned some English and French at the hotel, Chin was able to find a housekeeping position at the home of a young French bank clerk; Chin's wife worked as their laundress. The clerk's wife allowed them—Chin, his wife, and baby Rosalie—to live in the servants' quarters at the back of the house. The French couple had a daughter the same age as Rosalie. But Chin's wife died during a cholera epidemic and so did the banker's little girl. The grieving Frenchwoman offered to look after Rosalie for a few days until Chin found an amah, and became so fond of Rosalie that even after Chin hired an amah, she continued to spoil the child.

"She had been a music teacher in France and she taught Rosalie to sing and play a little bit of piano," Chin said, "to speak French, read and write a little bit. And also some English."

When the clerk left Shanghai for another posting, the wife wept over Rosalie, who was seventeen at the time. She gave Rosalie some small bits of jewelry and money, told her to take voice lessons. This, even though there was no respectable future for a girl onstage. It would be even worse for Rosalie, being of mixed race. The foreign woman knew no better and Rosalie was too young to fully understand. Yet a career in opera was Rosalie's greatest desire and Chin could not dissuade her.

Chin went to work for Mason Burnett at Lennox Manor. He gave Rosalie part of his wages to help her rent a cheap room in the city and take voice lessons. When Mason gave the house to his son, Charles, Chin stayed on as Number One Boy. The only work Rosalie could find was as a nightclub singer, work she had to take if she wanted to stay in her rented room. She had come to realize there was no future for her in opera and that in Chinese society, actresses and singers were no better than prostitutes.

"I didn't like what she was doing, " Chin said. "I begged her to find work as a lady's maid, an amah, something respectable. Then one day the nightclub's owner threatened to fire Rosalie unless she brought in more customers."

Chin worried she would end up someplace worse than the Golden Rooster. When he realized Charles Burnett fancied himself a patron of the arts, he gave Charles the nightclub's card. He hoped Charles might patronize the Golden Rooster regularly.

"You know the rest," he said. "I had promised her no one would know she was my daughter so that she could concoct a more glamorous story for her stage career. She used the French clerk's last name for her stage name: Rosalie Roussel."

"But you don't know where Rosalie went when she ran away from Charles?" Lisan said. "No letters, not even one?"

"No. We had argued," Chin said. "She refused to leave Charles even though he had turned into a brute. I threatened to tell Charles the truth if she didn't leave him. I thought he'd divorce her if he knew she was merely a servant's child."

By then Chin was the only servant remaining at Lennox Manor. The others had left, their wages unpaid. Chin only stayed because of Rosalie, and now after their fight he left too. He went to see Mason Burnett and reported on the situation, and Mason went to see Charles. When he came back, he told Chin to go to Lennox Manor. Father and son had reconciled, and he told Chin to bring some food to the house and tidy things up. But when Chin arrived, he found Charles's body hanging in the foyer. There was no sign of Rosalie.

"Master Mason blames Rosalie for running off and breaking her husband's heart. That's what all Shanghai believes. She may never come back, but if she does, I hope she'll come looking for me here. Or she may write to me at this address." Chin's voice was forlorn.

"She will come back, Chin," Lisan said, "a daughter always needs her father." This was the longest conversation she'd ever had with Chin. The head servant seemed relieved to confide in someone, finally. She wished she hadn't burned Rosalie's diary. "I should go up and see if Mrs. Stanton needs anything."

"There is another thing, Miss Liu," he said, "about Master Thomas. Did the doctor know about his hair falling out? Wasn't he concerned? I ask because of something that happened when I worked at the hotel. A guest committed suicide by swallowing poison. I heard about it from other servants, how terribly she suffered from stomach pain. But the most curious thing: her hair had begun to fall out."

"I'm sure the doctor knows," Lisan assured him, "because I mentioned it to Mrs. Stanton. I could ask if she told Dr. Ellis." At the look on Chin's normally bland features, it dawned on her. "Are you thinking of the missing rat poison?"

Chin's eyes were troubled. Her thoughts flew to Mason and the argument she'd overheard outside Thomas's room. Mason needed money. Thomas had left money to the company in his will. "Chin, do you think Mr. Stanton is being poisoned?"

The grim look on his face was all the answer she needed.

An hour after Chin told Lisan about Rosalie, Thomas Stanton died.

The house servants who had been responsible for the sickroom had of course reported the invalid's details to their colleagues. The servants were an avid and superstitious audience, deliberating on every aspect of Thomas's condition. Caroline, they all agreed, had nursed her husband with utter constancy, sharing with her servants the disgusting work of cleaning up his vomit and diarrhea, of holding him while he screamed in pain. She had watched over him so carefully, with such attention, each sign of decline in Thomas creasing her forehead with fresh worry. She had more than earned her breaks, her short excursions into the city to buy some perfume, look at jewelry, stop for coffee and pâtisseries.

Lisan wasn't sure what to do. Caroline was on her own now, her husband's body with the undertakers. She was living in the house where her husband had been murdered. With his murderer. But without proof, how could Lisan bring up her suspicions about Mason Burnett? How could she ask Caroline to take her seriously? Most importantly, was Caroline in danger?

Then there was Masako Kyo's second visit—nothing to do with Lisan, Caroline had assured her, but what Lisan had overheard disturbed her.

And you're impersonating Caroline Vessey. Kyo had been just outside the front door, Lisan just coming along the hallway. Had she heard Kyo correctly? There was a lot Lisan didn't know but she did know that Kyo delighted in causing trouble.

If Master Liu's plan was still for her to leave Shanghai, Lisan only had a few days left at Lennox Manor. Not very long ago, she could never have imagined her life might change so radically. A new country, a new identity. A father. But even though revelations of her past hammered through her head, even as she struggled to fathom an uncertain future, it was Lennox Manor that consumed her thoughts. Both sleeping and waking, it was as though the house demanded something of her.

Zhao the cook and his son left the day after Thomas died. Zhao made his farewells to Lisan before going, an apologetic look on his face, explaining that he'd cooked enough food to last them several more days. Zhao rattled off the dishes he had made, some in the icebox, some in the pantry in covered containers. Beef stew, a baked ham, cold tongue, a pair of roast chickens, two kinds of soup, custard, and stewed fruit.

"This house is cursed, Miss Liu," he said, "but how could it not be, with Master Burnett's son committing suicide here? And now Master Thomas has died. You should leave too, before the ghost decides to haunt you."

"Zhao, Mr. Stanton wasn't haunted to death," she said with more than a little exasperation. "He died from . . . from parasites." And from an incompetent doctor who couldn't recognize signs of poisoning.

"He may have caught parasites," Zhao said ominously, "but in the end he died because the house is cursed. At first, he was getting better. I could tell. He was starting to eat more. And then his hair fell out. The ghost took him."

CAROLINE HAD WRITTEN an obituary, which she handed to Lisan, asking her to make sure it was hand-delivered to the *North China Herald.* It announced the date and time for Thomas's funeral at Bubbling Well Cemetery.

"Charles Burnett is buried there," Caroline said, "and Mason is giving Thomas the plot beside it. Mason bought it for himself but now it's for Thomas."

LISAN BUSIED HERSELF tidying the papers stacked on the walnut desk in Caroline's parlor. Caroline and Mason were in Shanghai making funeral arrangements, selecting a coffin and gravestone, speaking to the priest.

Lisan had canceled all upcoming engagements. However, she hadn't yet updated her own notebook. She had meant to do it so many times, and it didn't feel very important anymore after the tragedy of Thomas's death, nor would it matter once she left China, but the routine of tedious clerical work appealed to her right now. It felt calming. It helped keep the pounding headache at bay.

She copied the cancellations into her gray notebook; then, for the sake of thoroughness, she flipped back a few pages in Caroline's blue appointment book, making sure to duplicate anything Caroline might've added herself the previous week. A few of Caroline's notations were cryptic: initials, address, time of day, notes that only Caroline understood, perhaps a telephone call to make, or a card she needed to write personally for some occasion. However scant the information, Lisan copied it over.

"Miss Liu?" It was Chin, holding out a visiting card. "The gatekeeper just gave me this. Your friend is here but she doesn't want to come in. She asks you to meet her out at the gate."

The card was from Ju Ming. Lisan pulled on her coat and hurried out to the garden, negotiating between puddles. At the gate, Ju Ming waved at her from behind the sheltering tarp of a rickshaw. She motioned for Lisan to climb in.

"I'm so sorry, Lisan," she said, "but you're the only one I trust with this." She handed Lisan an envelope, the stamp already on. It was addressed to Ju Ming's father.

"What's going on, Ju Ming?" she said. "Are you in trouble?"

"I will be very soon." And dimples appeared for a moment on her friend's pretty face. "I'm running away from home, Lisan. With my lover. Oh please, don't look so shocked. I want you to be happy for me."

Ju Ming's words came out in a torrent as usual. She was in love with a journalist. He had been promoted to foreign correspondent at his newspaper and was moving to London. They couldn't bear being apart, so Ju Ming was going with him.

"I won't tell you how we're traveling, only that I'm on my way now to Jessfield Station. It's best if you don't know so you don't need to lie for me, should it come to that," Ju Ming said, "but could you mail this letter for me in two days? We'll be well away by then."

The shocked expression must've still been on Lisan's face because Ju Ming touched her cheek with one finger and smiled. "The family arranged my marriage years ago, but I can't go through with it anymore. I just can't. Will you do this for me? Just drop it in a mailbox the day after tomorrow. Oh, Lisan, to live in London! I've always wanted to travel. A life with more adventure than going to the Race Club or learning a new dance. Can you please be happy for me?"

"What's he like, your lover? Does he have a name?" Lisan said. "Is he Chinese? How did you meet?"

"He's Chinese, but I won't tell you his name," Ju Ming said. "We met at St. John's University. A lecture someone dragged me to attend. I spent the entire hour staring at him. I'm so happy we decided to elope. We couldn't go on meeting at hotels much longer. But what's happened here? The gatekeeper said a death in the family."

"Mr. Stanton died," Lisan said, "after a short illness."

"Oh, poor Mrs. Stanton," Ju Ming said, "so young to be widowed. You know, I thought of her the other day. I was on my way to meet . . . well, to a hotel, and there was a foreign woman standing in front of a shop, and she rather resembled your employer. But what would Mrs. Stanton be doing on a shabby street like the Rue Voisin, which is nothing but cheap hotels and cheap cafés? What will she do now, do you know?"

"She wants to travel and asked me to be her companion," Lisan said. "She says she wants to take me with her around the world. I think she's just grieving and coming up with wild ideas."

Ju Ming clasped her hands together. "Oh, but what a wonderful offer! If you do this, Lisan, you must come to London! There's so much more to tell you, but I must run or I won't make the train."

Lisan climbed off the rickshaw, watched it jounce along the road. A gloved hand waved at her, a jaunty gesture. She put Ju Ming's letter inside the pocket of her skirt and walked back to the house. Ju Ming, in her exuberant way, had chosen love and adventure, with a confidence that Lisan could only envy but not emulate. There was one thing she could hold on to though. Ju Ming would be in London. If she took up Caroline's offer, then she might visit London. She could say, "And we could visit my friend Ju Ming."

An idle daydream, when Lennox Manor and its melancholy past seemed determined to wrap around her like a shroud.

Back in her room, she draped her coat over the wooden chair and pulled it closer to the fireplace, then moved aside the fireplace screen to push another piece of wood into the firebox. She leaned her forehead against the window, felt the glass shudder from gusts of wind. The rain mocked her, pelted droplets against the windows like insults, creating a barrier between her and the world outside. There had never been such weather. The rain had gone on for so long it felt as though nothing ever dried properly, dampness seeped into every shirt and pillowcase, made every piece of upholstered furniture feel clammy.

She had borrowed one of Caroline's fashion magazines and sat up in bed to read it. The house, now bereft of servants except for Chin, was utterly silent. There were only the muted sounds of wind and rain outside beating on windows and roof tiles. Inside, not even the creak of footsteps on floorboards. Her head fell back against the pillows.

And then, instead of being in her room, she is outside in the garden standing in front of the mansion. There is no rain. Snow covers the grounds and Lennox Manor sparkles. Frost blankets its gabled roofs and shining icicles create a fringe along its eaves. Pale winter sun reflects with blinding brilliance from white-covered lawns. Even the dimmest corners of the garden seem filled with light, and frost on trees and shrubbery glitters as though sprinkled with diamonds. Smoke rises from chimneys and the frosted white of the roof shines under the clear cerulean sky.

She has entered a new nightmare. She waits for Charles and Rosalie to appear. The ornamental lake gleams and water ripples against a rowboat tied to a small dock. It should be a peaceful scene but there's sobbing that rises and fades. A figure in red slips between the willow trees, beckoning to her. Why won't this apparition leave her alone? *I can't do anything for you*, she screams in frustration, *how am I supposed to come find you?* But the wind carries her voice away.

Get out. Get out. Rosalie's voice is strained, as though it takes everything she has to utter these words.

A sensation of danger tightens in her chest, and she wakes up.

THE DREAM LEFT her puzzled. Not *Come find me* but *Get out*. Since coming back from Master Liu's, the feeling of coercion that besieged her had changed. At first a frantic roil of emotions, then a shift to something different. She no longer felt compelled to stay and fulfill some unknown task. And with this latest dream, she tentatively put a name to the sensation. It was a warning.

She only had a few days left in Shanghai anyway. She'd stay until after the funeral. Caroline would need her. Then she would leave Lennox Manor and its ghosts behind.

CHAPTER 29

THOMAS STANTON'S FUNERAL took place just three days after he died, at Bubbling Well Cemetery. Rain fell in dense sheets as gusts from the north chilled the air. Caroline pulled the fur scarf a little tighter around her neck. Standing under a pair of large umbrellas held by his two servants, the priest spoke a hasty service. Almost as soon as he mumbled the final prayers, the mourners began leaving, first offering quick words of condolence to Caroline and Mason before hurrying away to their vehicles.

Dr. Ellis walked with Caroline and Mason to their motorcar. "He should've been able to overcome any parasites," the doctor said, his voice plaintive. "He was getting better at first. His decline was so sudden."

"You're worried that I blame you," Caroline said, "but there's no need, Doctor. I know you did your best." Beside her, Mason stayed silent.

Mason climbed in after Caroline with a curt nod to the doctor, who stood forlorn under his dripping umbrella as their car pulled away. Caroline looked out the window to see that Lisan and Chin were getting into her car. She had insisted they take her car rather than rickshaws to the cemetery.

"Thank you for not holding a wake, Uncle Mason," Caroline said, turning back to face him. "I appreciate it. I'm exhausted from everything this past week and I couldn't deal with guests, no matter how sympathetic." And they'd lost most of their servants.

"We'll invite some friends over another time," he said, "for a quiet and private event to remember him by. Shall we lunch together before the lawyers come?"

"Yes, of course," she said. She didn't want to spend more time than necessary with Mason. But she was still feeling her way. The things she had to do now that she was a widow. The threat of Masako Kyo. Whether Mason would try to subvert the terms of Thomas's will. It seemed easier to agree for now.

"Good. Very good." Mason's eyes gleamed, and she wished she hadn't agreed.

The two vehicles reached Lennox Manor at the same time. Chin rushed out of the other automobile and hurried up the steps, unlocking the front door to hold it open for Caroline and Mason. Caroline asked Chin to serve lunch in an hour and said nothing more as he took their coats. Mason lumbered up the staircase and turned toward the east wing. No doubt to drink unobserved.

On the way up to her room, Caroline merely asked Lisan, "Who is left?"

"The remaining house servants went while we were at the funeral," Lisan said. "The cooks are gone; the gardener is still here, he's just gone out for a bit this morning. And Chin isn't going anywhere." Her tone changed ever so slightly at this last bit of information.

"Chin is so loyal to Mason," Caroline murmured, her face pale and haggard under the black veil. "I'm going to lie down, Lisan. Come and wake me in a half hour. We need to talk."

BUT SHE DIDN'T sleep. She lay on her bed, eyes wide open. She'd told Lisan that she wanted to rest, but it was really to get some time alone. She didn't want Lisan fussing over her, that sweet face all anxious and attentive. Nor did she wish to get into a conversation with Mason, whose manner toward her had changed.

Was it her imagination or was there something about his attentions that warranted this uneasy feeling? Over the past two days since Thomas died, Mason had become more overbearing, autocratic even, as though he owned her. Thomas was barely in the ground and he was already trying to assert himself.

She had always known she couldn't count on Mason to act in her best interests. Closing her eyes, Caroline ran through the events of the morning searching for insights. No, farther back. Mason's behavior had changed at some point before Thomas's funeral. It had been the day before the funeral. Caroline sighed and stretched her limbs, turned onto her side to look out the window. The rain-spattered glass obscured any view of the gardens. She was no longer in any doubt that something was going on with Mason. But what?

There was a discreet knock. "Mrs. Stanton?" Lisan's voice called softly from the door. "You asked me to come get you thirty minutes before lunch."

"Come in, Lisan," she called, getting up and going to the vanity. Lisan entered and, silently taking the brush from her, began brushing out her hair.

"Chin has laid out two place settings in the breakfast room." Lisan began twisting her hair up, anchoring the chignon with pins. "He's heated up the soup but the rest of the meal is cold. I'm afraid it's not the usual because the cook has left."

"I'm not hungry, and Uncle Mason is only interested in what's to drink." Caroline stared at her reflection in the mirror. A little pinched, but then, she had just lost her husband. Everyone knew she had been by his bedside for days, worrying over every symptom. "It's fine, Lisan. Let's not worry about the servant problem for the next day or so."

Lisan gave her a hesitant smile. "If you don't need anything else, Mrs. Stanton, I'll go deal with the correspondence that's come in today. There are many letters of condolence."

"Not yet, Lisan," Caroline said. "I've made up my mind and there's something I want to talk about again. Do you remember me saying that, should anything happen to Thomas, I wanted to travel? For both of us to travel?"

"Yes, Mrs. Stanton," Lisan said, "and I thanked you for the offer, but asked you to think it over when you were not so distraught."

"I've thought it over, Lisan," Caroline said. "I've decided to leave Lennox Manor, leave Shanghai. If for nothing else, I need to leave Shanghai for my own safety. Uncle Mason has become . . . overly protective. My offer stands. If you come with me, we can travel the world together. You'll have money, you can leave anytime you choose."

She waited as Lisan took a deep breath. "Mrs. Stanton, I will think on it, I promise. I'm as tired as you are of other people making decisions about my life too. When do you plan on leaving?"

"Tonight, Lisan," she said, "tonight. Mason's starting to think he can make my decisions for me, take over my life now that Thomas is gone. He can't, of course, but it's making me nervous. So first, I need to get away from this house. I'll move into the Astor House Hotel. You must come with me—even if you decide not to come traveling with me, you can't stay here alone with Mason if I'm not here."

Lisan looked startled. "Yes, of course, Mrs. Stanton. You're right. I should leave as well."

"Now, please bring down a couple of my valises and pack them," she said. "Just enough things for a few days. Mason and I are going to have lunch and then the lawyers are coming. Have Chin set up the dining room for a meeting."

"Yes, of course," Lisan said. "I will get your luggage from the attic. But I should tell you that both chauffeurs resigned while you were resting. Once they'd done their duty for the funeral."

"I know how to drive. We'll take my car into Shanghai," Caroline said, "and we'll leave after the meeting with the lawyers. I suspect Mr. Burnett will drink heavily after the meeting and never notice our escape."

CAROLINE AND MASON spoke very little over lunch: asparagus soup and a platter of cold ham with boiled potatoes, a small dish of pickled beets. Chin poured wine and then more wine for Mason. Caroline tried to catch Chin's eye, make him slow down, but Mason snarled.

"Bring that claret over, boy," he said, "can't you see my glass is empty?"

Chin looked pointedly at Caroline as he tipped the bottle into Mason's wineglass, then shrugged. He cleared the table, then poured coffee from the sideboard, the metal pot keeping hot over a small spirit lamp. He served them stewed plums, then bowed and silently left the dining room, carrying the tray of used plates.

"After all these years in China," Mason said, "I still can't get used to those servants and their cloth shoes. Always makes me feel they're sneaking around, spying on us."

"It's rather nice, I think," Caroline said, "to have such quiet, unobtrusive housekeeping."

"Well, my dear," Mason said, wiping his mouth, "we should discuss family finances."

"I don't know how you can talk about money, Uncle Mason," she said, "when Thomas is barely in the ground. And shouldn't we wait for the lawyers?"

"There are some things that can't wait, unfortunately," he said.

"Thomas was not just my nephew, he was also my business partner. For the sake of Burnett and Stanton Ltd., after his will is read we must execute on it as soon as possible."

"You mean, for the sake of your debts," Caroline said. "I can't see you carrying on the railway venture without Thomas. You haven't the engineering expertise, and face it—your business reputation is dire. No one will invest in the railway now; it was Thomas who brought credibility to the venture."

"Caroline, you speak like a member of the board," he said, and belched. "Little did I know when I urged Thomas to marry you that you were more than a pretty face and a fat inheritance. It all began with Andrew Grey, you know."

It was as though a cold hand clutched at her throat. "Really? That architect?" she said.

"Yes, yes," Mason said, his expression unreadable. "We met at my club."

Newly arrived in Shanghai, eager to talk up his New York connections and find himself some work, Grey befriended Mason. The two soon fell into the habit of playing cards together. Grey often boasted of the invitations he received to attend all the noteworthy events of New York's social season. One he'd mentioned was a party at the Dominics', where he'd met, very briefly, the Dominics' ward, Caroline Vessey. She was plain and awkward, Grey said, absolutely unmarriageable except for the fact that she would inherit a fortune. But the Dominics were extremely protective of her and wary of fortune hunters.

"Thomas was coming to Shanghai, taking the train to Seattle," Mason said, "and he cabled me after the railway disaster to say he was safe, and that obviously his travel plans were now delayed. Of course, I had read all the news articles I could find about the disaster, and when I looked through the list of survivors, I saw the name 'Caroline Vessey.' Who was now bereft of her prudent guardians."

Mason cabled Thomas back and urged him to marry Caroline. "I mean, why spend our own money on a railway venture when he could get his hands on someone else's inheritance?"

He peeked at her slyly as he poured cream into his coffee but Caroline said nothing.

"But you know that in the end, Thomas married for love," Mason said.

"He did," she said, "Thomas loved me."

"Indeed. He refused to spend your inheritance on the business. In fact, he dug into his own pockets. But it's still not quite enough. Nor is the amount he's left to the business. I'll need more, Caroline, to hire someone to take Thomas's place, to put in more capital and attract other investors."

"It doesn't change my decision, Mason," Caroline said. "When Thomas was alive, I wasn't comfortable about this venture. Now that he's gone, that puts you in charge and I'm even less confident. Take what's coming to you from his will, but I won't be putting any more money into this venture."

"But you will, oh, you will," Mason said, leaning across the table. "And you'll give me authorization to manage your personal finances. Because I know who you really are."

And there it was. The reason behind his changed conduct, why he'd been looking at her so covetously. She poured another cup of coffee. "Who am I, if not Caroline Stanton?"

"An impostor," Mason said, "and how do I know? Again, Grey."

A few nights after the party at Lennox Manor, Mason had gone to his club and played cards with Grey. By midnight, they were the only two left at the table, still drinking and playing. Grey lost and couldn't pay, but claimed he would come into a fortune very soon.

A certain lady would be giving him a great deal of money to preserve her reputation, he'd said, slurring his words. He was giving her a couple of weeks and then she'd pay him. Fifteen thousand dollars.

"You must be a very persuasive man, Grey," Mason had said, raising a glass.

"No, just that her indiscretions are worth a lot to keep secret," Grey replied, "especially after the evidence arrives. I've hired a detective to collect proof, and I expect it to arrive soon. Come see me at the end of the month for your money. It's all too delicious, Mason, it really is."

But then Grey was killed, murdered for unpaid debts.

Then Thomas died, leaving Mason uncertain where he stood financially. Suddenly he remembered Grey's blackmail scheme and wondered whether there was any truth to it. Perhaps he could take advantage of such information. Information worth a fortune, Grey had claimed. It was worth a try. It was an easy walk from Mason's club to Les Trois Lanternes.

"The police had already searched Grey's room," Mason said, "and taken away his mail as part of their investigations. But the concierge mentioned that some pieces of correspondence had come in for Grey since then and he'd been holding it in case the police came back. A small bribe and he gave them to me. Imagine my astonishment when I read the contents of a fat envelope from a New York detective."

She could only look at him, lips tightly pressed.

"Indeed, it's all too delicious, it really is." Mason stood up, pushing his chair back from the table. "So you'll do as I say. You'll give me the authority to manage your finances or I'll expose you as a fraud."

"If you do that," she said, "we will both suffer. If I can't access the money, you can't get anything from me."

"Oh, my dear girl," he said, "don't worry. I don't want to expose you. If I did, what would happen to all that lovely money that doesn't actually belong to you? Let me tell you something, dear girl. You're everything I could hope for in a woman. I only wish my son could've found someone like you. You're a clever one, just what he needed. Devious."

"How flattering." She had to get away from this man. "And you've just admitted you can't expose me."

"I said I didn't *want* to expose you. But if you force me, I will, and the difference, my dear," Mason said, his smile wide and affable, "is that I will be poor but a free man and you'll go to jail."

He stumbled a little on his way to the door, opened it, and turned around to look at her. "Poor old Grey, whatever he was extorting from you, he wasn't asking enough." Still chuckling, he lumbered down the hall toward the staircase, humming loudly "Land of Hope and Glory," his voice richly melodious.

She took a glass from the sideboard and poured herself a whiskey. Damn that Grey. A good thing he was dead; he would never have managed to keep a secret. Grey, then that false princess, and now Mason. Mason, who now possessed whatever evidence Grey had obtained.

What would her life have been like if she'd remained as Caroline Vessey's maid-companion? What if Caroline Vessey had lived? A girl who was shy and difficult around people. A pale ghost of a young woman who hated dinner parties and going outside. She'd fought so relentlessly against Mrs. Dominic's plans for a coming out ball that in the end her aunt had given up in despair, and made it known that Caroline suffered from a delicate constitution. Caroline had agreed to travel cross-country with her aunt and uncle only if she could bring her maid, her classmate.

Near the end, Caroline had become demanding to live with.

She had made some oblique comments about gratitude and charity. Their former relationship began disintegrating as Caroline began treating her more and more as a servant. Then Caroline dangled the prospect of an inheritance. "I've written you into my will," she said, a smirk on her pallid features, "a nice sum of twenty-five thousand when I die. For being a true and loyal friend, the only one who understands me."

It was a bribe, and they both knew it. So that no matter how badly Caroline Vessey treated her, she could never protest, never disobey, never leave or she'd jeopardize that twenty-five thousand dollars. And in the end, both the Vessey and Dominic fortunes had been handed to her, along with a new identity. A fur coat and a body found in the wrong compartment. That was all it took for her fortunes to change.

And now, there was Mason as well as Masako Kyo. She considered each of her would-be blackmailers. Kyo was not as much of a threat as Mason, because Mason was the one with the evidence. She had very little time.

CHAPTER 30

CAROLINE HAD HELD out friendship to Lisan. Had offered her the chance to leave Shanghai, to travel and see the world. Lisan wasn't sure yet. But tonight, when she and Caroline went to the Astor House Hotel, at least she would be away from Lennox Manor, break free from the feeling that now jangled at her nerves like a fire alarm. *Get out. Get out.*

She needed to start packing for Caroline, but first there was Ju Ming's letter to post. She nearly rang for Xiao Wu, then realized all the servants were gone. She hurried out to the gate and gave the gatekeeper a coin to take the envelope to the nearest letter box, which was out by Jessfield Road.

The elderly man fidgeted, looked down. "I won't be coming back, Miss," he said.

Another defection. She felt in her pocket for another coin, handed it to him. "That's all right. I will tell Chin. Just make sure you post that letter."

Lisan would pack for Caroline while she and Mason ate lunch. Then she would pack for herself, a task that would take all of ten minutes. Switching on the attic light, she looked around at the stacks of miscellaneous furniture, avoiding the pile of framed pictures in the corner. She pulled out a valise and a small suitcase for Caroline, then paused for a moment at the door on her way out. Her eyes swept the attic, trying to identify the prickling sensation that had prompted her to look around a second time. Something about the crates from New York.

The lid was back on the wooden crate, the one containing the Dominics' china, crystal, and silverware.

Lisan had deliberately left the wooden lid offset, the way she'd found it when she discovered the missing knife. Now the lid was neatly pulled over the rough slats of the container. Had one of the departing servants helped himself to some valuables before leaving? She lifted the lid and looked inside. The box with the carving set was back in place, tucked against the other boxes. She opened it, expecting the fork to be gone as well. Instead, the carving set was complete, both knife and fork. Someone had taken the knife and then put it back.

Lisan stared at the box, recalled what Caroline had said about small items going missing and then being returned. It had almost been enough to make her believe in ghosts. The knife had been returned very recently. The most rational explanation was that one of the servants had stolen the knife and then his courage failed when Chin began asking questions and he returned it. She would tell Chin, put his mind at ease.

She took the luggage to Caroline's dressing room and started packing. She only had to bring just enough for a few days and it didn't take long. Fortunately Caroline kept all her jewelry in a leather case like a hatbox. Lisan laid the case on top of the valise, straightened up, and stumbled, a moment of light-headedness. She hadn't eaten a thing yet today.

Her own packing could wait; she would make herself a quick lunch from the food Zhao had prepared.

There was a forlorn air to the kitchen, the empty chairs pushed neatly under the long tables, all the pots and pans put away. Only the smell of cooked rice and spices lingered to remind Lisan of the many convivial meals she had shared in there, the stove presided over by Zhao the cook, waving his ladle occasionally to make a point.

To her delight, Yao was standing at the stove, boiling water for tea. She couldn't contain her relief at the sight of him. The morning post had brought him a note from Master Liu and he had left Lennox Manor right away.

Yao held out a paper bag of dried sour plums, her favorite snack. She took one, savored its sour-salty taste before opening the pantry door. There she found some of Zhao's chicken and sticky rice, wrapped in bamboo leaf packets. She longed to eat them steamed and hot, the fragrance of bamboo leaves infusing the rice, but cold would have to do. She unwrapped one and put half in a bowl for herself, half in another for Yao.

"It's very quiet," he said, pouring water into a teapot. "Have we lost more servants? I ran into Chin on Brenan Road—he said he was going to the market to buy fresh vegetables for dinner. "

"It's just the two of us now and Chin," she said, handing him a bowl and chopsticks. "Even the gatekeeper has gone. Why did Master Liu want to see you?"

"News from Fourth Uncle," he said, digging into the rice. "The Pinkerton detectives found Prince . . . your father."

The detectives had sent a brief telegram to let Master Liu know they'd located Mr. Zheng. He'd been injured in a riot but was recovering very well.

"Yes, and a lucky thing it was," Yao said, shaking his head. "I heard rumors about a massacre in Mexico but had no idea Prince Tsai had been caught up in all that horror."

Three hundred Chinese killed. Shopkeepers and market gardeners, from an immigrant community with its own bank and a doctor. A community that had been peaceful, thriving, self-sufficient, and hardworking.

"Master Liu sent for me because he received a telegram from

your father, who is safely back in America now," Yao said. "He will be in Canada in time to greet you. Whatever Masako Kyo threatens, you'll be safe."

"You mean, no one would bother going all the way to Canada?" she said.

"Master Liu has a plan," Yao said. "He will say that you went to Foochow to attend college on your scholarship. But you'll never reach the college. A young woman, traveling alone in dangerous times—anything could've happened."

She nodded, understanding. "You know, Masako Kyo was here three days ago," Lisan said, "the day Thomas Stanton died."

"She came to see you again?" Yao's eyes were intent.

She shook her head. "No, some nonsense to do with Mrs. Stanton. When Kyo left, Mrs. Stanton was extremely upset."

"Well, never mind Mrs. Stanton. Master Liu wants you home right away," Yao said. "He wants you safely in hiding until you leave China. He sent me here with an automobile, which is just outside the gates."

Fourth Uncle had reported that Masako Kyo was now in Peking, where she wouldn't be able to resist boasting about her discovery: that she knew how to bring Prince Tsai back to court.

"But what about Master Liu?" It occurred to Lisan that her guardian was also at risk. "Isn't he also in danger? I mean, Prince Tsai's enemies, wouldn't they also try and use him? Force him to tell them where my father is?"

"It's hard to bully a member of the powerful Liu family," Yao said. "Master Liu would simply deny Kyo's assertions since she has no proof. The problem will be if anyone from court sees you. The resemblance to your mother is her proof."

"But I've been given another choice, you know," Lisan said, making up her mind. "Yao, Mrs. Stanton wants to leave Shanghai and travel the world. She's asked me to go with her, as a paid companion."

"You can't mean to actually go." Yao looked at her, aghast. "It's not what Master Liu wants. It's not what your father wants. I'm here to take you back to the villa."

What they wanted. What *they* wanted. Those words, those assumptions. When she was so tired, when there had just been a death in the house. When Charles and Rosalie and Lennox Manor were doing their best to drive her mad.

When Ju Ming was out there, following her heart and her adventuresome spirit.

"All my life, I've done what others wanted because I haven't had a choice," Lisan said. "Yao, when you saved me, you were saving me from my mother's decision to kill herself and her daughters. Her decision. Then I did whatever Master Liu wanted. But Mrs. Stanton has given me another choice."

"Lisan, it wasn't for trivial reasons that your father brought us to Master Liu," he said, his voice rising. "If his enemies catch up with you, you'll be putting your own father in danger. What sort of daughter are you?"

"Evidently not as good a daughter as you are a loyal servant," she retorted, "therefore if I'm kidnapped, why should my father turn himself in, reveal his whereabouts for such an ungrateful child?"

"Lisan, they could hurt you. Please," Yao said, the look on his face so helpless that she nearly relented.

"Then we must convince them I'm only an orphan, a street urchin Master Liu took in," she said, "and if everyone tells the same story, they'll believe it. Come, Yao. It's the same tale the whole Liu family and their friends have believed for the past decade. Now I must go and pack. We're leaving this afternoon and checking into the Astor."

"You can't go with Mrs. Stanton." He reached for her hand. "You may never see Shanghai again. I may never see you again."

She pulled her hand away. "But, Yao, you've never really seen who I am. I'm not Prince Tsai's daughter, I'm not. I don't remember anything of that life, even now. I have my own ambitions, modest though they are. Tell Master Liu that."

"Lisan," he said, "I'm going to drive away, run some errands for our journey, perhaps tell Master Liu what you just said. And then I'm coming back, because you'll have changed your mind by then. And if you're not here, I'll go to the Astor. And by the way, I may not know everything about you, Lisan, but I know you're intelligent and sensitive and compassionate. Please don't put your faith in a rich foreigner."

Lisan stayed in the kitchen after Yao left, washed up the dishes. She had wanted to run after him, tell him the only reason she'd leave China was for him, not for a father she didn't know. That she was tired and on edge, sorry for losing her temper. But that she'd meant what she had said about wanting a choice.

THE DOOR TO the dining room was closed. Caroline and Mason were in there with the lawyers. Lisan checked the breakfast room, saw the morning paper still lying on the sideboard. It was unlikely either Caroline or Mason had bothered reading any newspapers today. She picked up the *North China Herald*. She would take it to the small parlor and put it on Caroline's desk. She skimmed the pages while walking up the stairs. Andrew Grey's murder was still of interest—it was an ongoing investigation, and there were more details about the murder.

Police ask witnesses to come forward. If anyone was in the vicinity of 26 Rue Voisin near Les Trois Lanternes Hotel and saw anything unusual between 10:30 and 11:30 on the morn-

ing of March 22 please contact the Shanghai Municipal Police. Police are still searching for the murder weapon, which
they think is very likely a blade of six to eight inches, an inch
and a half wide, with a sharp, tapered tip.

Like the carving knife that had turned up again. But surely that
description fit any number of knives. Ju Ming's words echoed. *But
what would Mrs. Stanton be doing on a shabby street like the Rue
Voisin, which is nothing but cheap hotels and cheap cafés?* Instead of
continuing to the attic, Lisan went to her room and opened her gray
notebook, thumbed through the pages she had updated—not Caroline's upcoming engagements but the entries from a few days ago.

March 22. AG, 26 Rue V. 10.

The initials, the address. Did "10" mean ten in the morning?
Lisan shook her head. She needed to pack her own bag. As she
climbed slowly up the attic stairs, her mind kept flashing back
to Andrew Grey's gloating face, his taunting words. *I know your
secret.* And then to Masako Kyo's matter-of-fact accusation. *And
you're impersonating Caroline Vessey.* No, it was preposterous.

In the attic, she pulled out her carpetbag. But somehow, she
didn't get to the door. She found herself kneeling in front of the
pictures leaning against the wall, found her hand reaching out to
turn Rosalie's portrait around. The soft mouth looked as if Rosalie was about to say something, the eyes were alert, as though in
warning. Although her face looked straight out from the picture,
it seemed to Lisan that Rosalie was staring at the wooden crates
on the opposite wall. But she'd already been through the boxes of
silverware.

But not the second crate. The one marked *Caroline Vessey bedroom.* She lifted aside the lid and leaned it against the wall. At the very top was the cardboard box Caroline had dropped in panic when the rat ran across her foot. There was a label pasted to the box: *Miss Fielding's Finishing School for Young Ladies: Memories of 1905.* It contained a school yearbook. Glancing into the box, she noticed a few other similar cardboard boxes, labeled for previous years. She turned the pages of the yearbook. The first pages contained photographs of clubs and school activities. *Helping at St. Francis Orphanage. Tennis Tournament. Flower Arranging.* Girls dressed in uniforms of ruffled white pinafores over long plaid skirts, names listed in the caption below each photograph.

She turned the pages and then saw *Spring Musical: The Pirates of Penzance.* A photograph of the entire cast and chorus, the caption below listing their names, left to right. She scanned the names and there it was: Caroline Vessey, third row, second from the left. But the face in the third row was plain and thin, hair tucked into a frilly costume bonnet. Could it be a mistake? There were so many girls in the production, had the yearbook committee made a mistake labeling the picture? She looked at each face carefully, found Caroline in the front row. But the corresponding name on the list was not Caroline Vessey. *Eleanor Fontaine.*

On the next page, the photograph showed a pretty girl, undoubtedly the Caroline she knew, in a dress with puffy sleeves and a beribboned bonnet at the front of the stage, a few chorus members in the background. Lisan clearly recalled Caroline's words as she was getting ready to attend an evening performance. How much she had detested the Gilbert and Sullivan musicals at school. *It was* The Pirates of Penzance *and I sang the role of Mabel in an awful puffy yellow dress and bonnet.* Except that the names below this photograph didn't mention Caroline Vessey. *Eleanor Fontaine.*

Heart racing, she thumbed through the pages until she reached *Graduating Class of 1905.* Individual photos, no chance of mistaken identities. There were only two photographs she cared about. With a low cry, Lisan dropped the yearbook, which fell into the crate.

She sat on the floor, back against the wall, knees close to her chest. *You're impersonating Caroline Vessey.* Was this what the warning meant? That the woman Lisan knew as "Mrs. Stanton" had taken her classmate's identity, deceived a man into marrying her? Now she was preparing to leave Shanghai and continue her pretense, this time as a wealthy widow. Lisan had been about to travel the world with a woman who had lied about her identity. Her life could've become dependent on the goodwill of someone like that.

I know your secret, Andrew Grey had said. Was this the secret? Had he revealed that secret to Kyo? Why had Caroline—she couldn't think of her yet as *Eleanor*—met him on the day he was murdered? Perhaps it was simply a coincidence. But the carving knife in the other crate, its gleaming steel nestled in a velvet-lined slot, told her otherwise.

And there was something else. She pressed her back against the wall, trying to pinpoint the source of her unease. Caroline had seemed relieved at Thomas's death. And who could blame her when he'd suffered so much, when she had stayed up night after night to exhaustion, dark circles swelling under her blue-green eyes? Was it possible that . . . No, it was Mason, it had to be. Caroline wouldn't harm her own husband.

She had to leave Lennox Manor, and quickly. Thank goodness her few belongings would be easy to pack. Suddenly she understood the sensation of danger, of warning. It wasn't Charles's ghost trying to frighten her. *Come find me*, Rosalie had pleaded in those earlier dreams, willing Lisan to understand what she needed. And now Lisan was being warned to get out.

From across the room, Rosalie regarded her with sad eyes. She now seemed resigned to the fact that Lisan would never come find her. She wanted Lisan to get away from Lennox Manor. Away from the woman she called "Mrs. Stanton."

Oh, why had she been so stubborn with Yao? Why hadn't she gone home with him? She would tell Caroline she was resigning, like all the other servants. She would not accompany her to the hotel tonight. She'd carry her carpetbag to Jessfield Station, where any number of donkey carts and rickshaws were available for hire. Sometimes there were even taxis, and right now she was willing to pay the insane expense of riding in an automobile just to get back to Master Liu's. She'd walk all the way if she had to, in pouring rain. The thought of facing Mrs. Stanton was more daunting than the prospect of a three-hour walk.

But most important of all, she couldn't let the American woman suspect she'd discovered her secret. Andrew Grey was ample warning of that. Footsteps up the staircase sent her back to the wooden crate, frantically pulling the heavy wooden lid off the floor. But the attic door opened before she could replace the lid properly and it sat askew on the crate.

"Oh good, you're up here," Mrs. Stanton said. "The lawyers are gone. Mason had a drink or three, then went to his room to sleep it off. I looked at what you packed and it's perfect. Have you done your own packing yet?"

She stopped at the sight of Lisan and her eyes took in the wooden crate, its misaligned lid, Lisan's stricken face and trembling hands.

The blue eyes narrowed, glimmered green. She crossed the room to the crate, moved the lid aside, and smiled. "You were snooping through my yearbook," she said, picking it up.

Lisan couldn't deny it. The book had been lying at the top, not even in its cardboard box. And she couldn't hide the anxiety on her face. She nodded. "It's none of my business, Mrs. Stanton," she said. "I won't mention this to anyone."

"I should've burned these," Mrs. Stanton said, "but after seeing that rat, I hated coming up unless it was absolutely necessary."

It had been absolutely necessary to return the knife, Lisan thought, never taking her eyes off the woman. A stranger now. Someone dangerous.

"It was a risk," the American woman said, flipping through the pages. Her voice grew almost dreamy. "But not many people in New York outside the Dominic household knew Caroline Vessey. Mrs. Dominic always pestered her to improve her appearance, always wanted her to change her hair, select more flattering dresses, and to get out more. Get some exercise to correct her posture. It made her self-conscious so she often pretended to be unwell because she hated meeting people and rarely left the apartment."

The words poured out. How easy it had been to go along with what people assumed, how the little snatch of memory about Danby's dislike of caviar had clinched her identity for the Dominics' lawyer.

"It was a large party and I had to help with the serving," she said. "I was beside Caroline, holding a tray of hors d'oeuvres, when Mr. Dominic introduced Danby to Caroline. But, of course, Danby never noticed me, I was just the help."

The woman's words mesmerized Lisan. How she and Lisan had so much in common because they were both orphans, left destitute. How by working in the Dominic household, she had ensured she wouldn't starve but neither did she have a future, or a path to independence. She was locked into a life of servitude.

"Now tell me honestly, Lisan," she said, tossing the yearbook into the crate, "wouldn't you have been tempted to do the same? To seize such an opportunity to escape from a future where the best you could hope for was, what, paid companion to some rich, lonely spinster? A governess to spoiled children? Wife to some bank clerk or a grocer?"

"Tempted, yes," Lisan said, "but I couldn't be as bold. I'd be afraid that someone from my past might recognize me." Someone like Andrew Grey, perhaps.

Mrs. Stanton held out her hand to Lisan. "Now that you know my secret, you can hold it over me, do you realize that? But somehow that doesn't worry me, because I trust you. We'll travel the world together."

"Mrs. Stanton," Lisan said, not taking her hand, "I've thought it over and I'm sorry. I won't be going with you to the hotel. I must resign my position with you. And now I must go pack."

The blond head tilted, green eyes gazed at her. "But why? What's in Shanghai for you? You're overeducated for an orphan girl, undereducated for a teacher. Do you think you'll get a better offer for a better life?"

Lisan glanced across the attic at Rosalie's portrait, a ripple of fear gripping her even though Mrs. Stanton had not made any threatening moves.

"I've trusted you with my secrets, Lisan," she said, "and now are you going to trade silence for money like the others?" Her eyes glinted a deep, impenetrable green and her cheeks were flushed.

"No, Mrs. Stanton, I would never do that," Lisan said, keeping her voice steady, "and I understand why you became Caroline Vessey, why you took over her life. I do. I don't blame you for that. It didn't harm anyone."

"No, you're so right, Lisan," Mrs. Stanton said, musing, "impersonation is a crime, but it didn't harm a single person. And you should understand that I would do anything, anything, to hold on to this life. Well then, go pack your bag and come see me after; I shall write you a check for your wages."

<h1 style="text-align:center">CHAPTER 31</h1>

IT TOOK LISAN less than ten minutes to throw all her belongings into the carpetbag. She debated taking her books and decided against it. One final look around to make sure she hadn't left anything behind. She was sorry she'd burned the diary; she wished she had given it to Chin. But what could Chin do with it anyway—he couldn't read French.

He could read Chinese though. She would give him the translated pages. It wasn't as good as having his daughter's actual notebook but it was something. But Chin might not return before she left, so she'd leave the translation on the kitchen table for him, with an explanatory note.

She sat at the desk to write the note, but the bell from the small parlor sent Lisan hurrying up to Mrs. Stanton's summons.

"Here you go, Lisan, your wages," the American woman said, and handed her a sealed envelope. "I wish you all the best."

"Thank you, Mrs. Stanton," she replied, thinking that the best thing was to get out of this room, this house.

"Could you do one more thing before you leave?" Mrs. Stanton said. "Could you ask Mason to come see me, here in my parlor?"

"Yes, of course," she murmured, "right away."

It was only the second time she had crossed the landing to enter the east wing. She had no idea where she might find Mason, so she knocked on the door closest to the landing. After waiting a moment, she tried the next one, which she recalled was his study.

"Chin, is that you?" Mason bellowed from inside. "Where's the boy with my clean towels? Ah, it's you, Miss Liu, visiting my humble quarters."

"Mrs. Stanton requests that you see her, Mr. Burnett," Lisan said, backing farther out to the corridor. Even from the door, Lisan could detect the smell of whiskey. "She is in her private parlor."

A satisfied look came over his face. "A momentous occasion, an invitation to her private parlor." He heaved himself out of the leather armchair and looked around the floor, put his feet into a pair of ludicrously bright cloth slippers and headed out to the hall-way. He gave Lisan a quick pat on the rear, humming as he strode across the landing toward the small parlor.

Back in her room, she picked up her bags and gave in to relief. It was long past time to be gone. Away from this family of murderers. Then she heard a cry, followed by a loud crash. Then silence. Then her name, called out in desperation. The urgency of Mrs. Stanton's voice made Lisan rush to the parlor.

"Help! Lisan, help!" Mrs. Stanton's blond hair had come un-done and her cheeks were flushed. She stood at the threshold of the parlor door. "Mr. Burnett has collapsed. Get him some smell-ing salts, the ones inside the small cabinet. I will run downstairs to telephone Dr. Ellis." She held the door open for Lisan.

Mason lay crumpled in front of the fireplace, one arm flung out; the other lay across the side of his head, his bulky form was absolutely motionless. She hurried to the cabinet and opened the drawer to find the smelling salts. As she knelt beside Mason, the parlor door shut and a key turned in the latch.

Startled, she called out, "Mrs. Stanton?"

"Lisan?" came the reply from the other side of the door. "I'm sorry, my dear, I'm truly sorry. But you've disappointed me and I can't trust you anymore."

Lisan rushed to the door. "Mrs. Stanton? Mrs. Stanton!"

What was she going to do? Drive away with both Lisan and Mason still locked in the room? But Chin would come back at some point. And hopefully also Yao. She should've listened to him, left long ago, before all the small delays led her to this. Although the more she thought about it, the more she doubted that Mason had poisoned his nephew.

A groan brought her to Mason's side, where she rolled him onto his back and waved the smelling salts under his nose. As he jerked his face away from the glass vial, she saw blood on the side of his head. A heavy silver candlestick lay on the carpet, one of a pair on the mantel. Blood smeared the polished base.

"Mr. Burnett?" she asked, dabbing the blood with her handkerchief. "Can you hear me?"

He waved her away and sat up, holding on to the armchair, then pulled himself up into the chair, breathing heavily. She held out the bloodstained square of white cambric and he took it without a word, pressed it against the wound. She needed to find something to tie around his head and stop the bleeding.

Lisan took scissors out of the sewing box and examined the velvet drapes. They were lined with plain cotton. She cut away a panel of lining fabric and tore it into strips.

"You need to watch out for that one," Mason said. She wrapped the cloth around his head and over the folded handkerchief, keeping it tight against the wound. "She's not really Caroline Stanton. Where is she?"

"Please keep your hand against the handkerchief, sir," Lisan said, "and as for where she is, she was planning to check into the Astor Hotel for a few days before leaving Shanghai. I guess she doesn't want us interfering with her departure and that's one reason why she's locked us in this room."

Mason shook his head, winced. "You already knew she's an impostor?"

"Yes, but I found out only about half an hour ago," Lisan said, "and she guessed—she could tell I'd figured it out. I had been looking through her school yearbook. She offered to take me traveling with her as a paid companion, and I refused. I told her not to worry, that I wouldn't give away her secret. But obviously she doesn't trust me."

"She's a clever one," Mason said, "and this isn't over, you can be sure. I fear we are in danger, Miss Liu."

"When did you learn she was an impostor, sir?" This was the longest and most rational conversation she'd ever had with Mason. He seemed to have aged; his complexion was gray, and his entire face sagged.

"I found out about her the day after Thomas died," he said. "It was thanks to Andrew Grey, rest his soul."

Andrew Grey, who had been killed. A slow knot began hardening in her stomach. He'd been killed for knowing Mrs. Stanton's secret.

"She asked me whether I was going to trade silence for money like the others," Lisan said. "Blackmail? Were there others?"

"Grey wasn't the only one," Mason said. "I tried it too, once I got hold of Grey's evidence. My dear, somehow I don't think false Caroline will be content to leave us alive."

No, Lisan thought. Not when Mason could send the police after her. She tried opening a window but the wood frames were warped and refused to budge. The second window was no better; no matter how hard she tried, the sash wouldn't lift more than an inch. She was overcome with that familiar sensation again, more urgent this time, warning her to *get out, get out, get out.*

"You're right, Mr. Burnett," Lisan said, "she won't be content to leave us alive. Not when we both know." She ran to the parlor door and looked through the keyhole. The key wasn't in it. She put her ear to the floor and thought she could hear Mrs. Stanton's footsteps, first along the wooden floor, then a sharper clatter of shoes on hard marble. The main staircase. Mrs. Stanton was going downstairs. Lisan rushed to the window and the blond head emerged from under the porte cochere.

"She's headed for the garage to get her motorcar," Lisan said. "She's leaving."

But Mason didn't answer. His head was lolling to one side. "Dizzy," he mumbled, "but I hardly drank anything today. Sun's not yet over the yardarm, is it?"

"Mr. Burnett?" Lisan said. "How are you feeling?" But she didn't move away from the window.

"Like someone smashed a candlestick over my head, how do you think?" he said, sounding amused. He sat up straighter, pushing himself upright using the armrests. "Head hurts like hell, arms and legs won't move. Room too bright." A fit of coughing, which turned into retching. He wiped his mouth with a scrap of fabric.

"Damned inconvenient that all the servants have quit," Mason murmured. "Scared of ghosts, Chin said. Why are you Chinese so backward and superstitious? Present company excepted." He was sweating.

"Normally, the servants would not worry too much," she said, still looking out the window. "They'd make offerings to appease ordinary ghosts. But the ghost of a suicide is the worst kind, one that can't be appeased. His sole purpose is driving another person to suicide."

"Do you know," he said, "that time I saw you in the middle of the night, I thought you were Rosalie's ghost. Sometimes I think I see her, you know."

"Sometimes I think I see her too," Lisan said, glancing back at him. Was it possible that of all the people in this house, Mason was the only other person who felt a ghostly presence? But Charles had been his son. It made sense. "I've seen her in dreams and sometimes at night outside in the garden. Do you ever wonder where Rosalie went?"

"She didn't go anywhere, she's dead," Mason said. His hand moved to his chest and he coughed. "Charles killed her."

Lisan's legs gave way; she had to sit on the windowsill. Rosalie dead. "How? When?" was all she could manage to say.

"Miss Liu, I fear the worst," Mason said. His eyes were unfocused, struggling to stay open. "I don't know what that woman has in mind, but we will not leave here alive. Or at least I won't. So I will tell you how and when. Call it my confession."

Mason and Charles hadn't spoken in months, Mason living in his Shanghai apartment, Charles with Rosalie in Lennox Manor. He ignored Charles's pleas for money, and heard through the grapevine that his son was drinking heavily and had lost most of his friends, as much from ill temper as from the amounts he'd been borrowing. Then Chin, who had stayed at Lennox Manor, came to see him one morning and told him how low Charles had fallen.

Mason went to Lennox Manor for a last attempt to reason with Charles, one final offer: he'd pay all Charles's debts if he would divorce Rosalie. Even though it would bankrupt him, Mason was willing to do this for his son. He found the front door unlocked, the house empty. He followed the sound of weeping upstairs to the west wing, where he found Charles beside Rosalie's body.

"It was jealousy," Mason said, "jealousy and hurt pride. They had no money at all, so she'd gone back to the nightclub to sing again. He thought she was flirting with the customers, they had an argument, and he strangled her. He wasn't in his right mind, that's what he said."

It was Mason who decided they would bury Rosalie, then put about the story that she'd run away. Given how Charles had been behaving, no one would doubt that his wife couldn't take any more. Mason then drove back to his Shanghai apartment. He had an urgent meeting that evening with his banker, so he had Chin pack a suitcase and instructed him to bring it to Lennox Manor, along with some food for Charles. Mason would move back, look after his son.

And the next day, he would begin spreading the news that Rosalie had abandoned Charles. He would find some way later to annul the marriage.

Instead, when he returned to Lennox Manor, Chin was sitting on the front steps under the porte cochere. Mason opened the door to the sight of his son hanging in the foyer. There was a note on the mezzanine floor saying that he couldn't live without Rosalie and couldn't live with himself.

After Charles's funeral, Mason moved into Lennox Manor to make sure no one would find Rosalie's hastily dug grave. If only he'd been more accepting of his son's marriage—but all he'd ever wanted was for Charles to marry well, because the way things were going with Mason's business, soon he'd have nothing to leave Charles.

"Chin stayed on with me for three years," Mason said, "the only servant with any common sense, any loyalty." His head drooped and he closed his eyes. The confession had exhausted him, physically and emotionally, but something else was wrong. His skin looked loose and gray, his lips paler than before.

Lisan had to reconsider her assumptions. All this time, the dreams, the apparitions, the urgent sensation to remain in Lennox Manor. It hadn't been Charles's spirit haunting her. It had been Rosalie. *Come find me.* Lisan understood now.

Lisan heard a rumbling sound and rushed to the window. The Adler coupé rolled out of the garage, the reverberations of its engine clearly audible through the glass panes. It drove under the porte cochere and stopped. Then she heard the muffled slam of an automobile door closing. But the engine was still running. Mrs. Stanton wasn't leaving the automobile parked there for long.

Lisan rattled the latch of the window that she'd managed to open just an inch. She pulled up at the brass grips again, to no avail. *Get out, get out, get out.* The sensation of danger was so strong that when she heard footsteps in the hallway outside, she wouldn't have been surprised if Mrs. Stanton had opened the door with a gun in her hand. Lisan put her ear to the door. She heard the footsteps slow down, a deliberate pause between footfalls. An odor drifted through the gap in the door frame, a familiar smell, but she couldn't put her finger on it. Then a clanging sound, like metal landing on the floor, and the swift patter of shoes running down marble steps. Lisan hurried back to the window in time to see the Adler drive away and out the gates.

So Mrs. Stanton had gone without speaking to them again, without any further threats. Was she really just leaving them in the house? Obviously, she wasn't anticipating anyone coming back to Lennox Manor anytime soon, or she wouldn't have driven off.

Lisan looked over at Mason, who was definitely not well. He slumped against the chair, his entire body limp. Chin would come back soon, and hopefully Yao as well. They needed to get Mason to a doctor as quickly as possible. She had to make sure anyone coming through the gates came up directly to this room. She could turn on the electric lights but she would also light an oil lamp, use it to signal from the window as soon as she saw either of them come in. She had to draw their attention to this window. Cold air came through the glass panes and she shivered. The fireplace was nothing but embers now; the fire set in the morning had burned down and there were no more logs. Yet the odor of smoke seemed stronger than a few minutes ago.

The strange odor. It was lamp oil. A horrible realization crossed her mind, a memory of the day she'd helped Mrs. Stanton inventory kitchen supplies. All those metal tins of lamp oil. Gallons and gallons of it. She ran to the parlor door. Wisps of smoke curled in through the gaps.

"Mr. Burnett," she cried, "can you stand? We must get out of here."

Mason struggled to sit up, blinked at the urgency of her voice, then cursed when he saw the smoke. "If there's a fire behind the door, that's not the way to go." He fell back against the chair. "My dear, you need to get a window open. By any means. And you must somehow climb out."

By now they could hear a roar from the fire in the hallway outside, growing louder by the minute.

"You don't have much time," Mason said, leaning on one elbow. "Try using the fireplace poker. Wedge the end under the window sash and lever it up."

She managed to raise the window another six inches, enough for her to get both hands firmly under the frame to lift it. She pushed, stretching her arms over her head until the window was completely open. She leaned over the sill to look. There was nothing below or around the window, no trellis, no columns or ledges to cling to and climb down, just a sheer drop.

The roar of the blaze outside in the corridor wasn't the only sound anymore—now there was the occasional exploding tinkle of glass as wall sconces fell victim to the heat. Perhaps she could cut the curtains into strips and tie them into a rope. But how long would that take? She stared despairingly down at the ground, so far down.

Get out, get out, get out.

She craned her neck to look at the windows below. They'd been left open and smoke was drifting out. There was smoke wafting from under the porte cochere too. The front door was open. Mrs. Stanton had left the downstairs doors and windows open so that the breeze could fan the flames and spread their destruction faster.

A rickshaw was hurtling up the driveway, the passenger poking the rickshaw puller with his umbrella to make him run faster.

"It's Chin, Mr. Burnett," she cried. "It's Chin!" She waved frantically, then snatched up a cushion and waved it, hoping the bright colors would catch his eye. The rickshaw came to a halt by the flower beds and Chin leaped out, trampling over shrubs to stand in the gravel below her window, horrified eyes scanning the front of the house.

"Can you get to the other side, to the east wing?" he called up.

"We can't get out of this room," Lisan shouted. "We're locked in and the hallway is on fire."

"How? How did this happen?" He seemed utterly overwhelmed.

"Whatever you're going to do, do it quick," Mason wheezed from behind. "The door is on fire. Is it just Chin? Can he get a ladder?"

"Never mind how it happened," Lisan called down. "Can you get a ladder? Mr. Mason is locked in with me and he's very ill."

"I don't know, ladders are for outside and I only know where everything is for inside," Chin said helplessly. "I can look in the gardening shed." He vanished around the side of the house. The rickshaw puller rested against his vehicle, catching his breath and staring up at the burning house.

"What's happening?" Mason said, coughing. Smoke from the burning door was now pushing into the parlor.

"He's gone to find a ladder," Lisan said. "Mr. Burnett, come closer to the window and get away from the smoke."

"Afraid not, my dear." He grimaced. "I've lost all feeling in my arms and legs. Think I've had a heart something or other."

"Let's try, all the same," she said, "we must get you away from the smoke. Perhaps I could push you, chair and all." She'd only managed to move the chair a couple of feet when a loud blast from an automobile horn drew her to the window. She waved and shouted at the top of her voice. Yao leaped out of the car, not bothering to shut the door or turn off the engine.

"I saw the smoke from a mile away," he called. "The fire department should be on its way. They'll get you down."

But both of them could see that unless the fire trucks came in the next few minutes, they would be too late. Cinders from the fire were blowing across the garden, tiny glowing sparks that would've set shrubs and branches on fire if the grounds weren't dripping wet from the morning's rain.

"Chin's gone to get a ladder from the garden shed," she said, "but that's no help for Mr. Burnett. He's suffered some sort of stroke and can't even stand."

"We don't have a ladder tall enough to reach you," Yao said.

From behind her, Mason grunted, "How many men are out there now?"

"Yao the gardener, the rickshaw driver, and Chin." Chin had come back without a ladder, shaking his head.

"Tell them not to let the rickshaw driver leave," Mason said, "then pull the drapes off the curtain rod. Do it, just do it, girlie." He was gasping more than speaking now.

Lisan tugged at the heavy fabric, yanking it down and away from the wall. It all came down, drapes, rod, and even the bracket. "Throw it all down to them. Tell them to use it like a net, three of them can stretch it out below the window. Tell them to hold it out, wide as they can."

Yao nodded at her shouted instructions and wrapped one corner of the fabric around his fist. Chin and the rickshaw driver did the same. A triangle of gold velvet rippled below her and Lisan edged herself to the window, climbed onto the sill, reached for the top of the window frame to steady herself.

"Now jump, my girl," Mason said, "you haven't much time." He had crawled from the chair to the window.

But she couldn't move. The acrid smell of smoke, the heat behind her, the roar of the fire licking up the wallpaper and consuming the walnut desk, the sharp small explosions of sound as crystal shattered. The familiar nightmare enveloped her and Lisan squeezed her eyes shut, clutched at the window frame.

Her short, chubby legs trudge up a staircase, but this time, when she looks up, she sees the face of the person gripping her hand. It's her eldest sister. A rounded face and generous mouth. The veranda they hurry along is familiar to her, she knows it's the third floor of the palace, her mother's quarters. But a section of the red-painted railing is missing and now she sees her other sister, recognizes the high cheekbones and arched eyebrows. Then her mother kneels beside her. Features that echo her own, a sweet smile curving her lips. Lisan will never forget those faces now.

Her mother smiles at her, ties a silk scarf around her eyes. Something drops onto her shoulders, tightens a bit around her neck. A murmured few words from her mother, her eldest sister's hand holding hers, trembling.

Now jump, her mother says.

Now jump, another voice says. Rosalie's voice. *Get out. Come find me. Now jump.*

Lisan opened her eyes. Yao was shouting, pleading for her to hurry. Something at the back of the house exploded. She released her hands from the window frame and let herself go, landing in a flurry of golden velvet. The men lowered the makeshift net to the ground and Yao picked her up, set her down by the car. He ran back to the two others, who were already picking up the curtain again, wrapping the fabric tightly around their fists. It was Mason's turn.

"Mr. Burnett," Yao called. "We're ready for you. Jump!"

But Mason shook his head. He gave a quick salute with two fingers and his head slid below the windowsill, vanished from sight.

"Get away from the house, Miss Liu," Chin said, still looking up at the window as though willing Mason to come back. "It's dangerous to be so close. Master Burnett! Come to the window!"

With a clatter of wood and tiles, part of the roof caved in. The rickshaw puller dashed for his vehicle, straw sandals splashing through puddles. He ran for the gates, rickshaw jolting behind him.

"Get inside the car!" Yao cried. Lisan stumbled her way into the back of the vehicle, Chin right behind her. They were halfway to the gates when Yao stopped. They all turned to watch the rest of the roof catch fire. Even if the fire truck arrived now, there was no hope for the wooden structure. The hothouse and all its tropical flowers, the library and its books, the ballroom with the shining parquet floors and sparkling chandeliers. The attic with its secrets. And the portrait of Rosalie.

"But what about Mr. Burnett?" Lisan said. "We should stay and tell the firemen someone is in there."

"Lisan, it's too late for Mr. Burnett," Yao said, "and we need to get you away from here, now. It's best if you're not here when the fire department arrives. I'm taking you home. Chin, come with us. I'm certain Master Liu will let you stay until you decide what to do next." He turned the car onto Brenan Road. "Lisan, what happened?"

"I don't even know where to begin," she said, "but Caroline Stanton isn't Caroline Stanton."

By the time they reached the city, she had blurted out what she knew and what she'd guessed about what Mrs. Stanton had done. "That wasn't necessarily in the best and most logical order, but . . ."

"But it's been quite a day," Yao said, "and you've just escaped from a murderer."

"Who tried to kill you and Master Mason," Chin murmured. "She's a monster. And now the house is gone." He sounded forlorn.

"You're thinking of your daughter, that when she comes back that's where she'll come to find you," Lisan said, turning around to face him. "But oh, Chin, she won't be coming back. I'm so sorry. Mr. Burnett confessed everything to me."

Chin looked out the window the entire time as she told him what had befallen Rosalie. His face was ashen but he didn't say anything.

At the villa, the old gatekeeper was dozing as usual and Yao drove the car directly into the garage.

"Stay here until I come back," he said. "I must speak first with Master Liu. And stay out of sight."

Lisan got out of the vehicle. "Old Mah," she said, shaking her head in the direction of the gate, "still Shanghai's most hopeless gatekeeper."

"Where did they bury my daughter?" Chin said. "Did Mr. Mason tell you?"

Comprehension jolted through her like lightning. *Come find me.* That was what Rosalie meant. Not to go looking for her somewhere outside Shanghai, but to find her grave so that she could have a proper burial with all the proper funeral rites. A real grave in a spot where the people who loved her could pray for her, bring offerings, and sweep her grave during the Ching Ming Festival.

"No, he didn't tell me," she said, thinking of the willow trees by the lake and how in her dreams Rosalie's ghost always lingered there. "Chin, did you ever feel her presence? Your daughter's, I mean."

He shook his head. "No. I wish I had. To hear or see her again, just one more time."

CHAPTER 32

THE MORNING AFTER the fire, Master Liu handed Lisan a newspaper, *Xinwen Bao*, and pointed to the article about the blaze that destroyed Lennox Manor. Lisan scanned the lines.

> . . . mansion belonging to Liu Fanzhu, leased by prominent businessman Mason Burnett . . . Mason Burnett's body found in the ruins . . . Liu Lisan, female, age 19, working as a secretary . . . missing, presumed perished in the fire. . . . body not yet found but parts of the house collapsed . . . piles of wood that are still burning . . . fire is now considered contained and the fire department says it will soon burn itself out.

She read it again, more carefully this time, and looked up at Yao and Master Liu. "But this is wrong," she said, "I didn't die in the fire. Can you correct this mistake? It shouldn't be difficult since your nephew is editor in chief."

There was silence from both men. "Lisan," Master Liu said, "I was the one who told my nephew to report that you'd died in the fire."

"I don't understand," she said, "why did you do that?" But the moment the question left her lips, she realized she should've known.

"To get you out of danger," Yao said. "To send you to your father without anyone coming after you or him."

Because everyone, most importantly Masako Kyo, would believe Lisan had died in the fire. Shanghai's other Chinese newspapers had picked up information from the *Xinwen Bao* article. *Liu Lisan, age 19, working as a secretary.* The foreign language papers mentioned only that a female servant was missing, presumed perished in the fire.

"So now if Masako Kyo talks, it's her word against that of someone from a wealthy and respected clan," Master Liu said, "and her evidence, which is you, will be dead. I can simply repeat what we've always said: that I found you on the streets. That I haven't seen or heard from Prince Tsai in decades."

False papers for both Lisan and Yao were ready. They would enter Canada and settle in the city of Victoria, British Columbia, Lisan traveling as Zheng Lei, daughter of Zheng Fong Hu, her father's identity all these years.

"He will be waiting for you in Victoria," Master Liu said. "Only two more days, and your ship leaves."

Yao was going with her to Canada. She took a deep breath. Yao had been loyal to her father all these years, had stayed behind in Shanghai to keep an eye on her, and now he would join them. It was because of her father, she told herself, he was going because of her father, there was no other reason why.

"In the meantime," Master Liu continued, "both of you must stay indoors and out of sight until it's time to board your ship. Fourth Uncle is the only one in the family who knows about you, that you're not actually dead."

"But what about Mrs. Stanton?" Lisan said. "We must tell the police about her before she gets out of Shanghai. I can't prove she killed Andrew Grey or poisoned her husband, but I know she tried to kill me and Mason Burnett."

"Lisan, no," Yao said. "You're in hiding now. Even the servants don't know you're here, that you're still alive."

She looked around the dining room and realized how quiet it was, how quiet the house had been the previous night. Chin had brought in the breakfast congee and dishes, not Master Liu's house servant.

When Yao had asked Chin and Lisan to stay in the garage until he had spoken to Master Liu, they'd assumed it was about Chin joining the household. Yao had briefed Master Liu quickly on the situation. Master Liu's modest staff consisted of a cook, two house servants, and the gatekeeper, none of whom lived at the villa. Master Liu told his servants to eat an early supper and then take three days off, starting immediately after supper. Thus, the servants were safely out of the way; they'd been enjoying a meal in the kitchen when Yao brought Lisan and Chin into the house.

"Then you must be the one to tell police what Mrs. Stanton did, Master Liu," Lisan said. "She's an impostor and, for the sake of preserving her identify, set the house on fire. Mason Burnett's death is on her hands."

Master Liu shook his head. "Lisan, without your testimony, we have nothing to tell them. And I know nothing about Mrs. Stanton if you're supposed to be dead."

"But she'll be getting away with murder!" Lisan said.

"Listen to me, Lisan," Yao said, "the knife, the photographs from her school days, they've all gone in the fire. Even if you made your accusations, where is the evidence?"

"The fire offers an opportunity for your disappearance to be absolute and clean," Master Liu said, "a better story than a mere change of identity."

What else could she do? She nodded agreement.

"One more thing . . . yes, here it is," Master Liu said, taking a small cloth bag from his coat pocket. "Your father gave me these to keep in safety for you, Lisan."

Inside was a string of large wooden beads linked with brass

findings, each bead the size of a large chestnut and carved with Buddhist symbols. The beads were as familiar to Lisan as her own face.

"Those are the beads from your ancestral altar," she said, lifting them from the bag. "They were around the Goddess of Mercy."

Master Liu took the beads from her. He held one carved wooden bead between his fingers as if to show her a magic trick. He twisted the wooden sphere and it opened in two halves. The bead was hollow and contained what appeared to be a wad of cotton. He handed it to her. Its center was hard, smooth. She unwrapped the cotton and found a large pink pearl.

"Fifty-four beads, fifty-four pearls," Master Liu said, "all perfectly matched. Each extremely valuable on its own. Sold together, worth a fortune. Your father wanted you to have these, Lisan. In case anything happened to him, this was to have been yours. It was to have been yours in any case."

She stared at the pink sphere, its soft glow, the perfect shape. She couldn't imagine what the entire string might be worth.

Master Liu cleared his throat. "You should also know," he said, "that I've set aside a sum for you. When you're settled in Canada, when your father has determined the best way to keep funds for you, I'll send it over. You know you're the closest I have to a daughter."

"Master Liu, to tell the truth, you're more father to me than my own father," she said. "I can't help but feel anxious about meeting him. I feel so unprepared."

"Ah." He smiled. "But he is equally nervous about meeting you. Think on it for a bit. I find it helpful to write things down. Perhaps you could do that on the ship, write down the questions you want to ask. About your family, about your future, about his expectations. About your own expectations."

That was the hardest part. Lisan didn't know her father, didn't know anything about Canada. How could she have realistic expectations? But now she was free of Lennox Manor, of Rosalie's ghost. The feeling of compulsion was gone, the fog that had trapped her mind and bound her will to the mansion had lifted. Because in the end, Rosalie's ghost had chosen to warn her, to save her.

And now Lisan had a debt to repay.

"Master Liu, I wish to ask you a favor," she said. "It's about Chin and his daughter. Please help him find his daughter's unmarked grave and give her a proper funeral."

Lisan had woken up in the gray hours of the morning and realized she knew exactly where Mason and Charles had buried Rosalie. Her ghost had been telling her all along. The apparition always drifted over to the willow trees at the edge of the lake. Before vanishing into mist Rosalie would always pause on the shoreline between two trees that grew a little bit apart from the others. It was where Mason often stopped during his walks around the garden. Knowing Rosalie's fate, Lisan now suspected Mason went to check that the rising waters hadn't eroded the ground, that the body interred so hastily was not exposed. She was certain Mason and Charles had buried Rosalie beside the two willows.

She described the spot to Master Liu and to Chin, but she didn't tell them about Rosalie's ghost, letting them assume it was Mason's nocturnal wanderings that made her so certain of the location.

"We will look for your daughter's grave as soon as the fire department has finished," Master Liu assured Chin. "Since my Fourth Brother owns the property, it won't be a problem."

THE GATES TO Master Liu's villa were closed, his servants away. Inside the villa, Chin went about cleaning and dusting, as though already part of the household. Outside, rainfall muffled the sounds of the street beyond the garden walls. Lisan took an umbrella from the porcelain stand by the front door, and when she stepped outdoors, had to hold it almost sideways to fend off the driving rain. Yao was in the garden shed. Lisan couldn't understand why he was content to work as a gardener when he was clearly qualified to do much more.

As she opened the door to the garden shed he looked up with a smile, then continued pressing soil into a shallow pot. Lisan seated herself on a wooden bench by the charcoal brazier. Almost as soon as she settled, the stray cat that slept in the garden shed got up from the floor beside the brazier and jumped into her lap, where it purred contentedly, resuming its nap.

"Is Canada really the right place for us, Yao?" Lisan said. "What if we don't like it there? How can it ever feel like our home?"

"For now, you're going so you and your father can be safe," he said. "A revolution is coming, Lisan, and it will be a long and confusing time before China is peaceful again. Then we can come back, if we still want to."

"So many unknowns, Yao," she said. "I want to see my father but I'm also afraid of what he's like. Perhaps I'll disappoint him." She stroked the cat, taking consolation from its soft fur. It was an old cat now; it had been in its prime when it first came to live here, shortly after her first cat died.

"Your father did take part in your upbringing, you know," Yao said. "It was his idea that you attend St. Clare's and that Master Liu let you have more independence. You couldn't possibly disappoint him."

Yao sat on the bench and put an arm around her shoulders. She leaned against him, comforted by his warmth, his kindness. Her life would be upended shortly, but for now, for another few minutes, she was with Yao, whose friendship sustained her more than food, more than sleep. But in the next moment, he moved away.

"I'm sorry, Princess," he said, "I forgot myself."

"Yao, we've been . . . been friends, equals while at Lennox Manor," she said, "and now you decide to get formal? My father gave up his title and position. He's a common citizen now and so am I. And you know how I feel about the monarchy."

"That foreign girls' school," he said in mock disapproval, "all those notions about democracy and how superior principles allowed Western nations to dominate Asia. Rather than because they forced their military might upon us."

"You're changing the subject," she said. "Please, no more of this calling me 'Princess.' For one thing, it would be terrible for our new identities if you slip up."

He laughed, then said, "You look better today. Not so tired."

To her surprise, she realized he was right. She hadn't suffered from any bad dreams, she'd slept the whole night without waking, and for the first time in weeks she felt fully alert. Her life was going to change completely in so many ways, and while the prospect was daunting, she didn't feel as overwhelmed as before. Perhaps because she was rested, or perhaps she was getting used to the idea.

She pointed at the shallow container. "Why are you planting a new *penjing* when we're leaving so soon?"

"Because I'm taking it with me," he said. "Perhaps it will live for a hundred years, starting its life here in Shanghai, cared for by future generations in Canada."

IN THE TWO days since the fire, Fourth Uncle produced documents that would ease their entry into Canada. All the legal papers, but also letters of introduction and telegrams confirming arrangements, and for Yao, a bank account. The Chinese community in Victoria was growing, its small Chinatown eager to welcome new arrivals. The Liu name opened doors, even in Canada.

Unlike the United States, Canada still allowed immigration

from China, although there was a head tax of five hundred dollars. Yao would enter under his own name and his own identity.
Once there, he hoped to find work as a gardener. Their contacts
in Victoria had assured them that given Yao's qualifications, his
chances were good. A wealthy family by the name of Butchart
owned a property with a huge garden the size of a public park
and had hired several of their gardeners from Victoria's Chinese
community.

Mr. Zheng, previously of the Liu Motorcar Import Company,
would set up a Chinese art and antiques business in Victoria's
Chinatown. Lisan could work at the shop or try for a job at the
new Great Qing Overseas Chinese Public School, thanks to her
knowledge of both English and Chinese.

ROSALIE WAS BURIED when the freighter was three days out of
Shanghai. Lisan knew this because of the feeling that swept her up
like a wave, lifting her on a surge of relief. She gripped the railing
and closed her eyes, spoke a silent prayer to the gods. She pic-
tured Rosalie gazing out from the portrait, her expression serene,
at peace. The wave subsided and pulled away, leaving Lisan with a
sensation of gratitude. Then nothing. Not the slightest prickle of
obligation, of sadness or fear.

Her hand felt in the pocket of her coat for the envelope. Master
Liu had given it to her on the eve of their departure, something
her father had asked him to do before she left China. The envelope
contained a letter and a photograph. She hadn't shared its contents with Master Liu or with Yao. Not yet. In his letter, her father
apologized for the past decade.

I had lost my family, all except for you. I had lost faith in my
countrymen, my government, in the role of the Emperor. All

was bitterness. Leaving China was not just for your safety. I didn't feel capable of being a parent.

The photograph was of her family. Not in formal Manchu court robes but in ordinary clothing. Her parents sat on a carved bench side by side, relaxed and smiling. Her father's arm rested lightly around her mother's shoulder; her mother's hands were folded demurely in her lap. With them, three girls, the youngest on her father's lap. She had studied each face over and over, their unclouded smiles and rounded cheeks, the arch of their brows, her sisters' and her own. The way her parents leaned ever so slightly toward each other, as though they wanted to be closer.

Gradually, with each day on the ocean, scraps of memory had returned. Of chasing her older sisters around the courtyard garden; being dressed for a party in a heavy, embroidered gown; of riding a horse, her father sitting on the saddle behind her, the safest feeling in the world. The memories were rapidly filling in with more details: the azaleas at the perimeter of the courtyard garden and the goldfish in its pond, the covered walkway around the courtyard where she could run and play when rain dripped off the eaves or when the sun burned too hot. Her world had been so small and now she was crossing the Pacific. She put the letter and photograph back in her coat pocket.

"What are you thinking about?" Yao joined her at the railing. "Of course, there is so much to think about, what a question."

The Jade Line freighter carried cargo and had room for a dozen paying passengers, but Lisan and Yao were the only ones. Fourth Uncle had made sure of that.

"I think my memories are coming back," she said. "Just in bits and pieces though."

"But it's coming back, which is better than not at all," he said.

"Soon you'll remember your father, your family. Good memories, not just sad ones."

"Yes. Yes, I think, I believe, our family was happy."

"There's something else, isn't there?" he said. "It's Mrs. Stanton, isn't it?"

"You mean Eleanor Fontaine," she said, wishing she were a child so that she could stamp her feet in frustration. "Yao, she's an impostor and a murderer, and she is out there spending money that's not hers, and there's no way to prove she's a killer. Where's the justice in that?"

"Leave her fate to the gods, Lisan," he said. "There's nothing you can do."

There was one other thing she had to know. "Yao, did you agree to come only because of my father? Because he's your master?"

He looked at her and reached out a hand. "Of course not. I wanted a chance at a future of my own. With you, if at all possible. A chance at a life of our own."

A life of our own, she thought and took his hand, felt his fingers squeeze hers gently. Then he put his arm around her and she turned her gaze to the ocean, to the first glimmers of sunlight rising from the horizon.

CHAPTER 33

THE FIRST PASSENGER steamship out of Shanghai was bound for Bangkok, and the idea of Siam appealed to Eleanor more than Singapore or Tokyo, so Bangkok was where she disembarked. The climate was hotter than anything she'd ever experienced, but the wicker peacock chair was more comfortable than a velvet-padded seat, and under the shelter of a canvas awning, the terrace's marble tiles were cool under her bare feet. As evening approached, a breeze came off the Chao Phraya River and it was almost refreshing. A pair of palm trees spread their leaves like large fans and lent privacy, shielding her from any eyes straining for a glimpse of the mysterious, wealthy woman who had checked into the Oriental Hotel.

Such freedom.

She closed her eyes, enjoying her solitude, the knowledge that from now on, no one would disturb her unless she allowed it. During her last days in Shanghai, staff at the Astor House Hotel had been instructed to give Mrs. Stanton complete privacy; they were all aware of the recent tragedies she had suffered. They'd even managed to turn away Mrs. Easton—although that had required the hotel manager's intervention. She'd had only one visitor, one she couldn't avoid, but it had been useful: an officer from the Shanghai Municipal Police force.

He wanted her help to understand how the fire at Lennox

Manor might've started. It was deliberately set, he said, apologetically. So she explained that after her husband died, she had felt very uncomfortable living there on her own with a man who wasn't a blood relation, not only because of how things might look but also because Mason Burnett was behaving strangely.

"You know his son died under very tragic circumstances three years ago," she said to the sympathetic young officer, an Englishman. "Mr. Burnett grew very close to Thomas and put all his hopes on their business partnership. I believe he regarded my late husband as a second son. When Thomas died, Mr. Burnett seemed all right until after the funeral, but I realize now he was just barely hanging on."

Mason, she explained, was a heavy drinker who became very difficult and abusive when inebriated. His alcohol habit had become so bad their servants had left. On the day of the fire, he started drinking at lunch, and became increasingly morose, saying there was no point in life anymore.

"Frankly, I felt alarmed by his behavior," she said, "so I packed very quickly, just a few things, and left as soon as I could. My maid stayed behind to pack the rest of my belongings. I was going to send a carriage back for her, along with a porter to carry away trunks and larger pieces of luggage. Oh, I blame myself for not taking her with me."

"Now, now, Mrs. Stanton," the officer said, "how could anyone have known that Mr. Burnett would burn down his own home? Obviously, he was suicidal. I imagine it runs in the family."

The resulting piece in the *North China Herald* had been most satisfactory. The story put all the blame for the fire on Mason, while also stressing that he had been grief-stricken and not in his right mind. She left a few farewell notes for the hotel concierge to send before boarding her ship; nobody would question her desire to leave Shanghai, a place that had brought so much sorrow.

She had been living in the suite at the Oriental Hotel for the past two weeks. The riverside hotel was the most modern and luxurious in all of Siam, the management and staff discreetly considerate of her situation. She required solitude, she explained, she was in retreat and needed to be away from other guests. Her suite on the upper floor featured a large terrace with a view of the river and the gleaming orange roofs and gilded, bell-shaped towers of Bangkok's many temples. It was all so pleasant she had stayed a week longer than planned.

But it was time to move on. Andrew Grey had given her a nasty scare, a reminder that she could never let down her guard. Grey and his evidence. She shook her head, recalling how much anxiety it had caused her, but in the end it turned out Mason had done her a favor by getting it from Grey's hotel.

The first thing she'd done after locking Lisan and Mason inside the small parlor was run to Mason's rooms and rummage through his belongings. She didn't have to search very long to find Grey's envelope of evidence. Mason had no imagination. He'd slid the brown paper package into his desk drawer—the top drawer, no less. It had been locked, but the key was under the blotter. A quick look inside the envelope confirmed it contained the information from Grey's detective, information he definitely could've used to control her. She tucked the envelope inside her valise, then went to the garage to start up her motorcar. After bringing the vehicle under the porte cochere, she put her luggage inside and went back to the house.

She began setting the fire.

From the time she and Lisan had made an inventory of all the food and supplies, she knew there were metal cans of lamp oil in the storage room, enough to soak several carpets and the hems of drapes. Fire in the attic, she suspected, would speed things along. She made sure to pour enough onto the crates containing what she most wanted destroyed. She hoped the rats burned too.

She drove away feeling quite pleased. Her frugal head servant had kept a collection of candle stubs in a tin can, and after she had finished with the lamp oil, she lit a few candles on each floor. They'd burn down and set the flames going, but only after she was safely out of the house.

It was time to give the contents of the brown paper envelope a final farewell. She took out the papers and spread them on the wicker table. She hadn't wanted to carry that sort of documentation on her, not until she was safely out of Shanghai. As soon as she'd booked her stay in Bangkok, she had posted the package to herself, care of the Oriental Hotel, Bangkok. *Hold for Mrs. Stanton.*

The papers were familiar to her now: copies of photographs and documents, an invoice for services rendered, and a covering letter from the detective agency Grey had hired to hunt down this information.

Dear Mr. Grey:

Your instructions were to: identify a blond maidservant who worked for the Dominics in New York and who was killed in the same avalanche as the Dominics; trace her origins and determine how she came to work for the Dominics; provide photographs of both this servant and Caroline Vessey.

I spoke to one of the Dominics' former servants and learned that the young woman was Eleanor Fontaine, Caroline Vessey's maid and companion. The two were classmates at Miss Fielding's Finishing School for Young Ladies in Boston,

*but Miss Fontaine's parents died and their debts left her virtu-
ally penniless. Miss Vessey took her in.*

*At the school, I was able to find photographs of both Miss
Fontaine and Miss Vessey.*

Enclosed are copies of:

- *Miss Fontaine's birth certificate*
- *Photographs of Miss Fontaine and Miss Vessey from
  their time at school*
- *Obituary for Miss Fontaine's parents*
- *Obituary for Mr. and Mrs. Dominic, mention of Miss
  Fontaine also perishing in the disaster*

*All documents and photographs are copies of the originals,
notarized on the back to attest that they are faithful copies. I
trust these are sufficient to your needs. If we can be of further
assistance in this or other matters, please do not hesitate to
use our services again.*

She studied the photographs, remembering when they'd been
taken. Two graduation pictures. The first one almost made her
wince at the memory of hair pulled back so tightly it hurt. She
turned to the second one, a group photograph. A notary's stamp
in red ink marked the bottom right corner. A typed list of names
on a slip of paper was glued above the stamp. *Class of 1905. Front
row, left to right,* the students arranged in alphabetical order. Her
own face in the front row, Caroline in the very back row.

A photograph of her onstage, the caption on the back clear and
unequivocal: *The Pirates of Penzance, spring musical 1905, Eleanor Fontaine.*

The third photograph was the most damning of all, a close-up of six girls standing behind a table piled high with blankets, Caroline beside her, looking glum as always; the caption read: *The Helping Hands Club with blankets knitted for St. Francis's Orphanage. L to R: Caroline Vessey, Eleanor Fontaine . . .*

Grey had spotted the deception only because he had seen her and taken notice of her that one time in New York. Few others would've paid attention to a maidservant. In Grey's hands, this information would've allowed him to squeeze a fortune out of her; in Mason's hands, it would've forced her to sign over control of her fortune. One thing was certain: after all she'd done to secure her life, she wouldn't put up with any more threats. Not after she'd confronted Andrew Grey face-to-face. Of all her acts of self-preservation, that had been her boldest.

On the day of her dreaded rendezvous, she'd arrived well before the appointed time and slipped into the alley between the hotel and the bar next door. The alley was paved in brick, but only for the first ten feet or so. Farther in, the ground was all mud and filth. Stacks of wooden crates as tall as her head were piled around the side door of the hotel. She took the carving knife out of her bag and tucked it between two crates. Then she walked out of the alley and crossed the intersection to the tea shop, where she waited at the corner under a black umbrella, well back under the awning, anonymous and unnoticed by people hurrying out of the rain.

As she had suspected he would, Grey came out of the hotel and looked around. He stood on the sidewalk in front of the hotel to wait, looking around from under the faded canvas awning. He wasn't even wearing a raincoat; after all, they would be going inside. She took a deep breath and crossed the street.

She greeted him with tears in her eyes, begged him to reconsider, drew him under the shelter of the umbrella, all the while moving toward the alley.

"Please, let's not talk out here," she had pleaded, tugging him by the arm. "Please listen to me, I can't go in the hotel yet, there's something I need to show you, something to give you, it could change your mind. Come in here with me, just for a moment, away from other people." She babbled without stopping, not giving him time to reply or protest.

What did he have to fear from a woman caught in his trap, a woman desperately trying to save herself? Her entreaties only added to his enjoyment. He let her draw him under her umbrella and into the alley, followed her all the way to the pile of crates stacked by the side door, the crates that hid them from anyone walking along the street. He even took her umbrella when she pressed the handle into his hand so that she could open her bag.

"Something I need to show you, give you," she repeated, and put her free hand against the crates as though to steady herself, her green eyes holding him with their beseeching gaze. He'd smiled, then stumbled backward in astonishment against the brick wall when she pushed the knife between his ribs. He reached for her with one hand, the other still holding the umbrella, but she stepped away and Grey fell against the wall, slid down to the mud. He made a yelping sound when she yanked the knife from his chest and plunged it into his throat. Blood spurted onto the hem of her oilskin raincoat. She turned Grey over so he lay face down in a puddle, then wiped the knife on Grey's jacket before dropping it in her bag.

Then she picked up the umbrella and walked out of the alley, just a woman caught in the rain, hastening to her destination. It had been so surprisingly easy, had happened so quickly. Easy because not for a moment, not until it was too late, had Andrew Grey believed she was a danger to him.

She crossed the street but couldn't bring herself to leave, not just yet. She had an irrational fear that Grey might come staggering out of the alley, the same look of astonishment on his face, blood dripping from his throat. So instead she waited across from the hotel, moved along from shop to shop, until the man rushed out of the alley shouting for help and people ran outside to gather on the sidewalk. Only then did she leave.

In the cold downpour, even Shanghai's tenacious beggars weren't making an attempt to beseech for coins. She slipped off the raincoat and flung it over a woman huddled under a piece of cardboard, hurried away before the surprised woman could look up and see her. She turned the corner onto Avenue Paul Brunat and she was Caroline Stanton again, dressed in an expensive coat, on the way to her jeweler.

Back home, back inside her room, she washed the knife and hid it in the bag. One night, when she was sure Lisan had gone to bed, she climbed up to the attic and returned the knife to its box.

Getting rid of Andrew Grey, that had been preparation. Preparation and playacting, making him feel overconfident when she begged him for mercy.

But with Thomas, it had been luck and opportunity. Luck that Thomas had come down with intestinal parasites, which had opened up the opportunity. Luck again that Dr. Ellis had been too inept to recognize his original diagnosis was no longer the cause of Thomas's illness, and too stubborn to reconsider. She might've felt more kindly toward her husband if she hadn't overheard Mason commenting that he'd advised Thomas to marry Caroline for her money. She did not like being used. In a way, it was too bad. Thomas had been an indulgent husband. It had been a good life.

But no husband was best of all. She'd known since childhood that love and friendship meant little to her, although she could feign both quite well when needed. Personal attachments were useful when convenient. When there was opportunity.

After Lisan mentioned that the servants had noticed Thomas's hair falling out, she knew she couldn't have all the houseboys there as witnesses. It was so easy; they were so superstitious. Just the mention of objects being moved around and full-grown men panicked.

What sort of risk was she running now by continuing to impersonate Caroline Stanton? It was a risk, but one that diminished with each passing year. People's memories would dim, her own features alter with age. She would travel constantly, never stay too long in one place, perhaps hire a companion to fend off unwanted attention.

Now that she thought about it, perhaps it was just as well Lisan hadn't come with her. A wealthy American woman with a Chinese maid-companion, that was rather too memorable. It was too bad she couldn't travel alone, but that would attract too much attention as well. She'd find someone older, middle-aged and compliant, too timid to rock the boat.

Still, Lisan's reaction had been disappointing, especially when what she had offered was so generous. She empathized with the girl, an orphan. She had even admitted to being an impostor, proving to Lisan how much she was willing to trust her. In her own way she had been as fond of Lisan as she was capable of such emotion. She had felt strangely regretful to read in the Shanghai newspapers that the two bodies found in the burnt ruins of Lennox Manor were those of Mason Burnett and Liu Lisan.

In fact, when she drove away from Lennox Manor that final time, there had been a moment when she rather hoped Lisan would survive the fire. She had been fond of the girl.

AUTHOR'S NOTE

EVEN BEFORE I knew "Gothic" was a genre, I loved Gothic novels. *Jane Eyre, Rebecca, Wuthering Heights* are books I've read over and over. The genesis of *The Fourth Princess* began, as it so often does, during research for another novel when I came across photographs of grand, Western-style mansions in Shanghai. They seemed so incongruous and out of context. Some of the homes were enormous, set on many acres of land, a reflection of their owners' affluence and desire to replicate the grand country houses of Europe. The photos got me thinking about a gothic novel set in Shanghai, one that stayed within the parameters of the genre but set in China rather than in a Scottish castle. As soon as I saw a photograph of Dennartt, a mansion built in 1907 by prominent lawyer William Venn Drummond, I knew its image would inspire this story.

Less history, more atmosphere

I really had to hold back on history. During the first iteration of the book, it just didn't seem gothic enough, and I realized that there was too much about what was going on in China outside Lennox Manor. It's 1911 and the Qing empire is on its way out (China becomes a republic in 1912), there is talk of revolution, China is fragmenting into a nation carved up by warlords, and political intrigue abounds. My characters are aware of all the tumult around them, but in gothic fiction the focus has to be the danger from within: the location and/or its residents. One revision later, less history, more atmosphere, and the story was starting to feel like a gothic novel.

Education for Chinese girls

Lisan is a graduate of St. Clare's Hall, a fictional school for girls. There was, however, St. Mary's Hall, a Christian school for Chinese girls established in 1881 by missionaries, and McTyeire School, established in 1882. Tuition fees were expensive; consequently these two schools were called by Shanghai Chinese the "Christian Schools for Wealthy/Noble Maidens." During the timeline of the story, women's literacy is still a new thing and there are very few post-secondary institutions for young women—one reason why women whose families allowed it and who could afford it went abroad. Women's education advanced greatly after China became a republic and legally confirmed women's rights to education.

The real princess Masako Kyo

Princess Masako Kyo is loosely based on the controversial Qing dynasty princess Aisin Gioro Xianyu (1907–1948), also known by her Japanese name Kawashima Yoshiko. Her activities during World War II, thirty years after the timeline of this novel, were the stuff of scandal and, in the end, treason. Raised in Japan, she was executed by the Kuomingtang (Nationalist Party of China) as a Japanese spy.

The fourth princess

Sarah Pike Conger was the wife of Edwin Conger, American ambassador to the Qing court from 1898 to 1905. She was inside the Foreign Legation during the Boxer Rebellion but despite this experience, made continued efforts afterward to be friends with the Empress Dowager Cixi, who had encouraged the Boxers. Pike Conger wrote a memoir, *Letters from China*, about her time there; in it she describes touring the many dwellings inside the Forbidden City after Western forces took control. She entered a courtyard with three coffins holding the bodies of three princesses. Fearing what foreign soldiers would do, the three had thrown themselves down a well. Years later, when Pike Conger visited the Empress Dowager's court, she told this story to a group of ladies-in-waiting and one of them exclaimed that she had been there and tried to do the same, but the bodies of the first three had blocked the well. She was the fourth princess, and this incident gave the novel its title.

Penjing / bonsai

Although *bonsai* is the popular term for these miniature trees and treescapes, it's a Japanese word. In China they are called *penjing* and further defined by different classifications. The Montreal Botanical Garden owns a spectacular collection of *bonsai*, and it boggles the mind that gardeners tending these tiny specimens are envisioning decades into the future as they prune and wire the trees. At the same time, I've long thought of *penjing* as a metaphor for Chinese women of the past, their lives (and feet) shaped by others. Just a thought.

The Wellington avalanche

The Dominics, Caroline Vessey, Eleanor Fontaine, and Thomas Stanton are fictional characters, but on March 1, 1910, an avalanche did roar down a mountainside in the Cascades near Stevens Pass in Washington State, killing ninety-six passengers, trainmen, and employees of the Great Northern Railway. The town of Wellington, where the trains were stopped, was subsequently renamed "Tye" because it didn't want future train passengers to forever associate the town with tragedy.

During rescue operations, the general manager of the Great Northern Railway offered a special train and his private car to take the injured back to Spokane and a proper hospital. Mention of this "private car" led to a rabbit hole of research about the luxurious train carriages built by the Pullman Company. It seemed to me that the snobbish Mrs. Dominic would insist on a personal car so that she wouldn't need to mix with common folk.

Chinese government and railways

Belatedly, the inward-looking Imperial government in China came to realize that reliable transportation was necessary to modernization. Unfortunately, between political resistance by traditionalists, incompetence, and corruption, Chinese efforts to build railways failed, and it was foreign nations with business interests in China that actually developed a working network of railways.

By the early 1900s the Qing government was broke; it supported various and sometimes conflicting schemes for railway investment. The one that interested Thomas and Mason was a scheme whereby foreign investors would "lend" money to the government for railway expansion. The government would then allow the foreign business to build and operate the railway, and the government would pay back the original loan with their share of profits from railway revenues.

References:

The White Cascade: The Great Northern Railway Disaster and America's Deadliest Avalanche by Gary Krist

Manchu Princess, Japanese Spy: The Story of Kawashima Yoshiko, the Cross-Dressing Spy Who Commanded Her Own Army by Phyllis Birnbaum

Letters from China by Sarah Pike Conger

Bonsai | Penjing: The Collections of the Montréal Botanical Garden by Danielle Ouellet

For images of 1900s Shanghai and its mansions, see my website: www.janiechang.com/books/fourthprincess/fourthprincess-gallery

ACKNOWLEDGMENTS

AFTER A DOZEN years, I feel truly fortunate that Harper-Collins Publishers continue to support my books. Thank you, Jennifer Brehl and Iris Tupholme. I feel very lucky to have you as editors.

The only reason this book even made it to a second revision is because of editor Janice Zawerbny, who spent almost as much time talking me off the ledge as she did editing. Thank you so much for your skills, insights, and friendship.

Many thanks to Alice Tibbetts, Neil Wadhwa, Amelia Wood, and all the wonderful professionals in the marketing and PR teams at William Morrow and HarperCollins Canada. With so many books being published every year and fewer outlets for promotion, the job of getting a book discovered by readers is tougher than it's ever been; please know that I appreciate the talent, time, and effort you put in for every author and every book. Every book, not just mine.

Sometimes, I still pinch myself that my agent, Kevan Lyon, agreed to stand in my corner and take me on as her client. Thank you, Kevan.

We all rely on community to keep us grounded and sane. During the writing of *The Fourth Princess*, a personally difficult time, I've never needed community more. To my dear Lyonesses, the best ever group of fierce and talented author friends who always have each other's backs, thank you for being so patient, supportive, and understanding, even when I'm wailing about some ridiculous small frustration. Special shout-outs to Kate Quinn, Jennifer Robson, Susan Juby, Weina Dai Randel, Kate Hilton, Alan Bradley, Rachel McMillan, Aimie K. Runyan, Stephanie Dray, Claire Mulligan, Roberta Rich, June Hutton—many thanks for your friendships and the joy of your books.

To Geoffrey: your support means the world to me.